The Best
AMERICAN SHORT STORIES 2002

GUEST EDITORS OF
THE BEST AMERICAN SHORT STORIES

1978 TED SOLOTAROFF
1979 JOYCE CAROL OATES
1980 STANLEY ELKIN
1981 HORTENSE CALISHER
1982 JOHN GARDNER
1983 ANNE TYLER
1984 JOHN UPDIKE
1985 GAIL GODWIN
1986 RAYMOND CARVER
1987 ANN BEATTIE
1988 MARK HELPRIN
1989 MARGARET ATWOOD
1990 RICHARD FORD
1991 ALICE ADAMS
1992 ROBERT STONE
1993 LOUISE ERDRICH
1994 TOBIAS WOLFF
1995 JANE SMILEY
1996 JOHN EDGAR WIDEMAN
1997 E. ANNIE PROULX
1998 GARRISON KEILLOR
1999 AMY TAN
2000 E. L. DOCTOROW
2001 BARBARA KINGSOLVER
2002 SUE MILLER

The Best AMERICAN SHORT STORIES® 2002

Selected from
U.S. and Canadian Magazines
by SUE MILLER
with KATRINA KENISON

With an Introduction by Sue Miller

HOUGHTON MIFFLIN COMPANY
BOSTON • NEW YORK 2002

Visit our Web site: www.houghtonmifflinbooks.com.

ISSN 0067-6233
ISBN 0-618-11749-0
ISBN 0-618-13173-6 (pbk.)

Printed in the United States of America

DOC 10 9 8 7 6 5 4 3 2 1

"Nobody's Business" by Jhumpa Lahiri. First published in *The New Yorker,* March 12, 2001. Copyright © 2001 by Jhumpa Lahiri. Reprinted by permission of the author.

"Digging" by Beth Lordan. First published in *The Atlantic Monthly,* September 2001. Copyright © 2001 by Beth Lordan. Reprinted by permission of the author.

"In Case We're Separated" by Alice Mattison. First published in *Ploughshares,* Vol. 27, Nos. 2 & 3. Copyright © 2001 by Alice Mattison. Reprinted by permission of The Wylie Agency, Inc.

"Billy Goats" by Jill McCorkle. First published in *Bomb,* No. 77. Copyright © 2001 by Jill McCorkle. Reprinted by permission of the author.

"Watermelon Days" by Tom McNeal. First published in *Zoetrope,* Vol. 5, No. 41. Copyright © 2001 by Tom McNeal. Reprinted by permission of Sterling Lord Literistic.

"Nachman from Los Angeles" by Leonard Michaels. First published in *The New Yorker,* November 12, 2001. Copyright © 2001 by Leonard Michaels, from *Of Mystery There Is No End.* Reprinted by permission of Riverhead Books, an imprint of Penguin Putnam, Inc.

"Bulldog" by Arthur Miller. First published in *The New Yorker,* August 13, 2001. Copyright © 2001 by Arthur Miller. Reprinted by permission of International Creative Management.

"The Rug" by Meg Mullins. First published in *The Iowa Review.* Copyright © 2001 by Meg Mullins. Reprinted by permission of the author.

"Family Furnishings" by Alice Munro. First published in *The New Yorker,* July 23, 2001. Copyright © 2001 by Alice Munro. Reprinted from *Hateship, Friendship, Courtship, Loveship, Marriage* by permission of Alfred A. Knopf, a division of Random House, Inc.

"Surrounded by Sleep" by Akhil Sharma. First published in *The New Yorker,* December 13, 2001. Copyright © 2001 by Akhil Sharma. Reprinted by permission of Georges Borchardt, Inc., for the author.

"Love and Hydrogen" by Jim Shepard. First published in *Harper's Magazine,* December 2001. Copyright © 2001 by Jim Shepard. Reprinted by permission of the author.

"Aftermath" by Mary Yukari Waters. First published by *Manoa,* Vol. 13, No. 1. Copyright © 2001 by Mary Yukari Waters. Reprinted by permission of the author.

Contents

Foreword

ALTHOUGH I READ short stories all year long, trying to keep abreast of the journals and literary magazines that course across my desk, I don't usually hunker down and get serious until right around Labor Day. As the days shorten and the weather turns, the annual reading deadline looms on the horizon, and I set aside all other tasks and get down to the business of reading. This year, of course, the end of summer was swiftly followed by the end of our national innocence. All of us who returned to work in the days and weeks that followed September 11 had to grapple with the changes the events of that day had wrought in our lives and endeavors. Projects that had seemed urgent just weeks before took a back seat to new priorities; work that had been fully engaging suddenly seemed less than compelling; it was hard to concentrate, harder still to figure out just what we should be doing. Instead of reading stories, I found myself drawn to the phone, to e-mail exchanges with distant friends, to snuggles with my husband and my kids, to long, heartfelt chats with my neighbor in the driveway. The human urge for connection seemed at odds with the stacks of magazines piled up in my office. For a while I couldn't even sit still, let alone give the short stories before me the careful attention they deserved. Friends reported, "I can read the newspaper, but I can't seem to read anything else." I knew exactly what they meant. Preoccupied with the unfathomable changes in our world at large, it was almost impossible to focus on the details of a smaller picture.

And then one fall day I came upon Michael Chabon's story "Along the Frontage Road." As I reached the end of this brief, bittersweet account of a father and son's expedition to choose a pumpkin from a roadside stand, I suddenly realized that I was holding my breath; not only that, I was praying for these characters, hoping with all my heart that each of them would receive grace, survive their losses, find love and understanding. The door back into stories had swung open. With that, I came to see that the kind of connection I'd been seeking was actually right in front of me, in stories that remind us that whatever happens, we aren't alone in the world, that our own fears and concerns are universal, that the details of our ordinary everyday lives do matter.

Throughout the weeks and months that followed, as old routines reasserted themselves and the numbness and shock many of us felt gave way to a new kind of heightened awareness, I was struck by the sheer depth and breadth of human experience portrayed in the stories I read each day. All of them had been written well before September 11, and yet often I found it hard to believe that this could be the case; the truths they spoke seemed so timely, so necessary now. Other times I was astonished by a story's timelessness, by a realization that an author's insights into the human condition were no less urgent in 2001 than they would be in any other decade, any other situation. Reading on, choosing stories that still seemed important, that still seemed necessary, or that were simply great fun to read, I came to see in some of these works nothing less than an antidote to terror. As James McKinley, the editor of *New Letters,* wrote to his readers, "We deceive ourselves if we believe that what's euphemistically called 'the tragic events of September 11' limn this nation any more than the coincident attack on the Pentagon or the anthrax onslaught define us. Ultimately, we are defined by what we create, not by what others destroy."

Here, then, are the stories of 2001, offered in the faith that we will continue to connect at the deepest levels through art, and that literature will remain as beneficial to the human community as any ideology, machine, or technological advance.

This year Sue Miller put aside her own fiction writing in order to read well over a hundred stories and compile this volume. She tackled the job with an open heart and an open mind, with the authors' names blacked out and no preconceptions about what kinds of stories she intended to choose. As she reveals in her introduction, she wondered if the stamp of her personality would be evident in her choices for this collection. "In fact," she writes, "I even looked forward to that possibility, with pleasure at the notion of discovering something about myself by those choices." With no agenda beyond finding the choicest works of fiction of 2001, Sue Miller did indeed bring a generous spirit and an astute judgment to her task: she has given us a richly varied, vigorous, highly readable collection, twenty stories that reaffirm the health of this quintessentially American form. We are grateful for her efforts, and for a volume that is much more than the sum of its parts.

The stories chosen for this anthology were originally published between January 2001 and January 2002. The qualifications for selection are (1) original publication in nationally distributed American or Canadian periodicals; (2) publication in English by writers who are American or Canadian, or who have made the United States or Canada their home; (3) original publication as short stories (excerpts of novels are not knowingly considered). A list of magazines consulted for this volume appears at the back of the book. Editors who wish their short fiction to be considered for next year's edition should send their publications to Katrina Kenison, c/o The Best American Short Stories, Houghton Mifflin Company, 222 Berkeley Street, Boston, MA 02116.

K.K.

Introduction

I WAS FORCED to write short stories by the exigencies of my life at a certain moment. Of course, that's not true; it's just how I felt. For one thing, I didn't have to write a word if I didn't want to. No one was either asking to read what I wrote or offering to pay me for it, and the choice to write — which I was barely aware of making — was my own. I wound up writing short stories because I didn't feel I had the time or the imaginative energy left to me — after being a mother, having a job, and running a house — to undertake the longer kind of work, the work of the novel, to which I felt more suited. Almost arbitrarily felt more suited, I would have to say. In any case, I wrote short stories for a number of years of my life, and when I was almost finished doing that — though I'm not sure even now that I'm shut of the form — I was lucky enough to have a collection of them published.

I had occasion recently to reread that book (I was trying to decide on a story to read aloud in front of an audience), and what struck me about the stories after all these years was what an odd collection, in fact, they make. How different they are, one from another — in tone, in subject matter, in structure, even in length. Motley.

This may not be how the collection would be received by others now, of course; and actually, it wasn't received that way when it was published, by and large. The reviewer in the Sunday *Times Book Review,* I recall, saw the stories as unitary. They were, she wrote, too much about sex and too little about love. (Ouch. This was only my second book, and it was hard to feel so keenly that the reviewer didn't care for my work. But I consoled myself that if ever a negative remark might help sell a book, "too much about sex" might be just that remark.)

Still, I do think that writers often come around, willy-nilly, to doing, recognizably, what they do, even when they're struggling hardest to do something new and fresh. This has happened to me sometimes with the novels I've written. After several years' work I'll produce something that feels like a bold step off into new terrain; there's the long wait, it gets published, and the reviews say, essentially, "Oh, here she comes, doing that again."

I wondered, then, if the same stamp of personality would be evident in my choices for this collection. In fact, I even looked forward to that possibility, with pleasure at the notion of discovering something about myself by those choices. It was a small part of my motivation in saying yes to the job of editor — the first part being simply delight in having been asked, and the second being the notion that I might learn something about where the American short story was, what was going on with it at this moment in its history and in ours. But the third, yes, had to do with the idea that I might in some way meet myself through the stories I had chosen.

And after all, there must be some measure of hope in the editors who put this book together annually at Houghton Mifflin that such a mark, such an aesthetic or moral stamp, will be palpable — or why choose a different writer every year? Why choose a writer at all, except to have the book shaped somehow by what his taste is, what his standards are? (Of course, the book is shaped too by what is Out There this year, and that's pure chance, combined in some measure, I suppose, with the pressures of the zeitgeist and the power, or lack of it, of some prevailing aesthetic of and for the short story.)

As I've looked over past volumes of this collection, though, it strikes me that they don't evenly wear the impress of their editor's sensibility. Or at least not apparently so. And it further strikes me that the volumes I admire most wear it least; that the stories in these collections — the ones I like best — only seem excellent, each in its quite distinctive way, and not to have been chosen with any particular demands being placed on them except that: excellence. It seems reasonable to me that this should be so — that range and excellence should be available without a recognizable editorial imprimatur. After all, most of what a writer is likely to admire in others' work is what she herself is unable to do, and this always encompasses a wider range of kinds of writing than what she is able to do.

And so, after I'd made my decisions, it was, oddly, with some relief that I discovered I could learn exactly nothing about my aesthetic-in-the-short-story by reading through all the stories I'd chosen. In the aggregate they had no voice, they didn't speak; separately, they certainly did — but each was a perfect representative only of its own instance.

For example, I chose two stories about a deal that gets made and then goes awry. Both involve treacherous behavior. But what could be more different tonally than Leonard Michaels's bemused, almost rueful account of Nachman's foot-dragging and largely unconscious inability to keep the deal he's made in "Nachman from Los Angeles," and the story of John Henderson's agonized alteration of the terms of his bargain and then the terrible price he exacts for that generosity in Karl Iagnemma's "Zilkowski's Theorem"?

Or, to move further to the ends of another spectrum, what could you say about Melissa Hardy's "The Heifer," so full of horrific events endured and indeed created by her otherwise stoic, even silent characters, that you could also say about Michael Chabon's "Along the Frontage Road," which slowly and elliptically reveals some measure of the human feeling underlying its seemingly ordinary behavior: the choosing of a Halloween pumpkin by a boy and his father, and their simple exchanges as they make this decision — except that both stories are wonderfully done?

There are two dog stories (and this may say more about me as a person, if not a reader, than any other choices I made), but Richard Ford's "Puppy," an account of a marriage revealed through the tale of what a couple does with a dog abandoned to their care, drew me because of the meandering, Peter Taylor-ish unreliability of the narrator; whereas what drew me to Arthur Miller's story, "Bulldog," was the funny and unexpected and completely exhilarating account of the birth of creative impulse that ends it.

Alice Munro is always utterly distinctive in the tone and fluid structure of her stories (I had a teacher once who referred to that quality as the Munro doctrine — he disapproved), and "Family

Furnishings" is no exception, landing as it does at its conclusion on a moment that would have been midway in the chronology of the story but that aptly captures what we know only by then to be simultaneously false and utterly true of the narrator's assumptions about the meaning and aims of her life to come.

But distinctive too is Jim Shepard's astonishing "Love and Hydrogen," the story of an illicit love affair set in the fantastic, enclosed, and doomed universe aboard the *Hindenburg* in 1937, or Tom McNeal's "Watermelon Days," which takes us to the Dust Bowl era in South Dakota to depict the beautiful and unexpected momentary reprieve of a difficult marriage, or Carolyn Cooke's "The Sugar-Tit," set on Beacon Hill in impoverished gentility, an account of another complicated marriage told in brilliant language (a tenor rising above "the rest of the men's voices, in the quivery way of oil on water") — an account that ends with an act of the bitterest fidelity.

Three of the stories speak of love and the immigrant experience, but with emphases so different as to make you forget the thematic connection — from Jhumpa Lahiri's young graduate students wounding and exposing each other within their almost hermetically sealed-off universe of part-time jobs and study and improvised meals, to Edwidge Danticat's Haitian lovers, reunited after a separation of seven years, alternating between their pleasure in being together again and the powerful sense of things unspoken and perhaps unspeakable between them, to the sense Beth Lordan gives us in "Digging" of the generations of hidden and lost hopes and sorrows that lie under the lives of the Irish American couple whose meeting and marriage she describes.

I found Jill McCorkle's story "Billy Goats" remarkable for the unusual choice of narrative voice — it's told mostly in the first-person plural; and for describing not so much a unique action, which usually gives shape to a story, as a pattern of habitual actions which make up the ordinary life of an ordinary place; and for the blessing pronounced on that ordinary life by the story's ending. And I found E. L. Doctorow's "A House on the Plains" remarkable for almost exactly the opposite qualities — its quite particular narrator, its long and intricate plot, the pace of its withholding and its revealing, and the sense of a simultaneously admirable and repugnant fidelity running under the dark and complicated events.

There's "The Red Ant House," by Ann Cummins, remarkable for being told in the quirky and slightly stylized voice of a child, about two girls trying to take control of their disordered lives by exposing themselves to the local bachelor (yes!); and Alice Mattison's elegant and very funny story about a woman finding a kind of grace in giving up control of her life, "In Case We're Separated." And there's "Surrounded by Sleep," by Akhil Sharma, an at once amusing and sad story about a boy slowly understanding the small consolations possible within what he's also slowly comprehending as the horrific callousness of a world that has dealt catastrophe to his family. There's a nearly plotless meditation on the necessary and painful evanescence of memory, set lovingly in the shifting world just after the Second World War in Japan — "Aftermath," by Mary Yukari Waters — and a neatly plotted tale of loss and the need for yearning in human life — "The Rug," by Meg Mullins — which ends with one of the most indelible images in the collection.

They are fine, these powerful and distinctive stories, and my only fear in invoking what seems to me unique or startling about each one is that I may have been reductive. If that's the case, I apologize to the writers of these stories, which I admire for so much more than the qualities that make them so markedly different one from another.

But different they are, as they should be. Mongrel (that dog again!), nearly polyglot in its variety of style, this collection says nothing clear about the American short story today except that it's healthy and strong and still exploring its realist roots (there were almost no experimental works in the 150 or so stories Katrina Kenison sent on to me). That it's being written by every ethnic version of American there is, about every ethnic version of the American experience there is. That it's being enthusiastically embraced by young writers and reclaimed by older ones. That it's being written by men and women in almost equal numbers, and that it's being written equally about the present and the near past and the long ago. Perhaps the stories written next year or in the few years following will reflect more about what we are thinking of at this moment as our changed world — or perhaps we'll find the world changed less than we thought. In any case, these stories, whose creation preceded that change, seem to belong less intensely than those imaginary stories-to-be to a particular time. Indeed, it almost seems that none of these stories needed this particular moment in history to be born.

Far less, I'd argue, did they need this particular editor to notice them. There may be one or two you wouldn't have chosen, had you been editing; there may be one or two I would have chosen differently if the circumstances under which I chose had been different — if I'd read certain stories in some other order or in some other room or mood. If I'd read them all at 5 P.M. on a sunny day, for example. Well, yes. But since I've come to the end of this process with these twenty on my list, it seems to me that they were the inevitable twenty. And having now reread them several times over as a collection, I've confirmed that, for myself anyway.

And confirmed something else. These stories arrived in my life at an odd time. I'd been working for six months on a nonfiction book, my first ever; then, seconds after I turned that in, I was sent on the road to flog the novel I'd finished months earlier. By the end of the tour I hadn't written fiction in almost a year, and sometimes I thought that if one more sweetly inquisitive aspiring writer asked me where I got my ideas from, I'd cry out, "Oh God, I don't know. How would I know?" and exit stage left. I didn't do that. I hope I wouldn't do that; but it felt as though these stories arrived in the nick of time to make me believe again in that place — the place where ideas come from — and to teach me once more what we read fiction for. I'm grateful.

SUE MILLER

The Best
AMERICAN SHORT STORIES 2002

MICHAEL CHABON

Along the Frontage Road

FROM THE NEW YORKER

I DON'T REMEMBER where we used to go to get our pumpkins when I was a kid. I grew up in a Maryland suburb that, in those days, had just begun to lay siege to the surrounding Piedmont farmland, and I suppose we must have driven out to somebody's orchard or farm — one of the places we went to in the summer for corn and strawberries, and in the fall for apples and cider. I do remember the way that my father would go after our pumpkins, once we got them home, with the biggest knife from the kitchen drawer. He was a fastidious man who hated to dirty his hands, in particular with food, but he was also a doctor, and there was something grimly expert about the way he scalped the orange crania, excised the stringy pulp, and scraped clean the pale interior flesh with the edge of a big metal spoon. I remember his compressed lips, the distasteful huffing of his breath through his nostrils as he worked.

Last month I took my own son down to a vacant lot between the interstate and the Berkeley mudflats. Ordinarily no one would ever go to such a place. There is nothing but gravel, weeds, and the kind of small, insidious garbage that presents a choking hazard to waterfowl. It is a piece of land so devoid of life and interest that from January to October, I'm certain, no one sees it at all; it ceases to exist. Toward the end of the year, however, with a regularity that approximates, in its way, the eternal rolling wheel of the seasons, men appear with trailers, straw bales, fence wire, and a desultory assortment of orange-and-black or red-and-green bunting. First they put up polystyrene human skeletons and battery-operated witches, and then, a few weeks later, string colored lights and evergreen swags.

Or so I assume. I have no idea, actually, how this kind of business operates. There may be a crew of Halloween men, who specialize in pumpkins, and then one of Christmas men, who bring in the truck-loads of spruce and fir. The Halloween men may be largely Iranian and the Christmas men Taiwanese. And I don't know if someone actually owns this stretch of frontage, or if it lies, despised and all but invisible, open to all comers, a freehold for the predations of enterprising men. But I don't want to talk about the contrast between the idyllic golden falls of my Maryland youth and the freeway hum, plastic skeletons, and Persian music that spell autumn in the disjointed urban almanac of my four-year-old son. I don't want to talk about pumpkins at all, really, or about Halloween, or, God knows, about the ache that I get every time I imagine my little son wandering in my stead through the deepening shadows of a genuine pumpkin patch, in a corduroy coat, on a chilly October afternoon back in, say, 1973. I don't mean to imply that we have somehow rendered the world unworthy of our children's trust and attention. I don't believe that, though sometimes I do feel that very implication lodged like a chip of black ice in my heart.

Anyway, Nicky loves the place. Maybe there is something magical to him in the sight of the windswept gray waste transfigured by an anomalous outburst of orange. In past years, the rubber witch hands and grinning skulls had intimidated him, but not enough to prevent him from trying to prolong our visits past the limits of my patience and of my tolerance for the aforementioned ache in my chest. This year, however, was different, in a number of ways. This year he took the spooky decorations in stride, for one thing.

"Dad. Look. Look, Dad. There's a snake in that skull's eyehole," he said.

We were just getting out of the car. The gravel parking strip was nearly empty; it was four o'clock on a Monday afternoon, with three weeks still to go until Halloween. So I guess we were a little early. But we had both wanted to get out of the house, where ordinary sounds — a fork against a plate, the creak of a stair tread — felt like portents, and you could not escape the smell of the flowers, heaped everywhere, as if some venerable mobster had died. In fact the deceased was a girl of seventeen weeks, a theoretical daughter startled in the darkness and warmth of her mother's body, or so I imagine it, by a jet of cool air and a fatal glint of light. It was my wife who had suggested that Nicky and I might as well go and pick out the pumpkin for that year.

There was only one other car in the lot, a late-model Firebird, beer-cooler red. Its driver's-side door stood open. In the front passenger seat I saw a little boy, black, not much older than my Nicky. The Firebird's radio was on, and the keys were in the ignition: a sampled Clyde Stubblefield beat vied with the insistent pinging of the alarm that warned of the open car door. The little boy was looking out, toward a small brown structure beyond the wire fence that in my three years of visiting this forlorn place had escaped my attention completely. It was hardly bigger than a drive-in photomat. On its sign there was a picture of a fish struggling with a bobber and a hook and the single word *Bait.* From the muscle car, the bait shop, and a deadened air of resentment exuded by the kicking, kicking foot of the little boy left alone, I inferred that he was waiting for his father.

"What if that snake was for real?" Nicky said, pointing to the skull that sat atop a bale of straw. It was hollow, like the genuine article, and some clever person had arranged a rubber snake so that it coiled in and out of the eye sockets and jaws. Nicky approached it now, boldly, one hand plunged into the rear of his polar-fleece trousers to scratch at his behind.

"That would be very cool," I said.

"But it's only rubber."

"Thank goodness."

"Can we get a skull, too, and put a snake inside it?"

"We only do pumpkins in our family."

"Is that because we're Jewish?"

"Why, yes, it is," I said. "Come on, Nick." I tugged his hand out of his pants and gave him a helpful nudge in the direction of the pumpkins. "Start shopping."

The pumpkins lay spilled like marbles in scattered bunches around the cashier's stand, which was tiny, a rudimentary wooden booth painted red and white to remind somebody — myself alone, perhaps — of a barn. Straw bales stood posed awkwardly here and there, exuding a smell of cut grass, which only intensified my sense of having borne my son into a base and diminished world. There was also straw strewn on the ground, I suppose to provide a rural veneer for the demolition-rubble paving material of the vacant lot.

And there was a scarecrow, a flannel shirt and blue jeans hastily stuffed with crumpled newspaper, and token shocks of straw protruding from the cuffs and throat of the shirt. The legs of the blue jeans hung empty from the knee, like the trousers of a double amputee. The head was a pumpkin fitted out with a *Friday the 13th*–style goalie's mask. I forbid myself, absolutely, to consider the proposition that in the orchards of my youth it would never have occurred to anyone to employ a serial-killer motif as a means of selling Halloween pumpkins to children.

Nicky walked slowly among the pumpkins, pondering them with the toe of his sneaker. If the past two years were any guide, he was not necessarily looking for the largest, the roundest, or the most orange. The previous lucky victims had both been rather oblong and irregular, dented and warty specimens that betrayed their kinship to gourds, and scarred with that gritty cement that sometimes streaks the skin of pumpkins. Last year's had not even been orange at all but the ivory that lately seemed, at least in our recherché corner of California, to have become popular. I had no idea what Nicky's criteria for selecting a pumpkin might be. But I had remarked certain affinities between my son and the character of Linus in *Peanuts,* and liked to imagine that he might be looking for the most sincere.

"Cute," said the man in the cashier's stand. He was of indeterminate ethnicity — Arab, Mexican, Israeli, Armenian, Uzbek — middle-aged, with a grizzled mustache and thick aviator-style glasses. He sat behind a table laid out with a steel cash box, a credit-card press, a cellular telephone, and five demonstration models, XS, S, M, L, and XL, priced according to size from ten to twenty-two dollars. "How old is he?"

"Four," I said.

"Cute," the pumpkin man said again. I agreed with him, of course, but the adjective was offered without much enthusiasm, and after that we let the subject drop. A door banged, and I looked across the lot. A man was walking from the bait shack out to the frontage road. He was tall and light-skinned, with a kettledrum chest and the kind of fat stomach that somehow manages to look hard: the body of a tight end. He wore white high-tops, big as buckets, barely recognizable as shoes. On his head was a Raiders cap, bill to the back, on his chin the quick sketch of a goatee. He nipped around the fence where it met the frontage road, approached the car from the driver's side, and dropped into the bucket seat, with his back to the boy. The boy said something, his voice rising at the end in a question. The man offered only a low monosyllable in reply. He reached one hand under his seat and felt around. A moment later his hand emerged, holding what looked to my not entirely innocent eye like a rolled zip-lock baggie. Then the man stood, and I heard the boy ask him another question that I couldn't make out.

"When I say so," the man replied. He walked back around the fence and disappeared into the bait shack. The boy in the Firebird turned and, as if he had felt me watching, looked over at me. We were perhaps twenty feet apart. There was no expression on his face at all. I suppressed an impulse to avert my gaze from his, though his blank stare unnerved me. Instead I nodded and smiled. He smiled back, instantly, a great big winning smile that involved every feature of his face.

"That your kid?" he said.

I nodded.

"He getting a pumpkin."

"Yep."

The boy glanced over at the bait shack. Then he threw his legs across the driver's seat and slid himself out of the car. He was a handsome kid, dark and slender, with a stubbly head and big, sleepy eyes. His clothes were neat and a little old-fashioned, stiff blue jeans rolled at the ankle, a sweater vest over a white-collared shirt, as if he had been dressed by an aunt. But he had the same non-Euclidean shoes as his father, or as the man I assumed was his father. He took another look toward the bait shack and then walked over to where I was standing.

"What he going to be for Halloween?"

"He's still trying to make up his mind," I said. "Maybe a cowboy."

"A cowboy?" He looked appalled. It was a hopelessly lame, outmoded, inexplicable thing for a little boy to want to be. I might as well have said that Nicky was planning to go trick-or-treating as a Scotsman, or as Johnny Appleseed.

"Or he was thinking maybe a cat," I said.

I felt something bump against my leg: it was Nicky, pressing his face to my thigh. I looked down and saw that he was carrying a remarkably tiny, rusty-red pumpkin, no bigger than a grapefruit. "Hey, Nick. What's up?"

There was, heavily, profoundly, no reply.

"What's the matter?"

The voice emerged from the fabric of my pant leg.

"Who is that guy you're talking to?"

"I don't know," I said. I smiled again at the kid from the Firebird. For some reason, I never feel whiter than when I am smiling at a black person. "What's your name?"

"Andre," he said. "Why he got such a little one?"

"I don't know."

"How he going to fit a candle in that midget?"

"That's a very good question," I said. "Nicky, why did you choose such a small one?"

Nicky shrugged.

"Did you already get yours?" I said to Andre.

He nodded. "Got me a big pumpkin."

"Go on, Nick," I said. "Go find yourself a nice big pumpkin. Andre's right — you won't be able to put a candle in this one."

"I don't want a big pumpkin. I don't want to put a candle in it. I don't want you to cut it open with a knife."

He looked up at me, his eyes shining. A tear sprang loose and arced like a diver down his cheek. You would have thought I was asking him to go into the henhouse and bring me a neck to wring for supper. He had never before shown such solicitude for the annual sacrificial squash. But lately you never knew what would make Nicky cry.

"I want to call Mommy," he said. "On the cell phone. She will tell you not to cut up my pumpkin."

"We can't bother Mommy," I said. "She's resting right now."

"Why is she resting?"

"You know why."

"I don't want her to rest anymore. I want to call her. Call her, Dad. She'll tell you not to cut it up."

"It ain't alive," Andre argued. He was taking such an interest in our family's pumpkin choice that I was certain his earlier boast had been a lie. Andre had no big pumpkin waiting for him at home. His father was a drug dealer who would not bother to take his son shopping for a pumpkin. This conversation was as close to the purchase of an actual pumpkin as Andre had any reason to expect. These may not in fact have been certainties so much as assumptions, and racist ones at that. I will grant you this. But what kind of father would leave his kid alone in a car, with the door open, at the side of a road that skirted the edge of a luckless and desolate place? What kind of man would do that? "It don't hurt them to be cut."

"I want this one," said Nicky. "And I'm going to name it Kate."

I shook my head.

"You can't do that," I said.

"Please?"

"No, honey," I said. "We don't name our pumpkins."

"We don't believe in it?"

"That's right." I did not want him telling all the people who set foot on our front porch the name that we had been tossing around the house over the past month or so, with an innocence that struck me now as wanton and foolish. My wife and I were given no real choice in the matter, and yet every time I look at Nicky's fuzzy knees poking out of his short pants, or smell peanut butter on his breath, or attend to his muttered nocturnal lectures through the monitor that we have never bothered to remove from his bedroom, I cannot shake the feeling that in letting ourselves be persuaded by mere facts and statistics, however damning, we made an unforgivable mistake. I had stood by once in an emergency room as doctors and nurses strapped my son, flailing, to a table to stitch up a gash in his forehead. I could picture, all too clearly, how your child looked at you as you betrayed him into the hands of strangers.

"Andre!"

The father was coming toward us, his gait at once lumbering and methodical. When I looked at him, I saw where Andre had learned to drain the expression from his face.

"What I tell you to do?" he said, softly but without gentleness. He did not acknowledge me, Nicky, the ten thousand pumpkins that lay all around us. "Boy, get back in that car."

Andre said something in a voice too low for me to hear.

"What?"

"Can I get a pumpkin?" he repeated.

The question was apparently so immoderate that it could not be answered. Andre's father pulled his cap down more firmly on his head, hitched up his pants, and spat into the straw at his feet.

These appeared to be a suite of gestures intended to communicate the inevitable outcome if Andre did not return immediately to the car. Andre had reset his own face to zero. He turned, walked back to the Firebird, and got in. This time he went around to the big red door on his side of the car and heaved it open.

"Your son is a nice boy," I said.

The man looked at me, for the first and last time.

"Uh-huh," he said. "All right."

I was just another pumpkin to him — dumb and lolling amid the straw bales, in the middle of a place that was no place at all. He went to the car, got in, and slammed the door. The pinging of the alarm ceased. The engine came awake with a rumble, and the Firebird went scrabbling out of the lot and back onto the frontage road. Nicky and I watched them drive off. I saw Andre turn back, his eyes wide, his face alight and hollowed with an emotion that I could not help but interpret as reproach. I had abandoned him to a hard fate, one that I might at least have tried, somehow, to prevent. But there was nothing that I could have done. I didn't have any illusions about that. I dressed and fed my child, I washed his body, I saw that he got enough sleep. I had him inoculated, padded his knees and encased the twenty-eight bones of his skull in high-impact plastic when he got on his bicycle and pedaled down our street. But in the end, when the world we have created came to strap him to a table, I could only stand behind the doctors and watch.

I took Nicky's half-grown red runt and balanced it on my palm.

"Hey, Nick," I said. "Listen. You can name it Kate if you want to."

"I don't want it," Nicky said. "I want to get a bigger one."

"All right."

"Kate can have that one."

"All right."

"Because she didn't get to have a pumpkin, since she didn't get to ever be alive."

"Good thinking," I said.

"But I still don't want to cut it up," he said. Then he went back again into the world of pumpkins, looking for the one that would best suit his unknown purposes.

CAROLYN COOKE

The Sugar-Tit

FROM AGNI REVIEW

OF COURSE SHE WAS FURIOUS: while the beef roast browned in the oven she scrubbed the grandfather clock with steel wool and wax. She scrubbed the collars of her husband's shirts and ironed them for the Ladies' Aid. Then she walked up the hill to her father's apartment with the roast on a plate under silver paper.

He didn't answer when she rang the bell. He couldn't go far, he was nearly blind; twice he'd been struck by buses, and survived. Giddy Shortall walked across Beacon Street to the Athenaeum and asked there. Yes, Mr. Wentworth was in with the periodicals.

She left the roast with the man in the vestibule and found her father in a polished red chair. He could no longer make out words, but he was a man of habits and liked to hold some reading in his hands. She knelt by his chair and whispered, to preserve the silence of the room, "I've come with a beef roast." Mr. Wentworth looked at her as if she were insane and said, "Surely you know better than to come to the Athenaeum with a roast."

She led him across the street and took him up in the elevator to his twin rooms at the old Bellevue. She carved off a corner of the meat for him, and filled a tiny etched glass with the juices. Then she read aloud from a novel by his favorite author, Thackeray, scenes of imprudent love and impatient heirs. He would bend and write a check, she knew: his milky eyes watered as he drank and ate. But her father's imagination was more modest than Jack's and his checks were always too small.

Jack was not a suitable husband, Giddy's father pronounced early on. He was an *enthusiast,* meaning he wasn't serious, and

Giddy was a fool. But she had married for love, not money, and she remained loyal and rigid in her devotion while Jack's attentions drifted. Now he had an interest in a bottling company in Natick; now he was shipping off crayons to the children of the English. But years passed, and the more Jack stumbled and failed at business, and drank, and looked to other women for sympathy, the more Giddy's father came to believe that his son-in-law was marked by a noble and aristocratic heart — an almost Grecian flaw. As Mr. Wentworth grew old this conviction hardened and refined itself until, toward the end, he seemed to prefer Jack to Giddy. It became easier then to ask him for money.

She found his checkbook among the piles of papers on his desk. "Don't go near my things!" he shouted. But she paid no attention and laid a check on his blotter with a pen and told him sternly, "This is money owed to Paula Blodgett." Imagine, owing money to Paula! Mr. Wentworth lifted the pen and licked his lips. His old hand shook as he wrote.

On her way home she stopped to sit in the Public Garden, something she rarely did, though she lived just around the corner. Her legs still hung down from the bench: she wasn't five feet tall, a tiny person forty years of age. Spread out before her the Garden seemed brilliant, the new leaves luminous under the gray branches of the trees, a grid of tulips sprung up in the freezing air. There was the familiar ginkgo tree with its button knobs, oriental and severe.

She had sat on this bench when she was a little girl, waiting for her mother and father to come and get her after symphony. Every Friday afternoon she followed them through the Common and into the Public Garden, two gray suits of worsted sliced from the same bolt. It was always winter during symphony, brown sticks for trees after the leaves fell off, the sky a dull penciled gray. Wind blew through her gray wool coat, but there was nothing to do but wait: they told her to. Her father pointed with his stick to this bench, and she sat down. Her legs hung above the walk. "Don't budge from this spot until we return," he told her, and Giddy, obedient, never moved. Her mother and father went to hear *Messiah,* but there was no question of Giddy going into Symphony Hall. She had asthma: she might wheeze.

(Jack never believed a word of it. "Impossible!" he told her. "You would have been plucked up by the white slavers!" But no, she remembered her father's expression of rapture as he crossed the park. She had always felt perfectly safe in the Public Garden. You were then.)

Jack was dead. She still saw him vividly, however, enormous and enthusiastic after one of the Blodgetts' lunch parties, full of wine and gin and desperate to leave Paula Blodgett with a crush. The terrible vision rose up before her eyes. Jack broke away from the group in their camel hair and furs, ran away down the path and up to a policeman who stood at the edge of the Swan Boat pond. The policeman took a step forward in greeting; the black brim of his cap nodded up and down. Laughter blew through the thin air, laughter and Paula's voice calling, "Jack, Jack!" — laughing, encouraging him. Jack put out his arms and lifted the policeman up, kissed him on the mouth, embraced him! He would do anything to make Paula laugh. (She held her face in her hands and roared.) The policeman hung for a moment in Jack's arms and put two fingers to his lips. Then he seemed to lose his balance, and stepped backward; one foot sank into the icewater of the pond. The Blodgetts and some of their guests pulled him out immediately and surrounded him.

Giddy slid forward on the bench until her feet touched ground. Light glinted off the gold rims of Jack's glasses and flashed as he moved toward her, his hands out like a beggar's. He seemed happy to see her. She walked toward him, unlatching the knob of her fishing creel, and handed him her handkerchief, which was still moist from the Blodgetts' gin. "You'd better blow your nose," she said.

A police car pulled up to the Arlington Street gate. The party of men and women put the policeman into the passenger seat, and he was driven away. Even Ned Blodgett said there was no harm done.

Giddy dressed carefully for lunch at the Blodgetts'. The last time she wore a brown worsted suit and a string of cultured pearls. Paula was quite bohemian herself, she was a free spirit; but she was also an imperial person who would cut you dead if you weren't correct.

Giddy presented herself to Jack in the kitchen. Was a baby blue scarf at her throat too much? Yes, he said, it was. She flung off the scarf with all her force, but it drifted and landed in a bowl of pippin apples. "Everyone adores you, darling, you're perfect," Jack assured her, smiling. He kneeled on the floor in front of her while she tied a tight bow around his neck. He was over six feet tall, a giant. Adore her? He adored her: the way the iron ramrod of her will butted up against the fortress of her reserve. The sweaters she knit for him turned out too tight, or the sleeves too long. He wore them everywhere: he adored her. But it was Paula he loved. When Giddy finished with his bow tie, she tugged the loops and slapped him on the shoulder. She was always rather physical, rather violent, with him.

Jack stood up and smashed his head on the doorjamb. She saw him bleeding, waving her away, making her look. She mopped his temple with a piece of an old nightgown from her ragbag. These rooms were too small for him. It was like a Dutch house, every room on a different floor. It was old and charming. (But for him it was crowded and tight!) Jack's arms hung down at his sides, the woolly cuffs of his sweater covering the backs of his hands. He seemed indifferent to his wound, cocked his head away from Giddy's Band-Aid and her swabbing hand.

"Stop bleeding!" she told him. "We'll be late!"

They were already late. Two men from Skinner had just left with her mother's tambour desk. At noon Giddy was still pulling treasures from the secret drawers — letters, stamps, her son's report cards from school. Two men came and wrapped the desk in a quilted silver pad, lifted it up, and took it out. But it wasn't enough — one desk. Jack needed an enormous amount of money for his business. He needed a ship — a ship — to carry all the crayons he would send to the children of England. Even as she stuck a Band-Aid on his forehead she saw him looking cagily through the door to the dining room, assessing the red Sarouk. He blew his nose into a dingy-looking handkerchief. "Here," said Giddy, and he put it in her hand.

He held out her coat, and she backed into it, struggling with the tight sleeves, then the globular buttons. She followed him out. He didn't bother with an overcoat; he lived to suffer. Above him outdoors rose the old ailanthus, her favorite tree, tall and erect; it had — she had read this somewhere — a *handsome habit.* Most of the ailanthuses had been chopped down years ago because their blossoms stank and fouled the old cisterns on the roofs. But it turned out the flowers of the female had no scent; the rankness was in the male.

Under the tree she reached up and touched his forehead where an orange stain of Mercurochrome had spread outside the confines of the bandage. "They'll think you got drunk and fell down," she told him. Her fears — what people would think — amused him. He smiled and rose above her.

"Maybe I *will* get drunk and fall down," he said.

They walked uphill. It was spring, still bitterly cold. One side of the street bloomed with magnolias, pink tongues and gray branches against the bricks. Forsythia, pussy willows — Giddy loved the look of flowers without leaves, something lush growing on a stick.

Paula and Ned Blodgett lived in a rosy brick building with a modest bow front and a few old lavender panes. Giddy saw right away that her own costume was too prim; Paula wore a Chinese pajama in red and purple mixed with other colors. She carried a drink in her hand and greeted her guests with a worldly, croupy laugh.

Giddy and Jack had to climb a flight of stairs and put their coats down on a bed. Bill Dooling was there smoking, and Paula said in her imperial voice, "Put out your cigarette, please, Bill. This is my bedroom!" It was a bold thing to say, but Paula was very bold. Her people were loyalists who fled to Maine in the Revolution: they wanted a king. Giddy could hear it in Paula's voice when she said "my bedroom!" She gave out favors, took what she wanted; she talked like a king.

They drank cocktails in a room filled with charming antiquities from Salem and prizes from the East Indies and hundreds of Greek things. On the mantel an urn showed Zeus about to carry off Ganymede. Swords poked out of the umbrella stand, and there was an old piano with unusually wide keys, which had belonged to some famous big-handed pianist. Giddy's friends towered above her, their bosoms wrapped in loopy Irish tweeds thick as bathmats, or in woolly sweaters. They talked about where the best pies came from — Brookline; Plasticine deviled eggs bobbed on the ends of their fingers, crystal triangles of gin bobbed in the air. The room shuddered with laughter.

Giddy rubbed her suit with a handkerchief — gin had rained down the side of someone's glass — and released a whiff of naphthalene from the mothballs she kept in her pockets. She stuffed the wadded cloth into her little wicker fishing creel. The creel was not proper or correct, but Giddy was devoted to it. Jack had brought it back from England, and it had her initials embroidered in yarn above the clasp.

Jack drifted away from her and landed near a low table of canapés, deviled eggs, stuffed celery, and olives. His liquid tenor rode above the rest of the men's voices, in the quivery way of oil on water. He went on about the crayon business — why did he go on? No one asked to hear it — about all the pigments and vats, the problem of shipping, about the ship that would take the crayons to the little children in England. Giddy sipped her drink and listened to him become enthusiastic, to the high sound of his implacable happiness. (Did it sound to Paula like happiness?) There he was in a circle of men, his face rosy and his blue eyes hard; his glasses glittered. He pulled out his handkerchief and honked into it.

Since she could remember, Giddy had washed out handkerchiefs full of stuff from men's noses. First her father's nose, then Jack's.

He stood in front of the fireplace turning Paula's Greek urn in his hands in such a casual way that Giddy was afraid he might drop it. He laughed; a beaming hot happiness came off him. "What do you make of this, darling?" he asked her.

She pinched the sleeve of his sweater in her fingers.

"Two cocktails is plenty," she told him.

He looked at her tragically, to remind her (she supposed) that he was a tragic man, a failure in business, and unfaithful; none of his passions were perfectly requited, and Giddy would never understand him. "Two is not enough!" he said. He held the urn uncertainly.

"Here," Giddy told him, and he put it in her hand.

He spotted Martha Sargent sitting on a needlepoint chair with her yarn bag, drinking a martini and casting on for a sleeve. "Women spinning out the threads of fate — terrifying!" he called to her.

"Terrifying for *you,* maybe," she told him, jabbing at him with her knitting needle. Giddy sat down. She and Martha talked about their children, Giddy's boy and Martha's girl, Ruth, who went to the same school where Giddy's father had taught — and had led the crusade against admitting girls. Ruth was a rather manly child, very strong and argumentative. Giddy's son was the most decent boy in the school — everyone said so.

Giddy herself had studied at home, except for a few months when she attended a school that met only outdoors, in the fresh air. The school attracted her father, who was transcendental. But Giddy failed to thrive outdoors; she caught pneumonia, and almost died. She never went back, and through what would have been her high school years she had "conversations" with her father. Giddy was his only "pupil" by then. Every morning he read aloud to her from a small Greek book. He interrupted his reading to ask her questions as they came to him. Was the point of architecture to reflect society or reform it? Reflect or reform? Summarize or improve? The library was a populist palace: was that good? The people went. They went indeed! He had himself seen in the Bates Reading Room a woman with a kerchief round her head, reeking of urine from her voluminous skirts, ask for the definitive *Larousse!* The murals by Sargent were very bad, didn't Giddy think so? Or did she adore them? What was the purpose of art? What did she think of love between men?

The school was wickedly expensive, but Giddy insisted that her son go, that he live in a castle at school. He came home weekends — her decent, perfect, beautiful boy. She loved him fiercely, more than she had ever loved anyone.

Jack drew some of the men into the conversation, which veered immediately to the subject of ancient Greece. Ned Blodgett in particular was crazy about Greece; he had studied it with the illustrious So-and-So. Ned was always writing epigrams and variations on Greek themes and firing them off to the men in the mail.

Martha Sargent drew herself up and said it made her furious to hear about the Golden Age of Greece as the height of human achievement, et cetera. "What woman would choose to return to the ancient world?" she asked, with real feeling. No one had an answer. Martha said, "You boys are on your own then!" and went off to help serve lunch.

"Oh, but you are hard and narrow, woman!" Jack called after her.

"Martha's all for the girls, you know," Bill Dooling said.

Jack looked down and seemed delighted to find Giddy there.

"But Giddy," he said, "we live in the Athens of America. Wasn't the Parthenon built by a Harvard man?"

"No!" Giddy told him definitely. She would not let him make a joke of her; but he wouldn't let go. Giddy should know, he insisted — she was keen on architecture. The men turned their attention to her, their benign smiles and pinkish eyes beaming down on her like soft reading lamps. Who built the Parthenon?

"Who then?" Jack pressed her.

She really didn't know. Bulfinch? (They all laughed loudly to show that they were with her. She was charming, she was adorable!) She blamed herself; her father knew all about the buildings. He had books — she could have read them. She hardly remembered the Parthenon, though she and Jack visited Greece, on a ship, before their son was born. She hated Athens: there was a hill there, at the top of the city, but the picture of it that came to Giddy's mind was deficient, only crumbling columns and that visible yellow heat under which the old marble trembled. On the ship Jack claimed to be charmed by her detachment from the oppressive march of ages. "Victorians swooned at Athens!" he cried at the dinner table; "My bride remained unmoved." An extremely tall woman from England, who made trouble by eating only vegetables and called everyone "love," took Giddy aside and told her *sarcasm* was a Greek word. "It means torn apart by dogs, love."

In her berth at night Giddy stared into the oscillating Greek darkness. Was Jack a dog? Would he tear her apart? But then she was sick among all the Cyclades, too sick to wonder, and Jack brought her ginger ale, and made her laugh with a tale of the Englishwoman demanding a fried tomato at Crete.

It was the last time Giddy and Jack traveled together; after that he had only gone to England alone — exploring, he called it. She hardly knew what he did there — he said he sold crayons, which was hard to imagine. He took them to the schoolrooms of the English children; he told Giddy the children had never seen such crayons, such colors, before. She would like to have gone along, to have seen the children, to have helped him, but business was always going badly and the time was never right. Besides, Jack pointed out, she had their son to take care of, although he spent the week at school.

*

Of course it turned out the Parthenon was built by a Greek. Jack took the joke as far as he could, and then, when it was too late, Bill Dooling said, "*Stop* it, Jack." He rushed so hard to Giddy's defense, arms and legs flying toward her, that he turned over a candlestand and a luster pitcher smashed. "God, I'm a bull in a china shop," Bill said, and set the table right. Giddy, lowest to the ground, picked up the broken pieces of the pitcher and held them in her fist. Martha Sargent appeared in the doorway with a ham.

Giddy carried the remains of the pitcher into the kitchen. She held the pieces up to Paula, who was talking to a woman in woolly clothing who had left her husband to study at the Divinity School. "I liked the one in the — sordid trousers," the woman was saying. "I liked *him* very much." Their eyes were wet with laughter.

"We had an accident," Giddy said, but Paula hardly looked down. She just reached out her hand, her fingers banded with platinum. "Don't worry about it, dear," she said, as if Giddy had broken the pitcher, as if Giddy were careless!

Paula leaned into the woolly woman, laughing, the broken shards of the luster pitcher jutting out from between her fingers in their jewels. "You want to put him in a bath and bathe him," Paula said. Giddy opened her mouth to speak, but there was nothing to add. They liked a man in sordid trousers, that was all. They wanted to put him in a bath and bathe him.

She ate her lunch on a needlepoint stool beside the piano, her feet splayed out and her knees touching to make a sturdy lap for Paula's Spode plate. Beside her at the piano Bill Dooling thumped away and grunted instead of clearly singing words. He had perfect pitch and a wild style that was almost obscene. His playing rose up around her ears and she heard him say, *I like you, Giddy. I like your eyes. I like your mouth. I like the way you look at me.*

Meaningless words, like the words of a song. Giddy wasn't sure she heard them at all. She finished her lunch and laid the plate carefully on a side table. She removed her inhaler from her fishing creel and misted her lungs.

Jack called over, "Why don't you turn up the heat, Bill?" but instead Bill played some lonely-sounding chords and looked at Giddy. "What can I give you?" he asked.

"'These Foolish Things,'" she said.

He played that, then "Georgia on My Mind," then "I Might Be Your Once in a While," then "Your Feet's Too Big." His eyes seemed to contract and grow redder. "You're sad?" she asked him.

He shook his head, his hands spread over the wide keys. "It's that — I've never played so well," he said.

He began to play again, but he didn't sing. Paula called to him from across the room. Finally Bill realized that his playing drowned her out, and he stopped. "What are we doing?" he asked.

"Jack needs you for a small adventure," Paula called over, "and I need you to supervise. He's gone already, quick! I'll meet you downstairs!"

Giddy stood up in alarm. "Bill, I wish you wouldn't egg him on," she said.

But all his melancholy had left him, and he was suddenly full of good nature. "Come on, don't be a dull girl," he said.

They went upstairs to get their coats. Giddy was struggling with her sleeves when Bill Dooling's arms suddenly tightened around her. She felt his large, heavy head on her shoulder, the bone at the tip of his chin bearing down. His hands reached around her waist and held her. "You are an angel," he said, patting her like a puppy. "Really, I never played so well." That was all; he seemed grateful. Then he thumped after her down the stairs.

It was a frigid day and everyone moved quickly. Giddy saw Paula and Jack up ahead. Jack had no overcoat, only his ridiculous knitted sweater; beneath her coat Paula's pajamas drifted around her ankles. As they crossed the street, Bill offered his elbow and Giddy hooked her arm around it. Jack called back to Bill, "We're going to play a game!" Bill excused himself from Giddy and ran loyally after Jack.

It was the famous joke Jack and Bill Dooling played on the maids. They went to a certain house on West Cedar Street and rang the bell. When the maid came to the door, they announced that they had come for the settee. "We have come for the settee!" There was no trouble at all. They went in the doorway, and when they came out again they had the settee with them, one man at each end of it. The maid held the door open and watched them walk down the hill, not far, cross the street with the thing between them, and ring another bell. Paula Blodgett followed behind them, one bare hand covering her mouth in a gesture of mild amusement. Jack rang the second bell. "We have come with the settee!" and of course the maid stood aside. The houses were all perfectly different, all stuffed with antiquity, all green walls or white walls or red walls. In went Jack and Bill Dooling with the settee. This was the joke — trust, obedience! How could any harm be done?

Later, Ned Blodgett helped Giddy get Jack the few blocks home, up the steps, into the narrow house. He chatted pleasantly with Giddy as if nothing were the matter. He held Jack up by his shoulder and his arm, and got him upstairs and into bed. Then he left them. But twenty minutes later Jack was back downstairs, surprising Giddy, who leaned over a cookie tin at the kitchen counter, crumbs falling from her mouth. Jack laughed at her and poured gin into a juice glass. "Honestly, Giddy," he said. "I never knew anyone with such a sweet tooth as you. You do love the little sweetie-pie, the sugar-tit. Don't you, darling?"

She hit him with a rolled-up newspaper. "Aren't you ashamed of what you've done? I'm surprised you can bear to let your own son see you," she told him. He looked at her, surprised. Their son was away at school. There was no one to see him but her.

She sold off the red Sarouk. The dining room floor looked bare without it; the room sounded hollow at meals. Her son asked about it when he came home from school. "The rug is gone," Giddy told him, "to a museum!"

"Why?" he asked her, and looking into his blank, good-natured face she saw how tractable he would be. She found herself angry with him, barely able to conceal her rage.

"It was two hundred years old — the best of its kind!" she said.

But immediately afterward Jack's business failed, and Paula threw him over. Not for that reason, Giddy felt sure — what did Paula care for Jack's success? He came to Giddy with the news, his thin hair standing up on top of his head. "There!" he told her. "She won't have me anymore. She's thrown me over! That's what you wanted, isn't it?" He was wild, inconsolable, *enthusiastic* — it was true.

Jack failed; he died. She found him in his bed with the pineapple posts when she came home with her shopping. He was covered in blood, horrible — but the moment she shut the door she doubted her eyes. Fortunately, her son was away at school. She called Bill

Dooling, who knew the mayor and the police. The cause of death was written up as Jack's heart, a natural cause for a man of forty-eight. No one questioned it at all, and though her son took the loss badly, he pitched a perfect game the next afternoon at school. "You can't let your teammates down," she told him. "You'll find they make you sit on the bench."

Jack left a sum of money to Paula in his will; not a great deal of money, but even so, Giddy had to go to her father to get it. It was a terrible humiliation for Paula, who cut Giddy dead at the memorial service and never spoke to her again.

ANN CUMMINS

The Red Ant House

FROM MCSWEENEY'S

THE FIRST TIME I saw this girl she was standing at the bottom of the coal pile. I thought she was a little wrinkled dwarf woman with her cheeks sucked in and pointed chin. She had narrow legs and yellow eyes. They had just moved into the old Perino house on West 2nd. This was the red ant house.

"I'm having a birthday," the girl said. She was going around the neighborhood gathering up children she didn't know for her birthday party. She told us they had a donkey on the wall and beans in a jar.

"What kind of beans?" I asked her.

She shrugged.

"Hey, you guys," I said to my brothers, "this bean wants us to go to her birthday party."

"My name's not Bean."

"What is it then?"

"Theresa Mooney."

"You don't look like a Theresa Mooney."

She shrugged.

"Hey, you guys. This girl named Bean wants us to go to her birthday party."

She didn't say anything then. She turned around and started down the street toward her house. We followed her.

In her yard was a grease monkey. Her yard was a junker yard with car parts and cars all over the place, and a grease monkey was standing up against one car, smoking a cigarette.

"Joe," the little dwarf girl says, "what do you think of a name like Bean?"

He considered it. The man was a handsome man with slick black hair and blue eyes, and he gave the dwarf a sweet look. I couldn't think of how such a funny-looking child belonged to such a handsome man. "It's an odd one," he said. The girl looks at me, her eyes slant. "One thing about a name like that," he said, "it's unusual. Everybody would remember it."

That idea she liked. She looks at me with a little grin. She says, "My name is Bean."

Just as if the whole thing was her idea.

Rosie Mooney was this Theresa's mother. When she moved in she had not known there would be ants in the house. These were the ants that had invaded the Perinos' chickens two summers before. Nobody wanted to eat chicken after that.

The ants came through the cracks in the walls. Rosie Mooney had papered those walls with velveteen flower wallpaper. She had a red room and a gold room. She had wicked eyes to her, Rosie Mooney, could look you through and through.

These were trashy people, I knew. They had Christmas lights over the sink. They had hodgepodge dishes, and garlic on a string, and a book of matches under one table leg to make it sit straight. When the grease monkey came in, he kissed Rosie Mooney on the lips, a long wormy kiss, and then he picked the birthday girl up, swung her in a circle.

For us, he took off his thumbs.

"It is an optical illusion," the girl told us.

He could also bend his thumbs all the way back, could tie his legs in a knot, and could roll his eyes back and look at his brain.

"Your dad should be in the circus," I told the girl.

"He's not my dad."

"What is he?"

She shrugged.

The grease monkey laughed. It was the sort of shamefaced laugh where you put two and two together you come up with sin.

There were two prizes for the bean jar event, one for a boy, one for a girl. The boy's prize was a gumball bank. Put a penny in, get a ball of gum. When the gum was gone you'd have a bank full of pennies. Either way, you'd have something.

The girl's prize was a music box. I had never seen such a music box. It was black with a white ivory top made to look like a frozen pond, and when you wound it up, a white ivory girl skated over the top. It was a nice box.

We were all over that jar, counting the beans. It was me, my brothers, the Stillwell boys, the Murpheys, and the Frietags. As I was counting, I thought of something. I thought, *This jar is an optical illusion.* That was because there would be beans behind the beans. It occurred to me that there would be more beans than could be seen, thousands more.

The grease monkey was the official counter. He had written the exact number on a piece of tape and stuck it to the bottom of the jar. We all had to write our numbers down and sign our names. I wrote five thousand. When Joe read that, everybody laughed.

"There are beans behind the beans," I informed them.

"This one's a shrewd one," the grease monkey said. "She's thinking." But when he turned the jar over, the number on the tape said 730. This Joe winked at me. "Don't want to be thinking too hard, though."

I just eyeballed him.

"You want to count them? You can count them if you want," he said.

"I don't care to."

He grinned. "Suit yourself."

And he awarded the music box to the birthday girl, who had written 600. Then I knew the whole thing had been rigged.

The birthday girl's mother said, "Theresa, I bet you'd like some other little girl to have the music box, since you have birthday presents. Wouldn't you?"

She didn't want to.

"That would be the polite thing," she said. "Maybe you'd like to give it to Leigh."

"I don't want it," I said.

This Theresa looked at me. She looked at the grease monkey. He nodded, then she held the box out to me.

But I didn't want it.

My mother was down sick all that summer. The doctor prescribed complete bed rest so the baby would stay in. For the last three years, she had gone to bed again and again with babies that didn't take.

Up until that point, there were six of us children.

There was Zip, named for my grandmother, Ziphorah. Zippy loved me until I could talk. "You used to be such a sweet child," she would say. "We used to dress you up and take you on buggy rides and everybody said what a sweet child you were. Whatever happened to the sweet child?"

There was Wanda, named for my other grandmother. Wanda was bald until she was five, and my father used to take every opportunity to bounce a ball on her head.

There was me, Leigh Rachel, named by the doctor because my parents drew a blank. I'm the lucky one. Once when I was a baby I jumped out a window — this was the second-story window over the rock cliff. My mother, who was down sick at the time, had a vision about it. I was already gone. By the time she got herself out of her bed and up the stairs, I was in flight, but she leaped across the room, stuck her arm out, caught me by the diapers, just as she'd seen it in the vision.

Another time, I survived a tumble down Bondad Hill in my grandpa's Pontiac. We both rolled like the drunk he was. Drunks I know about. My dad's dad was one, and my mom's dad was another. I never knew my dad's mom. She weighed three hundred pounds and died of toxic goiter. My mom's mom weighed seventy-five at the time of her death. Turned her face to the sky and said, "I despise you all." Irish like the rest of us.

There were the boys, Thomas Patrick, Raymond Patrick, Carl Patrick.

Then there were the ones who didn't take. One of these I saw, a little blue baby on a bloody sheet. My mother said, "Help me with these sheets," to Wanda, but Wanda couldn't stop crying, so I helped pull the sheet away from the mattress, and my mother wadded the sheet up.

I said, "We should bury that sheet."

She said, "It's a perfectly good sheet. We'll wash it."

Then she took a blanket and went into the living room and wrapped herself up in it. When my father came home he found her half bled to death.

My mother has Jewish blood in her. When they took her to the hospital, a Jewish man, Mr. Goldman, gave blood. He was the only Jew in town.

*

That summer my mother had cat visions. She would begin yelling in the middle of the night. She would come into our dreams: "The cats have chewed their paws off. They are under the bed."

"Mother, there are no cats."

"Look under the bed. See for yourself."

But we didn't want to.

Each day that summer I had to rub my mother's ankles and legs before I could go out to see the shadow, Theresa Mooney, who had started living in my back yard. I woke up in the morning, there she was on the swing or digging in the ground with a spoon.

Once out of the house, I didn't like to go back. If I sneaked back in for any little thing, I had to rub the legs again. This was my job. Zip's job was to clean the house.

Wanda cooked. Grilled cheese on Mondays, frozen pot pie on Tuesdays, Chef Boyardee ravioli on Wednesdays, frozen pot pie on Thursdays, and fish sticks on Fish Fridays. Saturdays were hamburger and pork-and-bean days, and Sundays, Sick Slim brought trout that he caught in the river. Sick Slim had a movable Adam's apple and finicky ways. He used to exchange the fish for loaves of my mom's homemade bread until he found out that she put her hands in the dough. After that, he didn't care for bread, though he still brought the fish. "I never thought she would have put her hands in it," I heard him tell my father.

Slim was my dad's army buddy. He built his house on West 1st, way back from the street, right up against Smelter Mountain. Slim didn't want anybody at his back, that's what my dad said.

We knew a secret on him. My brother Tom saw this with his own eyes. A woman drove to West 1st where Sick Slim lived. She had a little blond girl with her, and when the girl got out of the car, Tom saw that she was naked. The mother didn't get out of the car. The little girl walked up that long sidewalk to the porch and up the steps to Slim's house and knocked on the door, and Slim opened the door, and he gave the girl money.

Slim was a bachelor and didn't have anything to spend his money on except naked children and worms for fish.

We all thought it would be a good idea to try and get some of Slim's money. My brothers thought I should take my clothes off and go up to his door, though I didn't care to. But I thought

Theresa might like to make a little money, so I told her that there was a rich man on West 1st who would give us twenty dollars if she took her clothes off and walked up the sidewalk and knocked on his door. She didn't know about that. She was not accustomed to taking off her clothes outside.

I said, "Do you know how much twenty dollars is?"

She didn't know. She was poor as a rat.

"You go first, then I'll go," she said.

"It's my idea." I figured if it was her idea — which she didn't have any — then she could say who went first.

"Mama says not to get chilled," she said. She was prone to sore throats and earaches and whispering bones. Without notice, she would go glassy-eyed and stiff, and would lose her breath. When she caught it again, she'd say, "My bones are whispering."

"What are they saying?" I'd ask.

"They don't talk," she said. "They don't have words. Just wind."

"You are a delicate flower," I said to butter her up.

She liked that.

"I bet we could get thirty dollars for you. You're better looking than me."

She looked at me slant.

"It's easy," I said. "Don't think about it. You just think, *I am running through the sprinklers.* You don't think, *I am naked.* If you don't think about it, it's easy."

She told me she'd get beat if she took her clothes off outside.

"Maybe even forty dollars," I said, "because this particular gentleman likes itty-bitty things. Twenty for you, twenty for me. That's a lot of money. We could go places on that much money."

She thought about that. "I don't think we could go far on forty dollars."

"You got to look on the bright side. You're always looking on the dark side."

"No I'm not."

"You are doom and gloom and whispering bones. Just ask your whispering bones. They'll say you're doom and gloom."

"You go first," she said. "Then I'll go."

"Maybe I will."

"Okay," she said.

"Okay then."

*

My mother was curious about Theresa and her mother. "Where does little Terry go when her mama's working?" my mother asked me. "If we had any room at all, I'd have that child here. If we weren't doubled up already."

"Hang her on a hook," I said.

"Don't smart-mouth. Do you think she would like to come here?"

Mother thought all children should like to come to our house because it was so pleasant to have a big family. To have children to do the cooking, and cleaning, and leg rubbing. Her legs were yellow logs. I didn't like to touch them, and so I would think of them as yellow logs at Cherry Creek — the dried logs split by lightning with worm silk inside. I would close my eyes and rub the cold legs. Sometimes, if my mother didn't talk to me, if she only closed her eyes and breathed, I would forget I was in her room. I would put myself someplace else, Cherry Creek or Jesus Rock, and I would think of running my hands through soft things, the sand below Jesus Rock, or worm silk.

But mostly she talked. She wanted to know about Mooney and Joe. She wanted to know about Theresa.

When she talked, she would sit propped up on pillows, her belly a world under the sheet. Her eyes were all glitter.

"She doesn't stay with that man, does she?"

"Joe Martin is his name."

"I don't care to know his name."

"I don't know where she stays."

My mother sighed. Except for the belly, she couldn't put weight on. She had trouble keeping food down, and she didn't have the strength to wash her hair, so she kept it in a bandanna, one that bore the grease of her head.

"He has a wife and children, you know. Over in Dolores. I understand he has two little children. You mustn't say anything to the little girl, though. I'm sure she doesn't know. I understand," my mother said, "that he abandoned his family. I don't know how they make do.

"Now just look." She laughed and held her hands out to me. Her fingers were thick. The one ring finger was especially plumped out, and her wedding ring had sunk to the bone. "I have no circulation," she said, and she laughed again. They were cold, the fingers. "I'll be glad when this is over, Leigh. I guess we'll all be glad, won't we. Let's get some soap and get this ring off," she said.

I went for the soap and water. We soaped her hands good, and I started working the ring. She leaned back and closed her eyes. "Don't you love the sound?" she said.

"What sound?"

"Of the children playing. Listen to them." My brothers were kicking the can in the street. "You should be out, Leigh. Your poor old mom is all laid up, but you should be out. Why don't you go on out now?"

"Shall I tell Mr. Richter he has to come and cut this ring off your finger?"

"Go on out," she said, "and tell little Terry what I told you." She opened her eyes and smiled. "I know you want to." An ugly smile.

"I'm not going to say anything."

She shook her head. "I was wrong to tell you. I don't know why I told you. It was very, very wrong of me. I would not have told you if I were myself. You understand that?"

"Yes."

She frowned and shook her head. "It's only natural that you should go tell her now. A child cannot keep such a secret."

"You want me to tell her?"

"Of course I don't want you to tell her. But you will."

"No I won't."

"Yes you will. You cannot keep a secret."

I didn't say anything. Just soaped the fingers.

"Leigh?"

"What?"

"Can you keep it a secret?"

"Yes."

"Look at me."

I looked at her.

We looked at each other for a long time. She took my chin. She pinched it. She was pinching it. "You are the one," she said, "who cannot keep a secret. Am I right?"

"I can," I said, but she was pinching it. She shook my head back and forth.

"Here," she said. She pulled the sheet back. She put my face against her belly. The baby was kicking. "Feel that?" she said. "That's your blood, too." She put her hand on my cheek and held my face there. The baby stopped kicking, and my mother laughed.

"Well," she said, "it probably doesn't matter." She let me go. "It's just as well that little girl knows what kind of man is living under her roof."

"I can keep a secret."

She closed her eyes again, and leaned her head against the wall behind her.

She tried to twist the ring on her finger, but it wouldn't move. "I believe," she said, "we're going to have to cut this ring off. I cannot feel this finger anymore."

This was the summer they announced they were closing the mill. They were opening a new mill in New Mexico on an Indian reservation. Some workers got their walking papers. Some got transfers.

"What shall I do?" my father asked Wanda and me one night when we were walking down to the train depot. "Shall I take the transfer? Tell me what to do, and I'll do it."

We had to keep it secret because it was just the sort of news that would send my mother into a tizzy.

"It would mean a smaller house. You girls would all have to share one room, and the boys would have to share the other. But we'd eat good."

"What else could you do?" Wanda wanted to know.

He shrugged. "Collect the garbage?"

"You could do a lot of things," she said. She was against moving. Wanda was fourteen. She and Zippy had limbo parties for their friends in our living room. My brother Tom and I could out-limbo everybody because we were bendable beyond belief.

"You could work for the post office," Wanda said.

"I guess I could."

"Or the lumber mill."

"Mm-hm. Hate to let old Mike Reed down, though." Mike Reed was my father's boss. "That gentleman's done a lot for me. But I want to be fair to you kids, too. What do you think, Leigh?"

"Let's go."

"You'd have to leave all of your friends."

"That's okay."

"She doesn't have any friends," Wanda said.

"I do too."

"It's different if you're a little kid," she told my father.

"I think somebody's only thinking of herself," I said. He winked and took my hand. Wanda gave me a look.

"Good jobs are not that easy to come by," I said. My father squeezed my hand.

"We should put our fate in the hands of the Lord," I said.

He laughed. "Not bad advice," he said.

Wanda crossed her arms and just stared at the sidewalk in front of her.

On our way home we saw Joe at Lucky's Grill. We always stopped at Lucky's for ice cream on our way home. Joe was in a booth with a blond woman and two little boys. When he saw me a queer look came over him.

"That's the man who sniffs around Rosie Mooney," I said, "and I bet that's his wife and kids."

My father looked at Joe. "Wouldn't be the first time for old Joe Martin," he said quietly. He nodded and Joe nodded back.

"Mr. Martin, how you doing?" I called.

"I'm okay, Leigh. You?" The blond woman smiles. She's wearing red lipstick that makes her look like she's all lips. That's how blond this woman is.

"Can't complain," I said. "I haven't seen Rosie and Theresa Mooney in a while, though." The blond woman keeps smiling. She's smiling at her french fries.

"That old boy," I tell my father when we get outside, "probably has a wife in every state. Don't you think?"

My father put his hands in his pockets. "You shamed him, Leigh."

"Joe?" I hooted.

He looked at me. "You shamed me," he said.

Wanda dug her elbow into me. "You shamed that man's wife," she said.

I dug her back.

"She shamed them, didn't she, Dad?"

My father didn't say anything. He watched the air in front of him.

"God wouldn't spit you from his mouth," Wanda hissed.

Wanda's no saint. She'll knuckleball you in the back, and who are you going to scream to? The cats under the bed? The bloody cats?

Wanda's no saint, and Zip is no saint — *You used to be such a sweet child, we used to dress you up and take you in the buggy and everybody said what a sweet child you were, whatever happened to the sweet child?*

I'll tell you who's the saint. My father is the bloody saint. He'll say, "When I was over there in Guam? When I was fighting the Japansies? I walked to holy mass every day. I'd walk five miles if I had to. If it kilt me, I was going to holy mass."

So give the saint a hand.

The Bean was lying on our lawn, winding the music box. The skater skated. The Bean was keeping her finger on the skater head, and the music was chugalugging because she was pressing the head too hard.

"My dad'd never leave my mom," I was telling her. "He's a good Catholic."

The Bean sucked her cheeks.

"This is why you want the holy sacrament of matrimony in the house. To keep 'em from leaving."

She winds up that music box. Everywhere she goes, the music box goes. Terry was addicted to the skater on the pond.

"Joe'll be back, though," I told her to give her comfort. That morning we'd sat in the peach tree and watched Joe throw his clothes in the back of his truck while Rosie sat on the front porch and just smoked. "Don't you think?"

The Bean lay on her back and let the skater skate on her stomach. She closed her eyes.

"I mean, what'd he say? Did he say, 'I'm leaving you forever,' or did he say, 'I need time to think,' or did he say . . ."

She was holding the skater, letting her go, holding her, letting her go, and the music was revving up just to stop, and I said, "Am I invisible?" Because she hadn't said a word all morning. "Are you a mute?" I said.

She looked at me for a minute, then she screamed and laughed and the music box tumbled to the grass. "We're invisible!" she shouted. She flung her arms and legs out like an angel. "I'm a mute!" she yelled.

Then she started bawling. She says, "Don't look at me." She's put her hands over her face and she's bawling, a pitiful thing.

Me, I lay down next to her, and I didn't look at her, just lay there. The sky was blue-white. After a while she stopped bawling and started hiccupping. I said, "Got the chuck-a-lucks?" She sort of laughs and hiccups. "You know the difference between chuck-a-lucks and hiccups?"

I felt something scratchy on my hand, and it was her withered little paw. She whispered, "Leigh, you are my best friend."

I thought of how skinny she was, and how she'd probably never find anybody to marry her. I held her dry hand and we started to sweat.

I said, "I know what'll cheer us up."

She said, "What?"

I let go her hand, rolled over on my side, propped my head on my hand. I said, "That rich gentleman's money."

We both peed ourselves. I tried to hold it in, but the Bean's hot-footing down the sidewalk, doing a little sidewinder dance, trying to keep her knees together, her pointy bottom shining, and the pee's running down, and I don't know if she's laughing or crying, but I'm laughing so hard my stomach hurts. I peed his porch. Cars were honking. The Bean turned around and did a little dance for them, then scatted off around the house before we got the money. I pounded that door and rang the bell. He was in there. The shades were open and then they closed. He was in there shaking in his boots.

After a while we went for our clothes, but then this car stops at the curb, and this lady gets out, yells, "Hey!" We started running. I looked back, and the lady's my mom's friend, Mrs. Malburg, who makes oily donuts and eats them, fat Mrs. Malburg: "Hey, Leigh!" She is standing on the curb looking at the bush where our clothes are. She shades her eyes. She looks straight at us.

We hid in the little cave under Jesus Rock up there on Smelter Mountain. Theresa Mooney's moaning, "I'm dead." She's scrunched in the dirt, shivering up against the rock, and I don't tell her there are ants there in the shadows. Last year I buried a box of Crackerjacks there for a rainy day, but when the rainy day came, I dug them out and they were crawling with ants. I can't see Theresa Mooney's dirty feet where she's dug in. I don't know if the ants are awake.

The Bean moans, "I am dead, I'm dead, I'm dead." She says, "Will she tell?"

I start digging in the dirt with a stick. "Once," I told her, "there was an Indian maiden who got stole by the Calvary, and when she ran away back to her tribe, they buried her naked in an ant pile and the ants ate her. Her own people did that."

"That's not true," Theresa Mooney said.

I shrugged.

"First of all," she said, "ants can't eat people."

"You don't know about all the species," I told her. "Sugar ants, no. But these were not sugar ants."

She didn't say anything to that.

A train whistle was blowing — the Leadville train coming in. It was five o'clock. By now my dad would be home. He'd be sitting at the kitchen table with his boots unlaced, stirring his coffee. Wanda'd be taking the pot pies out of their boxes.

"Will she tell?" the Bean whispered.

Mrs. Malburg, muddy-eyed Mrs. Malburg, would be sitting across the table from my dad, giving him trouble. They would be talking in whispers so my mother wouldn't hear. "It is," I said, "against human nature to keep a secret."

The Leadville train whistled again. It was probably pulling into the depot.

I closed my eyes and listened hard.

"I'm cold," the Bean whispered.

"You can wrap yourself around me like a spider monkey," I told her. "I don't mind."

She crawled from the back of the cave and wrapped her ice cube self around me. She said, "You smell like yellow urine."

"So lick me," I said, and the Bean laughed.

I was listening for my brothers, who would be coming after us. Wanda would send them. She would say, *Jesus wouldn't spit you from his mouth.* They would all say it. "The Calvary is coming," I told the Bean. "Mark my word."

"We're dead," the Bean said.

"We are dead under Jesus Rock," I yelled so they'd know where to look.

"Shh!" the Bean hissed.

"This is Lazarus's cave!"

She unwrapped herself and scowled at me. She crawled to the edge of the hole, knelt there looking out, her little bottom tucked under her filthy heels. She stood up and stepped out in the sun. She stretched on her tiptoes and looked down the mountain. She turned around, her face twitching to go.

I crawled out, too. The evening breeze had a sting, and the sun was sitting on the mountain. Scrub oak leaves were crackling all around.

"Nobody's coming," she whispered. She squinted down the path.

"That," I said, "is an optical illusion."

At the bottom of the hill in the back of Sick Slim's house, a light went on, and then Sick Slim was standing at the window, looking up Smelter Mountain. We scatted back into the hole. Terry starts giggling and whimpering. "He saw us," she said. "We're trapped."

"Him?" I hooted. "He's blind." Then I remembered what my dad had said, how ever since he got back from playing soldier, Sick Slim didn't like anybody at his back. But we *were* at his back. Two naked children. I laughed.

"What?" the Bean said.

I crawled back out into the sun. I stood up and walked to the edge where he could see me good. I put my hands on my hips like King of the Mountain. I couldn't see his face, couldn't see him looking, but I knew he was.

I said, "Next time, we'll *make* him give us money."

"How?" the Bean said.

I didn't know exactly how. It was coming to me. It was a dream in the distance.

EDWIDGE DANTICAT

Seven

FROM THE NEW YORKER

NEXT MONTH WOULD make it seven years since he'd last seen his wife. Seven, a number he despised but had discovered was a useful marker. There were seven days between paychecks, seven hours, not counting lunch, spent each day at his day job, seven at his night job. Seven was the last number in his age — thirty-seven. And now there were seven hours left before his wife was due to arrive. Maybe it would be more, with her having to wait for her luggage and then make it through the long immigration line and past customs to look for him in the crowd of welcoming faces on the other side of the sliding doors at JFK. That is, if the flight from Port-au-Prince wasn't delayed, as it often was, or canceled altogether.

He shared an apartment in the basement of a house in East Flatbush, Brooklyn, with two other men. To prepare for the reunion, he had cleaned his room. He had thrown out some cherry-red rayon shirts that he knew she would hate. And then he had climbed the splintered steps to the first floor to tell the landlady that his wife was coming. His landlady was also Haitian, a self-employed accountant.

"I don't have a problem with your wife coming," she had told him. She was microwaving a frozen dessert. "I just hope she is clean."

"She is clean," he said.

The kitchen was the only room in the main part of the house that he'd ever seen. It was spotless, and the dishes were neatly organized in glass cabinets. It smelled of pine-scented air freshener.

"Did you tell the men?" she asked. She opened the microwave

and removed two small plastic plates of something that vaguely resembled strawberry cheesecake.

"I told them," he said.

He was waiting for her to announce that she would have to charge him extra. She had agreed to rent the room to one person, not two — a man she'd probably taken for a bachelor.

"I don't know if I can keep this arrangement if everyone's wife starts coming," she said.

He could not speak for the two other men. Michel and Dany had wives, too, but he had no idea if or when those wives would be joining them.

"A woman living down there with three men," the landlady said. "Maybe your wife will be uncomfortable."

He wanted to tell her that it was not up to her to decide whether or not his wife would be comfortable. But he had been prepared for this, too, for some unpleasant remark about his wife. Actually, he was up there as much to give notice that he was looking for an apartment as to announce that his wife was coming. As soon as he found one, he would be moving.

"Okay, then," she said, opening her silverware drawer. "Just remember, you start the month, you pay the whole thing."

"Thank you very much, Madame," he said.

As he walked back downstairs, he scolded himself for calling her Madame. Why had he acted like a servant who had been dismissed? It was one of those class things from home that he couldn't shake. On the other hand, if he had addressed the woman respectfully, it wasn't because she was so-called upper class, or because she spoke French (though never to him), or even because after five years in the same room he was still paying only three hundred and fifty dollars a month. If he had addressed the woman politely that day, it was because he was making a sacrifice for his wife.

After his conversation with the landlady, he decided to have a more thorough one with the men who occupied the other two rooms in the basement. The day before his wife was to arrive, he went into the kitchen to see them. The fact that they were wearing only white, rather sheer, loose boxers as they stumbled about bleary-eyed concerned him.

"You understand, she's a woman," he told them. He wasn't worried that she'd be tempted — they were skin and bones — but if she was still as sensitive as he remembered, their near nakedness might embarrass her.

The men understood.

"If it were my wife," Michel said, "I would feel the same."

Dany simply nodded.

They had robes, Michel declared after a while. They would wear them.

They didn't have robes — all three men knew this — but Michel would buy some, out of respect for the wife. Michel, at forty, the oldest of the three, had advised him to pretty up his room — to buy some silk roses, some decorative prints for the walls (no naked girls), and some vanilla incense, which would be more pleasing than the air fresheners the woman upstairs liked so much.

Dany told him that he would miss their evenings out together. In the old days, they had often gone dancing at the Rendez-Vous, which was now the Cenegal nightclub. But they hadn't gone much since the place had become famous — Abner Louima was arrested there, then beaten and sodomized at a nearby police station.

He told Dany not to mention those nights out again. His wife wasn't to know that he had ever done anything but work his jobs — as a day janitor at Medgar Evers College and as a night janitor at Kings County Hospital. And he wasn't going to tell her about those women who had occasionally come home with him in the early-morning hours. Those women, most of whom had husbands, boyfriends, fiancés, and lovers in other parts of the world, had never meant much to him anyway.

Michel, who had become a lay minister at a small Baptist church near the Rendez-Vous and never danced there, laughed as he listened. "The cock can no longer crow," he said. "You might as well give the rest to Jesus."

"Jesus wouldn't know what to do with what's left of this man," Dany said.

Gone were the late-night domino games. Gone was the phone number he'd had for the past five years, ever since he'd had a phone. (He didn't need other women calling him now.) And it was only as he stood in the crowd of people waiting to meet the flights arriving simultaneously from Kingston, Santo Domingo, and Port-au-Prince that he stopped worrying that he might not see any delight or recognition in his wife's face. There, he began to feel some actual joy, even exhilaration, which made him want to leap forward and grab every woman who vaguely resembled the latest pictures she had sent him, all of which he had neatly framed and hung on the walls of his room.

They were searching her suitcase. Why were they searching her suitcase? One meager bag, which, aside from some gifts for her husband, contained the few things she'd been unable to part with, the things her relatives hadn't nabbed from her, telling her that she could get more, and better, where she was going.

She had kept only her undergarments, a nightgown, and two outfits: the green princess dress she was wearing and a red jumper that she'd gift-wrapped before packing so that no one would take it. People in her neighborhood who had traveled before had told her to gift-wrap everything so that it wouldn't be opened at the airport in New York. Now the customs man was tearing her careful wrapping to shreds as he barked questions at her in mangled Creole.

"Ki sa l ye?" He held a package out in front of her before opening it.

What was it? She didn't know anymore. She could only guess by the shapes and sizes.

He unwrapped all her gifts — the mangoes, sugarcane, avocados, the orange- and grapefruit-peel preserves, the peanut, cashew, and coconut confections, the coffee beans, which he threw into a green bin decorated with drawings of fruits and vegetables with red lines across them. The only thing that seemed as though it might escape disposal was a small packet of trimmed chicken feathers, which her husband used to enjoy twirling in his ear cavity. In the early days, soon after he'd left, she had spun the tips of the feathers inside her ears, too, and discovered that from them she could get *jwisans,* pleasure, an orgasm. She had thought to herself then that maybe the foreign television programs were right: sex was mostly between the ears.

When the customs man came across the small package of feathers, he stared down at it, then looked up at her, letting his eyes linger on her face, mostly, it seemed to her, on her ears. Obviously, he had seen feathers like these before. Into the trash they went, along with the rest of her offerings.

By the time he was done with her luggage, she had little left. The suitcase was so light now that she could walk very quickly as she carried it in her left hand. She followed a man pushing a cart, which tipped and swerved under the weight of three large boxes. And suddenly she found herself before a door that slid open by itself, parting like a glass sea, and as she was standing there the door closed again, and when she moved a few steps forward it opened, and then she saw him. He charged at her and wrapped both his arms around her. And as he held her she felt her feet leave the ground. It was when he put her back down that she finally believed she was really somewhere else, on another soil, in another country.

He could tell she was happy that so many of her pictures were displayed on the wall facing his bed. During the ride home, he had nearly crashed the car twice. He wasn't sure why he was driving so fast. They dashed through the small talk, the inventory of friends and family members and the state of their health. She had no detailed anecdotes about anyone in particular. Some had died and some were still living; he couldn't even remember which. She was bigger than she had been when he left her, what people here might call chubby. It was obvious that she had been to a professional hairdresser, because she was elegantly coiffed with her short hair gelled down to her scalp and a fake bun bulging in the back. She smelled good — a mixture of lavender and lime. He had simply wanted to get her home, if home it was, to that room, and to reduce the space between them until there was no air for her to breathe that he wasn't breathing, too.

The drive had reminded him of the one they had taken to their one-night honeymoon at the Ifé Hotel, when he had begged the uncle who was driving them to go faster, because the next morning he would be on a plane for New York. That night, he'd had no idea that it would be seven years before he would see her again. He'd had it all planned. He knew that he couldn't send for her right away, since he would be overstaying a tourist visa. But he was going to work hard, to find a lawyer and get himself a green card, and then send for his wife. The green card had taken six years and nine months. But now she was here with him, staring at the pictures on his wall as though they were of someone else.

"Do you remember that one?" he asked, to reassure her. He was pointing at a framed eight-by-twelve of her lying on a red mat by a tiny Christmas tree in a photographer's studio. "You sent it last Noël?"

She remembered, she said. It was just that she looked so desperate, as if she were trying to force *him* to remember *her.*

"I never forgot you for an instant," he said.

She said that she was thirsty.

"What do you want to drink?" He listed the juices he had purchased from the Cuban grocer down the street, the combinations he was sure she'd be craving, papaya and mango, guava and pineapple, cherimoya and passion fruit.

"Just a little water," she said. "Cold."

He didn't want to leave her alone while he went to the kitchen. He would have called through the walls for one of the men to get some water, if they were not doing such a good job of hiding behind the closed doors of their rooms to give him some privacy.

When he came back with the glass, she examined it, as if for dirt, and then gulped it down. It was as though she hadn't drunk anything since the morning he'd got on the plane and left her behind.

"Do you want more?" he asked.

She shook her head.

It's too bad, he thought, that in Creole the word for love, *renmen,* is also the word for like, so that as he told her he loved her he had to embellish it with phrases that illustrated the degree of that love. He loved her more than there were seconds in the years they'd been apart, he babbled. He loved her more than the size of the ocean she had just crossed. To keep himself from saying more insipid things, he jumped on top of her and pinned her down on the bed. She was not as timid as she had been on their wedding night. She tugged at his black tie so fiercely that he was sure his neck was bruised. He yanked a few buttons off her dress and threw them aside as she unbuttoned his starched and ironed white shirt, and though in the rehearsals in past daydreams he had gently placed a cupped hand over her mouth, he didn't think to do it now. He didn't care that the other men could hear her, or him. Only for a moment did he think to feel sorry that it might be years before the others could experience the same thing.

He was exhausted when she grabbed the top sheet from the bed, wrapped it around her, and announced that she was going to the bathroom.

"Let me take you," he said.

"Non non," she said. "I can find it."

He couldn't stand to watch her turn away and disappear.

He heard voices in the kitchen, her talking to the men, introducing herself. He bolted right up from the bed when he remembered that all she had on was the sheet. As he raced to the door, he collided with her coming back.

There were two men playing dominoes in the kitchen, she told him, dressed in identical pink satin robes.

He left early for work the next day, along with the other men, but not before handing her a set of keys and instructing her not to let anyone in. He showed her how to work the stove and how to find all the Haitian stations on the AM/FM dial of his night-table radio. She slept late, reliving the night, their laughter after she'd seen the men, who, he explained, had hurried to buy those robes for her benefit. They had made love again and again, forcing themselves to do so more quietly each time. Seven times, by his count — once for each year they'd been apart — but fewer by hers. He had assured her that there was no need to be embarrassed. They were married, before God and a priest. This was crucial for her to remember. That's why he had seen to it on the night before he left. So that something more judicial and committing than a mere promise would bind them. So that even if their union had become a victim of distance and time, it could not have been easily dissolved. They would have had to sign papers to come apart, write letters, speak on the phone about it. He told her that he didn't want to leave her again, not for one second. But he had asked for the day off and his boss had refused. At least they would have the weekends, Saturdays and Sundays, to do with as they wished — to go dancing, sightseeing, shopping, and apartment-hunting. Wouldn't she like to have her own apartment? To make love as much as they wanted and not worry that some men in women's robes had heard them?

At noon, the phone rang. It was him. He asked her what she was doing. She lied and told him that she was cooking, making herself something to eat. He asked what. She said eggs, guessing that there must be eggs in the refrigerator. He asked if she was bored. She said no. She was going to listen to the radio and write letters home.

When she hung up, she turned on the radio. She scrolled between the stations he had pointed out to her and was glad to hear people speaking Creole. There was music playing, too — *konpa* by a group named Top Vice. She switched to a station with a talk show. She sat up to listen as some callers talked about a Haitian American named Patrick Dorismond who had been killed. He had been shot by a policeman in a place called Manhattan. She wanted to call her husband back, but he hadn't left a number. Lying back, she raised the sheet over her head and through it listened to the callers, each one angrier than the last.

When he came home, he saw that she had used what she had found in the refrigerator and the kitchen cabinets to cook a large meal for all four of them. She insisted that they wait for the other men to drift in before they ate, even though he had only a few hours before he had to leave for his night job.

The men complimented her enthusiastically on her cooking, and he could tell that this meal made them feel as though they were part of a family, something they had not experienced in years. They seemed to be happy, eating for pleasure as well as sustenance, chewing more slowly than they ever had before. Usually they ate standing up, Chinese or Jamaican takeout from places down the street. Tonight there was little conversation, beyond praise for the food. The men offered to clean the pots and dishes once they were done, and he suspected that they wanted to lick them before washing them.

He and his wife went to the room and lay on their backs on the bed. He explained why he had two jobs. It had been partly to fill the hours away from her, but also partly because he had needed to support both himself here and her in Port-au-Prince. And now he was saving up for an apartment and, ultimately, a house. She said that she, too, wanted to work. She had finished a secretarial course; perhaps that would be helpful here. He warned her that, because she didn't speak English, she might have to start as a cook in a restaurant or as a seamstress in a factory. He fell asleep mid-thought. She woke him up at nine o'clock, when he was supposed to start work. He rushed to the bathroom to wash his face, came back, and changed his overalls, all the while cursing himself. He was stupid to have overslept, and now he was late. He kissed her goodbye and ran out. He hated being late, being lectured by the night manager, whose favorite reprimand was "There's tons of people like you in this city. Half of them need a job."

She spent the whole week inside, worried that she'd get lost if she ventured out alone, that she might not be able to retrace her steps. Her days fell into a routine. She'd wake up and listen to the radio for news of what was happening both here and back home. Somewhere, not far from where she was, people were in the streets, marching, protesting Dorismond's death, their outrage made even greater by the fact that the Dorismond boy was the American-born son of a well-known singer, whose voice they had heard on the radio back in Haiti. "No justice, no peace!" she chanted while stewing chicken and frying fish. In the afternoons, she wrote letters home. She wrote of the meals that she had made, of the pictures of her on the wall, of the songs and protest chants on the radio. She wrote to family members, and to childhood girlfriends who had been so happy that she was finally going to be with her husband, and to newer acquaintances from the secretarial school, who had been jealous. She also wrote to a male friend, a neighbor who had come to her house three days after her husband had left to see why she had locked herself inside.

He had knocked for so long that she'd had no choice but to open the door. She was still wearing the dress she'd worn to see her husband off. When she collapsed in his arms, he had put a cold compress on her forehead and offered her some water. She had swallowed so much water so quickly that she'd vomited. That night, he had lain down next to her, and in the dark had told her that this was love, if love there was — having the courage to abandon the present for a future that one could only imagine. He had assured her that her husband loved her.

In the afternoons, while she was writing her letters, she would hear someone walking back and forth on the floor above. She took to pacing as well, as she waited for the men to come home. She wanted to tell her husband about that neighbor who had slept next to her for those days after he'd left and in whose bed she had spent many nights after that. Only then would she feel that their future would be true. Someone had said that people lie only at the beginning of relationships. The middle is where the truth resides. But there had been no middle for her husband and herself, just a beginning and many dream-rehearsed endings.

He had first met his wife during carnival in the mountains in Jacmel. His favorite part of the festivities was the finale, on the day before Ash Wednesday, when a crowd of tired revelers would gather on the beach to burn their carnival masks and costumes and feign weeping, symbolically purging themselves of the carousing of the preceding days and nights. She had volunteered to be one of the official weepers — one of those who wailed convincingly as the carnival relics turned to ashes in the bonfire.

"Papa Kanaval ou ale?" "Where have you gone, Father Carnival?" she had howled, with real tears running down her face.

If she could grieve so passionately on demand, he thought, perhaps she could love even more. After the other weepers had left, she stayed behind until the last embers of the bonfire had dimmed. It was impossible to distract her, to make her laugh. She could never fake weeping, she told him. Every time she cried for anything, she cried for everything else that had ever hurt her.

He had traveled between Jacmel and Port-au-Prince while he was waiting for his visa to come through. And when he finally had a travel date, he had asked her to marry him.

One afternoon, when he came home from work, he found her sitting on the edge of the bed in that small room, staring at the pictures of herself on the opposite wall. She did not move as he kissed the top of her head. He said nothing, simply slipped out of his clothes and lay down on the bed, pressing his face against her back. He did not want to trespass on her secrets. He simply wanted to extinguish the carnivals burning in her head.

She was happy when the weekend finally came. Though he slept until noon, she woke up at dawn, rushed to the bathroom before the men could, put on her red jumper and one of his T-shirts, then sat staring down at him on the bed, waiting for his eyes to open.

"What plan do we have for today?" she asked when they finally did.

The plan, he said, was whatever she wanted.

She wanted to walk down a street with him and see faces. She wanted to eat something, an apple or a chicken leg, out in the open with the sun beating down on her face.

As they were leaving the house, they ran into the woman whose footsteps she had been hearing all week long above her head. The woman smiled coyly and said, "*Bienvenue.*" She nodded politely, then pulled her husband away by the hand.

They walked down a street filled with people doing their Saturday food shopping at outside stalls stacked with fruits and vegetables.

He asked if she wanted to take the bus.

"Where to?"

"Anywhere," he said.

From the bus, she counted the frame and row houses, beauty-shop signs, church steeples, and gas stations. She pressed her face against the window, and her breath occasionally blocked her view of the streets speeding by. She turned back now and then to look at him, sitting next to her. There was still a trace of sleepiness in his eyes. He watched her as though he were trying to put himself in her place, to see it all as if for the first time, but could not.

He took her to a park in the middle of Brooklyn, Prospect Park, a vast stretch of land, trees, and trails. They strolled deep into the park, until they could see only a few of the surrounding buildings, which towered like mountains above the landscape. In all her daydreams, she had never imagined that there would be a place like this here. This immense garden, he told her, was where he came to ponder the passing seasons, lost time, and interminable distances.

It was past seven o'clock when they emerged from the park and headed down Parkside Avenue. She had reached for his hand at 5:10 P.M., he had noted, and had not released it since. And now, as they were walking down a dimly lit side street, she kept her eyes upward, looking into the windows of apartments lit by the indigo glow of television screens. When she said she was hungry, they turned onto Flatbush Avenue in search of something to eat.

Walking hand in hand with her through crowds of strangers made him long for his other favorite piece of carnival theater. A bride and groom, in their most lavish wedding clothing, would wander the streets. Scanning a crowd of revelers, they would pick the most stony-faced person and ask, "Would you marry us?" Over the course of several days, for variety, they would modify this request. "Would you couple us?" "Would you make us one?" "Would you tie the noose of love around our necks?" The joke was that when the person took the bait and looked closely, he or she might discover that the bride was a man and the groom a woman. The couple's makeup was so skillfully applied that only the most observant could detect this.

On the nearly empty bus on the way home, he sat across the aisle from her, not next to her as he had that morning. She pretended to keep her eyes on the night racing past the window behind him. He was watching her again. This time he seemed to be trying to see *her* as if for the first time, but could not.

She, too, was thinking of carnival, and of how the year after they'd met they had dressed as a bride and groom looking for someone to marry them. She had disguised herself as the bride and he as the groom, forgoing the traditional puzzle.

At the end of the celebrations, she had burned her wedding dress in the bonfire and he had burned his suit. She wished now that they had kept them. They could have walked these foreign streets in them, performing their own carnival. Since she didn't know the language, they wouldn't have to speak or ask any questions of the stony-faced people around them. They could perform their public wedding march in silence, a silence like the one that had come over them now.

E. L. DOCTOROW

A House on the Plains

FROM THE NEW YORKER

MAMA SAID I WAS thenceforth to be her nephew, and to call her Aunt Dora. She said our fortune depended on her not having a son as old as eighteen who looked more like twenty. Say Aunt Dora, she said. I said it. She was not satisfied. She made me say it several times. She said I must say it believing that she had taken me in since the death of her widowed brother Horace. I said, I didn't know you had a brother named Horace. Of course I don't, she said with an amused glance at me. But it must be a good story if I could fool his son with it.

I was not offended as I watched her primp in the mirror, touching her hair as women do, although you can never see what afterward is different.

With the life insurance, she had bought us a farm fifty miles west of the city line. Who would be there to care if I was her flesh-and-blood son or not? But she had her plans and was looking ahead. I had no plans, I had never had plans, just the inkling of something, sometimes, I didn't know what. I hunched over and went down the stairs with the second trunk wrapped to my back with a rope. Outside, at the foot of the stoop, the children were waiting with their scraped knees and socks around their ankles. They sang their own dirty words to a nursery rhyme. I shooed them away and they scattered off for a minute, hooting and hollering, and then of course came back again as I went up the stairs for the rest of the things.

Mama was standing at the empty bay window. While there is your court of inquest on the one hand, she said, on the other is your court of neighbors. Out in the country, she said, there will be no one to jump to conclusions. You can leave the door open and the window shades up. Everything is clean and pure under the sun.

Well, I could understand that, but Chicago to my mind was the only place to be, with its grand hotels and its restaurants and paved avenues of trees and mansions. Of course, not all Chicago was like that. Our third-floor windows didn't look out on much besides the row of boarding houses across the street. And it is true that in the summer people of refinement could be overcome with the smell of the stockyards, although it didn't bother me. Winter was another complaint that wasn't mine. I never minded the cold. The wind in winter blowing off the lake went whipping the ladies' skirts like a demon dancing around their ankles. And winter or summer you could always ride the electric streetcars if you had nothing else to do. I above all liked the city because it was filled with people all a-bustle, and the clatter of hooves and carriages, and with delivery wagons and drays and peddlers and the boom and clank of freight trains. And when those black clouds came sailing in from the west, pouring thunderstorms upon us so that you couldn't hear the cries or curses of humankind, I liked that best of all. Chicago could stand up to the worst God had to offer. I understood why it was built — a place for trade, of course, with railroads and ships and so on, but mostly to give all of us a magnitude of defiance that is not provided by one house on the plains. And the plains is where those storms come from.

Besides, I would miss my friend Winifred Czerwinska, who stood now on her landing as I was going downstairs with the suitcases.

Come in a minute, she said, I want to give you something. I went in and she closed the door behind me. You can put those down, she said of the suitcases.

My heart always beat faster in Winifred's presence, I could feel it and she knew it too and it made her happy. She put her hand on my chest now and she stood on tiptoes to kiss me with her hand under my shirt feeling my heart pump.

Look at him, all turned out in a coat and tie. Oh, she said, with her eyes tearing up, what am I going to do without my Earle? But she was smiling.

Winifred was not a Mama type of woman. She was a slight, skinny thing, and when she went down the stairs it was like a bird hopping. She wore no powder or perfumery except, by accident, the confectionery sugar that she brought home on her from the bakery where she worked behind the counter. She had sweet cool lips, but one eyelid didn't come up all the way over the blue, which made her not as pretty as she might otherwise be. And of course she had no titties to speak of.

You can write me a letter and I will write back, I said.

What will you say in your letter?

I will think of something, I said.

She pulled me into the kitchen, where she spread her feet and put her forearms flat on a chair so that I could raise her frock and fuck into her in the way she preferred. It didn't take that long, but even so while Winifred wiggled and made her little cat sounds I could hear Mama calling from upstairs as to where I had gotten.

We had ordered a carriage to take us and the luggage at the same time rather than sending it off by the less expensive American Express and taking a horsecar to the station. That was not my idea, but how much money we had after Mama bought the house only she knew. She came down the steps under her broad-brim hat and widow's veil and held her skirts at her shoe tops as the driver helped her into the carriage.

We were making a grand exit in full daylight. This was pure Mama as she lifted her veil and glanced with contempt at the neighbors looking out from their windows. As for the nasty children, they had gone quite quiet at our display of elegance. I swung up beside her and closed the door and at her instruction threw a handful of pennies on the sidewalk and I watched the children push and shove one another and dive to their knees as we drove off.

When we had turned the corner, Mama opened the hatbox I had put on the seat. She removed her black hat and replaced it with a blue number trimmed in fake flowers. Over her mourning dress she draped a glittery shawl in striped colors like the rainbow.

There, she said. I feel so much better now. Are you all right, Earle?

Yes, Mama, I said.

Aunt Dora.

Yes, Aunt Dora.

I wish you had a better mind, Earle. You could have paid more attention to the Doctor when he was alive. We had our disagreements, but he was smart for a man.

*

The train stop of La Ville was a concrete platform and a lean-to for a waiting room and no ticket-agent window. When you got off, you were looking down an alley to a glimpse of their Main Street. Main Street had a feed store, a post office, a white wooden church, a granite stone bank, a haberdasher, a town square with a four-story hotel, and in the middle of the square on the grass the statue of a Union soldier. It could all be counted because there was just one of everything. A man with a dray was willing to take us, and he drove past a few other streets where first there were some homes of substance and another church or two but then, as you moved further out from the town center, there were only worn-looking one-story shingle houses with dark porches and little garden plots and clotheslines out back with only alleys separating them. I couldn't see how, but Mama said there was a population of over three thousand living here. And then, after a couple of miles through farmland, with a silo here and there, off a straight road leading due west through fields of corn, there swung into view what I had not expected: a three-story house of red brick with a flat roof and stone steps up to the front door like something just lifted out of a street of row houses in Chicago. I couldn't believe anyone had built such a thing for a farmhouse. The sun flared in the windowpanes, and I had to shade my eyes to make sure I was seeing what I saw. But that was it in truth, our new home.

Not that I had the time to ponder, not with Mama settling in. We went to work. The house was cobwebbed and dusty and it was rank with the droppings of animal life. Blackbirds were roosting in the top floor, where I was to live. Much needed to be done, but before long she had it all organized and a parade of wagons was coming from town with the furniture she'd Expressed and no shortage of men willing to hire on for a day with hopes for more from this grand good-looking lady with the rings on several fingers. And so the fence went up for the chicken yard, and the weed fields beyond were being plowed under and the watering hole for stock was dredged and a new privy was dug, and I thought for some days Mama was the biggest employer of La Ville, Illinois.

But who would haul the well water and wash the clothes and bake the bread? A farm was a different life, and days went by when I slept under the roof of the third floor and felt the heat of the day still on my pallet as I looked through the little window at the stars and I felt unprotected as I never had in the civilization we had retreated from. Yes, I thought, we had moved backward from the world's progress, and for the first time I wondered about Mama's judgment. In all our travels from state to state and with all the various obstacles to her ambition, I had never thought to question it. But no more than this house was a farmer's house was she a farmer, and neither was I.

One evening we stood on the front steps watching the sun go down behind the low hills miles away.

Aunt Dora, I said, what are we up to here?

I know, Earle. But some things take time.

She saw me looking at her hands, how red they had gotten.

I am bringing an immigrant woman down from Wisconsin. She will sleep in that room behind the kitchen. She's to be here in a week or so.

Why? I said. There's women in La Ville, the wives of all these locals come out here for a day's work, who could surely use the money.

I will not have some woman in the house who will only take back to town what she sees and hears. Use what sense God gave you, Earle.

I am trying, Mama.

Aunt Dora, God damn it.

Aunt Dora.

Yes, she said. Especially here in the middle of nowhere and with nobody else in sight.

She had tied her thick hair behind her neck against the heat and she went about now loose in a smock without her usual women's underpinnings.

But doesn't the air smell sweet, she said. I'm going to have a screen porch built and fit it out with a settee and some rockers so we can watch the grand show of nature in comfort.

She ruffled my hair. And you don't have to pout, she said. You may not appreciate it here this moment with the air so peaceful and the birds singing and nothing much going on in any direction you can see. But we're still in business, Earle. You can trust me on that.

And so I was assured.

*

By and by we acquired an old-fashioned horse and buggy to take us to La Ville and back when Aunt Dora had to go to the bank or the post office or when provisions were needed. I was the driver and horse groom. He, the horse, and I did not get along. I wouldn't give him a name. He was ugly, with a swayback and legs that trotted out splayed. I had butchered and trimmed better-looking plugs than this in Chicago. Once in the barn when I was putting him up for the night he took a chomp in the air just off my shoulder.

Another problem was Bent, the handyman Mama had hired for the steady work. No sooner did she begin taking him upstairs of an afternoon than he was strutting around like he owned the place. This was a problem, as I saw it. Sure enough, one day he told me to do something. It was one of his own chores. I thought you was the hired one, I said to him. He was ugly, like a relation of the horse, and he was shorter than you thought he ought to be, with his long arms and big gnarled hands hanging from them.

Get on with it, I said.

Leering, he grabbed me by the shoulder and put his mouth up to my ear. I seen it all, he said. Oh yes. I seen everything a man could wish to see.

At this I found myself constructing a fate for Bent the handyman. But he was so drunkly stupid I knew Mama must have her own plan for him, or else why would she play up to someone of this ilk, and so I held my ideas in abeyance.

In fact, I was by now thinking I could wrest some hope from the wide loneliness of this farm with views of the plains as far as you could see. What had come to mind? An aroused expectancy or suspense that I recognized from times past. Yes. I had sensed that whatever was going to happen had begun. There was not only the handyman. There were the orphan children. She had contracted for three from the do-good agency in New York that took orphans off the streets and washed and dressed them and put them on the train to foster homes in the midland. Ours were comely enough children, though pale: two boys and a girl, with papers that gave their ages, six, six, and eight, and as I trotted them to the farm they sat up behind me staring at the countryside without a word. They were installed in the back bedroom on the second floor, and they were not like the miserable children from our neighborhood in the city. These were quiet children except for the weeping they were sometimes given to at night, and by and large they did as they were told. Mama had some real feeling for them, Joseph and Calvin and the girl, Sophie, in particular. There were no conditions as to what faith they were to be brought up in nor did we have any in mind. But on Sundays Mama took to showing them off to the Methodist church in La Ville in the new clothes she had bought for them. It gave her pleasure and also bespoke of her pride of position in life. Because it turned out, as I was learning, that even in the farthest reaches of the countryside you lived in society.

And in this great scheme of things my Aunt Dora required Joseph, Calvin, and Sophie to think of her as their Mama. Say Mama, she said to them. And they said it.

Well, so here was this household of us, ready-made, as something bought from a department store. Fannie was the imported cook and housekeeper, who by Mama's design spoke no English but understood well enough what had to be done. She was heavyset, like Mama, with the strength to work hard. And besides Bent, who skulked about by the barns and fences in the sly pretense of work, there was a real farmer out beyond who was sharecropping the acreage in corn. And two mornings a week a retired county teacher woman came by to tutor the children in reading and arithmetic.

Mama said one evening, We are an honest-to-goodness enterprise here, a functioning family better off than most in these parts, but we are running at a deficit, and if we don't have something in hand before winter the only resources will be the insurance I took out on the little ones.

She lit the kerosene lamp on the desk in the parlor and wrote out a personal and read it to me: "Widow offering partnership in prime farmland to dependable man. A modest investment is required." What do you think, Earle?

It's okay.

She read it again to herself. No, she said. It's not good enough. You've got to get them up off their ass and out of the house to the credit union and then on a train to La Ville, Illinois. That's a lot to do with just a few words. How about this: "Wanted!" That's good, it bespeaks urgency. And doesn't every male in the world think he's what is wanted? "Wanted — Recently widowed woman with a bountiful farm in God's own country has need of Nordic man of sufficient means for partnership in same."

What is Nordic? I said.

Well, that's pure cunning right there, Earle, because that is all they got in the states where we print this — Swedes and Norwegies just off the boat. But I'm letting them know a lady's preference.

All right, but what's that you say there — "of sufficient means"? What Norwegie off the boat'll know what that's all about?

This gave her pause. Good for you, Earle, you surprise me sometimes. She licked the pencil point. So we'll just say "with cash."

We placed the personal in one paper at a time in towns in Minnesota and then in South Dakota. The letters of courtship commenced, and Mama kept a ledger with the names and dates of arrival, making sure to give each candidate his sufficient time. We always advised the early-morning train, when the town was not yet up and about. Besides my regular duties, I had to take part in the family reception. Each of them would be welcomed into the parlor and Mama would serve coffee from a wheeled tray, and Joseph, Calvin, and Sophie, her children, and I, her nephew, would sit on the sofa and hear our biographies conclude with a happy ending, which was the present moment. Mama was so well spoken at these times I was as apt as the poor foreigners to be caught up in her modesty, so seemingly unconscious was she of the greatheartedness of her. They by and large did not see through to her self-congratulation. And of course she was a large handsome woman to look at. She wore her simple finery for these first impressions, a plain, pleated gray cotton skirt and a starched white shirtwaist and no jewelry but the gold cross on a chain that fell between her bosoms, and her hair was combed upward and piled atop her head in a state of fetching carelessness.

I am their dream of Heaven on earth, Mama said to me along about the third or fourth. Just to see how their eyes light up standing beside me looking out over their new land. Puffing on their pipes, giving me a glance that imagines me as available for marriage — who can say I don't give value in return?

Well, that is one way to look at it, I said.

Don't be smug, Earle. You're in no position. Tell me an easier way to God's blessed Heaven than a launch from His Heaven on earth. I don't know of one.

And so our account in the La Ville Savings Bank began to compound nicely. The late-summer rain did just the right thing for the corn, as even I could see, and it was an added few unanticipated dollars we received from the harvest. If there were any complications to worry about, it was that fool Bent. He was so dumb he was dangerous. At first, Mama indulged his jealousy; I could hear them arguing upstairs, he roaring away and she assuring him so quietly I could hardly hear what she said. But it didn't do any good. When one of the Norwegies arrived, Bent just happened to be in the yard where he could have a good look. One time there was his ugly face peering through the porch window. Mama signaled me with a slight motion of her head and I quickly got up and pulled the shade.

It was true Mama might lay it on a bit thick. She might coquette with this one, yes, just as she might affect a widow's piety with that one. It all depended on her instinct for the particular man's character. It was easy enough to make believers of them; if I had to judge them as a whole I would say they were simple men, not exactly stupid but lacking command of our language and with no wiles of their own. By whatever combination of sentiments and signatures, she never had anything personal intended but the business at hand, the step-by-step encouragement of the cash into our bank account.

The fool Bent imagined Mama looking for a husband from among these men. His pride of possession was offended. When he came to work each morning, he was often three sheets to the wind, and if she happened not to invite him upstairs for the afternoon siesta he would go home in a state, turning at the road to shake his fist and shout up at the windows before he set out for town in his crouching stride.

Mama said to me on one occasion, The damned fool has feelings.

Well, that had not occurred to me in the way she meant it, and maybe in that moment my opinion of the handyman was raised to a degree. Not that he was any less dangerous. Clearly he had never learned that the purpose of life is to improve your station in it. It was not an idea available to him. Whatever you were, that's what you would always be. So he saw these foreigners who couldn't even talk right not only as usurpers but as casting a poor light on his existence. Were I in his position, I would learn from the example of these immigrants, and think what I could do to put together a few dollars and buy some farmland for myself. Any normal person would think that. Not him. The only idea that got through his thick skull was that he lacked the hopes of even the lowest foreigner. So I would come back from the station with one of them in the buggy and the fellow would step down, his plaid suit and four-in-hand and his derby proposing him as a man of sufficient means, and it was like a shadow and sudden chilling as from a black cloud came over poor Bent, who could understand only that it was too late for him — everything, I mean, it was all too late.

And, finally, to show how dumb he was, he didn't realize it was all too late for them, too.

Then everything green began to fade off yellow, the summer rains were gone, and the wind off the prairie blew the dried-out topsoil into gusty swirls that rose and fell like waves in a dirt sea. At night the windows rattled. At first frost, the two little boys caught the croup.

Mama pulled the Wanted ad back from the out-of-state papers, saying she needed to catch her breath. I didn't know what was in the ledger, but her saying that meant our financial situation was improved. And now, as I supposed with all farm families, winter would be a time for rest.

Not that I was looking forward to it. How could I, with nothing to do?

I wrote a letter to my friend Winifred Czerwinska, in Chicago. I had been so busy until now I hardly had the time to be lonely. I said that I missed her and hoped before too long to come back to city life. As I wrote, a rush of pity for myself came over me and I almost sobbed at the picture in my mind of the Elevated trains and the lights of the theater marquees and the sounds I imagined of the streetcars and even of the lowings of the abattoir where I had earned my wages. But I only said I hoped she would write me back.

I think the children felt the same way about this cold countryside. They had been displaced from a greater distance away in a city larger than Chicago. They could not have been colder huddled at some steam grate than they were now, with blankets to their chins. From the day they arrived, they wouldn't leave one another's side, and though she was not croupy herself, Sophie stayed with the two boys in their bedroom, attending to their hackings and wheezes and sleeping in an armchair in the night. Fannie cooked up oatmeal for their breakfasts and soup for their dinners, and I took it upon myself to bring the tray upstairs in order to get them talking to me, since we were all related in a sense and in their minds I would be an older boy orphan, taken in like them. But they would not talk much, only answering my friendly questions yes or no in their soft voices, looking at me all the while with some dark expectation in their eyes. I didn't like that. I knew they talked among themselves all the time. They were smart. For instance, they knew enough to stay out of Bent's way when he was drinking. But when he was sober they followed him around. And one day I had gone into the stable, to harness the horse, and found them snooping around in there, so they were not without unhealthy curiosity. Then there was the unfortunate matter of one of the boys, Joseph, the shorter, darker one — he had found a pocket watch and watch fob in the yard, and when I said it was mine he said it wasn't. Whose is it then, I said. I know it's not yours, he said as he finally handed it over. To make more of an issue of it was not wise, so I didn't, but I hadn't forgotten.

Mama and I were nothing if not prudent, discreet, and in full consideration of the feelings of others in all our ways and means, but I believe children have another sense that enables them to know something even when they can't say what it is. As a child I must have had it, but of course it leaves you as you grow up, it may be a trait children are given so that they will live long enough to grow up.

But I didn't want to think the worst. I reasoned to myself that were I plunked down so far away from my streets among strangers who I was ordered to live with as their relation, in the middle of this flat land of vast empty fields that would stir in any breast nothing but a recognition of the presiding deafness and dumbness of the natural world, I, too, would behave as these children were behaving.

And then, one stinging cold day in December, I went into town to pick up a package from the post office. We had to write away to Chicago for those things it would not do to order from the local merchants. The package was in, but there was also a letter addressed to me, and it was from my friend Winifred Czerwinska.

Winifred's penmanship made me smile; the letters were thin and scrawny and did not keep to a straight line but rose and fell while slanting in a downward direction, as if some of her mortal being was transferred to the letter paper. And I knew she had written from the bakery because there was some powdered sugar in the folds.

She was so glad to hear from me and to know where I was. She thought I had forgotten her. She said she missed me. She said she was bored with her job. She had saved her money and hinted that she would be glad to spend it on something interesting, like a train ticket. My ears got hot reading that. In my mind I saw Winifred squinting up at me, I could almost feel her putting her hand under my shirt to feel my heart the way she liked to do.

But on the second page she said maybe I would be interested in news from the old neighborhood. There was going to be another inquest, or maybe the same one reopened.

It took me a moment to understand she was talking about the Doctor, Mama's husband in Chicago. The Doctor's relatives had asked for his body to be dug up. Winifred found this out from the constable, who knocked on her door as he was doing with everyone. The police were trying to find out where we had gone, Mama and I.

I hadn't gotten your letter yet, Winifred said, so I didn't have to lie about not knowing where you were.

I raced home. Why did Winifred think she would otherwise have to lie? Did she believe the bad gossip about us? Was she like the rest of them? I thought she was different. I was disappointed in her, and then I was suddenly very mad at Winifred.

Mama read the letter differently. Your Miss Czerwinska is our friend, Earle. That's something higher than a lover. If I have worried about her slow eye being passed on to the children, if it shows up, we will just have to have it corrected with surgery.

What children, I said.

The children of your blessed union with Miss Czerwinska, Mama said.

Do not think Mama said this merely to keep me from worrying about the Chicago problem. She sees things before other people see them, she has plans going out through all directions of the universe, she is not a one-track mind, my Aunt Dora. I was excited by her intentions for me as if I had thought of them myself. Perhaps I had thought of them myself as my secret, but she had read my secret and was now giving her approval. Because I certainly did like Winifred Czerwinska, whose lips tasted of baked goods and who loved it so when I fucked into her. And now it was all out in the open, and Mama not only knew my feelings but expressed them for me, and it only remained for the young lady to be told that we were engaged.

I thought then her visiting us would be appropriate, especially as she was prepared to pay her own way. But Mama said, Not yet, Earle, everyone in the house knew you were loving her up, and if she was to quit her job in the bakery and pack a bag and go down to the train station even the Chicago police, as stupid as they are, they would put two and two together.

Of course, I did not argue the point, though I was of the opinion that the police would find out where we were regardless. There were indications all over the place, not anything as difficult as a clue to be discerned only by the smartest of detectives, but bank-account transfers, forwarding mail, and such. Why, even the driver who took us to the station might have picked up some remark of ours, and certainly a ticket-seller at Union Station might remember us, Mama being such an unusual-looking woman, very decorative and regal to the male eye, she would surely be remembered by a ticket-seller who would not see her like from one year to the next.

Maybe a week went by before Mama expressed an opinion about the problem. You can't trust people, she said, it's that damn sister of his who didn't even shed a tear at the grave. Why, she even told me how lucky the Doctor was to have found me so late in life.

I remember, I said.

And how I had taken such good care of him.

Which was true, I said.

Relatives are the fly in the ointment, Earle.

Mama's not being concerned so much as she was put out meant that we had more time than I would have thought. Our quiet lives of winter went on as before, though as I watched and waited she was obviously thinking things through. I was satisfied to wait even though she was particularly attentive to Bent, inviting him in for dinner as if he was not some hired hand but a neighboring farmer.

And I had to sit across the table on the children's side and watch him struggle to hold the silver in his fist and slurp his soup and pity him the way he had pathetically combed his hair down and tucked his shirt in and the way he folded his fingers under when he happened to see the dirt under his nails. This is good eats, he said aloud to no one in particular, and even Fannie, as she served, gave a little humph, as if, despite having no English, she understood clearly enough how out of place he was here at our table.

Well, as it turned out there were things I didn't know. For instance, that the little girl, Sophie, had adopted Bent, or maybe made a pet of him as you would any dumb beast, but they had become friends of a sort and she had confided to him remarks she overheard in the household. Maybe if she was making Mama into her mama she thought she was supposed to make the wretched bum of a hired hand into her father, I don't know. Anyway, there was this alliance between them that showed to me that she would never rise above her unsavory life in the street as a vagrant child. She looked like an angel, with her little bow mouth and her pale face and gray eyes and her hair in a single long braid that Mama herself did every morning, but she had the hearing of a bat and could stand on the second-floor landing and listen all the way down the stairs to our private conversations in the front parlor. Of course, I knew that only later. It was Mama who learned that Bent was putting it about to his drinking cronies in town that the Madame Dora they thought was such a lady was his love slave and a woman on the wrong side of the law back in Chicago.

Mama, I said, I have never liked this fool, though I have been holding my ideas in abeyance for the fate I have in mind for him. But here he accepts our wages and eats our food then goes and does this?

Hush, Earle, not yet, not yet, she said. But you are a good son to me, and I can take pride that as a woman alone I have bred in you the highest sense of family honor. She saw how troubled I was. She hugged me. Are you not my very own knight of the Round Table? she said. But I was not comforted; it seemed to me that forces were massing slowly but surely against us in a most menacing way. I didn't like it. I didn't like it that we were going along as if everything was hunky-dory, even to giving a grand Christmas Eve party for the several people in La Ville whom Mama had come to know

— how they all drove out in their carriages under the moon that was so bright on the plains of snow that it was like a black daytime, the local banker, the merchants, the pastor of the First Methodist church, and other such dignitaries and their wives. The spruce tree in the parlor was imported from Minnesota and all alight with candles, and the three children were dressed for the occasion and went around with cups of eggnog for the assembled guests. I knew how important it was for Mama to establish her reputation as a person of class who had flattered the community by joining it, but all these people made me nervous. I didn't think it was wise having so many rigs parked in the yard, and so many feet tromping about the house, or going out to the privy. Of course, it was a lack of self-confidence on my part, and how often was it that Mama had warned me nothing was more dangerous than that, because it was translated into the face and physique as wrongdoing, or at least defenselessness, which amounted to the same thing. But I couldn't help it. I remembered the pocket watch that the little sniveling Joseph had found and held up to me, swinging it from its fob, I sometimes made mistakes, I was human, and who knew what other mistakes lay about for someone to find and hold up to me.

But now Mama looked at me over the heads of her guests. The children's tutor had brought her harmonium and we all gathered around the fireplace for some carol singing. Given Mama's look, I sang the loudest. I have a good tenor voice and I sent it aloft to turn heads and make the La Villers smile. I imagined decking the halls with boughs of holly until there was kindling and brush enough to set the whole place ablaze.

Just after the New Year, a man appeared at our door, another Swede with his Gladstone bag in his hand. We had not run the Wanted ad all winter, and Mama was not going to be home to him, but this fellow was the brother of one of them who had responded to it the previous fall. He gave his name, Henry Lundgren, and said his brother Per Lundgren had not been heard from since leaving Wisconsin to look into the prospect here.

Mama invited him in and sat him down and had Fannie bring in some tea. The minute I looked at him I remembered the brother. Per Lundgren had been all business. He did not blush or go shy in Mama's presence, nor did he ogle. Instead he asked sound questions. He had also turned the conversation away from his own circumstances, family relations, and so on, which Mama put people through in order to learn who was back home and might be waiting. Most of the immigrants, if they had family, it was still in the Old Country, but you had to make sure. Per Lundgren was close-mouthed, but he did admit to being unmarried, and so we decided to go ahead.

And here was Henry, the brother he had never mentioned, sitting stiffly in the wing chair with his arms folded and the aggrieved expression on his face. They had the same reddish fair skin, with a long jaw and thinning blond hair, and pale woeful-looking eyes with blond eyelashes. I would say Henry here was the younger by a couple of years, but he turned out to be as smart as Per, or maybe even smarter. He did not seem to be as convinced of the sincerity of Mama's expressions of concern as I would have liked. He said his brother had made the trip to La Ville with other stops planned afterward to two more business prospects, a farm some twenty miles west of us and another in Indiana. Henry had traveled to these places, which is how he learned that his brother never arrived for his appointments. He said Per had been traveling with something over two thousand dollars in his money belt.

My goodness, that is a lot of money, Mama said.

Our two savings, Henry said. He comes here to see your farm. I have the advertisement, he said, pulling a piece of newspaper from his pocket. This is the first place he comes to see.

I'm not sure he ever arrived, Mama said. We've had many inquiries.

He arrived, Henry Lundgren said. He arrived the night before so he will be on time the next morning. This is my brother. It is important to him, even if it costs money. He sleeps at the hotel in La Ville.

How could you know that? Mama said.

I know from the guestbook in the La Ville hotel, where I find his signature, Henry Lundgren said.

Mama said, All right, Earle, we've got a lot more work to do before we get out of here.

We're leaving?

What is today, Monday. I want to be on the road Thursday the latest. I thought with the inquest matter back there we were okay at least to the spring. This business of a brother pushes things up a bit.

I am ready to leave.

I know you are. You have not enjoyed the farm life, have you? If that Swede had told us he had a brother, he wouldn't be where he is today. Too smart for his own good, he was. Where is Bent?

She went out to the yard. He was standing at the corner of the barn, peeing a hole in the snow. She told him to take the carriage and go to La Ville and pick up half a dozen gallon cans of kerosene at the hardware. They were to be put on our credit.

It occurred to me that we still had a goodly amount of our winter supply of kerosene. I said nothing. Mama had gone into action, and I knew from experience that everything would come clear by and by.

And then, late that night, when I was in the basement, she called downstairs to me that Bent was coming down to help.

I don't need help, thank you, Aunt Dora, I said, so astonished that my throat went dry.

At that they both clomped down the stairs and back to the potato bin, where I was working. Bent was grinning that toothy grin of his as always, to remind me he had certain privileges.

Show him, Mama said to me. Go ahead, it's all right, she assured me.

So I did, I showed him. I showed him something to hand. I opened the top of the gunnysack and he looked down it.

The fool's grin disappeared, the unshaven face went pale, and he started to breathe through his mouth. He gasped, he couldn't catch his breath, a weak cry came from him, and he looked at me in my rubber apron and his knees buckled and he fainted dead away.

Mama and I stood over him. Now he knows, I said. He will tell them.

Maybe, Mama said, but I don't think so. He's now one of us. We have just made him an accessory.

An accessory?

After the fact. But he'll be more than that by the time I get through with him, she said.

We threw some water on him and lifted him to his feet. Mama took him up to the kitchen and gave him a couple of quick swigs.

Bent was thoroughly cowed, and when I came upstairs and told him to follow me he jumped out of his chair as if shot. I handed him the gunnysack. It was not that heavy for someone like him, he held it in one hand at arm's length, as if it would bite. I led him to the old dried-up well behind the house, where he dropped it down into the muck. I poured the quicklime in and then we lowered some rocks down and nailed the well cover back on, and Bent the handyman, he never said a word but just stood there shivering and waiting for me to tell him what to do next.

Mama had thought of everything. She had paid cash down for the farm but somewhere or other got the La Ville bank to give her a mortgage, and so when the house burned it was the bank's money. She had been withdrawing from the account all winter, and now that we were closing shop she mentioned to me the actual sum of our wealth for the first time. I was very moved to be confided in, like her partner.

But really it was the small touches that showed her genius. For instance, she had noted immediately of the inquiring brother, Henry, that he was in height not much taller than I am. Just as in Fannie the housekeeper she had hired a woman of a girth similar to her own. Meanwhile, at her instruction, I was letting my dark beard grow out. And at the end, before she had Bent go up and down the stairs pouring the kerosene in every room, she made sure he was good and drunk. He would sleep through the whole thing in the stable, and that's where they found him, with his arms wrapped like a lover's arms around an empty can of kerosene.

The plan was for me to stay behind for a few days just to keep an eye on things. We have pulled off something prodigious that will go down in the books, Mama said. But that means all sorts of people will be flocking here and you can never tell when the unexpected arises. Of course, everything will be fine, but if there's something more we have to do you will know it.

Yes, Aunt Dora.

Aunt Dora was just for here, Earle.

Yes, Mama.

Of course, even if there was no need to keep an eye out you would still have to wait for Miss Czerwinska.

This is where I didn't understand her thinking. The one bad

thing in all of this is that Winifred would read the news in the Chicago papers. There was no safe way I could get in touch with her now that I was dead. That was it, that was the end of it. But Mama had said it wasn't necessary to get in touch with Winifred. This remark made me angry.

You said you liked her, I said.

I do, Mama said.

You called her our friend, I said.

She is.

I know it can't be helped, but I wanted to marry Winifred Czerwinska. What can she do now but dry her tears and maybe light a candle for me and go out and find herself another boyfriend?

Oh, Earle, Earle, Mama said, you know nothing about a woman's heart.

But anyhow I followed the plan to stay on a few days, and it wasn't that hard with a dark stubble and a different hat and a long coat. There were such crowds nobody would notice anything that wasn't what they'd come to see, that's what a fever was in these souls. Everyone was streaming down the road to see the tragedy, they were in their carriages and they were walking and standing up in drays, people were paying for anything with wheels to get them out there from town, and after the newspapers ran the story they were coming not just from La Ville and the neighboring farms but from out of state in their automobiles and on the train from Indianapolis and Chicago. And with the crowds came the hawkers to sell sandwiches and hot coffee, and peddlers with balloons and little flags and whirligigs for the children. Someone had taken photographs of the laid-out skeletons in their crusts of burlap and printed them up as postcards for mailing, and these were going like hotcakes.

The police had been inspired by the charred remains they found in the basement to look down the well and then to dig up the chicken yard and the floor of the stable. They had brought around a rowboat to dredge the water hole. They were really very thorough, they kept making their discoveries and laying out what they found in neat rows inside the barn. They had called in the county sheriff and his men to help with the crowds, and they got some kind of order going, keeping people in lines to pass them by the open barn doors so everyone would have a turn, it was the only choice the police had if they didn't want a riot, but even then the oglers went around back all the way up the road to get into the procession again — it was the two headless remains of Madame Dora and her nephew that drew the most attention, and of course the wrapped bundles of the little ones.

There was such heat from this population that the snow was gone from the ground, and on the road and in the yard and behind the house and even into the fields where the trucks and automobiles were parked everything had turned to mud so that it seemed even the season was transformed. I just stood and watched and took it all in, and it was amazing to see so many people with this happy feeling of spring, as if a population of creatures had formed up out of the mud especially for the occasion. That didn't help the smell any, though no one seemed to notice. The house itself made me sad to look at, a smoking ruin that you could see the sky through. I had become fond of that house. A piece of the floor hung down from the third story, where I had my room. I disapproved of people pulling off the loose brickwork to take home for a souvenir, there was a lot of laughing and shouting, but of course I did not say anything. In fact, I was able to rummage around the ruin without drawing attention to myself, and sure enough I found something — it was the syringe, for which I knew Mama would be thankful.

I overheard some conversation about Mama, what a terrible end for such a fine lady who loved children was the gist of it. I thought as time went on, in the history of our life of La Ville I myself would not be remembered very clearly. Mama would become famous in the papers as a tragic victim mourned for her good works, whereas I would be noted down only as a dead nephew. Even if the past caught up with her reputation and she was slandered as the suspect widow of several insured husbands, I would still be in the shadows. This seemed to me an unjust outcome considering the contribution I had made, and I found myself for a moment resentful. Who was I going to be in life now that I was dead and not even Winifred Czerwinska was there to bend over for me?

Back in town at night, I went behind the jail to the cell window where Bent was and I stood on a box and called to him softly, and when his bleary face appeared I ducked to the side where he couldn't see me and whispered these words: "Now you've seen it all, Bent. Now you have seen everything."

I stayed in town to meet every train that came through from Chicago. I could do that without fear — there was such a heavy traffic all around, such swirls of people, all of them too excited and thrilled to take notice of someone standing quietly in a doorway or sitting on the curb in the alley behind the station. And, as Mama told me, I knew nothing about the heart of a woman, because all at once there was Winifred Czerwinska, stepping down from the coach, her suitcase in her hand. I lost her for a moment through the steam from the locomotive blowing across the platform, but then there she was in her dark coat and a little hat and the most forlorn expression I have ever seen on a human being. I waited till the other people had drifted away before I approached her. Oh my, how grief-stricken she looked, standing by herself on the train platform with her suitcase and big tears rolling down her face. Clearly she had no idea what to do next, where to go, who to speak to. So she had not been able to help herself when she heard the terrible news. And what did that mean except that if she was drawn to me in my death she truly loved me in my life. She was so small and ordinary in appearance, how wonderful that I was the only person to know that under her clothes and inside her little rib cage the heart of a great lover was pumping away.

Well, there was a bad moment or two. I had to help her sit down. I am here, Winifred, it's all right, I told her over and over again, and I held my arms around her shaking, sobbing wracked body.

I wanted us to follow Mama to California, you see. I thought, given all the indications, Winifred would accept herself as an accessory after the fact.

RICHARD FORD

Puppy

FROM THE SOUTHERN REVIEW

EARLY THIS PAST SPRING someone left a puppy inside the back gate of our house, and then never came back to get it. This happened at a time when I was traveling up and back to St. Louis each week, and my wife was intensely involved in the AIDS marathon, which occurs, ironically enough, around tax time in New Orleans and is usually the occasion for a lot of uncomfortable, conflicted spirits, which inevitably get resolved, of course, by good will and dedication.

To begin in this way is only to say that our house is often empty much of the day, which allowed whoever left the puppy to do so. We live on a corner in the fashionable historical district. Our house is large and old and conspicuous — typical of the French Quarter — and the garden gate is a distance from the back door, blocked from it by thick ligustrums. So to set a puppy down over the iron grating and slip away unnoticed wouldn't be hard, and I imagine was not.

"It was those kids," my wife said, folding her arms. She was standing with me inside the French doors, staring out at the puppy, which was seated on the brick pavement looking at us with what seemed like insolent curiosity. It was small and had slick, short coarse hair and was mostly white, with a few triangular black side-patches. Its tail stuck alertly up when it was standing, making it look as though it might've had pointer blood back in its past. For no particular reason, I gauged it to be three months old, though its legs were long and its white feet larger than you would expect. "It's those ones in the neighborhood wearing all the black," Sallie said.

"Whatever you call them. All penetrated everywhere and ridiculous, living in doorways. They always have a dog on a rope." She tapped one of the square panes with her fingernail to attract the puppy's attention. It had begun diligently scratching its ear, but stopped and fixed its dark little eyes on the door. It had dragged a red plastic dust broom from under the outside back stairs, and this was lying in the middle of the garden. "We have to get rid of it," Sallie said. "The poor thing. Those shitty kids just got tired of it. So they abandon it with us."

"I'll try to place it," I said. I had been home from St. Louis all of five minutes and had barely set my suitcase inside the front hall.

"Place it?" Sallie's arms were folded. "Place it where? How?"

"I'll put up some signs around," I said, and touched her shoulder. "Somebody in the neighborhood might've lost it. Or else someone found it and left it here so it wouldn't get run over. Somebody'll come looking."

The puppy barked then. Something (who knows what) had frightened it. Suddenly it was on its feet barking loudly and menacingly at the door we were standing behind, as though it had sensed we were intending something and resented that. Then just as abruptly it stopped and, without taking its dark little eyes off us, squatted puppy-style and pissed on the bricks.

"That's its other trick," Sallie said. The puppy finished and delicately sniffed at its urine, then gave it a sampling lick. "What it doesn't pee on it jumps on and scratches and barks at. When I found it this morning, it barked at me, then it jumped on me and peed on my ankle and scratched my leg. I was only trying to pet it and be nice." She shook her head.

"It was probably afraid," I said, admiring the puppy's staunch little bearing, its sharply pointed ears and simple, uncomplicated pointer's coloration. Solid white, solid black. It was a boy dog.

"Don't get attached to it, Bobby," Sallie said. "We have to take it to the pound."

My wife is from Wetumpka, Alabama. Her family were ambitious, melancholy Lutheran Swedes who somehow made it to the South because her great-grandfather had accidentally invented a lint shield for the ginning process that ended up saving people millions. In one generation the Holmbergs from Lund went from being dejected, stigmatized immigrants to being moneyed gentry with snooty Republican attitudes and a strong sense of entitlement. In Wetumpka there was a dog pound, and stray dogs were always feared for carrying mange and exotic fevers. I've been there; I know this. A dogcatcher prowled around with a ventilated, louver-sided truck and big catch net. When an unaffiliated dog came sniffing around anybody's hydrangeas, a call was made and off it went forever.

"There aren't dog pounds anymore," I said.

"I meant the shelter," Sallie said privately. "The SPCA — where they're nice to them."

"I'd like to try the other way first. I'll make a sign."

"But aren't you leaving again tomorrow?"

"Just for two days," I said. "I'll be back."

Sallie tapped her toe, a sign that something had made her unsettled. "Let's not let this drag out." The puppy began trotting off toward the back of the garden and disappeared behind one of the big brick planters of pittosporum. "The longer we keep it, the harder it'll be to give it up. And that *is* what'll happen. We'll have to get rid of it eventually."

"We'll see."

"When the time comes, I'll let *you* take it to the pound," she said.

I smiled apologetically. "That's fine. If the time comes, then I will."

We ended it there.

I am a longtime practitioner before the federal appeals courts, arguing mostly large, complicated negligence cases in which the appellant is a hotel or a restaurant chain engaged in interstate commerce, which has been successfully sued by an employee or a victim of what is often some terrible mishap. Mostly I win my cases. Sallie is also a lawyer, but did not like the practice. She works as a resource specialist, which means fundraising, for by and large progressive causes: the homeless, women at risk in the home, children at risk in the home, nutrition issues, et cetera. It is a far cry from the rich, *arriviste*-establishment views of her family in Alabama. I am from Vicksburg, Mississippi, from a very ordinary although solid suburban upbringing. My father was an insurance-company attorney. Sallie and I met in law school at Yale, in the seventies. We have always thought of ourselves as lucky in life, and yet in no way extraordinary in our goals or accomplishments. We are simply southerners from sturdy, supportive families who had the good fortune to get educated well and who came back more or less to home, ready to fit in. Somebody has to act on that basic human impulse, we thought, or else there's no solid foundation of livable life.

One day after the old millennium's end and the new one's beginning, Sallie said to me — this was at lunch at Le Périgord on Esplanade, our favorite place — "Do you happen to remember" — she'd been thinking about it — "that first little watercolor we bought, in Old Saybrook? The tilted sailboat sail you could barely recognize in all the white sky. At that little shop near the bridge?" Of course I remembered it. It's in my law office in Place St. Charles, a cherished relic of youth.

"What about it?" We were at a table in the shaded garden of the restaurant, where it smelled sweet from some kind of heliotrope. Tiny wild parrots were fluttering up in the live-oak foliage and chittering away. We were eating a cold crab soup.

"Well," she said. Sallie has pale, almost animal-blue eyes and translucently caramel northern European skin. She has kept away from the sun for years. Her hair is cut roughly and parted in the middle, like some Bergman character from the sixties. She is forty-seven and extremely beautiful. "It's completely trivial," she went on, "but how did we ever know back then that we had any taste? I don't really even care about it, you know that. You have much better taste than I do in most things. But why were we sure we wouldn't choose that little painting and then have it be horrible? Explain that to me. And what if our friends had seen it and laughed about us behind our backs? Do you ever think that way?"

"No," I said, my spoon above my soup, "I don't."

"You mean it isn't interesting? Or eventually we'd have figured out better taste all by ourselves?"

"Something like both," I said. "It doesn't matter. Our taste is fine and would've been fine. I still have that little boat in my office. People pass through and admire it all the time."

She smiled in an inwardly pleased way. "Our friends aren't the point, of course. If we'd liked sad-clown paintings or put antimacassars on our furniture, I wonder if we'd have a different, *worse* life now," she said. She stared down at her lined-up knife and spoons. "It just intrigues me. Life's so fragile in the way we experience it."

"What's the point?" I had to return to work soon. We have few friends now in any case. It's natural.

She furrowed her brow and scratched the back of her head, using her index finger. "It's about how altering one small part changes everything."

"One star strays out of line and suddenly there's no Big Dipper?" I said. "I don't really think you mean that. I don't really think you're getting anxious just because things might have gone differently in your life." I will admit this amused me.

"That's a very frivolous way to see it." She looked down at her own untried soup and touched its surface with the rim of her spoon. "But yes, that's what I mean."

"But it isn't true," I said, and wiped my mouth. "It'd still be the thing it is. The Big Dipper or whatever you cared about. You'd just ignore the star that falls and concentrate on the ones that fit. Our life would've been exactly the same, despite bad art."

"You're the lawyer, aren't you?" This was condescending, but I don't think she meant it to be. "You just ignore what doesn't fit. But it wouldn't be the same, I'm sure of that."

"No," I said. "It wouldn't have been exactly the same. But almost."

"There's only one Big Dipper," she said, and began to laugh.

"That we know of, and so far. True."

This exchange I give only to illustrate what we're like together — what seems important and what doesn't. And how we can let potentially difficult matters go singing off into oblivion.

The afternoon the puppy appeared, I sat down at the leathertop desk in our dining room where I normally pay the bills and diligently wrote out one of the hand-lettered signs you see posted on laundromat announcement boards and stapled to telephone poles alongside advertisements for new massage therapies, gay health issues, and local rock concerts. PUPPY, my sign said in black Magic Marker, and after that the usual data, with my office phone number and the date (March 23). This sheet I Xeroxed twenty-five times on Sallie's copier. Then I found the stapler she used for putting up the AIDS marathon posters, went upstairs and got out an old braided leather belt from my closet, and went down to the garden to take the puppy with me. It seemed good to bring him along while I stapled up the posters about him. Someone could recognize him, or just take a look at him and see he was available and attractive and claim him on the spot. Such things happen, at least in theory.

When I found him he was asleep behind the ligustrums in the far corner. He had worked and scratched and torn down into the bricky brown dirt and made himself a loll deep enough that half of his little body was out of sight below ground level. He had also broken down several ligustrum branches and stripped the leaves and chewed the ends until the bush was wrecked.

When he sensed me coming forward, he flattened out in his hole and growled his little puppy growl. Then he abruptly sat up in the dirt and aggressively barked at me in a way that — had it been a big dog — would've alarmed me and made me stand back.

"Puppy?" I said, meaning to sound sympathetic. "Come out." I was still wearing my suit pants and white shirt and tie — the clothes I wear in court. The puppy kept growling and then barking at me, inching back behind the wrecked ligustrum until he was in the shadows against the brick wall that separates us from the street. "Puppy?" I said again in a patient, cajoling way, leaning in among the thick green leaves. I'd made a loop out of my belt, and I reached forward and slipped it over his head. But he backed up farther when he felt the weight of the buckle, and unexpectedly began to yelp — a yelp that was like a human shout. And then he turned and began to claw up the bricks, scratching and springing, his paws scraping and his ugly little tail jerking, at the same time letting go his bladder until the bricks were stained with hot, terrified urine.

Which, of course, made me lose heart, since it seemed cruel to force this on him even for his own good. Whoever had owned him had evidently not been kind. He had no trust of humans, even though he needed us. To take him out in the street would only terrify him worse, and discourage anyone from taking him home and giving him a better life. Better to stay, I decided. In our garden he was safe and could have a few hours' peace to himself.

I reached and tried to take the belt loop off, but when I did he bared his teeth and snapped and nearly caught the end of my thumb with his little white incisor. I decided just to forget the whole effort and go about putting up my signs alone.

I stapled up all the signs in no time — at the laundromat on Barracks Street, in the gay deli, outside the French patisserie, inside the coffee shop and the adult news on Decatur. I caught all the telephone poles in a four-block area. On several of the poles and all the message boards I saw that others had lost pets too, mostly cats. *Hiroki's lost. We're utterly disconsolate. Can you help? Call Jamie or Hiram at . . .* Or, *We miss our Mittens. Please call us or give her a good home. Please!* In every instance as I made the rounds I stood a moment and read the other notices to see if anyone had reported a lost puppy. But (and I was surprised) no one had.

On a short, disreputable block across from the French Market, a section that includes a seedy commercial strip (sex shops, T-shirt emporiums, and a slice-of-pizza outlet), I saw a group of the young people Sallie had accused of abandoning our puppy. They were, as she'd remembered, sitting in an empty store's doorway, dressed in heavy, ragged black clothes and thick-soled boots with various chains attached and studded wristlets, all of them — two boys and two girls — pierced, and tattooed with Maltese crosses and dripping knife blades and swastikas, all dirty and utterly pointless but abundantly surly and apparently willing to be violent. These young people had a small black dog tied with a white cotton cord to one of the boys' heavy boots. They were drinking beer and smoking but otherwise just sitting, not even talking, simply looking malignantly at the street or at nothing in particular.

I felt there was little to fear, so I stopped in front of them and asked if they or anyone they knew had lost a white-and-black puppy with simple markings in the last day, because I'd found one. The boy who seemed to be the oldest and was large and unshaven, with brightly dyed purple-and-green hair cut into a flattop — the one who had the dog leashed to his boot — this boy looked up at me without obvious expression. He turned then to one of the immensely dirty-looking, fleshy, pale-skinned girls crouched farther back in the grimy door stoop, smoking — this girl had a crude cross tattooed into her forehead like Charles Manson is supposed to have — and asked, "Have you lost a little white-and-black puppy with simple markings, Samantha? I don't think so. Have you? I don't remember you having one today." The boy had an unexpectedly youthful-sounding, nasally midwestern accent, the kind I'd been hearing in St. Louis that week, although it had been high-priced attorneys who were speaking it. I know little enough about young people, but it occurred to me that this boy was possibly one of these lawyers' children, someone whose likeness you'd see on a milk carton or a Web site devoted to runaways.

"Ah, no," the girl said, then suddenly spewed out laughter.

The big, purple-haired boy looked up at me and produced a disdainful smile. His eyes were the darkest, steeliest blue, impenetrable and intelligent.

"What are you doing sitting here?" I wanted to say to him. "I know you left your dog at my house. You should take it back. You should all go home now."

"I'm sorry, sir," the boy said, mocking me, "but I don't believe we'll be able to help you in your important search." He smirked at his three friends.

I started to go. Then I stopped and handed him a paper sign and said, "Well, if you hear about a puppy missing anywhere."

He said something as he took it. I don't know what it was, or what he did with the sign when I was gone, because I didn't look back.

That evening Sallie came home exhausted. We sat at the dining room table and drank a glass of wine. I told her I'd put my signs all around, and she said she'd seen one and it looked fine. Then for a while she cried quietly because of disturbing things she'd seen and heard at the AIDS hospice that afternoon, and because of various attitudes — typical New Orleans attitudes, she thought — voiced by some of the marathon organizers, which seemed callous and constituted right things done for wrong reasons, all of which made the world seem — to her, at least — an evil place. I have sometimes thought she might've been happier if we had chosen to have children or, failing that, if we'd settled someplace other than New Orleans, someplace less parochial and exclusive, a city like St. Louis, in the wide Middle West — where you can be less personally involved in things but still be useful. New Orleans is a small town in so many ways. And we are not from here.

I didn't mention what the puppy had done to the ligustrums, or the kids I'd confronted at the French Market, or her description of them having been absolutely correct. Instead I talked about my work on the Brownlow-Maisonette appeal, and about what good colleagues all the St. Louis attorneys had turned out to be, how much they'd made me feel at home in their understated, low-key offices and how this relationship would bear important fruit in our presentation before the Eighth Circuit. I talked some about the definition of negligence as it is applied to common carriers, and about the unexpected latter-day reshapings of general tort-law paradigms in the years since the Nixon appointments. And then Sallie said she wanted to take a nap before dinner and went upstairs, obviously discouraged from her day and from crying.

Sallie suffers, and has as long as I've known her, from what she calls her war dreams — violent, careering, antic, destructive Technicolor nightmares without plots or coherent scenarios, just sudden drop-offs into deepest sleep accompanied by images of dismembered bodies flying around and explosions and brilliant flashes and soldiers of unknown armies being hurtled through trap doors and hanged or thrust out through bomb bays into empty, screaming space. These are terrible things I don't even like to hear about and that would scare the wits out of anyone. She usually awakes from these dreams slightly worn down, but not especially spiritually disturbed. And for this reason I believe her to be constitutionally very strong. Once I convinced her to go lie down on Dr. Merle Mackey's well-known couch for a few weeks and let him try to get to the bottom of all the mayhem. Which she willingly did. Though after a month and a half Merle told her — and told me privately at the tennis club — that Sallie was as mentally and morally sturdy as a racehorse, and that some things occurred for no demonstrable reason, no matter how Dr. Freud had viewed it. In Sallie's case, her dreams (which have always been intermittent) were just the baroque background music of how she resides on the earth and didn't represent, as far as he could observe, repressed memories of parental abuse or some kind of private disaster she didn't want to confront in daylight. "Weirdness is part of the human condition, Bob," Merle said. "It's thriving all around us. You've probably got some taint of it. Aren't you from up in Mississippi?" "I am," I said. "Then I wouldn't want to get *you* on my couch. We might be there forever." Merle smirked like somebody's presumptuous butler. "No, we don't need to go into that," I said. "No, sir," Merle said, "we really don't." Then he pulled a big smile, and that was the end of it.

After Sallie was asleep I stood at the French doors again. It was nearly dark, and the tiny white lights she had strung up like holiday decorations in the cherry laurel had come on by their timer and delivered the garden into an almost Christmasy lumination and loveliness. Dusk can be a magical time in the French Quarter — the sky so bright blue, the streets lush and shadowy. The puppy had come back to the middle of the garden and lay with his sharp little snout settled on his spotted front paws. I couldn't see his little feral eyes, but I knew they were trained on me, where I stood watching him, with the yellow chandelier light behind me. He still wore my woven leather belt looped to his neck like a leash. He seemed as peaceful and as heedless as he was likely ever to be. I had set out some Vienna sausages in a plastic saucer, and beside it a red plastic mixing bowl full of water — both where I knew he'd find them. I assumed he had eaten and drifted off to sleep before emerging, now that it was evening, to remind me he was still here, and possibly to express a growing sense of ease with his new surroundings. I was tempted to think what a strange, unpredictable experience it was to be him, so new to life and without essential defenses, and in command of little. But I stopped this thought for obvious reasons. And I realized, as I stood there, that my feelings about the puppy had already become slightly altered. Perhaps it was Sallie's Swedish tough-mindedness influencing me; or perhaps it was the puppy's seemingly untamable nature; or possibly it was all those other signs on all the other message boards and stapled to telephone poles, signs that seemed to state in a cheerful but hopeless way that fate was ineluctable, and character, personality, will, even untamable nature were only its accidental byproducts. I looked out at the little, low, diminishing white shadow motionless against the darkening bricks, and I thought: All right, yes, this is where you are now, and this is what I'm doing to help you. In all likelihood it doesn't really matter if someone calls, or if someone comes and takes you home and you live a long and happy life. What matters is simply a choice we make, a choice governed by time and opportunity and how well we persuade ourselves to go on until some other powerful force overtakes us. (We always hope it will be a positive and wholesome force, though it may not be.) No doubt this is another view one comes to accept as a lawyer — particularly one who enters events late in the process, as I do. I was, however, glad Sallie wasn't there to know about these thoughts, since it would only have made her think the world was a heartless place, which it really is not.

The next morning I was on the TWA flight back to St. Louis. Though later the evening before, someone had called to ask if the lost puppy I'd advertised had been inoculated for various dangerous diseases. I had to admit I had no idea, since it wore no collar. It *seemed* healthy enough, I told the person. (The sudden barking spasms and the spontaneous peeing didn't seem important.) The caller was clearly an elderly black woman — she spoke with a deep Creole accent and referred to me once or twice as "baby," but otherwise she didn't identify herself. She did say, however, that the puppy would be more likely to attract a family if it had its shots and had been certified healthy by a veterinarian. Then she told me about a private agency uptown that specialized in finding homes for dogs with elderly and shut-in persons, and I dutifully wrote down the agency's name — "Pet Pals." In our overly lengthy talk she went on to say that the gesture of having the puppy examined and inoculated with a rabies shot would testify to the good will required to care for the animal and increase its likelihood of being deemed suitable. After a while I came to think this old lady was probably completely loony and kept herself busy dialing numbers she saw on signs at the laundromat and yakking for hours about lost kittens, macramé classes, and Suzuki piano lessons, things she wouldn't remember the next day. Probably she was one of our neighbors, though there aren't that many black ladies in the French Quarter anymore. Still, I told her I'd look into her suggestion and appreciated her thoughtfulness. When I innocently asked her name, she uttered a surprising profanity and hung up.

"I'll do it," Sallie said the next morning as I was putting fresh shirts into my two-suiter, making ready for the airport and the flight back to St. Louis. "I have some time today. I can't let all this marathon anxiety take over my life." She was watching out the upstairs window down to the garden again. I'm not sure what I'd intended to happen to the puppy. I suppose I hoped he'd be claimed by someone. Yet he was still in the garden. We hadn't discussed a plan of action, though I had mentioned the Pet Pal agency.

"Poor little pitiful," Sallie said in a voice of dread. She took a seat on the bed beside my suitcase, let her hands droop between her knees, and stared at the floor. "I went out there and tried to play with it this morning, I want you to know this," she said. "It was while you were in the shower. But it doesn't know *how* to play. It just barked and peed and then snapped at me in a pretty hateful way. I guess it was probably funny to whoever had him that he acts that way. It's a crime, really." She seemed sad about it. I thought of the sinister blue-eyed, black-coated boy crouched in the fetid doorway across from the French Market with his new little dog and his three acolytes. They seemed like residents of one of Sallie's war dreams.

"The Pet Pal people will probably fix things right up," I said, tying my tie at the bathroom mirror. It was unseasonably chilly in St. Louis, and I had on my wool suit, though in New Orleans it was already summery.

"If they *don't* fix things up, and if no one calls," Sallie said gravely, "then you have to take him to the shelter when you come back. Can we agree about that? I saw what he did to the plants. They can be replaced. But he's really not our problem." She turned and looked at me on the opposite side of our bed, whereon her long-departed Swedish grandmother had spent her first marriage night long ago. The expression on Sallie's round face was somber but decidedly settled. She was willing to try to care about the puppy because I was going away and she knew it would make me feel better if she tried. It is an admirable human trait, and undoubtedly how most good deeds occur — because you have the occasion, and there's no overpowering reason to do something else. But I was aware she didn't really care what happened to the puppy.

"That's exactly fine," I said, and smiled at her. "I'm hoping for a good outcome. I'm grateful to you for taking him."

"Do you remember when we went to Robert Frost's cabin?" Sallie said.

"Yes, I do." And surely I did.

"Well, when you come back from Missouri, I'd like us to go to Robert Frost's cabin again." She smiled at me shyly.

"I think I can do that," I said, closing my suitcase. "Sounds great."

Sallie bent sideways toward me and extended her smooth, perfect face to be kissed as I went past the bed with my baggage. "We don't want to abandon that," she said.

"We never will," I answered, leaning to kiss her on the mouth. And then I heard the honk of my cab at the front of the house.

Robert Frost's cabin is a great story about Sallie and me. The spring of our first year in New Haven, we began reading Frost's poems aloud to each other, as antidotes to the grueling hours of reading cases on replevin and the rule against perpetuities and theories of intent and negligence — the usual shackles law students wear at exam time. I remember only a little of the poems now, twenty-six years later: "Better to go down dignified / With boughten friendship at your side / Than none at all. Provide, provide!" We thought we knew what Frost was getting at: that you make your way in the world and life — all the way to the end — as best you can. And so at the close of the school year, when it turned warm and our classes were over, we got in the old Chrysler Windsor my father had given me and drove up to where we'd read Frost had had his mountainside cabin in Vermont. The state had supposedly preserved it as a shrine, though you had to walk far back through the mosquito-y woods and off a winding logger's road to find it. We wanted to sit on Frost's front porch in some rustic chair he'd sat in, and read more poems aloud to each other. Being young southerners educated in the North, we felt Frost represented a kind of old-fashioned but indisputably authentic Americanism, vital exposure we'd grown up exiled from because of race troubles and because of absurd preoccupations about the South itself, practiced by people who should know better. Yet we'd always longed for that important exposure, and felt it represented rectitude-in-practice, self-evident wisdom, and a sense of fairness expressed by an unpretentious bent for the arts. (I've since heard Frost was nothing like that, but was mean and stingy and hated better than he loved.)

When Sallie and I arrived at the little log cabin in the spring woods, it was locked up tight, with no one around. In fact it seemed to us like no one ever came there, though the state's signs seemed to indicate this was the right place. Sallie went around the cabin looking in the windows until she found one that wasn't locked. And when she told me about it, I said we should crawl in and nose around and read the poem we wanted to read and let whoever came tell us to leave.

But once we got inside, it was much colder than outside, as if the winter and something of Frost's true spirit had been captured and preserved by the log and mortar. Before long we had stopped our reading — after doing "Design" and "Mending Wall" and "Death of the Hired Man" in front of the cold fireplace. And partly for warmth we decided to make love in Frost's old bed, which was made up as he might've left it years before. (Later it occurred to us that possibly nothing had ever happened in the cabin, and maybe we'd even broken into the wrong cabin and made love in someone else's bed.)

But that's the story. That was what Sallie meant by a visit to Robert Frost's cabin — an invitation to me, upon my return, to make love to her, an act that the events of life and years sometimes can overpower and leave unattended. In a moment of panic, when we thought we heard voices out on the trail, we jumped into our clothes and by accident left our Frost book on the cold cabin floor. No one, of course, ever turned up.

That night I spoke to Sallie from St. Louis, at the end of a full day of vigorous preparations with the Missouri lawyers (whose clients were reasonably afraid of being put out of business by a $250 million class-action judgment). She, however, had nothing but unhappy news to impart. Some homeowners were trying to enjoin the entire AIDS marathon because of a routing change that went too near their well-to-do Audubon Place neighborhood. Plus one of the original organizers was now on the verge of death (not unexpected). She talked more about good-deeds-done-for-wrong-reasons among her hospice associates, and also about some plainly bad deeds committed by other rich people who didn't like the marathon and wanted AIDS to go away. Plus nothing had gone right with our plans for placing the puppy into Pet Pals.

"We went to get its shots," Sallie said sadly. "And it acted perfectly fine when the vet had it on the table. But when I drove it out to Pet Pals on Prytania, the woman — Mrs. Myers, her name was — opened the little wire gate on the cage I'd bought, just to see him. And he jumped at her and snapped at her and started barking. He just barked and barked. And this Mrs. Myers looked horrified and said, 'Why, whatever in the world's wrong with it?' 'It's afraid,' I said to her. 'It's just a puppy. Someone's abandoned it. It doesn't understand anything. Haven't you ever had that happen to you?' 'Of course not,' she said, 'and we can't take an *abandoned* puppy anyway.' She was looking at me as though I was trying to steal something from her. 'Isn't that what you do here?' I said. And I'm sure I raised my voice to her."

"I don't blame you a bit," I said from wintry St. Louis. "I'd have raised my voice."

"I said to her, 'What are you here for? If this puppy wasn't abandoned, why would *I* be here? I wouldn't, would I?'

"'Well, you have to understand we really try to place the more mature dogs whose owners for some reason can't keep them, or are being transferred.' Oh God, I hated her, Bobby. She was one of these wide-ass Junior League bitches who'd gotten bored with flower arranging and playing canasta at the Boston Club. I wanted just to dump the dog right out in the shop and leave, or take a swing at her. I said, 'Do you mean you won't take him?' The puppy was in its cage and was being completely quiet and nice. 'No, I'm sorry, it's untamed,' this dowdy, stupid woman said. 'Untamed!' I said. 'It's an abandoned puppy, for fuck's sake.'

"She just looked at me then as if I'd suddenly produced a bomb and was jumping all around. 'Maybe you'd better leave now,' she said. I'd probably been in the shop all of two minutes, and here she was ordering me out. I said, 'What's wrong with you?' I *know* I shouted then. I was so frustrated. 'You're not a pet pal at all,' I shouted. 'You're an enemy of pets.'"

"You just got mad," I said, happy not to have been there.

"Of course I did," Sallie said. "I let myself get mad because I wanted to scare this hideous woman. I wanted her to see how stupid she was and how much I hated her. She did look around at the phone as if she was thinking about calling 911. Someone I know came in then. Mrs. Hensley from the Art League. So I just left."

"That's all good," I said. "I don't blame you for any of it."

"No. Neither do I." Sallie took a breath and let it out forcefully into the receiver. "We have to get rid of it, though. Now." She was silent a moment, then she began. "I tried to walk it around the neighborhood using the belt you gave it. But it doesn't know how to be walked. It just struggles and cries, then barks at everyone. And if you try to pet it, it pees. I saw some of those kids in black sitting on the curb. They looked at me like I was a fool, and one of the girls made a little kissing noise with her lips, and said something sweet, and the puppy just sat down on the sidewalk and stared at her. I said, 'Is this your dog?' There were four of them, and they all looked at each other and smiled. I know it was theirs. They had another dog with them, a black one. We just have to take him to the pound, though, as soon as you come back tomorrow. I'm looking at him now, out in the garden. He just sits and stares like some Hitchcock movie."

"We'll take him," I said. "I don't suppose anybody's called."

"No. And I saw someone putting up new signs and taking yours down. I didn't say anything. I've had enough with Jerry DeFranco about to die, and our injunction."

"Too bad," I said, because that was how I felt — that it was too bad no one would come along and out of the goodness of his heart take the puppy in.

"Do you think someone left it as a message?" Sallie said. Her voice sounded strange. I pictured her in the kitchen, with a cup of tea just brewed in front of her on the Mexican tile counter. It's good she set the law aside. She becomes involved in ways that are far too emotional. Distance is essential.

"What kind of message?" I asked.

"I don't know," she said. Oddly enough, it was starting to snow in St. Louis, small dry flakes backed — from my hotel window — by an empty, amber-lit cityscape and just the top curve of the great silver arch. It is a nice cordial city, though not distinguished in any way. "I can't figure out if someone thought we were the right people to care for a puppy, or were making a statement showing their contempt."

"Neither," I said. "I'd say it was random. Our gate was available. That's all."

"Does that bother you?"

"Does what?"

"Randomness."

"No," I said. "I find it consoling. It frees the mind."

"Nothing seems random to me," Sallie said. "Everything seems to reveal some plan."

"Tomorrow we'll work this all out," I said. "We'll take the dog, and then everything'll be better."

"For us, you mean? Is something wrong with us? I just have this bad feeling tonight."

"No," I said. "Nothing's wrong with us. But it *is* us we're interested in here. Good night, now, sweetheart."

"Good night, Bobby," Sallie said in a resigned voice, and we hung up.

*

That night in the Mayfair Hotel, with the window shades open to the early-spring snow and orange-lit darkness, I experienced my own strange dream. In my dream I'd gone on a duck-hunting trip into the marsh that surrounds our city. It was winter and early morning, and someone had taken me out to a duck blind before it was light. These are things I still do, as a matter of fact. But when I was set out in the blind with my shotgun, I found that beside me on the wooden bench was one of my law partners, seated with his shotgun between his knees and wearing strange red canvas hunting clothes — something you'd never wear in a duck blind. And he had the puppy with him, the same one that was then in our back garden awaiting whatever its fate would be. And my partner was with a woman, who either was or looked very much like the actress Liv Ullmann. The man was Paul Thompson, a man I (outside my dream) have good reason to believe once had an affair with Sallie, an affair that almost caused us to split apart without our even ever discussing it, except that Paul, who was older than I am and big and rugged, suddenly died — actually in a duck blind, of a terrible heart attack. It is a thing that can happen in the excitement of shooting.

In my dream Paul Thompson spoke to me and said, "How's Sallie, Bobby?" I said, "Well, she's fine, Paul, thanks," because we were pretending he and Sallie didn't have the affair I'd employed a private detective to authenticate — and almost did completely authenticate. The Liv Ullmann woman said nothing, just sat against the wooden sides of the blind seeming sad, with long straight blond hair. The little white-and-black puppy sat on the duckboard flooring and stared at me. "Life's very fragile in the way we experience it, Bobby," Paul Thompson, or his ghost, said to me. "Yes, it is," I said. I assumed he was referring to what he'd been doing with Sallie. (There had been some suspicious photos, though to be honest, I don't think Paul really cared about Sallie. Just did it because he could.) The puppy, meanwhile, kept staring at me. Then the Liv Ullmann woman herself smiled in an ironic way.

"Speaking about the truth tends to annihilate truth, doesn't it?" Paul Thompson said to me.

"Yes," I answered. "I'm certain you're right." And then for a sudden instant it seemed like it had been the puppy who'd spoken Paul's words. I could see his little mouth moving after the words were already spoken. Then the dream faded and became a different dream, which involved the millennium fireworks display from New Year's Eve, and didn't stay in my mind like the Paul Thompson dream did, and does even to this day.

I make no more of this dream than I make of Sallie's dreams, though I'm sure Merle Mackey would have plenty to say about it.

When I arrived back in the city the next afternoon, Sallie met me at the airport, driving her red Wagoneer. "I've got it in the car," she said as we walked to the parking structure. I realized she meant the puppy. "I want to take it to the shelter before we go home. It'll be easier." She seemed as though she'd been agitated but wasn't agitated now. She had dressed herself in aqua walking shorts and a loose pink blouse that showed her pretty shoulders.

"Did anyone call?" I asked. She was walking faster than I was, since I was carrying my suitcase and a box of brief materials. I'd suffered a morning of tough legal work in a cold, unfamiliar city and was worn out and hot. I'd have liked a vodka martini instead of a trip to the animal shelter.

"I called Kirsten and asked if she knew anyone who'd take the poor little thing," Sallie said. Kirsten is her sister, and lives in Andalusia, Alabama, where she owns a flower shop with her husband, who's a lawyer for a big cotton consortium. I'm not fond of either of them, mostly because of their simpleminded politics, which includes support for the Confederate flag, prayer in the public schools, and the abolition of affirmative action — all causes I have been outspoken about. Sallie, however, can sometimes forget she went to Mount Holyoke and Yale and step back into being a pretty, chatty southern girl when she gets together with her sister and her cousins. "She said she probably *did* know someone," Sallie went on, "so I said I'd arrange to have the puppy driven right to her doorstep. Today. This afternoon. But then she said it seemed like too much trouble. I told her it *wouldn't* be any trouble for *her* at all, that *I'd* do it or arrange it to be done. Then she said she'd call me back, and didn't. Which is typical of my whole family's sense of responsibility."

"Maybe we should call her back," I said as we reached her car. We had a phone in the Wagoneer. I wasn't looking forward to visiting the SPCA.

"She's forgotten about it already," Sallie said. "She'd just get wound up."

When I looked through the back window of Sallie's Jeep, the puppy's little wire cage was sitting in the luggage space. I could see his white head, facing back, in the direction it had come from. What could it have been thinking?

"The vet said it's going to be a really big dog. Big feet tell you that."

Sallie was getting in the car. I put my suitcase in the back seat so as to not alarm the puppy. Twice it barked its desperate little high-pitched puppy bark. Possibly it knew me. Though I realized it would never have been an easy puppy to get attached to. My father had a neat habit of reversing propositions he was handed as a way of assessing them. If a subject seemed to have one obvious outcome, he'd imagine the reverse of it; if a business deal had an obvious beneficiary, he'd ask who benefited but didn't seem to. Needless to say, these are valuable skills lawyers use. But I found myself thinking — except I didn't say it to Sallie — that though we may have thought we were doing the puppy a favor by trying to find it a home, we were really doing ourselves a favor by presenting ourselves to be the kind of supposedly decent people who do that *sort* of thing. I am, for instance, a person who stops to move turtles off busy interstates, or picks up butterflies in shopping-mall parking lots and puts them into the bushes to give them a fairer chance at survival. I know these are pointless acts of pointless generosity. Yet there isn't a time when I do it that I don't get back in the car thinking more kindly about myself. (Later I often work around to thinking of myself as a fraud, too.) But the alternative is to leave the butterfly where it lies expiring, or to let the big turtle meet annihilation on the way to the pond, and in doing these things let myself in for the indictment of cruelty or the sense of loss that would follow. Possibly, anyone would argue, these issues are too small to think about seriously, since whether you perform these acts or don't perform them, you always forget about them in about five minutes.

Except for weary conversation about my morning at Ruger, Todd, Jennings, and Sallie's rerouting victory with the AIDS race, which was set for Saturday, we didn't say much as we drove to the SPCA.

Sallie had obviously researched the address, because she got off the interstate at an exit I'd never used and that immediately brought us down onto a wide boulevard with old cars parked on the neutral ground and paper trash cluttering the curbs down one long side of some brown-brick housing projects where black people were outside on their stoops and wandering around the street in haphazard fashion. There were a few dingy-looking barbecue and gumbo cafés, and two tire-repair shops where work was taking place out in the street. A tiny black man standing on a peach crate was performing haircuts in a dinette chair set up on the sidewalk, his customer wrapped in newspaper, and some older men had stationed a card table on the grassy median and were playing in the sunlight. There were no white people anywhere. It was a part of town, in fact, where most white people would've been afraid to go. Yet it was not a bad section, and the Negroes who lived there no doubt looked on this world as something other than a hopeless place.

Sallie took a wrong turn off the boulevard and onto a rundown residential street of pastel shotgun houses where black youths in baggy trousers and big black sneakers were playing basketball without a goal. The boys watched us drive past but said nothing. "I've gotten us off wrong here," she said in a distracted, hesitant voice. She is not comfortable around black people when she is the only white — which is a residue of her privileged Alabama upbringing, where everything and everybody belonged to a proper place and needed to stay there.

She slowed at the next corner and looked both ways down a similar small street of shotgun houses. More black people were out washing their cars or waiting at bus stops in the sun. I noticed this to be Creve Coeur Street, which was where the *Times-Picayune* said an unusual number of murders occurred each year. All that happened at night, of course, and involved black people killing other black people for drug money. It was now 4:45 in the afternoon, and I felt perfectly safe.

The puppy barked again in his cage, a soft, anticipatory bark, then Sallie drove us a block farther and spotted the street she'd been looking for — Rousseau Street. The residential buildings stopped there, and old, dilapidated two- and one-story industrial uses began: an offshore pipe manufactory, a frozen seafood company, a shut-down recycling center where people had gone on leaving their garbage in plastic bags. There was also a small, windowless cube of a building that housed a medical clinic for visiting sailors off foreign ships. I recognized it because our firm had once represented the owners in a personal-injury suit, and I remembered grainy photos of the building and my thinking that I'd never need to see it up close.

Near the end of this block was the SPCA, which occupied a long, glum, red-brick warehouse-looking building with a small red sign by the street and a tiny gravel parking lot. One might've thought the proprietors didn't want its presence too easily detected.

The SPCA's entrance was nothing but a single windowless metal door at one end of the building. There were no shrubberies, no disabled slots, no directional signs leading in, just this low, ominous, flat-roofed building with long factory clerestories facing the lot and the seafood company. An older wooden shed was attached on the back. And a small sign I hadn't seen because it was fastened too low on the building said: YOU MUST HAVE A LEASH. ALL ANIMALS MUST BE RESTRAINED. CLEAN UP AFTER YOUR ANIMAL. IF YOUR DOG BITES A STAFF MEMBER YOU ARE RESPONSIBLE. THANKS MUCH.

"Why don't you take him in his cage," Sallie said, nosing up to the building, becoming very efficient. "I'll go in and start the paperwork. I already called them." She didn't look my way.

"That's fine," I said.

When we got out I was surprised again at how warm it was, and how close and dense the air felt. Summer seemed to have arrived during the day I was gone, which is not untypical of New Orleans. I smelled an entirely expectable animal gaminess combined with a fish smell and something metallic that felt hot and slightly burning in my nose. And the instant I was out into the warm, motionless air I could hear barking inside the building. I assumed the barking was triggered by the sound of a car arriving. Dogs trained themselves to the hopeful sound of motors.

Across the street from the SPCA were other shotgun houses I hadn't noticed. Elderly black people were sitting in metal lawn chairs on their little porches, observing me getting myself organized. It would be a difficult place to live, I thought, and quite a lot to get used to with the noise and the procession of animals coming and going.

Sallie disappeared through the unfriendly little door, and I opened the back of the Wagoneer and hauled out the puppy in his cage. He stumbled to one side when I took a grip on the wire rungs, then barked several agitated, heartfelt barks and began clawing at the wires and my fingers, giving me a good scratch on the knuckles that almost caused me to drop the whole contraption. The cage, even with him in it, was very light, though my face was so close I could smell his urine. "You be still in there," I said.

For some reason, and with the cage in my grasp, I looked around at the colored people across the street, silently watching me. I had nothing in mind to say to them. They were sympathetic, I felt sure, to what was going on and thought it was better than cruelty. I had started to sweat because I was wearing my business suit. I awkwardly waved a hand toward them, but of course no one responded.

When I had maneuvered the cage close to the metal door, I for some reason looked to the left and saw down the grimy alley between the SPCA and the sailors' clinic to where a round steel canister was attached to the SPCA building by large corrugated aluminum pipes, all of it black and new-looking. This, I felt certain, was a device for disposing of animal remains, though I didn't know how. Probably some incinerating invention that didn't have an outlet valve or a stack — something very efficient. It was an extremely sinister thing to see and reminded me of what we all heard years ago about terrible vacuum chambers and gassed compartments for dispatching unwanted animals. Probably they weren't even true stories. Now, of course, it's just an injection. They go to sleep, feeling certain they'll wake up.

Inside the SPCA it was instantly cool, and Sallie had almost everything done. The barking I'd heard outside had not ceased, but the gamy smell was replaced by a loud disinfectant odor that was everywhere. The reception area was a cubicle with a couple of metal desks and fluorescent tubes in the high ceiling, and a calendar on the wall showing a golden retriever standing in a wheat field with a dead pheasant in its mouth. Two high school–age girls manned the desks, and one was helping Sallie fill out her documents. These girls undoubtedly loved animals and worked after school and had aspirations to be vets. A sign on the wall behind the desks said PLACING PUPPIES IS OUR FIRST PRIORITY. This was here, I thought, to make people like me feel better about abandoning dogs. To make forgetting easier.

Sallie was leaning over one of the desks, filling out a thick green document, and looked around to see me just as an older, stern-faced woman in a white lab coat and black rubber boots entered from a side door. Her small face and both her hands had a puffy but also a leathery texture that southern women's skin often takes on — too much sun and alcohol, too many cigarettes. Her hair was dense and dull reddish brown and heavy around her face, making her head seem smaller than it was. This woman, however, was extremely friendly and smiled easily, though I knew just from her features and what she was wearing that she was not a veterinarian.

I stood holding the cage until one of the high school girls came around her desk and looked in it and said the puppy was cute. It barked so that the cage shook in my grip. "What's his name?" she said, and smiled in a dreamy way. She was a heavyset girl, very pale, with a lazy left eye. Her fingernails were painted bright orange and looked unkempt.

"We haven't named him," I said, the cage starting to feel unwieldy.

"We'll name him," she said, pushing her fingers through the wires. The puppy pawed at her, then licked her fingertips, then made little crying sounds when she removed her finger.

"They place sixty-five percent of their referrals," Sallie said over the forms she was filling out.

"Too bad it id'n a holiday," the woman in the lab coat said in a husky voice, watching Sallie finish. She spoke like somebody from across the Atchafalaya, somebody who had once spoken French. "Dis place be a ghost town by Christmas, you know?"

The helper girl who'd played with the puppy walked out through the door that opened onto a long concrete corridor full of shadowy, metal-fenced cages. Dogs immediately began barking again, and the foul animal odor entered the room almost shockingly. An odd place to seek employment, I thought.

"How long do you keep them?" I said, and set the puppy's cage on the concrete floor. Dogs were barking beyond the door, one big-sounding dog in particular, though I couldn't see it. A big yellow tiger-striped cat that apparently had free rein in the office walked across the desktop where Sallie was going on writing and rubbed against her arm, and made her frown.

"Five days," the puffy-faced Cajun woman said, and smiled in what seemed like an amused way. "We try to place 'em. People be in here all the time, lookin'. Puppies go fast 'less they something wrong with them." Her eyes found the cage on the floor. She smiled at the puppy as if it could understand her. "You cute," she said, then made a dry kissing noise.

"What usually disqualifies them?" I said, and Sallie looked around at me.

"Too aggressive," the woman said, staring approvingly in at the puppy. "If it can't be housebroke, then they'll bring 'em back to us. Which isn't good."

"Maybe they're just scared," I said.

"Some are. Then some are just little naturals. They go in one hour." She leaned over, hands on her lab-coat knees, and looked in at our puppy. "How 'bout you," she said. "You a little natural? Or are you a little scamp? I b'lieve I see a scamp in here." The puppy sat on the wire flooring and stared at her indifferently, just as he had stared at me. I thought he would bark, but he didn't.

"That's all," Sallie said, and turned to me and attempted a hospitable look. She put her pen in her purse. She was thinking I might be changing my mind, but I wasn't.

"Then that's all you need. We'll take over," the supervisor woman said.

"What's the fee?" I asked.

"Id'n no fee," the woman said, and smiled. "Remember me in yo' will." She squatted in front of the cage as if she was going to open it. "Puppy, puppy," she said, then put both hands around the sides of the cage and stood up, holding it with ease. She made a little grunting sound, but she was much stronger than I would've thought. Just then another blond helper girl, this one with a metal brace on her left leg, came humping through the kennels door, and the supervisor just walked right past her, holding the cage, while the dogs down the long, dark corridor started barking ecstatically.

"We're donating the cage," Sallie said. She wanted out of the building, and I did, too. I stood another moment and watched as the woman in the lab coat disappeared along the row of pens, carrying our puppy. Then the green metal door closed, and that was all there was to the whole thing. Nothing very ceremonial.

On our drive back downtown we were both, naturally enough, sunk into a kind of woolly, disheartened silence. From up on the interstate, the spectacle of modern, southern city life and ambitious new construction where once had been a low, genteel old river city seemed particularly gruesome and unpromising and probably seemed the same to Sallie. To me, who labored in one of the tall metal-and-glass enormities — I could actually see my office windows in Place St. Charles, small, undistinguished rectangles shining high up among countless others — it felt alien to history and to my own temperament. Behind these square mirrored windows, human beings were writing and discussing and preparing cases, and on other floors were performing biopsies, CAT scans, drilling out cavities, delivering news both welcome and unwelcome to all sorts of other expectants — clients, patients, partners, spouses, children. People were in fact there waiting for *me* to arrive that very afternoon, anticipating news of the Brownlow-Maisonette case — where *were* things, how were our prospects developing, what was my overall *take* on matters, and what were our hopes for a settlement (most of my "take" wouldn't be all that promising). In no time I'd be entering their joyless company and would've forgotten about myself here on the highway, peering out in near despair because of the fate of an insignificant little dog. Frankly, it made me feel pretty silly.

Sallie suddenly said, as though she'd been composing something while I was musing away balefully, "Do you remember after New Year's that day we sat and talked about one thing changing and making everything else different?"

"The Big Dipper," I said as we came to our familiar exit, which quickly led down and away through a different poor section of darktown that abuts our gentrified street. Everything had begun to seem more manageable as we neared home.

"That's right," Sallie said, as though the words *Big Dipper* reproached her. "But you know, and you'll think this is crazy. It *is*, maybe. But last night when I was in bed, I began thinking about that poor little puppy as an ill force that put everything in our life at a terrible risk. And we were in danger in some way. It scared me. I didn't want that."

I looked over at Sallie and saw a crystal tear escape her eye and slip down her soft, rounded pretty cheek.

"Sweetheart," I said, and found her hand on the steering wheel. "It's quite all right. You put yourself through a lot. And I've been gone. You just need me around to do more. There's nothing to be scared about."

"I suppose," Sallie said resolutely.

"And if things are not exactly right now," I said, "they soon will be. You'll take on the world again the way you always do. We'll all be the better for it."

"I know," she said. "I'm sorry about the puppy."

"Me too," I said. "But we did the right thing. Probably he'll be fine."

"And I'm sorry things threaten me," Sallie said. "I don't think they should, then they do."

"Things threaten all of us," I said. "Nobody gets away unmarked." That is what I thought about all of that then. We were in sight of our house. I didn't really want to talk about these subjects anymore.

"Do you love me?" Sallie said, quite unexpectedly.

"Oh yes," I said, "I do. I love you very much." And that was all we said.

A week ago, in one of those amusing fillers used to justify column space in one of the trial lawyers' journals I look at just for laughs, I read two things that truly interested me. These are always chosen for their wry comment on the law, and are frequently hilarious and true. The first one I read said, "Scientists predict that in five thousand years the earth will be drawn into the sun." It then went on to say something like "so it's not too early to raise your malpractice insurance," or some such cornball thing as that. But I will admit to being made oddly uncomfortable by this news about the earth — as if I had something important to lose in the inevitability of its far-off demise. I can't now say what that something might be. None of us can think about five thousand years from now. And I'd have believed none of us could *feel* anything about it either, except in ways that are vaguely religious. Only I did, and I am far from being a religious man. What I felt was very much like the sensation described by the old saying "Someone just walked on your grave." Someone, so it seemed, had walked on my grave five thousand years from now, and it didn't feel very good. I was sorry to have to think about it.

The other squib I found near the back of the magazine, behind the Legal Market Place, and it said that astronomers had discovered the oldest known star, which they believed to be fifty million light-years away, and they had named it the Millennium Star for obvious reasons, though the actual millennium had gone by with hardly any change in things that I'd noticed. When asked to describe the chemical makeup of this Millennium Star — which of course couldn't even be seen — the scientist who discovered it said, "Oh, gee, I don't know. It's impossible to reach that far back in time." And I thought — sitting in my office with documents of the Brownlow-Maisonette case spread all around me and the hot New Orleans sun beaming into the window I'd seen from my car when Sallie and I were driving back from delivering the puppy to its fate — I thought, "*Time?* Why does he say *time,* when what he means is space?" My feeling then was very much like the feeling from before, when I'd read about the earth hurtling into the sun — a feeling that so much goes on everywhere all through time, and we know only a laughably insignificant fraction about any of it.

The days that followed our visit to the SPCA were eventful days. Sallie's colleague Jerry DeFranco did, of course, die. And though he had AIDS, he died by his own dispirited hand, in his little garret apartment on Kerlerec Street, late at night before the marathon, in order, I suppose, that his life and its end be viewed as a triumph of will over pitiless circumstance.

On another front, the Brownlow appellants decided very suddenly and unexpectedly to settle our case rather than face years of extremely high lawyers' fees and of course the possibility (though not a good one) of enduring a crippling loss. I had hoped for this, and look at it as a victory.

Elsewhere, the marathon went off as planned, and along the route Sallie had wanted. I unfortunately was in St. Louis and missed it. A massacre occurred, the same afternoon, at a fast-food restaurant not far from the SPCA, and someone we knew — a black lawyer — was killed. And during this period I began receiving preliminary feelers about a federal judgeship I'm sure I'll never get. These things are always bandied about for months and years, all sorts of persons are put on notice to be ready when the moment comes, and then the wrong one is chosen for completely wrong reasons, after which it becomes clear that nothing was ever in doubt. The law is an odd calling. And New Orleans a unique place. In any case, I'm far too moderate for the present company running things.

Several people did eventually call about the puppy, having seen my signs, and I directed them all to the animal shelter. I went around a time or two and checked the signs, and several were still up along with the AIDS marathon flyers, which made me satisfied, but not very satisfied.

Each morning I sat in bed and thought about the puppy, waiting for someone to come down the list of cages and see him there alone and staring, and take him away. For some reason, in my imaginings, no one ever chose him — not an autistic child, nor a lonely, discouraged older person, a recent widow, a young family with roughhousing kids. None of these. In all the ways I tried to imagine it, he stayed there.

Sallie did not bring the subject up again, although her sister called on Tuesday and said she knew someone named Hester in Andalusia who'd take the puppy; then the two of them quarreled so bitterly that I had to come on the phone and put it settled.

On some afternoons, as the provisional five waiting days ticked by, I would think about the puppy and feel utterly treacherous for having delivered him to the shelter. Other times I'd feel that we'd given him a better chance than he'd have otherwise had, either on the street alone or with his previous owners. I certainly never thought of him as an ill force to be dispelled, or a threat to anything important. To me life's not that fragile. He was, if anything, just a casualty of the limits we all place on our sympathy and our capacity for the ambiguous in life. Though Sallie might've been right — that the puppy had been a message left for us to ponder: something someone thought about us, something someone felt we needed to know. Who or what or in what way that might've been true, I can't quite imagine. Though we are all, of course, implicated in the lives of others, whether we precisely know how or don't.

On Thursday night, before the puppy's final day in the shelter, I had another strange dream. Dreams always mean something obvious, and so I try as much as I can not to remember mine. But for some reason this time I did, and what I dreamed was again about my old departed law partner, Paul Thompson, and his nice wife,

Judy, a pretty, buxom blond woman who'd studied opera and sung the coloratura parts in several municipal productions. In my dream Judy Thompson was haranguing Paul about some list of women's names she'd found, women Paul had been involved with, even in love with. She was telling him he was an awful man who had broken her heart, and that she was leaving him (which did actually happen). And on her list — which I could suddenly, as though through a fog, see — was Sallie's name. And when I saw it there, my heart started pounding, pounding, pounding, until I sat right up in bed in the dark and said out loud, "Did you know your name's on that goddamned list?" Outside, on our street, I could hear someone playing a trumpet, a very slow and soulful version of "Nearer Walk with Thee." And Sallie was there beside me, deep asleep. I of course knew she'd done it, deserved to be on the list, and that probably there *was* such a list, given the kind of reckless man Paul Thompson was. As I said, I had never spoken to Sallie about this subject and had, until then, believed I'd gone beyond the entire business. Though I have to suppose now I was wrong.

This dream stayed on my mind the next day, and the next night I had it again. And because the dream preoccupied my thinking, it wasn't until Saturday after lunch, when I had sat down to take a nap in a chair in the living room, that I realized I'd forgotten about the puppy the day before, and that all during Friday many hours had passed, and by the end of them the puppy must've reached its destination, whatever it was to be. I was surprised to have neglected to think about it at the crucial moment, having thought of it so much before then. And I was sorry to have to realize that I had finally not cared as much about it as I'd thought.

MELISSA HARDY

The Heifer

FROM DESCANT

THE HEIFER was a pretty brindle, white with flecks of red and black and gray. She was dainty, with ears that flickered and eyes like wavering, dark jelly. An intelligent-seeming heifer, sweet-smelling, like grass.

"I shall name her Olga," Aina told her new husband. This was after her little sister Olga Lappi back in Finland, whom she would never see again now that she had come all the way to New Ontario to marry Uwe Pahakka. "Truly, I have never before seen so beautiful a cow," she swore, stroking the heifer's sides, where the short hair felt like silk.

Uwe beamed. He knew that this was a fine compliment, coming from a girl whose family owned a dairy farm. "I think that she looks like you," he commented.

"Do you really?" Aina asked, shy and pleased.

Uwe had come out to Canada four years ago from Finland, leaving Aina behind. She was only fourteen at the time and her parents said that she could follow her young suitor only when he had legal title to a farm, the documents to prove it, and money for her passage. They had their reasons for these strictures. Uwe's father had been feckless and his mother had drifted off into a kind of untidy madness later in her life. "The Pahakkas are not good stock," her father had advised his protesting daughter.

The Lappis thought that they had heard the last of Uwe when he disappeared into that great hole in the world which was sucking up all the young men, North America. Surely such a disorganized, unsatisfactory boy, given to momentary riotous enthusiasms and sudden prolonged bouts of melancholy, could not succeed in making a life for himself in such a hard new place as Canada.

Indeed, Aina heard from her lover but twice in the four years that elapsed between his departure and the arrival of the letter requesting her hand in marriage.

In his first letter, dated six months after his departure, he wrote that he had decided to go round the Horn of South America in order to make his fortune prospecting gold in the Yukon. "Everybody is going," he told her.

In his second letter, dated two months after the first, he advised his fiancée that he had changed his mind. "No need to go to the Klondike," he assured her. "There are plenty of rocks right here in Ontario."

In fact, Uwe, who was in Toronto at the time, working on a construction crew, had hopped the train north when silver was discovered near Mile 103 on the TN&O Railroad and had managed, through sheer haphazardness, to stake several solid claims before the area filled up with prospectors. He sold the claims for a good price and, after talking to a Frenchman who wanted to sell his land and move back to Quebec, put the proceeds toward the purchase of the farm.

Accordingly, enclosed with the third letter, the one that arrived a full four years after his emigration, asking for her hand, was another, written on the stationery of the Government of Ontario, testifying to the fact that Uwe Pahakka indeed held title to a farm located in the township of Cobalt, New Ontario. Also enclosed was a money order, to be used toward Aina's passage to the New World.

"We are very fortunate," Uwe wrote his fiancée. "The land is partially cleared and there is a house already."

When the letter arrived in their little village, tied with string it was so fat, Aina had practically forgotten Uwe. After all, she had not heard from him in three years. Lately she had thought she might marry another boy — the sturdy, towheaded son of a neighboring farmer. He had courted her off and on for the past two years, furtively at first, then more openly as time passed and still Uwe did not write. There had been talk between the two fathers of ceding some pasturage as Aina's dowry. Both men felt that the deal was to their advantage.

However, the idea of leaving her family and her village and everything that was familiar to her in order to move to a new country where everything was not old like it was in Finland and eroded with scrubbing . . . This idea caught in the girl's imagination and grew and grew until it became so large that she was hard put to squeeze anything in alongside it. The notion of moving to Canada and marrying Uwe Pahakka filled her brain to bursting.

In place of the childish affection she had once felt for Uwe, a whole new love began to assemble itself out of bits and pieces and snatches of memory. Some of these memories were of things that had actually happened — wildflowers that he had one day picked for her and given her by the stone wall near her father's well, words of endearment he had actually spoken in her ear when nobody was looking. Others were of events that she had wished had transpired, sentiments that she had hoped he might one day express. Like a woman who has gone blind during her lover's absence, Aina attempted to remember Uwe by passing her fingers over the contours of a stranger's face, repeating to herself until she was sure of it, "Yes! It is! There can be no mistake! It must be! Surely it is my darling!"

In no time at all and in this way, Aina managed to conceive so great a passion for her former lover that it could not be denied, not even by fathers bent on swapping land for grandchildren. When old Lappi refused to allow Aina to travel to Canada to marry Uwe and threatened to return to him his money order by the next post, she fasted for two months, until she had grown so frail that she could no longer rise from her bed without assistance or stand without fainting.

"It is clear that she is determined to starve herself to death if you will not let her marry young Pahakka," observed Father Hongo, the village pastor (Father Hongo frequently found it convenient to discern God's will in obstinance and other forms of resistance). "You had better let her go, or her blood will be on your hands."

It was only then that Aina's father finally agreed to allow the girl to depart for Canada. He did not want the death of his daughter on his conscience, and besides, there was little Olga coming on to sixteen. She might do very nicely for the neighbor's son in a year or two, if his father was still interested in that pasturage.

The victorious Aina traveled by boat to Montreal and by train to

Toronto, where Uwe met her at Union Station. They were married on the following day, October 14, 1910, by a Finnish pastor who had been to seminary with Father Hongo and to whom the old minister had written, saying that this was a reasonably good thing, Aina marrying Uwe, though perhaps not so good as it might be.

Following the ceremony, the newlyweds climbed on board the new TN&O, and sixteen long hours later disembarked at the new town of Cobalt, which, at that time, was little more than a collection of rough log shanties separated by charred stumps.

Uwe hired a two-seater democrat and a big plow horse from what passed for the livery shop, laid in supplies at the general store — seven bags of flour, one hundred pounds of sugar, a fifty-pound tin of lard, a fifty-pound bag of salt, one case each of dried apples, peaches, apricots, raisins, and currants, a bag each of rice and beans and potatoes, a wooden tub of corn syrup with a spout for pouring, and a side of salt pork. "We won't go into town much, once the snow comes," he advised her, cramming the provisions, with no little difficulty, into the back of the rickety two-seater. Then, climbing onto the seat beside Aina, he drove the ten miles to the farm down a raw red road which, where it was swale, was corduroyed with tamarack posts and chinked with moss, and where it wasn't, ran like a river of sticky mud a foot and a half deep.

"Road's better when it freezes," Uwe explained. "It will freeze soon." They had to stop twice to push the buggy several hundred feet to a tidier patch of ground.

As they drove through this new land of Canada, Aina sat straight and tall, observing how the forest pressed in to either side of the road with an attentiveness honed all the sharper for trepidation. The forest was dense, boreal, at once dark and light, pointed and tall. Cedar and poplar and whitewood and tamarack, spruce and balsam with a thick undergrowth of scrappy maple and willow and alder. From a cedar swamp nearby, a whippoorwill called plosively. In the clear, chill air of the northern autumn the bird's cry sounded as round as a silvery bell.

Then, at length, there it was, the farm, formerly the property of Gui Rancourt, now of Uwe Pahakka: a tarpaper shanty huddled down in a clearing around which a scattering of ragged outbuildings — a privy, a cowshed, a roothouse — gravitated like shaggy dancers move around a center. Out back of the shack stretched a field of blackened stumps and, to the west, a ramshackle barn made of what appeared to be sticks lashed together.

"Do you like it?" Uwe asked proudly. He beamed. "I thought I'd build a sauna out back in the spring. There's a pond there — deep and cold. And you will have a milk cow. I'm getting you one from a neighbor, but we thought we'd wait until it was a few months older before separating it from the herd. We can see it though. I will take you there tomorrow when we return the hack. My wedding present to you."

That was how Aina first learned of the heifer, and so she had clapped her hands and laughed aloud and, turning to her new husband, kissed him squarely on the mouth in spite of the fact that the black shack looked squatting and evil to her and the field beyond the barn baneful, like a cemetery of wooden crosses burned by a careless and disdainful enemy.

For the next three months Aina waited for the day on which Uwe would lead the heifer across the dooryard to her. It was difficult not to dwell on the subject, as the dainty, sweet-eyed cow was all Uwe could think of to talk about to his new wife . . . and all Aina had left to hope for now that her dearest wish — to join her childhood sweetheart in Canada and marry him — had apparently been granted.

For this reason, whenever a silence began to gape between the two, like a chasm soundlessly riven through the rock on which they stood and through which they might plunge to a muffled doom . . . Whenever they found themselves standing in the middle of the tiny cabin (sixteen by twenty feet), staring at one another with eyeballs burned bald and raw from earlier eye-wars and chimney smoke, both poised to speak, both wondering if what was in their hearts to say would somehow manage to smuggle itself out in a packet of words so artfully arranged that, finally, the other would understand and forgive and they could both walk away from each other and this place for once and for all . . . Whenever Uwe felt that he must somehow atone for bringing Aina so far from her family to live alone with a man as simple and, well, uneventful as himself in a little tarpaper shack in the middle of a frozen wilderness so glaringly white that it razed the corneas of a man's eye and so cold that it made of his fingers and his toes wood . . . Or whenever he decided that he might snowshoe into Cobalt to the blind pig to lift a pint or two of that good Calgary Ale (a man's privilege!) and play a little blackjack (a fellow could go stir-crazy sitting in a shack all the long winter with nothing to do and only a sour-faced girl to keep him company!) . . . Then it was that Uwe would go on and on about the heifer and what a beauty she was and how everything would be all right once the cow was on the farm. "She'll be a companion to you," he assured Aina. "You'll see!"

For by that time it was clear that Uwe was not, nor could he ever be, a true companion to Aina.

Beginning with their reunion in Toronto and marriage, and extending over November, December, and January of that year, the love that had driven Aina to leave home and come to Canada to marry Uwe Pahakka began to dry up and blow away, like arid earth which no roots hold in place. The lover whom she had remembered had, of course, never really existed, and the man who was Uwe Pahakka proved no substitute for this exemplary phantom. Uwe was, upon closer scrutiny, not so handsome as she had recollected, nor, if the truth be told, handsome at all. Yes, he was tall — six foot three or four (he had to stoop when he was inside the shack or skin his pate on the log beams of the ceiling) — but he was also ungainly. His pants' legs were always too short, as were his sleeves, exposing big knobs of ankles and wrists. His hair was so blond as to be almost white, but it was thinning and clung to his skull in stray wisps. There was no center to his pale eyes — this was disconcerting — and his teeth were spaced too far apart.

In addition, her husband reminded Aina of an old woman, rattling brittly on and on about nothing at all and given to endless repetition. When he became excited, he flushed a deep, turkey red and stammered, spraying saliva everywhere. Conversely, when his spirits were low or Aina had spoken sharply to him, he would lie down on the prickly, sharp-smelling mattress she had woven of balsam boughs and, rolling onto his side facing the wall, pull his knees up toward his chest, moaning softly. He would whimper like this for hours until she was of a mind to beat him to death with a shovel.

Finally, Uwe was, in Aina's estimation, intolerably lazy, and though he had made good on the silver claims up around Mile 103, he might as well have washed his hands in the money they brought him, for all those dollar bills that they had fetched ran through his big, clumsy fingers just like water.

All these ponderings and ruminations came to a head one morning in early February when Aina woke, wincing into the cold gray light of a new day, with Uwe heavy and damp beside her in knubbled gray long johns, and thought to herself, tight-lipped, *Aina Lappi, you have made a terrible mistake!*

Then she lay very still beside her huge, unlovable husband and listened to the ice on the lake boom and the trees split with the cold — pop! — just like that! right down the middle. The wind spat and hissed inside the stovepipe like an animal cornered in its burrow, determined to defend its young, and Aina began to plot her escape.

By mid-February, Aina, figuring that the heifer was now old enough to be moved to the farm, sent Uwe to fetch the cow from Farmer Lanthier.

"You'll see," he told Aina. "When Olga is here, you will have no more worries. You will be the happiest woman in New Ontario."

Unfortunately, there was a problem.

"Well, my friend," Farmer Lanthier told Uwe, "you could say that it's this way." Recognizing that Uwe's French was sparse, he spoke slowly and made elaborate gestures. "As for me, old Lanthier, I live on this side of the river and you . . . you live on that." He pointed to here as being his feet and there as being somewhere to the west of his barn.

"Yes," Uwe agreed, nodding vigorously to indicate that he understood.

"To get from this side of the river to that, you must first cross the river," Lanthier continued, again pointing here and there and making an undulating motion with his hands to indicate waves.

Once more Uwe was in agreement. "Yes, yes," he said.

"The ice," said Lanthier. *"La glace. Les vaches n'aiment pas la glace. Non. Non. Pas de tout."*

Uwe did not understand. "What? What?" he asked.

"Idiot!" declared Lanthier. "The cow will not cross glare ice. Trust me, my friend, she will walk on a mirror first!"

Dejected, Uwe returned home without the cow.

"It's no use," he said to his wife. "Lanthier says that Olga will not cross the glare ice."

"What?" Aina demanded. "The cow will not cross the ice? This man is trying to rob you! He is trying to cheat you! You have already paid him for the cow a long time ago and now he will try to sell her again, to somebody else! Go back to him tomorrow and tell him that you want my cow now."

"But Aina," Uwe protested. He did not want to go back to Lanthier's so soon. He was tired — Lanthier's farm was four miles east on the Cobalt road, which made the journey eight miles on snowshoes. Besides, the farmer had called him an idiot and, worse, had treated him like one. Uwe took offense at that. "If Lanthier is right and Olga hates the ice, how am I to make her cross the river?"

"Of course he is right," snapped Aina impatiently. "Canadian cows are no different from Finnish cows. I don't know why I didn't think of it myself when you told me you were fetching her in February. But it is all right. I will make Olga boots!"

"Boots for a cow?" Uwe asked incredulously.

"Boots with spikes," Aina clarified. "That way, she will not be afraid to cross the ice."

"It is glare ice," Uwe reminded her.

"I know what I am talking about," insisted Aina.

The next day, Aina made four boots from three-ply leather, which she studded with two-inch spikes. This task took her most of the day, as it was difficult to anticipate what size boot might fit Olga and how it might be lashed to her leg in such a way that the heifer would be unable to kick it off.

The following day, Aina rose an hour before dawn and made Uwe get up too so that they could snowshoe together to the Lanthier homestead. She had determined to fetch the cow home herself and to do so immediately so that Lanthier could not resell her cow. She was certain that was what the Frenchman intended.

Uwe complained bitterly the entire journey. "Farmer Lanthier will say that we are crazy, making boots for cows . . . and he will be right! I will be the laughingstock of the entire township! Aina! Aina!" (Long as his legs were, Uwe had trouble keeping up with his small, quick wife, who had made him carry not only the makeshift cow boots in his packsack, but also his own extra pair of hobnailed boots, for her to wear when the time came for leading Olga across the ice. "I will need traction," she had then explained.)

"What?' Aina now retorted. "You don't want to wait till spring, do you, when the ice melts and you must build a raft to float her across the torrent? Cows do not like water any more than they like ice!"

Uwe grumbled and yanked at his packsack. The big spikes hammered into the cow boots tore at the canvas from the inside and, despite his heavy Red River coat, clawed at the skin of his back.

"This I have to see!" said Farmer Lanthier when the Pahakkas had made their intentions known through what broken French Uwe, in his deep humiliation, could muster, such as *vache* and *glace* and *les choses, vous savez, pour les pieds comme ça,* pointing to his big feet. Aina, still convinced that the Frenchman intended to cheat her of her cow, underscored these communications with a selection of dire and threatening gestures.

"Ring the dinner bell, Louise!" Lanthier told his wife, though it was just half past nine in the morning. "I have nine children, and I want them all to see a cow wearing boots," he explained to Uwe. Then he threw his head back and laughed aloud.

When all the Lanthiers' nine children had assembled expectantly on the bank of the river, Farmer Lanthier threw a threadbare Hudson Bay blanket over Olga's back, tied a rope about her neck, and led her to Aina. *"Voilà, madame,"* he said. *"Votre vache!"*

Aina took the rope he offered her, handed it to Uwe, and sat down on the ground next to the cow.

"Your boots," she instructed Uwe.

Reluctantly, with a sideways glance at the unruly crowd of Lanthiers, Uwe fished his extra pair of hobnailed boots out of his packsack and handed them to Aina. She pulled them on over her rubber moccasins, lacing them up tightly. The boots were much too large for her, but the distance she must go in them was short. What was important was that they grip the ice.

"Olga will never consent to wear boots," Uwe hissed at Aina. "You bring disgrace on me, yourself, Finland!"

Aina thrust out her hand. "Olga's boots!" she ordered. "One at a time."

Uwe rummaged around in the packsack and brought forth a boot. Aina, having been uncertain about left and right, front and back as regards a cow's hoof, had made them all the same — a leather cup into the bottom of which a square of wood had been fitted to serve as a kind of sole. Two-inch spikes had been driven down through this sole so that they protruded out the other side. Around two of the spikes, placed on the left and right side of the sole, rawhide thongs had been tied. Aina intended to lash the boot to the cow's leg by means of these thongs. Lifting Olga's hoof, she carefully fitted the leather cup onto it. Olga tried to kick, but Aina held her leg firmly.

"Now, you hold this leg," she shouted in Finnish to the biggest Lanthier boy. *"Vite! Vite!"* After repeating the command several times and pointing, she managed to convey to the boy her intention. He ran over and, dropping to his knees, seized Olga's leg and held it firmly while Aina tied the boot to it. Indicating to the boy to continue holding on to the heifer's leg, she then moved to the heifer's left front foot and fitted the next boot, pointing to another one of Lanthier's children, a girl of about eight hunkered down to watch the show. *"Vite!"* she cried. "You there! *Vite!"* The girl sprang to her feet at once and bounded over to Olga. Dropping to her knees, she seized Olga's left front leg.

In this fashion and with the assistance of Lanthier's children, Aina managed to fit Olga with the homemade boots in about a quarter of an hour, despite the bewildered cow's plaintive protests — alarmed at finding herself two inches taller than she was accustomed to being and perched precariously on twenty spikes, the heifer rolled her big, soft eyes and bawled plaintively, pitching her weight backward, forward, and sideways in a desperate attempt to free herself of the four pairs of hands restraining her.

"Tell them: at the count of three, let go," Aina instructed Uwe, who, after several false starts, managed to convey this strategy to the children holding down the cow. Then Aina stood, and grasping the rope tied around Olga's neck, she ventured out onto the ice as far as the rope extended — about four feet. The ice was smooth, mirror-bright, and as white as an eyeball. She nodded to Uwe to indicate that she was ready.

"Un, deux, trois!" cried Uwe.

Aina ground the heels of her hobnailed boots into the glare ice, leaned back, and pulled with all her might. The children released Olga's legs, falling back into the snow, and the cow came skittering desperately out onto the ice, her legs tangling and chips of green ice flying. But Aina did not pause. She knew that if she stopped, the cow would also stop, so she backed off across the river as fast as she could, sliding and skidding and dragging Olga along with her. Olga, meanwhile, convinced that she had miraculously escaped some dire fate when she had broken free of the children's grasp, tottered gingerly after Aina, her ears flapping, her tail flicking, and her spiked boots making a *rat-a-tat-tat* sound like hail hitting a roof.

In a moment's time they were on the other side of the river (it was, after all, not a very big river), and Olga, staggering desperately from right to left, kicked first one leg, then another in an attempt to free herself of the spiked boots.

On the opposite bank, the Lanthiers and Uwe cheered and clapped and jumped up and down. "Bravo!" cried the children.

"There, there," Aina advised the cow. Kneeling beside her, she caught at her front leg and began to untie the rawhide thong. "You're all right now, my Olga. You will never have to wear boots again."

Uwe jogged across the ice to join Aina.

"How smart you are, Aina!" Uwe congratulated his wife. "How did you know that the cow would wear boots?"

"I didn't," said Aina shortly, not looking up at him but unlashing a second boot. "But I wanted my cow."

On the other side of the river, Lanthier turned to his wife. "Too bad about that heifer. I was going to sell her to Old Mercer next week. He took a fancy to her the last time he was here, and the Finn does not know enough to get a bill of sale when he buys livestock. Still, it was worth the money to see such a marvelous sight as a cow in boots."

Uwe was right about one thing. Olga was a companion to Aina, and once she came to the farm, Aina, who had been so glum and sour the whole winter long, seemed to Uwe almost happy. What he didn't know was that his little wife soothed herself to sleep at night thinking up ingenious ways to murder him in his sleep using ordinary household objects or such implements as one might find about a farm — the scythe he used for cutting the tall grass, for example, or the pitchfork with which he baled hay, or that coil of brass wire for snaring rabbits, or just that least little bit of lye poured into his whiskey jug. Once he almost obliged her when a bottle of assayer's acid in the back pocket of his trousers burst into flames over at the blind pig in Cobalt, but a drunk prospector rolled the big Finn up in a blanket and put out the fire. It was a long time before Uwe could sit comfortably on his left buttock, however, and that gave Aina some satisfaction.

As for Uwe, he watched his young wife sing her way busily

through her day, seemingly happy at her tasks and content, and he thought that he had been right to marry her after all, and wasn't it about time to go into town for nails or tarpaper or, better yet, for seed? Sooner or later he was going to need seed if he was going to farm this land. And he'd take up his snowshoes and say to Aina, "I'll be back tomorrow or maybe the next day."

"Yes, yes, go along, then," she would say, hoping that he might be eaten by a bear or attacked by wolves or catch his leg in a trap and freeze to death. One thing was for sure: a man could die a hundred ways in this wilderness.

At the first touch of the vernal sun, in late May of that year, the entire countryside around the farm grew loose and wobbly in its joints, like an overcooked fowl. The snow sunk and shrank with loud sighs. Bare patches of soggy ground spread like brown stains on the previously white face of the land. A brook pulsed through every ravine; a river twisted through every valley. On the river, water stretched in shining pools a foot deep across the ice, while the muskegs thereabout grew bottomless and quaked, as if with some deep hunger. The half-cleared field out back became a lake, the stumps that littered it submerged by a good foot and a half of water.

By this time, Aina was pregnant. She would not have known of her condition had not Madame Lanthier looked twice at her that time she came buying eggs and said as much. After consulting with several neighbor ladies, whom she had convened for the express purpose of determining how far along Aina was through pantomime, discussion, and examination, Madame Lanthier concluded that the girl was due sometime in October. These particulars were conveyed with some difficulty to Aina, who still spoke no English nor French.

Aina's feelings about her condition were mixed. On the one hand, she was pleased that she should soon have additional companionship in the form of a child; on the other hand, having a baby in tow would make escape from Uwe more difficult.

As for Uwe, the revelation at once delighted and panicked him. "A son!" he exalted. "The Pahakka line will live on in our child!" On occasions when his mood was less sanguine, he despaired, "Another mouth to feed! And I have a hard enough time feeding a woman and a cow!"

"The cow feeds herself," Aina pointed out. "And I feed you."

*

After a week of trying to clear the field using a big dray horse he had rented by the day from Farmer Lanthier, Uwe gave up. "This land is useless, and what am I going to grow anyway?" he asked Aina. "Potatoes, like Old Lanthier? Turnips? The growing season is too short and the soil is too full of rocks. No, I am going up to Golden City and see if I can get work at that Hollinger mine there. I hear they're hiring every able-bodied man that walks through the dry-room door. Maybe I'll do some prospecting first. That's the way to get rich: find gold. Drill, blast, scale, and timber . . . Farming is for fools. Later, I'll send for you."

Mining accidents were not infrequent, Aina mused. There were gas leaks, and she had heard of hoist cables breaking, hurtling miners to their death, and rock exploding when a miner bit his drill into the side of a drift and hit a missing hole. As for prospectors, they tended to just wander off.

"Buy me a pig and some chickens and I'll put in vegetables where you've cleared," she told Uwe. "Then you can go to the Porcupine and we will have eggs and bacon and ham too, once the winter comes. The baby is not due until the fall. Olga and I will be fine."

So Uwe bought a fat piglet from Farmer Lanthier and a rooster and two speckled hens and, in mid-June of 1911, packed his packsack and caught the railroad spur north to Golden City.

It started as a ground fire, burning perhaps for weeks in the moss and humus that made up the forest floor around the tarpaper shack. The air smelled acrid, as if lightning had just struck a nearby tree. Aina's eyes smarted for days.

"The summer is hot, too hot," Madame Lanthier observed, sniffing the air and blinking. "It's a summer for fire, all right."

In July, a surface fire boiled up from the humus, a lick of flame that caught and held the attention of the bush. It spread, eating the deadfalls and windrows over a two- to three-hectare radius to the west of Aina and Uwe's farm.

"You can contain a brush fire," Farmer Lanthier reassured her. "It's the crown fires you have to watch out for. Thank the Blessed Virgin there's no wind."

Of course, all Aina understood was *fire* and the fact that Farmer Lanthier didn't seem to be too alarmed. The Lanthiers did want Aina to stay with them, however. "We insist," they said. "Just till the fire is contained."

But Aina shook her head. "I have left my Olga at home," she told them, "and the pig and the chickens. I must go back."

The Lanthiers, of course, only understood that she had refused their offer. "Stupid woman," exclaimed Farmer Lanthier, watching Aina pole across the river on the raft he had spiked together that spring out of dry jack pines.

For the following three days, men from the township fought the surface fire, hauling buckets of water from the river and digging trenches. Then, on the third night, the wind picked up and blew flames upward into the tall tops of the trees. The gas and chemicals in the burning leaves exploded, generating strong winds, which in turn drove the fire before them; flames leapt from tree to tree like frenzied dancers. At the same time, the surface fire abated; the new crown fire had sucked the air beneath the treetops up into itself to feed on, creating a kind of vacuum along the ground.

Unlike the brush fire, which had gone about its destruction in a slow, methodical fashion, cropping the undergrowth as sheep or cattle will systematically graze a field, the crown fire was chaotic and greedy. By midnight, the corduroy road leading to Aina's house was lined by blazing fires that roared like a dozen freight trains converging on the same crossing at once. She could hear nothing over the fire's high, insistent shriek, and the heat from the blaze scorched her skin as red as the noonday sun might. The night was as bright as day, fire lit and teeming with shadows.

Aina doused the tarpaper shack with well water in the hopes that this might keep it from catching fire; then she poured a bucket of water over her own head to keep stray sparks from igniting her hair and clothing. Hastily she assembled a bundle — her good dress, an extra pair of shoes, some tiny garments that she had sewn for the baby, a gold locket that had belonged to her maternal grandmother, and some crumpled banknotes — rolled it up in a blanket, and buried it in a shallow hole she scraped out with her hands in the dirt floor in the roothouse. She figured that as the floor of the roothouse was three feet below ground level, it might withstand fire better than the shack.

Leaving the roothouse, she let the pig out of its sty and the chickens out of their coop. The pig promptly began to bury himself in the cool, moist manure pile next to the stick barn. The hens and the rooster, after a few moments of confused rushing back and forth and clucking and flapping, did the same, though less systematically.

Finally, Aina doused another blanket with water and, holding it over her head, ran through the boiling smoke toward the half-cleared field where she had put Olga out to pasture a few hours before. "I am coming, Olga!" she called to the heifer, but the fire's roar was so loud that she could not hear herself cry out; her words were swallowed up in the horrible howl.

Just as she reached the field, she stumbled over a root and pitched forward onto her hands and knees into the sticky mud of the half-plowed earth. To the west, the fire snapped and licked its way along the stump fence that separated the clearing from the forest. A hot pinecone exploded; its flying fragments drove into her cheek; she cried out; the fragments stung like shrapnel.

Then, as she was struggling to rise, an undulating serpent of flame coiled through the fire-lit sky high above her, idle as a kite that drifts and hangs upon the air before suddenly it plunges. Aina rose to her knees in the mud, transfixed by the sight of the serpentine flame, unable to move as it spiraled down toward her, frightened, but not knowing how to avoid it, which way to twist or turn so that it might not fall on her. In fact, it slid past her shoulder by little more than a hand's breadth and died, writhing, like some damned and tormented soul, in the muck beside her.

Aina gasped with relief, then blinked. Everything had gone dark, indistinguishable. She blinked again, but still could not separate images from the dull blackness that lay against her eyes. Unlike darkness, this blackness had no depth but was flat; it crowded close against her. She closed her eyes and felt them burn against the membrane that lined her eyelid. The flame's heat must have seared her corneas. She had heard of that happening — temporary blindness that might take weeks to heal, or hours. At any rate, for now Aina could not see.

"Olga! Olga!" she cried, reaching out with both hands to feel the space around her. Her fingers closed shut on air. "Olga! Are you there?" she shrieked into the gale.

The fire screamed back its wordless fury, a maddened monster that cannot be appeased but must howl and howl and destroy everything within its grasp.

Pushing herself up with one hand, Aina stood with difficulty, wobbling for a moment when she had found her feet. Six months gone with child, her body had grown ungainly; it was more difficult for her to find her balance than before, particularly now, when she could not see. Tentatively the Finnish woman stepped forward into the roaring nothingness before stumbling over another gnarled root. Cursing Uwe for not clearing the field, she ventured gingerly first this way, then that, feeling her way with her hands, but there were roots everywhere she turned, and charred stumps. The dried branches tore at her scorched skin. They seemed to surround her.

After a few moments of trying to find her way through the field of stumps with her hands, Aina gave up. She did not know which direction she was facing, where she had been, where she might hope to find the cow. "Olga!" she cried again, but without hope now of any reply. Weary and distraught, she sank down onto one knee, then both. Then she sat with her legs stretched out before her. Finally she dropped down onto her side in the cool muck of the open, haphazardly plowed field, pulled her knees up toward her belly, and drew the wet blanket over her head, shoulders, and torso. Miraculously, she slept.

Aina opened her eyes just a crack. They were very sore, but by squinting and shading them with her hand, she could just make out the outline of the sun, newly risen in the east. Glimpsed through the thick boil of settling smoke, it looked more like the moon than itself — a pale anemic disk, more reflective than radiant. *I am not blind after all,* she marveled.

Stiff and sore and still shading her eyes with her hands, for the light made them ache, Aina stood carefully and peered around the field. The soil was as dry as snuff under her feet and reflected heat like an oven. She took a step forward. At her footfall, ashes whirled up, clogging her nostrils. She sneezed, then coughed, then realized that the sound she heard inside her head was her ears ringing. Was the fire over, then? She could no longer hear its roar, nor could she see flames, just smoke and ash and the burned black shape of things . . .

Suddenly Aina stopped and stared straight ahead.

A black cow stood forlornly in the far northwest corner of the field.

Aina took a tentative stop toward her.

Who could this black cow be? she wondered. Not Olga. Olga was a brindled cow — red and gray and brown. Where had this black cow come from?

Aina took another step.

Was she one of Farmer Lanthier's cows? How had she crossed the river? Perhaps she belonged to someone else. There were new neighbors to the south . . .

Then it struck her. She stopped in her tracks, absorbing the blow by doubling over it and twisting to one side — it was as though she had been punched in the stomach, hard. "Olga?" she exhaled.

Slowly the cow turned its big head to look at her.

Afraid, but unable to stop herself, Aina stumbled headlong toward the heifer. "Olga," she pleaded.

The cow lowed.

Aina crept up alongside the burned heifer. She looked first at one side of her, then the other. Then, assembling the fragments of her remaining courage, she reached out with shaking fingers to touch Olga's blackened coat. As she had feared, her fingers came in contact not with Olga's sweet silky hide but a crisp, thick crust. Where Aina's fingers had touched the animal, the crust peeled off in a great welt, leaving a flaming red patch, raw and bare.

"Oh, Olga!" Aina exclaimed.

Moving to the front of the heifer, she stared hard into the animal's eyes. They were flat and opaque like stones, river rocks, not soft and jellylike as they had been before. Olga had not been so lucky as Aina. The fire had burned away her retinas. She was blind.

Aina dropped to her knees and, looking underneath the cow, cried aloud and then bit her hand in anguish. Olga's hooves and udders were utterly gone, burned away. "I don't understand," Aina whispered hoarsely to the heifer. "How can you even be alive?"

But Olga only lowered her head and blindly tried to browse the blackened grass with fumbling lips.

Aina rose to her feet, shaking so violently that she was not certain her body could contain her. Weeping, she staggered toward the roothouse, where Uwe kept a loaded shotgun — for wolves or bears or other fierce creatures that might threaten the farm.

Later that morning Uwe returned. He had heard about the fire up in Golden City and had commandeered a handcart and ridden the rails south to Cobalt to see if Aina needed any help.

"It's too bad you weren't able to save the house," he told her. She was crouched in the yard by the roothouse, watching disconsolately as the pig dug its way out of the manure pile. The rooster and one hen staggered around the yard, covered with dung. The other hen had died, somehow suffocated by smoke or manure or burned alive.

"Did you tell anyone where you were going?" Aina wanted to know.

Her voice was flat. She seemed worn out to Uwe. She didn't once look at him or seem excited to see him. To tell the truth, the Finn was not a little put out. He hadn't caused the fire, after all, and he had come as soon as he had heard.

"Not likely," Uwe reassured her. "The TN&O doesn't take kindly to a fellow borrowing their handcart."

"Good." Aina seemed satisfied.

Later, when Uwe's back was turned, Aina shot him. She used the same shotgun with which she had dispatched Olga; there were two shells in it, after all. She buried both her husband and the cow in a big hole in the field. It took her the better part of a day to dig the hole and another to fill it, but when it was done, she felt much better, though she still missed Olga.

The next day she dug up the bundle of clothing she had buried in the roothouse. The locket was blackened and the banknotes singed; still, there was enough money to tide her over until she could sell the farm.

In early October 1911, just a few days shy of her first wedding anniversary and after thirty-six hours of a difficult labor, Aina Pahakka gave birth to a plump, ice-eyed daughter whom she named Olga. Madame Lanthier brought the baby into the world, having had much experience in these matters.

Regrettably, Olga's father, Uwe Pahakka, had gone missing some months before. He had been last seen in the area of Golden City about the time of the Great Fire in Cobalt. Perhaps he had gone prospecting and lost his way in the bush. These things had been known to happen, and Uwe had always been a careless, easy sort of man, prone to mishaps and mistakes.

Or perhaps he had grown tired of married life and gone west.

The following spring, when he still hadn't turned up, Aina sold the farm to a settler from Southwestern Ontario and booked passage back to Finland with her young daughter.

"You can't say I didn't warn you," her father told her upon her arrival home. "I always knew that Uwe Pahakka was no good!"

Aina did not marry the farmer's sturdy towhaired son, about whom she had dreamed for so many months, for he was married already to her sister Olga. However, in time she married another farmer's son, to whom she quickly bore five children and with whom she came to own and maintain one of the very best dairy farms in their little region, with several strong bulls and many fine, brindled heifers.

KARL IAGNEMMA

Zilkowski's Theorem

FROM ZOETROPE

HENDERSON SLIPPED into the back of the half-full auditorium and settled into an empty chair, shielding his face with a tattered yellow notepad. Around him, mathematicians stood in groups of three and four, sipping coffee from Styrofoam cups and cracking jokes about variational calculus and Zermelo-Fraenkel set theory. Their dreary humor seemed perfectly suited to the auditorium, with its frayed orange carpeting and comfortless chairs and flickering fluorescent lights. *So this is Akron,* thought Henderson. It was neither better nor worse than he'd expected.

The conference was the same every year, the same three hundred people, the same dismal cities: Gdansk one year, then Belfast, now Akron. Where next — Mogadishu, perhaps? Teheran? Henderson recognized and disliked many of the faces he saw; he found these people infinitely more agreeable bound between the covers of journals, their moist handshakes and pungent breath eliminated, their grating voices smoothed by the uninflected diction of mathematics. Henderson ducked his head and scribbled idly on his notepad. He did not want any of his colleagues to notice him, but mostly he did not want to catch the eye of the speaker, Czogloz.

Czogloz was presenting a paper entitled "Perturbation Analysis of Weakly Nonlinear Systems," and as the clock swept past two o'clock he stepped to the podium and flipped on the overhead projector. He looked younger than Henderson had hoped he would: his hairline was anchored firmly to his temples, and his forehead was free of the frown-shaped wrinkles that marked most mathematicians. Four years of assistant professorship had not affected Czogloz much; this seemed unfair to Henderson. Czogloz was sporting a goatee, and wearing a tie made of some shiny purple material that Henderson thought totally inappropriate for a presentation on weakly nonlinear systems. The goatee, Henderson noted, gave Czogloz a demonic air.

"Welcome," Czogloz began, in his lush Hungarian accent. "It's good to see so many familiar faces." Henderson instinctively shrank deeper into his chair, but Czogloz was only following his notes; his gaze never left the podium. He launched smoothly into his presentation, first defining the problem with nitpicky precision, then briefly reviewing related research: Dobujinski's famous 1964 theorem, an obscure series of proofs by a Greek named Kaliardos. Then Czogloz cleared his throat and waded into his own research, his voice rising a half-octave and the words coming faster. Henderson surveyed the dim auditorium: he sensed a grudging respect, a retreat from the skeptical hostility that usually prevailed at the conference. He turned back to the projection screen and began scribbling desperately on his notepad, mentally probing the equations for a tender spot, a place where he could sink a lance.

Czogloz placed a transparency entitled "Summary and Conclusions" on the overhead projector, and as if awakening from a dream the audience shifted slightly. "So it has been shown," Czogloz said, "that stability can be analyzed using classical perturbation analysis, provided the system is weakly nonlinear and locally differentiable." He glanced up from his notes with a reserved but winning smile. "Now. Could I address any —"

"Question," Henderson said. His voice held a nervous, aggressive tone, but he didn't attempt to soften it. He'd been waiting for this moment for so long. "What about the invertibility of the matrix H? You haven't addressed the case where H is singular."

Czogloz peered into the murky reaches of the auditorium. "Could you be more specific, please?"

"Certainly," Henderson said. A few faces in the audience glanced back at him. "On transparency eleven, you claim that if the matrix B is positive definite, then H is nonsingular, but you don't discuss the case where B is positive *semi*-definite. And of course it's possible that for a dissipative system, B could be positive semi-definite. And thus H could be singular. And thus noninvertible."

Czogloz paused. Slowly he leafed through his transparencies until he reached number eleven. He placed it carefully on the overhead projector, then turned his back to the audience and stared up at the wide white projection screen. A murmur had surfaced in the auditorium, and there was a tautness in the sound that recalled for Henderson a movie dramatization of a public execution. Czogloz unconsciously stroked his goatee, studying the graceful unfolding of the problem, the ingenious substitution that landed it onto solid footing, then the minor but critical assumption Henderson had attacked.

"Yes, of course." Czogloz cleared his throat. His ears were glowing as if they'd been badly sunburned. "The condition of positive definiteness can be viewed as a restriction of the method. A limitation."

"A limitation? It would seem that your subsequent results are invalidated."

Now the auditorium was silent except for the patient hum of the overhead projector fan. Czogloz nodded stiffly. "That may be correct. I'll have to consider more thoroughly the . . . implications."

An appreciative rumble rose from the audience. This type of drama was rare, and always welcome: it would be recounted in hushed whispers at the next conference, and the next, and the next after that. Henderson would be viewed with a mixture of fear and respect; his own presentations would become targets for mathematical headhunters. Henderson knew this. He also knew there would be a small crowd awaiting him at the end of the presentation, so before Czogloz could clear his throat forcefully enough to regain the audience's attention, he slipped out the back door.

In his damply air-conditioned Marriott room that evening, as Henderson was packing his garment bag and sipping minibar champagne — a reward for his cruel but delicious victory that afternoon — the telephone rang.

Czogloz's voice held a cheerful lilt. "Hello, John. I hope I haven't disturbed you — you sound quite merry."

Henderson coughed harshly as champagne fizz tickled the back of his throat. He set the plastic tumbler down and wiped his mouth, his palms suddenly damp with perspiration. "Listen, Miklos: there's no point in getting worked up."

"Oh, no, I'm not worked up," Czogloz said. "In fact, I must thank you for pointing out my error this afternoon. In the taxi, going back to the hotel, I realized a solution that avoids the difficulty you pointed out. An extraordinary little solution, actually. It could open an entirely new area of research for me."

"Well. That's wonderful." Henderson stretched the telephone cord into the bathroom and grabbed his shaving kit and toothbrush and stuffed them into the garment bag. "I'm sorry, I can't talk right now, Czogloz. I'm leaving for the airport."

"In an ideal world," Czogloz continued, "you might have been slightly more . . . *discreet.* But there it is."

Beneath Czogloz's accent, Henderson thought he detected an alcohol-induced slur. The thought of Czogloz drunk made Henderson uneasy, and he quickly zipped his bag and scanned the empty room. "Well, I'm off. I'll see you at the next conference. Or around town, I suppose." Czogloz and Henderson both taught in Boston — Czogloz at a university downtown and Henderson at a technical college in the suburbs — but Henderson had managed to avoid Czogloz for the past four years.

"I thought we could meet," Czogloz said. "In the hotel bar. Shall we say . . . thirty minutes?"

"You're in this hotel?" Henderson glanced nervously at the locked door. "How did you know I was staying here?"

"John, my goodness — you're acting like a character in a horror movie. *Relax.* I'm down the highway, at the Comfort Inn. I'll buy you a drink — Wild Turkey bourbon, if I remember correctly."

"I don't think so, Czogloz. I'd love to catch up on old times, but I'm flying out at eight-thirty."

"There's a matter we should discuss." Czogloz's voice held a dull, melancholy note. It was the voice of a man announcing an unfortunate but inevitable piece of news. "It's Marya, actually."

At the sound of Marya's name a shiver began in Henderson's chest that scurried over every inch of his skin. He felt as though he'd been heated over glowing coals and then dunked into an ocean-sized bath of icewater. "What about Marya?"

Czogloz sighed — a deep, troubling soul-sigh. "Too much. Too much for the telephone."

Henderson slumped onto the bed, feeling a familiar ache of yearning and despair, and found himself face-to-face with his reflection in the armoire mirror. He studied the image dispassionately — the frayed hair, the flabby neck and too-small shirt, the nervous, darting tongue that even to Henderson seemed vaguely obscene — then turned slowly away. "Thirty minutes," he said finally. "I'll need to change my flight."

"Wonderful," Czogloz said. "Do that, John. Change your flight."

Henderson crossed the faded lobby of the Marriott Hotel and paused at the entrance of Chez Georges restaurant. Through the smoky glass doors he saw a row of figures hunched at the bar, and toward the far end he thought he spotted Czogloz's goatee and shiny tie. Henderson rested his hand on the door handle, then backed away and hurried to the men's room and stood in front of an unoccupied urinal and closed his eyes. His heart was fluttering as though he'd just climbed a dozen flights of stairs. Henderson stood at the urinal, exhaling deeply, until he noticed the man next to him frowning; then he flushed and splashed his face in the sink and marched back across the lobby toward Chez Georges, toward Czogloz.

Miklos Zoltan Czogloz, from Budapest via Louisville. They'd met as first-year graduate students at the Michigan Engineering Institute, two aggressive young theorists who disagreed about Marx and Irish beer but agreed that mathematics was a game — the most elaborate, wonderful game, like puzzling out riddles posed by God. That first semester, while ninety inches of snow buried the institute, Henderson and Czogloz sat across from each other at the pitted oak tables of the Bachman Library, working increasingly difficult equations until they could solve them without thinking, like concert pianists playing finger exercises. When the semester ended, they moved into the top half of a decaying Dutch colonial on Mill Street, four blocks from the mathematics building. They smashed a six-dollar bottle of Asti Spumante against the brick windowsill and howled into the frozen December night, and Czogloz christened the house Poincaré Manor, in honor of his favorite mathematician.

And then Henderson met Marya. Marya Zilkowski, from Bialystok, who *liked* mathematics but didn't *love* it, and worried more about whether her kielbasa — which she stuffed by hand, in the bathtub — had too much garlic or black pepper. It was never clear to Henderson why she'd enrolled in graduate school, but he didn't care; no matter why she'd come, he wanted her to stay. Henderson began avoiding the library and instead lay tangled with Marya in his narrow twin bed, listening to Charles Mingus albums or making strenuous love or sampling Polish recipes that Marya had learned from her *babcia.* She had a California-shaped birthmark, Henderson discovered; she was prone to irrational fits of laughter; she worried that her luxuriant country accent made her sound rude and unintelligent. Marya was flighty — she made important decisions impulsively, as if she were deciding which pair of socks to wear — and although this frustrated Henderson, he envied her ability to change her mind, to implicitly admit she'd been wrong. Marya in the evening would cook enormous platters of kapusta or bigos or pierogi, and Czogloz, returning from the mathematics building at midnight or 1 A.M., would accept a plate of food and sit with Marya and Henderson on the Salvation Army sofa and watch *Hogan's Heroes* reruns. Henderson and Czogloz spoke with unabashed optimism of the control-theory problems they would solve — it seemed only a matter of time — while Marya joked about her future restaurant, Mala Warszawa: Little Warsaw, Polish home cooking.

They lived in Poincaré Manor for two years, and during that third summer Henderson flew to Newark for an adaptive-control conference. Four days without Marya — he sat at the back of over-air-conditioned conference rooms, his blank notebook before him, and found himself imitating Marya's careless loopy signature. He wrote *Marya Henderson,* and the sight made him fidgety with excitement. He decided to skip the Friday presentations. It was an uncharacteristically impulsive decision. That Thursday evening at the airport, hurrying through the drab terminal, he felt a sense of supreme gratitude and wonder, the way he imagined Euler must have felt when he realized $e^{\pi i} + 1$ equaled exactly zero, nothing. His sneakers chirped against the tile floor, a sound that inexplicably brought tears to his eyes. At home, as he worked his key in the deadbolt, he thought he heard something odd — a familiar voice with an unfamiliar inflection — but he put it out of his mind. His hands trembled against the scratched brass lock.

There was a single terrible moment, when Henderson's garment bag slumped to the floor and Marya glanced up from the kitchen table. She was wearing a blue gingham apron and beneath it was naked. Czogloz was lying on the sitting-room floor with a plate of golabki beside him and a *Journal of American Mathematics* propped on his chest, and apart from a pair of red sweatsocks he too was naked. Henderson stepped back and pulled the door shut. He stood frozen for a moment — he heard Czogloz's plate clatter against the pine floorboards, and Marya cried *Czekaj!* in a strangled, unnatural tone — then Henderson was gone, scrambling down the stairs and across the dark quadrangle, toward the mathematics building and the safety of his empty office.

Later there was a telephone call, Marya hiccupping through tears and speaking in anxious half-Polish phrases. *I am stupid, kochana, I am sorry,* she'd said, over and over — but she hadn't offered to take him back. It was a plain, miserable fact: she loved Henderson but she loved Czogloz more. Flighty, flaky Marya had changed her mind. It wasn't something that made sense to Henderson, but then nothing that involved women and love had ever made sense to him. He began sleeping in his office, unable to bear the sight of Marya's bra uncoiled on the floor of Czogloz's room, the smell of her perfume — Chanel No. 5, a classic and melancholy scent — on Czogloz's hand towels in the bathroom. That December, when their lease was up, Henderson at midnight stuffed his clothes and textbooks and yellow notepads into eight liquor boxes and loaded them into a taxi, and moved into a studio across the river from the institute. And for the next eighteen months, when he saw Czogloz at a seminar or dissertation defense, they talked about ice hockey or control theory, and did not mention Marya's name.

But even now Henderson kept the single remaining relic of his and Marya's relationship — a pair of pink cotton panties — in the far reaches of his lower-right desk drawer. Some Friday afternoons, when the Evans Building was abandoned and the carillon had tolled its dirge, Henderson found himself closing his office door and leaning back in his armchair, into a slant of sunlight, with the panties crushed up under his chin. Although they'd been washed accidentally, years ago, sometimes Henderson thought he could smell Marya's eastern-European tang of garlic and dried leaves, her scent. On the back of the panties, near the tag, was a sight that never failed to twist Henderson's heart: the word MARYA penned in blurry blue ink. He thought he had never seen a name as beautiful or as tragic.

*

Czogloz, slouched against the bar, did not look as young as he had that afternoon during his presentation. His suit coat was thrown over a stool and his purple tie was loosened, and he wore the look of a traveler stranded overnight in an airport terminal. As Henderson crossed the room, Czogloz rose unsteadily, clutching the bar for support, then shook Henderson's hand with a slightly feminine grip.

"Good to see you, Miklos," Henderson said. "Love your tie."

Czogloz grinned wearily. "Hello, John. It's good to see you, too." There was a sincerity in his voice that Henderson found disarming. "I read your contraction-analysis paper in the *J.A.M.* Wonderful work."

"Not really," Henderson said. "A minor observation surrounded by well-known facts. It didn't deserve publication."

This was the truth and they both knew it, but Czogloz shrugged diffidently. He glanced down at the bar and spread his hands, a conciliatory gesture. "I must tell you, I am not angry about this afternoon. For a while, after the presentation — yes, I was somewhat . . . *perturbed.* But no more."

Czogloz was drinking what looked like cough syrup, and Henderson ordered another and a Wild Turkey for himself. When the drinks arrived, Henderson took a polite sip and said, "So. Marya."

"Marya." Czogloz tilted his glass, watching thick red liquid coat the walls of the tumbler. "We're finally getting married, in October. I don't know if you've heard."

"Hersch told me," Henderson said. "Congratulations. I wish you every happiness." His words were dull and lifeless, a parody of congratulations. "How is she?"

Czogloz frowned hard into his glass. "She was happy, until a few months ago. She was teaching a Polish cooking course at the BCAE. We put a down payment on a very nice condominium in the city. And then something happened. She 'found religion,' as she likes to say."

"My goodness," Henderson said. "And I have trouble even finding my car keys."

"That's funny," Czogloz said, without smiling. "I'd almost forgotten about your interesting sense of humor." Czogloz signaled for another drink and tapped the base of his tumbler against the bar until it arrived. "And now she is carrying things too far — even the priest agrees. She called Krakow last month to tell her mother about the time she stole six hundred thousand zlotys from her grandmother's purse. The poor woman! Seventy years old, listening to her only daughter tell her she's a thief."

"A conversion," Henderson mused. "Jesus. Who'd have guessed?" The bourbon was warming him into loquaciousness, and the strangeness of the story warmed him further. He was glad, he reflected, that he'd changed his flight and come tonight. "I suppose it's nice for her, but how many people is she hurting? Her mother, you. Who else?"

Czogloz nodded. "I was hoping you could help."

"And why would I do that?"

"For Marya. And for me. It is making things . . . difficult."

Henderson stirred his drink with his pinkie, then licked his finger. "Really? How difficult?"

Czogloz nodded, as if he'd been expecting the question. "She will no longer go to horror movies, which is something we both — we all — loved. She spends weeknights at Bible study or adoration, then berates me for not attending with her. She's begun listening to Christian folk music."

"That's it? Movies and shitty music?"

"She told me last week she was reconsidering the wedding."

Henderson paused with the bourbon nearly to his lips, then recovered and took a long, casual sip. He was not completely surprised; it was just like Marya to dither over something so important. Czogloz's lips were pursed; he was staring at the tall, ornate pepper mill that stood in an alcove behind the bar like a religious icon. "Do you know, John, that Catholics believe Jesus Christ rose from the dead?" Czogloz grinned bemusedly. "That he hopped up, stone dead, and strolled away? Remarkable."

Henderson could not imagine Marya kneeling in a church, or praying, or lifting a gaudy gold chalice to her lips; she was so thoroughly *carnal.* When he thought of Marya, he most often thought of cooking — the tightly rolled gawumpki, the swollen, bursting kielbasa, the thick Bulgarian wine — or he thought of sex.

Henderson had never been drawn to religion; the notion of a God seemed as abstract to him as nonlinear control theory did to most other people. Some late nights, the sheets in knots and his forehead filmed with sweat, Henderson found himself yearning for some nebulous *goodness* into which he could cast his irritation and anxiety and self-doubt. In his half-dreaming state he envisioned the faux-antique wishing well that stood in the lobby of the nearby McDonald's. When he woke the next morning, however, he felt a caustic mixture of skepticism and shame. For what was there to believe in? The ability of people to grow accustomed to even the cruelest discomfort. The dusky accumulation of regret with every passing year. The flow of electrons from low potentials to higher ones. Beyond that — what?

"There's more," Czogloz said. "There's the matter of her Ph.D."

The restaurant's jazzy music seemed to pause, and the other patrons' voices fell mute, as though they were speaking through cotton. Henderson watched Czogloz study the empty bottom of his glass. "She wants to give up her Ph.D. And she wants to announce the truth, in the *J.A.M.*"

Henderson clutched Czogloz's wrist. "Jesus, Miklos. Stop her."

"She's very serious about it," Czogloz said, extracting his wrist with a gentle but firm tug. "She says the situation has always made her feel terrible."

Henderson slumped against the bar and mechanically signaled for another round. He felt a numbness that went far beyond the effects of the bourbon. He felt like a dental patient dulled by Novocain, indifferently watching the world move before him.

"You know," Czogloz said, "I think it's the best work you've ever done. Zilkowski's Theorem — I *knew* it wasn't actually hers. She didn't care about it, it was nothing to her. And yet . . ." He trailed off. "Such beauty. A beautiful proof."

Henderson shrugged bleakly. "I was inspired, I suppose."

"It must have pained you to see it published under someone else's name."

"Not at all," he said, with more feeling than he'd intended. "I was happy for Marya. I wanted her to be happy."

"Happiness." Czogloz grinned ruefully. "A difficult condition to achieve."

It had started five months after Henderson moved out of Poincaré Manor: she'd called one chilly May morning, while Henderson was struggling against the impulse to draw the blinds and stay in bed until noon. Marya's voice sent a warm shiver down through his thighs. "Are you well?" she'd asked, and it was all he could do not to laugh bitterly. "Perfect," he'd said, eventually. "How are you?"

She told him about her mother's arthritis, about the hot, needling pains in her own wrists, about the pumpkin-colored sweater she'd knitted for her sister's son, Stefan. Her voice slipped into a languorous drawl, and suddenly it was as if she'd never done the thing she'd done: they talked about Reagan, and Charlie Parker. They talked about sex. She told him details about herself and Czogloz that Henderson could not bear to hear but that thrilled him nonetheless. But there was a problem, she admitted. Her dissertation — she was stuck. The feeling, she explained, was like trying to run a marathon without understanding how even to crawl. "Who knows? Maybe I'll return home," she said, with a sigh. "Maybe it's time to open Mala Warszawa."

"Don't," Henderson said. "Please don't. Give me six weeks — a month."

Henderson went to the library. Marya was studying a class of problems not too distant from his own research, and within a week he'd discovered some curious connections. That next Sunday, there was a feverish stretch of hours when equations seemed to fall all around him, like ripe fruit from a tree. He scribbled them down as fast as he could write. Monday morning, exhausted, he called Marya's apartment to tell her the news, but Czogloz answered the phone. Henderson closed his eyes and hung up.

It happened occasionally: the Ph.D. student who flared like a brilliant comet, then disappeared. Marya's dissertation committee, after her defense, convened for only seven minutes — seven minutes — then burst from the conference room to tell her she'd passed, that she was now Dr. Marya Zilkowski. And she had not published a single paper since.

"So," Czogloz said, setting his empty glass on the bar, "the final reason I called you tonight: Marya and I would like to invite you to dinner next week, at our condominium."

The thought of sitting down to dinner between Czogloz and Marya seemed so ludicrous to Henderson that he stared at Czogloz for a long moment without saying anything. "Dinner," he said finally.

"Marya's been experimenting with new recipes — Polish-French, Polish-Cantonese." Czogloz shrugged. "Fusion cuisine, I suppose."

Henderson rose unsteadily from the stool. He felt flustered, and weary. And drunk. "No French," he said. "No Cantonese — just Polish. Tell her I'll come only if she cooks plain Polish."

Czogloz nodded. "I'll ask her to make bigos." He looked up at Henderson with a clear-eyed expression that, for a moment, seemed almost wistful. "It was your favorite, I believe. Yes?"

"They were all my favorites," Henderson said.

The next night, back in Boston, Henderson reclined on his battered sofa and allowed his mind to explore the horrible and fascinating possibility of being exposed as the author of Zilkowski's Theorem. There would be a minor scandal; conversation in the coffee room at the next conference would fall to a hush when he entered. In a perverse way, Henderson realized, it would enhance his reputation. But tenure-review committees were not known for their wit or compassion.

Yet what would it matter? At worst, his tenure review would be scathing; he would be asked to find another job. Truth was, Henderson disliked academia. He disliked the bitchy tediousness of faculty meetings; he disliked the endless discussions with self-absorbed undergraduates, who were uncertain whether they should major in mathematics or Spanish literature. Often Henderson found himself nostalgic for his days as a graduate student, days when he'd spend eleven hours huddled in a study carrel, stopping only to microwave a frozen burrito or watch snow drift past the Bachman Library windows. It had been a lonely but painless existence.

The Russian theorists would understand, Henderson concluded idly. They would understand the concept of theorems written for the sake of romance. The Russians had an appreciation for the noble, doomed gesture, but others — the Germans, the Japanese, the Americans — who could say? Henderson willed his mind into a state of blankness. Outside his apartment window, a man spoke half of a conversation into a cellular phone. *Can't do eight hundred,* the man said. *Nine-fifty, absolute lowest. Break my balls lowest.* His life was simple, thought Henderson. He knew nothing of Zilkowski's Theorem.

He shuffled to the kitchen and poured a pint of milk into a saucepan, but the smell of it warming made his stomach curdle and he dumped it down the sink. He knelt, and from the far reaches of the cabinet retrieved a bottle of Wild Turkey. A gauzy film of dust lay over the bottle and made it seem ancient, an artifact from a less enlightened time. Henderson poured a tall finger of bourbon into a coffee mug and shuffled to the sitting room. He rifled through his cassettes and picked out one of Feynman's lectures, then flopped onto the sofa. The voice of the genius physicist filled the small apartment, but instead of soothing Henderson, as it usually did, it only made him feel suddenly and painfully aware of his own mediocrity. And yet Henderson didn't stop the cassette. Instead he got to his feet and turned the volume up — way up, blasting, loud enough for all the neighbors to hear.

Czogloz and Marya's condominium was on Commonwealth Avenue near Kenmore Square, and as Henderson peeled off the I-93 exit ramp he locked the doors, as he always did when he drove into the city. On the porch, listening to the muted chime of the doorbell, he found himself unhappily reviewing his recent conversation with Czogloz. He'd been taken advantage of again: enlisted to help pacify the woman who'd dumped him, by the man she'd dumped him for. That woman! Not only had she lured him into writing her dissertation, now she was punishing him for doing it. A bitter taste rose in Henderson's mouth, and he spat into the cluster of violet tulips alongside the porch. And people like Czogloz get National Science Foundation grants, he thought, while Henderson has to beg for research funding. He had subconsciously slipped into the third person, as he did during moments of severe anxiety.

The door opened and there was Czogloz: wearing faded jeans and a yellow polo shirt, looking decidedly more relaxed than he had in Akron. Behind him stood Marya. She had shrunk slightly, it seemed to Henderson, and her hair had darkened from iced-tea brown to near black, but otherwise she was the same woman he remembered with such painful specificity. She was wearing an orange blouse and a short black skirt, with sheer purple tights — an oddly sexy, Marya-like combination — and the sight of her standing before him caused in Henderson a warm, liquid rush of desire. She wiped her hands on a dishtowel and beamed at Henderson as he stepped inside.

"The brilliant scholar arrives! It's great to see you, John." She took him by the shoulders and kissed him, right cheek, then left, a one-two combination that left Henderson dizzy. "Come in, please — everything's ready."

Czogloz led Henderson through a quick tour of the condo —

unremarkable, save for a dim, musky bedroom strewn with tangled heaps of clothes, which Czogloz hurried past — then ushered him into an airy dining room with polished oak floorboards and a bay window. The room bore unmistakable traces of Czogloz and Marya — a framed mathematical journal offprint, a stereo cluttered with worn, sleeveless records — and the sight of such objects in close proximity piqued Henderson's displeasure. It was a warm evening and the windows were thrown open; the faint nasal rhythms of a Red Sox broadcast drifted in from a neighbor's television. Czogloz offered Henderson a glass of murky red wine, and Henderson downed it in three swallows. "You must be mortgaged to the hilt," he said to Czogloz. "Not bad for an assistant professor."

"The basement floods," Czogloz said, "and the radiators are temperamental. Other than that . . . we're happy."

Marya appeared from the kitchen with a tray of golabki. Golabki — a rush of intense sensation filled Henderson's chest, so suddenly that he thought he might sob. The memory of a particular August night came to him: golabki and the same thick red wine; he and Marya dining cross-legged on the floor, in the languorous heat, in their underwear; a scratchy Monk record blasting from the bedroom. That woman! He took a seat at the table and speared one of the cabbage rolls with his fork and bit it in half.

"I hope it's not too spicy," Marya said. "I remember you liked spicy."

Henderson turned to her. "So. Czogloz — Miklos — has told me about your conversion. I would say I'm happy for you, but that wouldn't be completely accurate."

Marya looked at Henderson with tender curiosity, like a child examining a small, injured animal. "Same old John. You never did like small talk, did you?" She sipped her wine and grinned. "I know, you think it's just one of my silly ideas. It's not. Truly."

"I suppose you want my approval for your 'announcement' in the *J.A.M.*? I suppose that's the purpose of this dinner?"

Now Marya laughed, and shot Henderson a wry glance. "John, please — I would like your approval, yes. I won't deny that."

"My approval," Henderson said. "Let me see: you publish a retraction, walk away with a clear conscience, and I get . . . what? Mocked by the tenure committee. Shunned at conferences."

"You get my gratitude," Marya said, covering his hand with hers.

"You get the knowledge that you've made me happy. That's all I can offer, John. What else do I have?"

"For God's sake," Henderson said, suddenly — infuriatingly — thrilled by Marya's touch. "Do you really think this is necessary? Think of all the fools with Ph.D.s, and you, an intelligent person who deserves one! It's a victimless crime."

"No crime is victimless," Marya said with a shrug. "When you find religion you begin to understand that."

Henderson shook his head in disgust: Marya had changed. She seemed duller, less spontaneous. And her accent, which had once sounded so alluringly foreign, had flattened into a quasi-American drawl. Beside Marya, Czogloz was staring out the bay window with a vacant, terminal expression on his face. Outside, the Red Sox broadcast had increased in volume, the surflike roar of the crowd washing over the commentators' chatter; it was tied at three in the fifth inning.

They finished the golabki in silence. Czogloz cleared their plates and emerged from the kitchen with bowls of steaming bigos, and when he departed to fetch another bottle of wine Henderson rested his elbows on the table and stared at Marya. "So now you want to be forgiven," he said. "I thought you people had priests for that."

Marya shot him a quick, tight-lipped glance. "It's a matter of conscience," she said quietly. "I did awful things, John. Cheating on you. Plagiarizing. Calling you in the morning when Miklos was gone. It wasn't right."

"It was nothing. Nothing happened! We talked about control theory, which — last time I checked — is not a sin."

"It was wrong. I was wrong to treat you the way I did." She nodded matter-of-factly, as Czogloz returned with the wine. "For several years I was very unhappy."

"And now you are happy," Henderson said.

Marya looked up at him, the expression on her face gliding from suspicion to resentment to tenderness, all within a half-second. "Yes," Marya said. "I'm happy."

Henderson started to speak, then shook his head and swallowed a long gulp of wine. He wanted Marya to be happy, but not this way; sneaking into happiness through the back door of religion was too easy, a fool's bargain. He felt a surge of angry restlessness. He downed the rest of the wine and wiped his mouth with the back of his hand.

"Okay, fine. I'll make you a deal." Henderson motioned toward the open window and the chatter of the baseball broadcast. "If the Red Sox win, you have my blessing. Publish your retraction. Ruin my career. Be happy. But if the Sox lose — sorry, Marya. I guess you'll just have to live with your conscience. Like the rest of us."

"John! What are you — what do you mean?" Marya asked. She and Czogloz were staring at him with horrified expressions on their faces. "Please, John, do this for me. For our friendship."

"Henderson," Czogloz hissed, "this is too important to trivialize. For all of us."

But Henderson leaned back in his chair and shrugged. For so long he'd played by the rules and lost; now he was willing to give fate a chance.

Czogloz stared at the television in the corner as if it were a strange contraption he'd never seen, then slowly flipped through the channels until he found the game. They moved their chairs around the table and watched in silence. The Red Sox scored in the sixth and eighth, but the Tigers tied it with a three-run homer in the top of the ninth. The game was tied at the end of nine innings, and went into extra innings. Marya sat forward in her chair, hugging herself in concentration, but Henderson found himself unable to focus his attention. He felt as vacant and detached as the Hood Dairy Company blimp on the screen, drifting high above the ballpark. He drank a third glass of wine and then a fourth, watching the dusk deepen through the bay window, the streaky pink and orange of the horizon recalling for him the freakish aurora borealises he'd seen so often at the institute. At one point he became aware of Czogloz studying him, but when he glanced over Czogloz turned away.

The Tigers eked out a run in the top of the eleventh — a single, a wild pitch, two sacrifice flies — and in the bottom of the inning the first two Red Sox grounded to the shortstop. A desperate rumble rose from the crowd. "What now?" Henderson said to the side of Marya's face. "What happens now? You go ahead with more confessions, you make yourself feel better, then what? What about the people around you? Forgiveness doesn't come so easily, Marya."

She didn't look at him. "Religion has as many unanswered questions as mathematics," Henderson insisted. "Wait and see."

Just then the volume leaped to a roar, and the camera panned sharply upward; Henderson spotted the ball arcing high above the stadium, a brilliant streak against the grainy sky. The ball seemed to hang motionless for an instant; then, as if swatted by an invisible hand, it began to plummet. Marya clapped her hands together in astonishment. The Detroit right fielder sprinted back to the warning track and then to the wall, and as the ball cleared the fence he leaped, his glove reaching back into the bullpen, then stumbled away from the fence with his glove held high. He'd caught the ball; a moan escaped from the Boston crowd. The Detroit right fielder pumped his fist and flipped the ball from his glove into his bare hand. He trotted slowly toward the dugout.

Czogloz released a hiss of breath. "I closed my eyes. I've always hated that aspect of sports, the tension." He seemed to want to say more but stayed quiet. On the screen, players were shaking hands with one another and shuffling toward the dugouts.

Henderson sat with his arms crossed over his chest. He turned to Marya, who seemed to be staring at something just beyond the television set. Her lips were drawn into a thin, determined line, and her hands were clasped, as if she were praying. "If I were a cruel man," Henderson said, "I'd point out a moral here."

"But you're not cruel. You're generous and intelligent, and kind." Marya took Henderson's hand. "You're not cruel, John. Are you?"

The next morning Henderson reclined in his stained leather chair, stirring a mug of coffee with the gnawed end of a ballpoint pen. It was not yet seven o'clock, and the Walter H. Layton Mathematics Building was quiet. Henderson had never been in his office quite so early, and was surprised at how much he enjoyed the deep, luxurious silence; soon the first graduate students would arrive, unshaven and reeking of last night's stir-fry, then the undergraduates with 8 A.M. lectures, then the staff assistants and UPS men, and the building would begin to exude its normal levels of tension and haste. Henderson sipped his coffee and studied the dusty vectors of sunlight arrayed across his desk. It occurred to him that he would miss his office, if he was asked to leave. It was the only place at the college he felt truly at ease.

The mailbox icon on his Unix desktop was blinking: one new message, from Czogloz, time-stamped 2:17 A.M. "Dear John," it began, and Henderson paused, momentarily taken aback at the sight of such a personal greeting.

> I am writing to thank you. You have made Marya very happy, and therefore you have made me very happy. A great weight has been lifted from her: she sits now at the table composing a menu for our wedding, which will be in May, and the smile on her face is truly wondrous. I have no words to describe it. You will be invited to the wedding, of course, and I hope you will attend.
>
> The editor of the *J.A.M.* has agreed to publish a brief note in the December issue regarding the "misunderstanding," as he terms it. I regret this. I regret also that Marya has drafted a letter to the regents of the Institute asking that they revoke her Ph.D. I was unable, finally, to discourage her.
>
> I must tell you that Marya believes you possess great kindness. I told her this is not true — I hope you understand. Because it is not true, is it? You are not kind. Marya claimed that your recent generosity was proof of the spirit working within you. I did not have a response to that statement. It seemed — dare I say? — plausible.
>
> I am too tired to write more, but must thank you again for what you've done. I do not completely understand why you've done it, but am grateful nonetheless. Thank you.
>
> Your friend,
> Miklos

Henderson reread the message, then clicked "delete." He switched off the computer. He leaned back in his chair, feeling vaguely certain that he should feel good about what he'd done — or what he'd allowed to happen — yet he did not feel good. For who, in the end, would benefit? Marya. Czogloz, by extension. And Henderson — as usual — would be left worse off, lower down, unhappier. Was it possible to find happiness in its pure state, unalloyed by sorrow? Sometimes it seemed so, but often Henderson was convinced it was impossible. Happiness was a zero-sum game: for one to become happy, another must find despair. For so long Henderson had been on the wrong side of the equation.

With this thought in his mind Henderson took a small padded envelope from his desk drawer and printed Czogloz's university address on it, then stuffed Marya's pink panties inside and stapled the envelope shut.

Outside, the sun had risen above the computer science building and a breeze was stirring the newly fallen leaves. Four students in identical blue T-shirts and khaki shorts were strolling down West Street, untroubled by the early-autumn chill and all it implied: syllabuses, homework, exams. New junior faculty, new emeriti. Tenure reviews. Arrivals and departures. Henderson watched them for a moment, envious of their cheery indifference, then hurried north, toward the faculty parking lot.

Driving across town, he switched on the radio but didn't bother tuning in to any particular station. He parked near the mathematics building of Czogloz's university and inside found an intercampus mailbox. He hesitated for a moment — the envelope resting on the lip of the mail slot, the panties' weight almost imperceptibly slight — then dropped the package in and double-checked to make sure it had reached bottom. No return address, no postmark, the monotonous blocky printing; Czogloz might suspect who'd sent it, but he'd never know for sure. *Fine,* thought Henderson. *Let him wonder.*

He hurried back to his car and drove, past the edge of campus, past the Portuguese neighborhood, to where the houses possessed a faded shabbiness. On a whim he turned down a leaf-strewn, deserted side street. He felt a dark tugging, of something like remorse, but he put it from his mind. He parked the car and began to walk, past a laundromat, then a bank, then a fish market. Across the street was a church, a steepled stone building with broad concrete steps and a bright stained glass window above the doors. A homeless man in an army fatigue jacket was sitting on the steps, smoking a cigarette. A sign near the sidewalk read JESUS SAVES SAT 6 SUN 9 1030 1215.

Henderson crossed the street and climbed the steps and pulled open the tall, heavy wooden doors. Inside, sunlight filtered dustily through rows of high windows and settled over the empty pews. The air smelled of incense and old, moist stones. He took a seat in the rearmost pew and stared straight up at the graceful geometry of the vaulted ceiling. It was a gorgeous place, he had to admit: the emptiness, the silence, the warm, dense air like a blanket draped over his shoulders. Somewhere outside, a car alarm squealed, the sound muffled and hollow in the cavernous church.

He recalled a story he'd once heard, about Euler's "proof" of God's existence to Diderot: $\frac{(a+b^n)}{n} = x$, so God must exist. Ridiculous, of course. But then there was Pascal's argument: that reasonable men should believe in God, because the potential payoff of heaven so far outweighed the risk of hell. Henderson sat with his hands clasped, biting his lower lip. If Pascal had known probability theory, he thought, he could have formalized his argument. It was a shame.

A young priest walked down the aisle carrying a pair of ivory candles, and Henderson found himself trying to catch his eye. The thought occurred to him that he, John Henderson, could join the priesthood. His body quivered at the thought, a sharp rush of fear and excitement. They took anyone who applied — wasn't there some rule? *Look at me,* Henderson thought, his gaze fixed on the priest's downcast face. He could join the priesthood and spend entire afternoons thinking about faith, about forgiveness. Yes. He could stand before a congregation, and tell them what it meant to be lonely and full of fear. *Look at me,* he thought. *Please. Look at me.*

But the priest hurried past, his cassock rustling softly.

JHUMPA LAHIRI

Nobody's Business

FROM THE NEW YORKER

EVERY SO OFTEN a man called for Sang, wanting to marry her. Sang usually didn't know these men. Sometimes she had never even heard of them. But they'd heard that she was pretty and smart and thirty and Bengali and still single, and so these men, most of whom also happened to be Bengali, would procure her number from someone who knew someone who knew her parents, who, according to Sang, desperately wanted her to be married. According to Sang, these men always confused details when they spoke to her, saying they'd heard that she studied physics, when really it was philosophy, or that she'd graduated from Columbia, when really it was NYU, calling her Sangeeta, when really she went by Sang. They were impressed that she was getting her doctorate at Harvard, when really she'd dropped out of Harvard after a semester and was working part-time at a bookstore in the square.

Sang's housemates, Paul and Heather, could always tell when it was a prospective groom on the phone. "Oh. Hi," Sang would say, sitting at the imitation-walnut kitchen table, rolling her eyes, coin-colored eyes that were sometimes green. She would slouch in her chair, looking bothered but resigned, as if a subway she were riding had halted between stations. To Paul's mild disappointment, Sang was never rude to these men. She listened as they explained the complicated, far-fetched connection between them, connections Paul vaguely envied in spite of the fact that he shared a house with Sang, and a kitchen, and a subscription to the *Globe*. The suitors called from as far away as Los Angeles, as close by as Watertown. Once, she told Paul and Heather, she had actually agreed to meet one of these men, and he had driven her north up I-93, pointing from the highway to the corporation he worked for. Then he'd taken her to a Dunkin' Donuts, where, over crullers and coffee, he'd proposed.

Sometimes Sang would take notes during these conversations, on the message pad kept next to the phone. She'd write down the man's name, or "Carnegie Mellon" or "likes mystery novels," before her pen drifted into scribbles and stars and ticktacktoe games. To be polite, she asked a few questions too, about whether the man enjoyed his work as an economist, or a dentist, or a metallurgical engineer. Her excuse to these men, her rebuttal to their offers to wine and dine her, was always the same white lie: she was busy at the moment with classes, its being Harvard and all. Sometimes, if Paul happened to be sitting at the table, she would write him a note in the middle of the conversation — "He sounds like he's twelve" or "Total dweeb" or "This guy threw up once in my parents' swimming pool" — waving the pad for Paul's benefit as she cradled the phone to her ear.

It was only after Sang hung up that she complained. How dare these men call? she'd say. How dare they hunt her down? It was a violation of her privacy, an insult to her adulthood. It was pathetic. If only Paul and Heather could hear them, going on about themselves. At this point, Heather would sometimes say, "God, Sang, I can't believe you're complaining. Dozens of men, successful men, possibly even handsome, want to marry you, sight unseen. And you expect us to feel sorry for you?" Heather, a law student at Boston College, had been bitterly single for five years. She told Sang the proposals were romantic, but Sang shook her head. "It's not love." In Sang's opinion, it was practically an arranged marriage. These men weren't really interested in her. They were interested in a mythical creature created by an intricate chain of gossip, a web of wishful, Indian-community thinking in which she was an aging, overlooked poster child for years of *bharat natyam* classes, perfect SATs. Had they had any idea who she actually was and how she made a living, in spite of her test scores, which was by running a cash register and arranging paperback books in pyramid configurations, they would want nothing to do with her. "And besides," she always reminded Paul and Heather, "I have a boyfriend."

"You're like Penelope," Paul ventured one evening. He had

lately been rereading Lattimore's Homer, in preparation for his orals in English literature the following spring.

"Penelope?" She was standing at the microwave, heating some rice. Paul watched as she removed the plate and mixed the steaming rice with a spoonful of the dark-red hot lime pickle that lived next to his peanut butter in the door of the refrigerator.

"From *The Odyssey*?" Paul said gently, a question to match her question. He was tall without being lank, with solid fingers and calves, and fine straw-colored hair. The most noticeable aspect of his appearance was a pair of expensive designer glasses, their maroon frames perfectly round, which an attractive salesgirl in a frame shop on Beacon Street had talked him into buying. Paul had not liked the glasses even as he was being fitted for them, and had not grown to like them since.

"Right, *The Odyssey*," Sang said, sitting down at the table. "Penelope. Only I can't knit."

"Weave," he said, correcting her. "It was a shroud Penelope kept weaving and unweaving, to ward off her suitors."

Sang lifted a forkful of the rice to her lips, blowing on it so that it would cool. "Then who's the woman who knits?" she asked. She looked at Paul. "You would know."

Paul paused, eager to impress her, but his mind had drawn a blank. He knew it was someone in Dickens, had the paperbacks up in his room. "Be right back," he said. Then he stopped, relieved. "*A Tale of Two Cities*," he told her. "Madame Defarge."

Paul had answered the phone the first time Sang called, at nine o'clock one Saturday morning in July, in reference to the housemate ad he and Heather had placed in the *Phoenix*. The call had roused him from sleep, and he had wondered, standing there, groggy in his bathrobe, what sort of name Sang was, half expecting a Japanese woman. It wasn't until she wrote out a check for her security deposit at the end of her visit that he saw that her official name was Sangeeta Biswas. This was the name he would see on her mail, on the labels of the thick, pungent *Vogue* magazines she received each month, and in the window of the electric bill she agreed to take on. Heather had been in the shower when Sang arrived and pressed the doorbell that chimed two solemn tones, so Paul had greeted her alone. She had worn her long hair loose, something Paul was to learn she rarely did, and as he walked behind her he had liked the way it clung protectively to her body, over the rise of her shoulder blades. She had admired the spectacular central staircase, as most everyone did, letting her hand linger over the banister. The staircase turned six times at right angles after every six steps, and was constructed of dark gleaming wood with the luster of cognac. It was the only thing of enduring beauty in the house, a false promise of what was above: ugly brown cabinets in the kitchen, moldy bathrooms with missing tiles, omnipresent oatmeal carpeting to protect the ears of the landlords, who lived below.

She had remarked on what a lot of space it was, pacing the landing before joining Paul in the vacant room. There was a built-in hutch in the corner, with Doric pilasters and glass-paned doors, which Sang opened and closed. Paul told her that the room had originally been the dining room, the cabinet intended to store china. There was a bathroom across the landing; Paul and Heather shared the larger one, upstairs. "I feel like I'm standing inside an empty refrigerator," she'd said, referring to the fact that the walls, once blue, had been painted over with a single coat of white; the effect, under the glare of the ceiling light, was stark and cold. She ran a hand along one wall and carefully removed a stray piece of tape. Once there had been an arched doorway connecting the room to the kitchen, since filled in, but Sang noted that the arch was still visible, like a scar in the plaster.

While she was there, the phone rang, another person replying to the ad, but by then she had handed over her deposit. She had met Heather, and the three of them had chatted in the living room with its peeling bay window and its soft filthy couch and its yellow papasan chair. They told her about their system for splitting up the chores, and about the landlords, both doctors at Brigham and Women's. They told her there was only one phone jack in the house, in the kitchen. The phone was attached to a cord so long that they could all drag it to their rooms, though at times the price to pay for dragging the cord too far was a persistent crackle.

"We thought about having another line put in, but it's pretty expensive," Heather said.

"It's not a big deal," Sang said.

And Paul, who seldom spoke on the phone to anyone, said nothing at all.

*

She had practically nothing to contribute to the house, no pots or appliances, nothing for the kitchen apart from an ailing hanging plant that shed yellow heart-shaped leaves. A friend helped her move in one Sunday, a male friend who was not, Paul gathered, her boyfriend (for she had mentioned one on her first visit, telling them that he was in Cairo for the summer visiting his parents, that he was Egyptian, and that he taught Middle Eastern history at Harvard). The friend's name was Charles. He wore high-top sneakers and a bright-orange bowling shirt, his hair tied back in a stubby ponytail. He was telling Sang about a date he'd had the night before, as they unloaded a futon, two big battered suitcases, a series of shopping bags, and a few boxes from the back of a pickup truck. Paul had offered to help, calling out from the deck where he was trying to read *The Canterbury Tales,* but Sang had said no, it was nothing. Their talk distracted him and yet he remained, watching Sang through the railing. Charles was teasingly forbidding her to buy too many things, so that moving out would be just as easy.

Sang had been laughing at him, but now she stopped, her expression pensive. She looked up at the house, a balled-up comforter in her arms. "I don't know, Charles. I don't know how long I'll be here."

"He still doesn't want to live together until you're married?"

She shook her head.

"What does he say?"

"That he doesn't want to spoil things."

Charles shifted the weight of the box he was carrying. "But he acknowledges the fact that you're getting married."

She turned back to the truck. "He says things like 'When we have kids, we'll buy a big house in Lexington.'"

"You've been together three years," Charles said. "So he's a little old-fashioned. That's one of the things you like about him, right?"

The next few nights, Sang slept on the couch in the living room, her things stored temporarily in the corner, in order to paint her room. Both Paul and Heather were surprised by this; neither of them had made an effort to do much to their rooms when moving in. For the walls, she had chosen a soothing sage green; for the trim, the palest lavender, a color that the paint company called "mole." It wasn't what she imagined a mole to look like at all, she told Paul, stirring the can vigorously on the kitchen counter. "What would you have named it?" she asked him suddenly. He could think of nothing. It was only upstairs, sitting alone at his big plywood desk, piled with thick books full of tissue-thin pages, that he thought of the ice cream his mother always ordered at Newport Creamery when his family went on Sunday nights for hamburgers. His mother had died years ago, his father soon after. They'd adopted Paul late in life, when they were in their fifties, so people had often mistaken them for his grandparents. That evening in the kitchen, when Sang walked in, Paul said, "Black raspberry."

"What?"

"The paint."

She had a small, slightly worried-looking smile on her face, a smile one might give a confused child. "That's funny."

"The name?"

"No. It's just a little funny the way you picked up a conversation we had, like, six hours ago, and expected me to remember what you were talking about."

As soon as Paul opened the door of his room the next morning, he detected the fresh yet cloying smell of paint, heard the swish of the roller as it moved up and down a wall. After Heather had left the house, Sang started to play music: one Billie Holiday CD after another. They were having a spell of sticky, sweltering days, and Paul was working in the relative cool of the living room, a few paces across the landing from Sang.

"Oh, my God," she exclaimed, noticing him on her way to the bathroom. "This music must be driving you crazy." She wore cut-off jeans, a black tank top with straps like those of a brassiere. Her feet were bare, her calves and thighs flecked with paint.

He lied, telling her he often studied to music. Because he noticed it was the kitchen she went to most often, to rinse her brushes or eat some yogurt out of a big tub, the second day he moved himself there, where he made a pot of tea and, much to her amusement, set the alarm on his wristwatch to know when to take out the leaves. In the afternoon, her sister called, from London, with a voice identical to Sang's. For a moment Paul actually believed it was Sang herself, mysteriously calling him from her room. "Can't talk, I'm painting my room sage and mole," she reported cheerfully to her sister, and when she replaced the receiver of the dark-brown phone there were a few of her mole-colored fingerprints on the surface.

He liked studying in her fleeting company. She was impressed with how far he'd got on his Ph.D. — she told him that after she had dropped out of Harvard a year ago, her mother had locked herself up in her bedroom for a week and her father had refused to speak to her. She'd had it with academia, hated how competitive it was, how monkish it forced one to become. That was what her boyfriend did, always blocking off chunks of his day and working at home with the phone unplugged, writing papers for the next conference. "You'll be good at it," she assured Paul. "You're devoted, I can tell." When she asked him what his exam entailed, he told her it would last three hours, that there would be three questioners, and that it would cover three centuries of English and European literature.

"And they can ask you anything?" she wanted to know.

"Within reason."

"Wow."

He didn't tell her the truth — that he'd already taken the exam the year before and failed. His committee and a handful of students were the only ones who knew, and it was to avoid them that Paul preferred to stay at home now. He had failed not because he wasn't prepared but because his mind had betrayed him that bright May morning, inexplicably cramped like a stubborn muscle that curled his foot during sleep. For five harrowing minutes, as the professors stared at him with their legal pads full of questions, as trains came and went along Commonwealth Avenue, he had not been able to reply to the first question, about comic villainy in *Richard III.* He had read the play so many times he could picture each scene, not as it might be performed on a stage but rather as the pale printed columns in his Pelican Shakespeare. He felt himself go crimson; it was the nightmare he had been having for months before the exam. His interrogators had been patient, had tried another question, which he had stammered miserably through, pausing in the middle of a thought and unable to continue, until finally one of the professors, white hair like a snowy wreath around his otherwise naked head, put out a hand, as might a policeman stopping traffic, and said, "The candidate's simply not ready." Paul had walked home, the tie he'd bought for the occasion stuffed into his pocket, and for a week he had not left his room. When he returned to campus, he was ten pounds thinner, and the department secretary had asked him if he'd fallen in love.

Sang had been living with them for a week when a suitor called. By then the painting was finished, the dreary room transformed. She was removing masking tape from the edges of the windowpanes when Paul told her someone named Asim Bhattacharya was calling from Geneva. "Tell him I'm not in," she said, without hesitating. He wrote down the name, spelled out carefully by the caller, who had said before hanging up, "Just tell her it's Pinkoo."

More men called. One asked Paul dejectedly if he was Sang's boyfriend. The mere possibility, articulated by a stranger, had jolted him. Such a thing had happened once before in the house, the first year Paul had lived there — two housemates had fallen in love, had moved out in order to marry each other. "No," he told the caller. "I'm just her housemate." Nevertheless, for the rest of the day he had felt burdened by the question, worried that he'd transgressed somehow, simply by answering the phone. A few days later, he told Sang. She laughed. "He's probably horrified now, knowing that I live with a man," she said. "Next time," she advised him, "say yes."

A week afterward, the three of them were in the kitchen, Heather filling a thermos with echinacea tea because she had come down with a cold and had to spend all day in classes, Sang hunched over the newspaper and coffee. The night before, she had locked herself up in her bathroom, and now there were some reddish highlights in her hair. When the phone rang and Paul picked up, he assumed it was another suitor on the line, for like many of Sang's suitors, the caller had a slight foreign accent, though this one was more refined than awkward. The only difference was that instead of asking for Sangeeta he asked to speak to Sang. When Paul asked who was calling, he said, in a slightly impatient way, "I am her boyfriend." The words landed in Paul's chest like the dull yet painful taps of a doctor's instrument. He saw that Sang was looking up at him expectantly, her chair already partly pushed back from the table.

"For me?"

He nodded, and Sang took the phone into her room.

"Boyfriend," Paul reported to Heather.

"What's his name?"

Paul shrugged. "Didn't say."

"Well, she must be happy as a clam," Heather remarked with some asperity, screwing the lid onto her thermos.

Paul felt sorry for Heather, with her red, chapped nose and her thick-waisted body, but more than that he felt protective of Sang. "What do you mean?" he said.

"Because her lover's back, and now she can tell all those other guys to fuck off."

The boyfriend was standing on the sidewalk with Sang, looking up at the house, as Paul returned on his bike from a day of photocopying at the library. A bottle-green BMW was parked at the curb. The couple stood with an assumed intimacy, their dark heads tilting toward each other.

"Keep away from the window when you change your clothes," Paul heard him say. "I can see through the curtain. Couldn't you get a room at the back?" Paul stepped off his bike at a slight distance from them, adjusted the straps of his backpack. He was uncomfortably aware that he was shabbily dressed — in shorts and Birkenstocks and an old Dartmouth T-shirt, his pale legs covered with matted blond hair. The boyfriend wore perfectly fitted faded jeans, a white shirt, a navy-blue blazer, and brown leather shoes. His sharp features commanded admiration without being imposing. His hair, in contrast, was on the long side, framing his face in a lavish, unexpected style. He looked several years older than Sang, Paul decided, but in certain ways he strongly resembled her, for they shared the same height, the same gilded complexion, the same sprinkle of moles above and below their lips. As Paul walked toward them, Sang's boyfriend was still inspecting the house, searching the yellow-and-ocher Victorian façade as if for defects, until he looked away suddenly, distracted by the bark of a dog.

"Your roommates have a dog?" the boyfriend asked. He took an odd, dancelike step to the left, moving partly behind Sang.

"No, silly," Sang said teasingly, running her hand down the back of his head. "No dogs, no smokers. Those were the only listings I called, because of you." The barking stopped, and the ensuing silence seemed to punctuate her words. There was a necklace around her neck, lapis beads she now fingered in a way that made Paul think they were a gift. "Paul, this is Farouk. Farouk's afraid of dogs." She kissed Farouk on the cheek.

"Freddy," Farouk said, nodding rather than extending a hand, his words directed more to Sang than to Paul. She shook her head.

"For the millionth time, I'm not calling you Freddy."

Farouk glanced at her without humor. "Why not? You expect people to call you Sang."

She was unbothered. "That's different. That's actually a part of my name."

"Well, I'm Paul, and that's pretty much all you can call me," Paul said. No one laughed.

Suddenly she was never at home. When she was, she stayed in her room, often on the phone, the door shut. By dinner, she tended to be gone. The items on her shelf of the refrigerator, the big tubs of yogurt and the crackers and the tabouli, sat untouched. The yogurt eventually sported a mantle of green fuzz, setting off shrieks of disgust when Sang finally opened the lid. It was only natural, Paul told himself, for the two of them to want to be alone together. He was surprised to run into her one day in the small gourmet grocery in the neighborhood, her basket piled high with food she never brought back to the house, purple net bags of shallots, goat cheese in oil, meat wrapped in butcher paper. Because it was raining, Paul, who had his car with him, offered her a ride. She told him no thank you and headed off to the T stop, a Harvard baseball cap on her head, hugging the grocery bag to her chest. He had no idea where Farouk lived; he pictured a beautiful house on Brattle Street, French doors and pretty molding.

It was always something of a shock to find Farouk in the house. He visited infrequently and seemed to appear and disappear without a trace. Unless Paul looked out the window and saw the BMW, always precisely parked under the shade of a birch tree, it was impossible to tell if he was there. He never said hello or goodbye; instead, he behaved as if Sang were the sole occupant of the house. They never sat in the living room, or in the kitchen. Only once, when Paul returned from a bike ride, did he see them overhead, eating lunch on the deck. They were sitting next to each other, cross-legged, and Sang was extending a fork toward Farouk's mouth, her other hand cupped beneath it. By the time Paul entered the house, they had retreated into her room.

When she wasn't with Farouk, she did things for him. She read through proofs of an article he'd written, checking it for typos. She scheduled his doctor's appointments. Once she spent all morning with the yellow pages, pricing tiles; Farouk was thinking of redoing his kitchen.

By the end of September, Paul was aware of a routine: Mondays, which Sang had off from the bookstore, Farouk came for lunch. The two of them would eat in her room; sometimes he heard the sounds of their talking as they ate, or their spoons tapping against soup bowls, or the nocturnes of Chopin. They were silent lovers — mercifully so, compared with other couples he'd overheard in the house through the years — but their presence soon prompted him to go to the library on Mondays, for he was affected nevertheless, embarrassed by the time her door had been partly open and he'd seen Farouk zipping his jeans. Three years had passed since Theresa, the one girlfriend he'd ever had. He'd dated no one since. Because of Theresa, he'd chosen a graduate school in Boston. For three months he had lived with her in her apartment on St. Botolph Street. For Thanksgiving he'd gone with her to her parents' house in Deerfield. It was there that it had ended. "I'm sorry, Paul, I can't help it, I just don't like the way you kiss me," she had told him once they'd gone to bed. He remembered himself sitting naked on one side of the mattress, in a room he was suddenly aware he was never again to see. He had not argued; in the wake of his shame, he became strangely efficient and agreeable, with her, with everyone.

Late one night Paul was in bed reading when he heard a car pull up to the house. The clock on his desk said twenty past two. He shut off his lamp and got up to look through the window. It was November. A full moon illuminated the wide, desolate street, lined with trash bags and recycling bins. There was a taxi in front of the house, the engine still running. Sang emerged from it alone. For close to a minute she stood there on the sidewalk. He waited by the window until she climbed up to the porch, then listened as she climbed the staircase and shut the door to her room. Farouk had picked her up that afternoon; Paul had seen her stepping into his car. He thought perhaps they'd fought, though the next day he detected no signs of discord. He overheard her speaking to Farouk on the phone in good spirits, deciding on a video to rent. But that night, around the same time, the same thing happened. The third night he stayed awake on purpose, making sure she got in okay.

The following morning, a Sunday, Paul, Heather, and Sang had pancakes together in the kitchen. Sang was playing Louis Armstrong on the CD player in her room while Paul fried the pancakes in two cast-iron skillets.

"Kevin's sleeping over tonight," Heather said. She'd met him recently. He was a physicist at MIT. "I hope that's okay."

"Sure thing," Paul said. He liked Kevin. He had been coming over often for dinner, and brought beers and helped with the dishes afterward, talking to Paul as much as he talked to Heather.

"I'm sorry I keep missing him. He seems really nice," Sang said.

"We'll see," Heather said. "Next week is our one-month anniversary."

Sang smiled, as if this modest commemoration were in fact something of much greater significance. "Congratulations."

Heather crossed her fingers. "I guess the next stage is when you assume you're going to spend weekends together."

Paul glanced at Sang, who said nothing. She got up, returning five minutes later from the cellar with a basket full of laundry.

"Nice Jockeys," Heather said, noticing several pairs folded on top of the pile.

"They're Farouk's," Sang said.

"He doesn't have a washing machine?" Heather wanted to know.

"He does," Sang said, oblivious of Heather's disapproving expression. "But it's coin-operated."

The arguments started around Thanksgiving. Paul would hear Sang crying into the phone in her room, the gray plastic cord stretched across the linoleum and then across the landing, disappearing under her door. One of the fights had something to do with a party Sang had been invited to, which Farouk didn't want to attend. Another was about Farouk's birthday. Sang had spent the day before making a cake. The house had smelled of oranges and almonds, and Paul had heard the electric beater going late at night. But the next afternoon he saw the cake in the trashcan.

Once, returning from school, he discovered that Farouk was there, the BMW parked outside. It was a painfully cold December day; early that morning the season's first flakes had fallen. Walking past Sang's room, Paul heard her raised voice. She was accusing: Why didn't he ever want to meet her friends? Why didn't he invite her to his cousin's house for Thanksgiving? Why didn't he like to spend the night together? Why, at the very least, didn't he drive her home?

"I pay for the cabs," Farouk said quietly. "What difference does it make?"

"I hate it, Farouk. It's abnormal."

"You know I don't sleep well when you're there."

"How are we ever going to get married?" she demanded. "Are we supposed to live in separate houses forever?"

"Sang, please," Farouk said. "Try to be calm. Your roommates will hear."

"Will you stop about my roommates," Sang shouted.

"You're hysterical," Farouk said.

She began to cry.

"I've warned you, Sang," Farouk said. He sounded desperate. "I will not spend my life with a woman who makes scenes."

"Fuck you."

Something, a plate or a glass, struck a wall and broke. Then the room went quiet. After much deliberation, Paul knocked softly. No one replied.

A few hours later, Paul nearly bumped into Sang as she was emerging from her bathroom, wrapped in a large dark-pink towel. Her wet hair was uncombed and tangled, a knot bulging like a small nest on one side of her head. For weeks he had longed to catch a glimpse of her this way, and still he felt wholly unprepared for the vision of her bare legs and arms, her damp face and shoulders.

"Hey," he said, sidling quickly past.

"Paul," she called out after a moment, as if his presence had registered only then. He turned to look at her; though it was barely past four, the sun was already setting in the living room window, casting a golden patch of light to one side of her in the hallway.

"What's up?" he said.

She crossed her arms in front of her, a hand concealing each shoulder. A spot on her forehead was coated with what appeared to be toothpaste. "I'm sorry about earlier."

"That's okay."

"It's not. You have an exam to study for."

Her eyes were shining brightly, and she had a funny frozen smile on her face, her lips slightly parted. He began to smile back when he saw that she was about to cry. He nodded. "It doesn't matter."

For a week Farouk didn't call, though when the phone rang she flew to answer it. She was home every night for dinner. She had long conversations with her sister in London. "Tell me if you think this is normal," Paul overheard her say as he walked into the kitchen. "We were driving one time and he told me I smelled bad. Sweaty. He told me to wash under my arms. He kept saying it wasn't a criticism, that people in love should be able to say things like that to each other." One day Charles took Sang out, and in the evening she returned with shopping bags from the outlets in Kittery. Another night she accepted an invitation to see a movie at the Coolidge with Paul and Heather and Kevin, but once they'd reached the box office she told them she had a headache and walked back to the house. "I bet you they've split up," Heather said, once they'd settled into their seats.

But the following week Farouk called when Sang was at work. Though Farouk hadn't bothered to identify himself, Paul called the bookstore, leaving her the message.

The relationship resumed its course, but Paul noticed that Farouk no longer set foot in the house. He wouldn't even ring the bell. He would pause at the curb, the engine of his car still running, beeping three times to signal that he was waiting for her, and then she would disappear.

Over winter break she went away, to London. Her sister had had a baby boy recently. Sang showed Paul the things she had bought for the baby: playsuits full of snaps, a stuffed octopus, a miniature French sailor's shirt, a mobile of stars and planets that glowed in the dark. "I'm going to be called Sang Mashi," she told him excitedly, explaining that *mashi* was the Bengali word for aunt. The word sounded strange on her lips. She spoke Bengali infrequently — never to her sister, never to her suitors, only a word here and there to her parents, in Michigan, to whom she spoke on weekends.

"How do you say *bon voyage*?" Paul asked.

She told him she wasn't sure.

Without her there, it was easier for Paul to study, his mind spacious and clear. His exam was less than six months away. A date and time had been scheduled, the first Tuesday in May, at ten o'clock, marked with an X on the calendar over his desk. Since summer he had worked his way yet again through the list of poems and critical essays and plays, typing summaries of them into his computer. He had printed out these summaries, three-hole-punched them, put them in a series of binders. He wrote further summaries of the summaries on index cards that he reviewed before bed, filed in shoeboxes. For Christmas he was invited to an aunt's house in Buffalo, as usual. This year, with his exam as an excuse, he declined the invitation, mailing off gifts. Heather was away too; she and Kevin had gone skiing in Vermont.

To mark the new year, Paul set up a new routine, spreading himself all over the house. In the mornings he reviewed poetry at the kitchen table. After lunch, criticism in the living room. A Shakespeare play before bed. He began to leave his things, his binders and his shoeboxes and his books, on the kitchen table, on certain steps of the staircase, on the coffee table in the living room. He was slouched in the papasan chair one snowy afternoon, reading his notes on Aristotle's *Poetics,* when the doorbell rang. It was a UPS man with a package for Sang, something from J. Crew. Paul signed for it and took it upstairs. He leaned it against the door of her room, which caused the door to open slightly. He closed it firmly, and for a moment he stood there, his hand still on the knob. Even though she was in London, he knocked before entering. The futon was neatly made, a red batik bedspread covering the top. The green walls were bare but for two framed Indian miniatures of palace scenes, men smoking hookahs and reclining on cushions, barebellied women dancing in a ring. There was none of the disarray he for some reason pictured every time he walked by her room; only outside, through the windows, was there the silent chaos of the storm. The snow fell in disorderly swirls, yet it covered the brown porch railing below, neatly, as if it were a painted trim. A single panel of a white seersucker curtain was loosely cinched with a peach silk scarf that Sang sometimes knotted at her throat, causing the fabric of the curtain to gather in the shape of a slim hourglass.

Paul untied the scarf, letting the curtain cover the windowpane. Without touching his face to the scarf, he smelled the perfume that lingered in its weave. He went to the futon and sat down, his legs extending along the oatmeal carpet. He took off his shoes and socks. On a wine crate next to the futon was a glass of water that had gathered bubbles, a small pot of Vaseline. He undid his belt buckle but suddenly the desire left him, absent from his body just as she was absent from the room. He buckled his belt again, and then slowly he lifted the bedspread. The sheets were flannel, blue and white, a pattern of fleur-de-lis.

He had drifted off to sleep when he heard the phone ring. He stumbled barefoot out of Sang's room, into the kitchen, the linoleum chilly.

"Hello?"

No one replied on the other end, and he was about to hang up when he heard a dog barking.

"Hello?" he repeated. It occurred to him it might be Sang, a poor connection from London. "Sang, is that you?"

The caller hung up.

That evening, after dinner, the phone rang again. When he picked it up he heard the same dog he'd heard earlier.

"Balthazar, shush!" a woman said as soon as Paul said hello. Her voice was hesitant. Was Sang in? she wanted to know.

"She's not here. May I take a message?"

She left her name, Deirdre Frain, and a telephone number. Paul wrote it down on the message pad, under Partha Mazoomdar, a suitor who'd called from Cleveland in the morning.

The next day Deirdre called again. Again Paul told her that Sang wasn't there, adding that she wouldn't be back until the weekend.

"Where is she?" Deirdre asked.

"She's out of the country."

"In Cairo?"

This took him by surprise. "No, London."

"In London," she repeated. She sounded relieved. "London. Okay. Thanks."

The fourth call was very late at night, when Paul was already in bed. He went downstairs, feeling for the phone in the dark.

"It's Deirdre." She sounded slightly out of breath, as if it were she, not he, who'd just rushed to the phone.

He flicked on the light switch, rubbing his eyes behind his glasses. “Um, as I said, Sang’s not back yet.”

“I don’t want to talk to Sang.” She was slurring her words, exaggerating the pronunciation of Sang’s name in a slightly cruel way.

Paul heard music, a trumpet crooning softly. “You don’t?”

“No,” she said. “Actually, I have a question.”

“A question?”

“Yes.” There was a pause, the clink of an ice cube falling into a glass. Her tone had become flirtatious. “So, what’s your name?”

He took off his glasses, allowing the room to go blurry. He couldn’t recall the last time a woman had spoken to him that way. “Paul.”

“Paul,” she repeated. “Can I ask you another question, Paul?”

“What?”

“It’s about Sang.”

He stiffened. Again she had said the name without kindness. “What about Sang?”

Deirdre paused. “She’s your housemate, right?”

“That’s right.”

“Well, I was wondering, then, if you’d know if — are they cousins?”

“Who?”

“Sang and Freddy.”

He put his glasses on again, drawing things into focus. He was unnerved by this woman’s curiosity. It wasn’t her business, he wanted to tell her. But before he could do that, Deirdre began quietly crying.

He looked at the clock on the stove; it was close to three in the morning. It was his own fault. He shouldn’t have answered the phone so late. He wished he hadn’t told the woman his name.

“Deirdre,” he said after a while, tired of listening to her. “Are you still there?”

She stopped crying. Her breathing was uneven, penetrating his ear.

“I don’t know who you are,” Paul said. “I don’t understand why you’re calling me.”

“I love him.”

He hung up, his heart hammering. He had the urge to take a

shower. He wanted to erase her name from the legal pad. He stared at the receiver, remnants of Sang's mole-colored fingerprints still visible here and there. For the first time since the winter break had begun, he felt lonely in the house. The call had to be a fluke. Some other Sang the woman was referring to. Maybe it was a scheme on behalf of one of her Indian suitors, to cast suspicion, to woo her away from Farouk. Before Sang had left for London, the fights had subsided, and things between Sang and Farouk, as far as Paul could tell, were still the same. In the living room, she'd been wrapping a brown leather satchel, a pair of men's driving gloves. The night before she'd left, she'd made a dinner reservation for the two of them at Biba. Farouk had driven her to the airport.

The ringing of the phone woke Paul the next morning. He remained in bed, listening to it, looking at the ashen branches of the tree outside his window. He counted twelve rings before they stopped. The phone rang half an hour later, and he ignored it again. The third time he was in the kitchen. When it stopped, he unplugged the cord from the jack.

Though he studied in silence for the remainder of the day, he felt fitful. Sitting in the kitchen that evening with a bricklike volume of Spenser, he was unable to concentrate on the lines, irritated by the footnotes, by how much there was left to learn. He wondered how many times Deirdre had tried to call him since he'd unplugged the phone. Had she given up? The calling felt obsessive to him, unhinged. He wondered whether she was the type to do something. To take a bottle of pills.

After dinner he plugged the phone back into the jack. There were no further calls. And yet his mind continued to wander. Something told him that she'd try again. He'd made the mistake of telling her when Sang would be back. Perhaps Deirdre was waiting to speak to her directly. Perhaps Deirdre would tell Sang the same thing she'd told him, about loving Farouk. Before going to bed, he poured himself a glass of Dewar's, a gift sent by his aunt in Buffalo. Then he dialed the number Deirdre had given him. She picked up right away, with a lilting hello.

"Deirdre, it's Paul."

"Paul," she said slowly.

"You called me last night. I'm Sang's housemate."

"Of course. Paul. You hung up on me, Paul." She appeared to be drunk again, but in a sunnier mood.

"Listen, I'm sorry about that. I just wanted to make sure you were okay."

Deirdre sighed. "That's sweet of you, Paul."

"And to ask you to please stop calling me," he said after a considerable pause.

"Why?" There was panic in her voice.

"Because I don't know you," he said.

"Would you like to know me, Paul?" she said. "I'm a very likable person."

"I have to go," he said firmly, hoping not to provoke her. "But maybe there's someone else you could talk to? A friend?"

"Freddy's my friend."

The mention of Farouk, the use of the nickname, unsettled Paul as it had the night before. Yesterday he'd surmised that Deirdre might be a student of Farouk's at Harvard, practically a teenager, infatuated with an older man. He imagined her sitting at the back of a lecture hall, visiting him in his office, getting the wrong idea. Now a simple, reasonable question, which was at the same time a poisoned question, formed in Paul's mind.

"So, how exactly do you know Farouk?" Paul asked lightly, as if they were chatting at a party.

He didn't think she'd tell him, thought she might even hang up on him as he had on her, but they slipped easily into a conversation. It was Deirdre who did most of the talking. She told Paul that she was from Vancouver originally, and that she'd moved to Boston in her twenties to study interior design. She'd met Farouk one Sunday afternoon a year and a half ago, when she was walking out of a café in the South End. He had followed her halfway down the block, tapped her on the shoulder, looked her up and down with unconcealed desire. "You can't imagine," Deirdre said, remembering it. "You can't imagine how something like that feels." Nevertheless, he'd been gentlemanly. For their first date, they had gone to Walden Pond. Afterward they had bought corn and tomatoes, and grilled salmon in her back yard. Farouk loved her home, an old farmhouse on five acres. He had asked her to draw up the plans for redoing his kitchen. On Labor Day they had hiked Mount Sunapee together. She said other things Paul listened to, unsure of how much he should believe. For either they were true and

Farouk and Deirdre were having a full-blown affair, or Deirdre was simply inventing it all, the way lonely, drunk people sometimes invent things. At one point he wandered into the hallway and opened Sang's door, making sure the curtain was tied as he'd remembered it.

"What about you?" Deirdre asked suddenly.

"What about me?"

"Well, here I am going on and you haven't said a thing. What are you like, Paul? Are you happy?"

He had sacrificed an hour to this woman. The edge of his ear ached from pressing the phone to it for so long. "This isn't about me." He swallowed, shutting the door to Sang's room. "It's about Sang."

"They're cousins, right?" Deirdre said. He could barely hear her. "Aren't they?"

The desperation with which she asked him brought with it a crushing certainty. He knew that all she had told him was true, the knowledge of something having gone terribly wrong leveling him the way his exam had. The way Theresa's words had.

"Sang and Farouk are not cousins," he said. He felt a strange, inward power as he spoke, aware that the information could devastate her.

She was silent.

"They're boyfriend and girlfriend, Deirdre," he said. "A serious couple."

"Oh yeah?" Her tone was challenging. "How serious?"

He thought for a moment. "They see each other four or five nights a week."

"They do?" To Paul's satisfaction, Deirdre sounded wounded by this information.

"Yes," he said, adding, "They've been together for over three years."

"Three?" The word trailed off weakly, in a way that made Paul wonder if she might cry again. But when she spoke next her voice was clear. "Well, we're a serious couple too. I picked him up from the airport yesterday when he came back from Cairo. I saw him tonight. He was here for dinner, here in my house. He made love to me on my staircase, Paul. An hour ago, I could still feel him dripping down my thighs."

*

Sang returned from London with presents for the house, KitKats in red wrappers, tea from Harrods, marmalade, chocolate-coated biscuits. A snapshot of her nephew went up on the refrigerator, his small smiling face pressed against Sang's. Paul, from his room, saw that it was Farouk who dropped her off at the house. Eventually Paul had gone downstairs, down the magnificent staircase, which he was now unable to descend without a fleeting image of Farouk naked on top of a woman who was not Sang. In the kitchen he opened his cupboard and pulled down the Dewar's.

"Wow. Things have really changed around here," Sang said, smiling, her eyebrows raised in amusement, watching him pour the drink.

"What do you mean?"

"You're drinking Scotch. If I'd known, I would have bought you some single-malt in duty-free, instead of the KitKats."

The thought of her buying him a gift depressed him. They were friendly, but they were not friends. He offered her a glass of the Scotch, which she accepted. They sat together at the table. She clinked her glass against his.

She began sorting through the mail Paul had collected for her. Her hair was a few inches shorter; she smelled intensely of a spicy perfume.

"I don't know any Deirdres," she said, reading her messages on the legal pad. "Did she say why she was calling?"

He'd drained his glass, and was already pacified by the drink. He shook his head.

"I wonder what I should do."

"About what?"

"Well, should I call her back?"

He stood up and opened the freezer to get ice cubes for a second drink. When he returned to the table, she was crossing out the name with a pencil. "Forget it. She's probably a telemarketer or something."

Avoiding Sang was easy. The university library, which Paul normally found so charmless, with its cement floors and gray metal shelves and carrels full of anonymous ballpoint philosophy, was where he began to spend his days. At home, he discovered that it was just as easy to take a sandwich up to his room. Winter gave way to a wet, reluctant spring, full of wind and slanted rains that lashed the window by Paul's bed. Whenever the phone rang, he didn't answer. In the first few days after Sang's return, he'd been convinced each time that it would be Deirdre, demanding to talk to Sang. But Deirdre never called. He waited for her voice, the things she had told him, to fade from his memory. But the conversations had lodged themselves stubbornly in his mind, alongside all the plays and poems and essays. He saw two people swimming in Walden Pond, their heads above the surface of the water. But then there was Sang, day after day, disappearing to eat dinner at Farouk's. There she was, sitting at the kitchen table, booking Farouk's tickets to Cairo for the summer, his credit-card number written on a sheet of paper. After two months, Deirdre still hadn't called, and Paul finally stopped fearing that she would.

Paul took the week of his spring break off from studying. "Stop cramming. That's probably what happened the first time. Go to the Caribbean," his adviser suggested. Instead, Paul stayed at home, but declared himself officially on vacation. He went to movies at the Brattle, spent two days making a cassoulet. He drove to Wellfleet one day, forcing himself not to take a book. He decided to ride out to Concord on his bike, to see Emerson's house; on Saturday morning, he discovered that the chain needed to be fixed, and he brought the bike up to the deck. When he looked up, Sang was standing there, the phone in her hands, the cord stretched as far as it could go.

"Something weird just happened," she said.

"What?"

"It was that Deirdre woman. The one you took the message from when I was away."

Paul bent down, pretending to root around for something in his toolbox. "She was asking for Farouk," Sang continued. "She says she's a friend of his, visiting from out of town."

"Oh. So that must have been why she was calling," he said, relieved to hear that this was all Deirdre had said.

"He's never mentioned a Deirdre."

"Oh."

Sang sat down in a beach chair, the phone in her lap, her body leaning into it. She straightened, staring at the phone, pressing numbers at random without picking up the receiver. "Farouk doesn't have any friends," she said. "Ever since I've known him, he's never introduced me to a single friend. I'm his only friend, really." She looked intently at Paul, and for a second he feared she was about to draw some sort of parallel, point out that Paul didn't have friends either. Instead, she said, "How did she get my number, anyway?"

She'd looked it up in Farouk's address book; Deirdre had confessed this to Paul. Farouk had made it easy for her, writing it under *S* for Sang, the name of the cousin he had mentioned in a way that had made her suspicious. Paul shook his head, standing up, squeezing the handbrakes on the bicycle. "Don't know. I guess I'd ask Farouk."

"Right. Ask Farouk." She stood up and went back into the house.

That evening, when Paul returned from Concord, he found Sang at the kitchen table. She said nothing as he went to the refrigerator to pull out the remains of the cassoulet.

"Farouk isn't in," she said, as if responding to a question on Paul's part. "He hasn't been in all day."

He lifted the lid of the baking dish and sprinkled a few drops of water on top of the cassoulet. "You want some of this?"

"No, thanks." She was frowning.

Paul put the cassoulet in the oven and poured a Scotch. The muscles in his arms and his thighs ached pleasantly. He wanted to take a shower before eating.

"So, when exactly did this Deirdre person call?" Sang said, stopping him as he walked out of the kitchen.

He turned to face her, pivoting on his heels. "I don't remember. It was when you were away."

"And did she say anything to you?"

"What do you mean?"

"What did she say to you, exactly?"

"Nothing. I didn't talk to her," he said, his pulse racing; he was thankful that he was already coated with sweat. "She just wanted you to call her back."

"Well, I can't call her back. She didn't even leave her number. It was weird. Did she sound like a weird sort of person to you?"

He remembered Deirdre's tears. "I love him," she'd told Paul, a perfect stranger. He looked at Sang, manipulating his face into an uncomprehending expression. "I'm not sure what you mean."

She sighed impatiently. "Can you hand me that?" she said, pointing to the message pad.

Paul watched as Sang began flipping through the pages that had been turned over, running her finger down each line.

"What are you looking for?" he said after a moment.

"Her number."

"Why?"

"I want to call her back."

"Why?"

She looked up at him, exasperated. "Because I want to, Paul. Is that okay with you?"

He went upstairs to take his shower. It wasn't his business, he told himself as the hot water washed over him, and, later, as he dried himself, then combed back his hair, enveloped in steam. When he came downstairs again, he found her on her hands and knees, going through the recycling bin, newspapers and magazines piled around her.

"Damn it," she said.

"Now what are you looking for?"

"The number. I remember ripping out that page for some reason. I think I threw it away." She began to put the newspapers and magazines back into the bin. "Damn it," she said again. She stood up, kicking the bin lightly with her foot. "I don't even remember her last name. Do you?"

He inhaled, as if to seal the information inside himself, but then he shook his head, relieved at the opportunity, at last, to be honest with her. He too had forgotten Deirdre's last name. It had been a name of one syllable, but apart from that detail it had vanished from his brain.

"Hey, Paul," Sang said after a moment. "Are you okay? I'm sorry if I sounded harsh back then."

He walked across the kitchen, opened the oven. "Don't worry about it."

Her stomach growled, loudly enough for Paul to hear. "God, I just realized I haven't eaten a thing today. I think I'll have some of that cassoulet, after all. Should I make a salad?" This would be their first dinner together alone, without Heather. He used to yearn for such an occasion. He used to feel clumsy and tongue-tied when Sang was in the room. Now he felt dread.

"I guess she was a little weird," he said slowly, gazing at the back of Sang's head, bent forward over the sink where she was ripping lettuce. She turned around.

"How? How did she seem weird to you?"

He was so nervous that for a terrible instant he worried that he might laugh out loud. Sang was regarding him steadily. The faucet was still running. She reached back to turn it off, and now the room was silent.

"She was crying," he said.

"Crying?"

"Um — yeah."

"Crying how?"

"Just — crying. Like she was upset about something."

Sang opened her mouth as if to speak, but for a while it simply hung open. "So let me get this straight. This woman Deirdre called and asked for me."

Paul nodded. "Right."

"And you said I wasn't there."

"Right."

"And then she asked you to have me call her back."

"Right."

"And then she started crying?"

"Yeah."

"And then what happened?"

"That was it. Then she hung up."

For a moment Sang seemed satisfied with the information, nodding slowly. Then she shook her head abruptly, as if to flick it away. "Why didn't you tell me this?"

He regretted having offered her the cassoulet. He regretted having ever picked up the phone that day. He regretted that Sang and not another person had moved into the room, into his house, into his life. "I did," he said calmly, drawing a line between them in his mind. "I told you she called."

"But you didn't tell me this."

"No."

She opened her eyes wide, incredulous. "Didn't it occur to you that I might want to know?"

He curled his lips together, looking away.

"Well?" she demanded, shouting at him now. "Didn't it?"

When he still did not reply, she marched up to him, her hands clenched in fists, and he braced himself for a blow, twisting his face to one side. But she didn't strike him. Instead she gripped the sides of her own head, as if to steady herself. "My God, Paul." Her voice was so shrill it was nearly inaudible. "What the hell is wrong with you?"

Now it was she who began to avoid him. For a few nights she was not at home. Paul saw her getting into Charles's truck with a weekend bag. Because Heather had by then all but officially moved in with Kevin, once again Paul found himself alone in the house. A week passed before he saw Sang again. Thinking himself alone, he hadn't bothered to shut his door. She came up to his room, wearing a pretty dress he'd never seen, a white cotton short-sleeved dress, fitted at the waist. The neck was square, showing off her collarbones. "Hey," she said.

"Hey." He had not missed her at all.

"Look. I just wanted to tell you that it's all a huge confusion. Deirdre really is an old friend of Farouk's, from way back. From college."

"You don't have to explain it to me," Paul said.

"She lives in Canada," Sang continued. "In Vancouver."

"I see."

"They talk, like, once a year. Farouk mentioned my name to her years ago, when we first got together, when he lived in another apartment, and she remembered it. She was trying to get in touch with him because she's getting married, and she wanted to send Farouk an invitation. She didn't have Farouk's new address or his number, and he's not listed. That's why she tried here."

She seemed strangely flattered, excited by her absurd explanation. Some color had come to her cheeks.

"There's only one thing, Paul."

He looked up. "What's that?"

"Farouk called Deirdre to ask about what you said."

"What I said?"

"About the crying." Sang shrugged her shoulders, dropped them carelessly. "He told me she has no idea what you were talking about." Her voice sounded compressed, the words running together quickly.

"Are you saying I made it up?"

She was silent.

For her sake, he'd told her about the crying. That night in the kitchen, watching her make the salad, he'd felt the walls collapsing around her. He'd wanted to warn her somehow. Now he wanted to push her from the door frame where she stood.

"Why would I make up a story like that?" He could feel a nerve on one side of his head throbbing.

Instead of arguing with him, she gave a sympathetic glance, letting her head rest against the door frame. "I don't know, Paul." It occurred to him that this was the first time she'd visited him in his room. For a moment she appeared to be searching for a free place to sit. She straightened her head.

"Did you really think it would make me leave him?"

"I didn't think it would make you do anything," Paul said. He was clenching his teeth now. His body felt heavy from her accusation, numb. "I didn't make it up."

"I mean, it's one thing for you to like me, Paul," she continued. "It's one thing for you to have a crush. But to make up a story like that?" She stopped, her mouth now straining into something that was not a smile. "It's pathetic, really. Pathetic!" And she walked out of the room.

When they crossed paths again, she didn't apologize for the outburst. She didn't appear angry, only indifferent. He noticed that a copy of the *Phoenix,* which she'd left on top of the microwave, was folded to the real-estate section, and that a few of the listings were circled. She came and went from Farouk's. She looked up at Paul briefly when she happened to see him, with a mechanical little smile, and then she looked away, as if he were invisible.

The next time Sang worked at the bookstore, Paul stayed up in his room until he heard her leave the house. Once she was gone, he went to the kitchen, emptying out the recycling bin, which had not been taken out all winter. He flipped though each magazine, unfolded every newspaper, searching for the sheet of paper with Deirdre's number. It would be like Sang, he thought, to look for it and not find it. But Paul couldn't find it either. He pulled out the white pages and opened them at random, searching for a Deirdre, not caring how ridiculous he was being. Then he remembered it.

Her last name. It swam effortlessly back to his memory, accompanied by the sound of Deirdre's voice as she introduced herself to him that night on the telephone months ago. He turned to the *F*'s, saw it there, a D. Frain, an address in Belmont. He dragged the nail of his index finger beneath the listing, leaving a faint dent in the paper.

He called the next day. He left a message on her machine, asking her to call him back. He felt giddy, having done it. In a way, it was his fear that Deirdre would not call him back, knowing that she too was now keeping her distance, that emboldened him to keep calling, to keep leaving messages. "Deirdre, this is Paul. Please call me," he said each time.

And then one day she picked up the phone.

"I need to talk to you," he said.

She recognized his voice. "I know. Listen, Paul?"

He cut her off. "It's not right," he said. He was sitting in a booth in the lobby of the library, watching as students flashed their ID cards to the security guard. He fished in his pocket for extra quarters. "I listened to you. I was kind to you. I didn't have to talk to you."

"I know. I'm sorry. It was wrong of me." She no longer sounded drunk or flirtatious or desperate or upset in any way. She was perfectly ordinary, polite but removed.

"I didn't even tell her the other stuff you told me." He saw that a student was standing outside the booth, waiting for him to finish. Paul lowered his voice. He felt mildly hysterical. "Remember all that stuff?"

"Look, please, I said I'm sorry. Can you hold on a second?" Paul heard a doorbell ring. After a minute she came back to the phone. "I have to go now. I'll call you back."

"When?" Paul demanded, afraid that she was lying to him, that it was a ploy to be rid of him. In January, when Paul had wanted to get off the phone with Deirdre, she had pleaded with him to stay on the line.

"Later. Tonight," she said.

"I want to know when."

She told him she'd call at ten.

The idea came to him immediately after getting off the phone, the receiver still in his hand. He left the library, went to the nearest

Radio Shack. "I need a phone," he told the salesman. "And an adapter with two jacks."

It was a night Sang worked at the bookstore; as usual, she was home by nine. She said nothing to Paul when she came into the kitchen to get her mail.

"I called Deirdre," Paul said.

"Why don't you stop involving yourself this way?" Sang said evenly, leafing through a catalogue.

"She's calling me at ten o'clock," Paul said. "If you want, you can listen in without her knowing. I got another phone and hooked it up to our line."

She dropped the catalogue, noticing the second phone. "Jesus, Paul," she hissed. "I can't fucking believe you."

She went into her room; at five to ten she came out and sat next to Paul. He'd set the phones together on the table. At exactly one minute past ten, both phones rang. Paul picked up one. "Hello?"

"It's me," Deirdre said.

He nodded, motioning to Sang, and slowly, carefully, Sang picked up the other phone and put it to her ear without allowing it to touch her. She held it unnaturally, the bottom of the receiver turned away from her mouth, pointed toward her shoulder.

"Like I said, Paul, I'm sorry for calling you. I shouldn't have," Deirdre said.

She seemed relaxed, willing to talk, in no apparent rush. Paul relaxed a little too. "But you did."

"Yes."

"And you cried about Farouk."

"Yes."

"And then you made me into a liar."

She was silent.

"You denied the whole thing."

"It was Freddy's idea."

"And you went along with it," Paul said. He was looking at Sang. She was pressing her top teeth into her lower lip in a way that looked painful.

"What was I supposed to do, Paul?" Deirdre said. "He was furious when he found out I'd called you. He refused to see me. He unplugged his phone. He wouldn't answer the door."

Sang put a palm against the table's edge, as if to push it away, but she ended up pushing herself back in her chair, scraping the linoleum. Paul put a finger to his lips, but then he realized that to Deirdre, it was he who'd made the sound. She kept talking.

"Listen, Paul, I'm sorry you're in the middle of all this. I really am sorry I called. It was just that Freddy kept telling me Sang was his cousin, and when I asked him to introduce me to her he refused. I didn't care at first. I figured I wasn't the only woman in his life. But then I fell in love with him." She wanted to believe him, she explained. She was a thirty-five-year-old woman, already married and divorced. She didn't have time for this.

"But I've ended it," she said matter-of-factly. "You know, there was a point when I actually believed he couldn't live without me. That's what he does to women. He depends on them. He asks them to do a hundred things, makes them believe his life won't function without them. That was him this afternoon when you called, still wanting to see me, still wanting to keep me on the side. He doesn't have any friends, you see. Only lovers. I think he needs them, the way other people need a family or friends." She sounded reasonable and reflective now, as if she were describing an affair she'd had years before. Sang's eyes were closed and she was shaking her head slowly from side to side. The dog was barking.

"That's my dog," Deirdre said. "He's always hated Freddy. He's the size of a football, but every time Freddy comes over he makes me put a guardrail across the stairs."

Sang inhaled sharply. She put the receiver down quietly on the table; then she picked it up again.

"I should go," Paul said.

"Me too," Deirdre agreed. "I think you need to tell her now."

He was startled, afraid Deirdre had discovered his trick, that she knew that Sang was listening in. "Tell her what?"

"Tell her about me and Farouk. She deserves to know. It sounds like you're a good friend of hers."

Deirdre hung up, and for a long time Paul and Sang sat there, listening to the silence. He had cleared himself with Sang, and yet he felt no relief, no vindication. Eventually Sang hung up her phone and stood up, slowly, but made no further movements. She looked sealed off from things, holding herself as if she still needed to be perfectly stealthy, as if the slightest sound or gesture would betray her presence.

"I'm sorry," Paul said finally.

She nodded and went to her room, shutting the door. After a while he followed her, stood outside. "Sang? Do you need anything?"

He remained there, waiting for her to reply. He heard her moving around the room. When the door opened, he saw that she had changed, into a black top with long tight-fitting sleeves. Her pink raincoat was draped over her arm, her purse hanging over her shoulder. "I need a ride."

In the car, she directed him, saying what to do and where to turn only at the last possible minute. They drove through Allston and down Storrow Drive. "There," she said, pointing. It was an ugly high-rise, bereft of charm and yet clearly exclusive, on the Cambridge side of the river. She got out of the car and started walking.

Paul followed her. "What are you doing?"

She speeded up. "I need to talk to him." She spoke in a monotone.

"I don't know, Sang."

She walked even faster, her shoes clicking on the pavement.

The lobby was filled with beige sofas and potted trees. There was an African doorman sitting at the desk who smiled at them, recognizing Sang. He was listening to a radio tuned to the news in French.

"Evening, miss."

"Hello, Raymond."

"Getting cold again, miss. Maybe rain later."

"Maybe."

She kept her finger pressed on the elevator button until it came, while she fixed her hair in the mirror opposite. On the tenth floor they stopped, then walked to the end of the hallway. The doors were dark brown, thickly varnished. She tapped the door knocker, which was like a small brass picture frame hinged to the surface. Inside, there was the sound of a television. Then there was silence.

"It's me," she said.

She tapped it again. Five consecutive taps. Ten. She pressed the top of her head against the door. "I heard her, Farouk. I heard Deirdre. She called Paul, and I heard her." Sang's voice was quavering.

"Please open the door." She tried the knob, a strong metal knob, which would not budge.

There were footsteps, a chain being undone. Farouk opened the door, a day's stubble on his face. He wore a flecked fisherman's sweater, corduroy pants, black espadrilles on bare feet. He looked nothing like a philanderer, just bookish and slight. "I did not invite you here," he said acidly when he saw Paul.

In spite of all he knew, Paul was stung by the words, unable to speak in his own defense.

"Please leave," Farouk said. "Please, for once, try to respect our privacy."

"She asked me," Paul said.

Farouk lurched forward, arms extended rigidly in front of him, pushing Paul away as if he were a large piece of furniture. Paul took a step back, then resisted, grabbing Farouk's wrists. The two men fell to the floor of the hallway, Paul's glasses flying onto the carpet. It was easy for Paul to pin Farouk to the ground, to dig his fingers into his shoulders. Paul squeezed them tightly through the thick wool of the sweater, feeling the give of the tendons, aware that Farouk was no longer resisting. For a moment Paul lay on top of him fully, subduing him like a lover. He looked up, searching for Sang, but she was nowhere. He looked back at the man beneath him, a man he barely knew, a man he hated. "All she wants is for you to admit it," Paul said. "I think you owe her that."

Farouk spat at Paul's face, a cold spray that made Paul recoil. Farouk pushed him off, went into his apartment, and slammed the door. Other doors along the hallway began to open. Paul could hear Farouk fastening the chain. He found his glasses and stood up, pressed his ear to the varnished wood. He heard crying, then a series of objects falling. At one point he could hear Farouk saying, "Stop it, please, please, it's not as bad as you think." And then Sang saying, "How many times? How many times did you do it? Did you do it here on the bed?"

A minute later the elevator opened and a man walked toward Farouk's apartment. He was a lean man with gray hair and a big bunch of keys in his hand. "I'm the super in this building. Who are you?" he asked Paul.

"I live with the woman inside," he said, pointing at Farouk's door.

"You her husband?"

"No."

The super knocked on the door, saying neighbors had complained. He continued to knock, rapping the wood with his knuckles until the door opened.

Inside was a hallway illuminated by track lights. Paul glimpsed a bright white kitchen without windows, a stack of cookbooks on the counter. To the right was a dining room, painted the same sage green as Sang's room. Paul followed the super into the living room. There was an off-white sofa, a coffee table, a sliding glass door that led to a balcony. In the distance was a view of the Citgo sign, draining and filling with color. There was a bookcase along one wall which had fallen to the floor, its books in a heap. The receiver of a telephone on a side table hung from a cord, beeping faintly, repeatedly. In spite of these things, the room had a barren quality, as if someone were in the process of moving out of it.

Sang was kneeling on an Oriental carpet, picking up the pieces of what appeared to have been a clear glass vase. She was shivering. Her hair was undone, hanging toward the floor, partly shielding her face. There was water everywhere, and the ruins of a bouquet of flowers, irises and tiger lilies and daffodils. She worked carefully with the glass, creating a pile of shards on the coffee table. There were petals in her hair and stuck to her face and neck, and plastered to the skin exposed above her black scoop-necked top, as if she had smeared them on herself like a cream. There were welts emerging above her neckline, fresh and bright.

The men stood there, looking at her, none of them saying anything. A policeman arrived, his black boots and his gun and his radio filling up the room, static from his radio replacing the silence. Someone in the building had called the station to complain, he said. He asked Sang, who was still on the floor, if Farouk had struck her. Sang shook her head.

"Do you live here?" he asked.

"I painted the walls," Sang said, as if that would explain everything. Paul remembered her painting her own room, barefoot, listening to Billie Holiday.

The policeman leaned over, inspecting the broken glass and flower debris on the carpet, noticing the welts on her skin. "What happened?"

"I bought them," she said, tears streaming quickly down her cheeks. Her voice was thick, ashamed. "I did this to myself."

After that, everything proceeded in an orderly way, with people moving in separate directions, not reacting to anyone else. The policeman filled out a form, then lent an arm and took Sang to the bathroom. The super left, saying something to Farouk about a fine. Farouk went to the kitchen, returning with a roll of paper towels and a garbage bag, and knelt by the carpet, cleaning up the mess Sang had made. The policeman looked at Paul, as if assessing him for the first time. He asked if Paul was an involved party.

"I'm her housemate," Paul replied. "I just gave her a ride."

The next morning Paul was awakened by the noise of a car door closing. He went to the window and saw the trunk of a taxi being pressed down by the driver's hand. Sang had left a note on the kitchen table: she was going to London to visit her sister. *Paul, thanks for yesterday,* it said. Along with this was a signed check for her portion of the rent.

For a few days nothing happened. He collected her mail. The bookstore called to ask where she was. Paul told them she had the flu. Two weeks later the bookstore called again. This time it was to fire her. The third week, Farouk began to call, asking to speak to her. He didn't identify himself, didn't press Paul when he said, night after night, "Sang's not in." He was polite to Paul, in a way he had never been before, saying thank you, that he'd try later. Paul relished these calls. He liked depriving Farouk of the knowledge of where Sang was. But then, one day when he called, Heather, holed up in the house that week to study for an exam, happened to answer and said, "She's left the country," putting an end to Farouk's calls.

At the end of the month, the rent was due. Paul and Heather didn't have enough to cover it. Instead of contacting Sang's parents, he looked up her sister's phone number in London on an old telephone bill. A woman answered who sounded just like her.

"Sang?"

The phone switched hands, and a man came on the line. "Who is this?"

"This is her housemate in America, in Brookline. Paul. I'm trying to reach Sang."

There was a long pause. After some minutes had passed, he wondered if he ought to hang up and try again. But then the man picked up the phone. He didn't apologize for the delay. "She's indisposed at the moment. I'm sure she'll appreciate your call."

Charles came that weekend to pack up Sang's things. He tossed her clothes into garbage bags, stripped the futon of its sheets, and asked Paul to help him put it out on the sidewalk. Wrapping the framed Indian miniatures in newspaper at the kitchen table, he told Paul he'd talked to Sang on the phone, said that she'd be living in London with her sister through the summer. "You know, I kept telling her to leave him. Can you believe, I never even met the guy?"

Charles loaded up the back of his truck, until all that was left of Sang in the house was the sage and mole paint on the walls of her room and the hanging plant over the dish drainer. "I guess that's everything," Charles said.

The truck disappeared, but Paul stood awhile longer, looking at the houses lining the street. Though Charles was her friend, she had not told him. She had not told Charles that Paul had known for months about Deirdre. That night at Farouk's apartment, after washing up in the bathroom, Sang had got down on all fours and crawled into Farouk's coat closet, weeping uncontrollably, at one point hitting herself with a shoe. She'd refused to emerge from the closet until the policeman lifted her by the armpits and dragged her forcefully from the apartment, telling Paul to see her home. Tiny pieces of flower petals and leaves were still stuck in her hair. She had taken Paul's hand in the elevator, and all the way back to the house. In the car she had cried continuously, with her head between her knees, not letting go of Paul's hand, gripping it even as he shifted gears. He had put the seatbelt on her; her body had been stiff, unyielding. She seemed to know, without looking up, when they had turned in to their road. By then she had stopped crying. Her nose was running. She wiped it with the back of her hand. A light rain had begun to fall, and within seconds the windows and the windshield seemed covered with scratches, similar to the ones she'd inflicted on herself, the drops beading up in small diagonal lines.

The day Paul passed his exams, two of his professors took him to the Four Seasons bar for a drink. He had many drinks that afternoon, ice-cold martinis on an unseasonably warm spring day. He drank them quickly on an empty stomach and little sleep the night before, and suddenly he was drunk. He had answered every question, passed with honors the three-hour ordeal. "Let's pretend it never happened," his committee told him, alluding to his previous embarrassment. After they left him, shaking hands a final time, patting him on the back for good measure, he went to the men's room, splashed water on his face. He pressed a plush white towel to his temples, sprayed himself with some cologne from a leather-encased bottle by the sink. Returning to the lobby, the reception desk, the massive bouquets of flowers, the well-dressed guests, the brass carts piled with expensive luggage — all of them had spun round him like a carousel, then floated one by one in an arc across his vision. For a while he stood watching these images appearing and fading like fireworks, not wanting them to end. He wanted money all of a sudden, enough of it to march up to the desk and request a room, a big white bed, silence.

Outside, he turned a corner, crossed a street. He walked toward Commonwealth Avenue, so different at this end from the way it was by the university. Here it was an elegant, tree-lined boulevard, flanked by spectacular homes, and benches on which to sit and admire the architecture. The cross streets progressed alphabetically, Berkeley, Clarendon, Dartmouth. He walked slowly, still drunk, looking now and then for a taxi to take him home. At Exeter Street, he noticed a couple on a bench. It was Farouk and a woman, willowy but haggard. Her bony nose was a little too large for her face. Her slim legs were crossed. Her eyes, a limpid turquoise blue, were topped with mascara-coated lashes, and she blinked rapidly, as if irritated by a grain of sand.

There was an empty bench across from them. Paul walked to it and sat down. Loosening his tie, he looked directly at Farouk. For this man, Deirdre had called a perfect stranger, made a fool of herself. For this man, Sang would rush from the house, had refused all her suitors. Because the suitors didn't know her, they hadn't had a chance. "It's not love," she used to say. They still called for her now and again, their voices eager, their intentions plain. "Do you know her number in London?" some asked, but Paul had thrown it away. His head tilting this way and that way, he studied Farouk carefully. Paul had lain on top of this man. He had felt those legs, that chest, beneath his own, had smelled his skin and hair and breath. It was a knowledge he shared with Sang and Deirdre, a knowledge each had believed to be her own. Farouk and the woman exchanged glances. Let them, Paul thought, smiling, a quiet snicker escaping him. There was nothing Farouk could do to stop him; not with this new woman at his side. He slouched down, his head against the wood of the bench now, allowing the afternoon sun to warm his body, his face. He was tempted to stretch out. He closed his eyes.

He felt a poke in the side of his arm. It was Farouk, standing in front of him.

"You should be grateful I didn't sue," Farouk said. He spoke precisely, yet without rancor, as if he were making casual conversation.

Paul rubbed his eyes behind his glasses, displacing them. "What?"

"You've damaged my shoulder. I had to get an MRI. I may need surgery." The woman, now standing a few feet behind Farouk, said something Paul was unable to hear.

"He should know," Farouk said to the woman, his voice rising unpleasantly. Then he shrugged, and they walked off together. There was something curious about the way they were walking, together and yet with a space between them. It was only then that Paul noticed a small yellow dog at the end of a very long leash, stretched taut in the woman's hand, pulling her along the path.

BETH LORDAN

Digging

FROM THE ATLANTIC MONTHLY

SO ONE DAY a farmer — his name was Seamus Sullivan, and this was in County Mayo, not far from Knock, where, when Seamus was fifteen, the Virgin had appeared — says to the wife, "I'm off up the field, then," and he goes off in his boots in the early afternoon with the dog at his heel and a shovel in his hand. His only idea is to be out there, as far from the house as he can go without leaving his own bit of land, digging; what he wants is the heft and smell and slide of his own earth at his command. He doesn't wonder whether a man can own something like land; he owns this field and the dirt within it, and the field goes straight down to the center of the earth.

So he goes after the roots of a furze bush. It's the first edge of spring, and thin lips of yellow show here and there on the bush. This digging is hard work, starting away from the thorny bush to make sure he's beyond the spread of the roots, but it's a long day ahead with nothing else he need do, and he dedicates himself to it. He's forty-five, still strong enough to spend the whole day driving the shovel in and piling the good dirt out. But the furze is a shallow weed, and after only an hour the excuse work is mostly done, the thorny bush as root-exposed as if he were planting it instead of casting it out. So he pulls it to the center of the field and sets it afire. Then he goes back to crouch beside his dug pit and roll a cigarette with his dog lolling beside him while the bush burns. It's a pitch-filled thing, a furze bush, so it burns hot and fast. As he tosses the damp end bit of tobacco and paper away, he sees the wife standing down by their house, shading her eyes to watch the last of the flames. Bridget is just a girl still after two years of being married to him, who's older than her husband ought to be. That's enough; he stands and takes up his shovel again.

Maybe the sun comes out for a few minutes, and he feels so good, digging in the thin sunlight in his field, that he wonders why he doesn't do this once a week. His muscles are limber, the rhythm steady, and then his shovel hits something not dirt. Even that, even the challenge of going now into the next layer of his land, where rocks will complicate the digging — even that feels good. He moves the shovel back a few inches and drives it in again and lifts up the dirt and sees there, mud-encrusted and bent, a chalice, the gold pale and shining where his shovel has struck it.

So there stands Seamus, rubbing the dirt from the cup with his broad, callused fingers for a few seconds before he looks guiltily down the slope to see if Bridget is still watching him. She isn't, so he has a chance to decide: Will he keep digging and see if he can find more? Will he take just this one thing? Will he have a good look and then, tenderly, tuck it back where it came from and replace the dirt and pray for the grass to grow over it all?

In this same midafternoon, in Cork instead of Mayo, Mary Alice O'Driscoll comes hurrying along the road into Clonakilty, tears in her pretty eyes. She's nineteen and a strapping girl, tall and strong, and she has dreams. This is a difficult situation, being a strapping girl with dreams, because nobody believes the combination is natural.

Her sister Rosie is the beauty, and people assume she has dreams, but Mary Alice is sturdy, and her mother, a practical woman, sees no reason for Mary Alice not to marry Jimmy Curtin, who owns his own boat and has the hope of a house when his father passes on. He's a hard worker and a decent man, and if Mary Alice would just be reasonable, she'd see that decency is quite a bit to get in a husband, and Jimmy's not that old, not forty yet, and he fancies the girl.

Mary Alice *is* reasonable, so she has already abandoned any number of dreams without ever having mentioned them to anyone — gracefulness, for example, and a piano, a quick wit in conversation, a holiday in Switzerland, and a wedding in Saint Colman's Cathedral, in Queenstown, the most beautiful thing she has ever seen and as far from Rosscarbery as she's ever been — but now her mother says she can't go to the dance on Saturday in Glandore. Missing the dance shouldn't matter, given all those other things she knows she'll never have, but it does matter. Mary Alice believes her heart is breaking. So she's on her way down the road to complain to her aunt Margaret, who was the strapping sister herself and knows where you end up if you don't hold on to some dream — where she is, housekeeper to the priest.

So here's Mary Alice, her head up so that the tears won't spill, tapping at the kitchen door of the priest's house, tapping and tapping, and not until Father Moran himself, a book in his hand, pulls open the door does she realize that she has come into town with her apron still on and her hair still in last night's plait. Not that Father Moran is tidy, standing there in his stockinged feet and his hair mussed as if he has just waked up and here it is almost time for his tea.

"Oh, Father," she says, "I'm sorry to bother you. I was looking for Aunt Margaret."

"You were, of course," he says, but because he has indeed only just waked from a doze in his chair, his voice is much curter than he intended, and Mary Alice loses her hold on her tears, and they fall from her pretty eyes in two silver lines down her face.

She has no idea how lovely she looks to Father Moran, who isn't a young man but also isn't old enough to be her father.

Father Moran himself hardly has any idea of how lovely she looks to him, at this dusky moment in the kitchen when her aunt Margaret isn't there and he's barely awake and can't tell exactly who he is, priest or man, but he manages to say, "Here, now, what's this all about?"

Mary Alice can't say what it's all about, not to him, not in his stockinged feet, and so she sobs four times, trying to think of an appropriate thing to say to a priest, and says, "I was thinking of Saint Colman's Cathedral."

Father Moran has seen Saint Colman's Cathedral, so he almost understands why this girl — he has known her name at some moment, though it escapes him now — weeps so hopelessly, and he's touched by it, and moved to transfer his book from his left hand to his right, and to reach his left hand out to touch and comfort her. He means to pat her shoulder in a fatherly, priestly gesture, but his hand takes itself instead to her cheek, where the tears are cool against her firm, warm skin.

As soon as she has spoken, Mary Alice begins actually to think of Saint Colman's, its soaring beauty, and how she'll never be a bride there, never have a life that includes a piano or quick wit or holidays, all because her mother won't allow her to go to the dance in Glandore this Saturday night, where some young man might magically appear who would love her, and when the priest's gentle hand touches her tears, she has no choice in the matter; she covers his hand with her own and presses it to her face, and before either of them is quite certain why or how such a thing could happen, his book is on the floor and their mouths are sweet together with salt tears on all their lips.

By now Seamus has come in for his tea, with his chest full of his secret. Bridget sees that he has got something going on, something that makes him feel big this evening, and she wonders about it as she cuts the bread. He's been nowhere, just up the field the whole afternoon, digging. She has her doubts about whether potatoes will grow there in the second field, the sun's so poor below the hill, but the potatoes are his business. What is hers is this house, this empty house, with no child in it.

"Come up," he says behind her, and she hears the dog clip from the corner and into his lap.

So, Bridget thinks. *So.* And she cuts the bread thicker. When she has finished, she cooks him a buttered egg and brings out the last jar of her sister's blackberry jam. Her sister has the five boys and two girls. "Is it Christmas?" he asks when he comes to the table, but he's gentle about it, and she smiles just a bit, pouring the tea. "The field's ready, is it?" she says, and he says it is, nearly.

After the meal he goes out with the dog and smokes again, looking up at the field where the cup and four gold bracelets lie hidden in the dirt, though he can feel their presence still behind his ribs. He has dug them a deeper hiding place up there, and will leave them for now. He has nowhere to sell them, and no idea how to explain where the money came from if he did. Besides, he thinks the gold isn't that kind of treasure. It's something else, and he has spent the afternoon trying to get it figured out — how the gold stands for something ancient and splendid and connected to him.

He has decided that when he's got it straight in his head, the time will come and he'll go to the priest and tell him what he's found, and ask him to write to the proper people so they can come and get it and take it to the museum. They'll make a card for it, he thinks, saying SEAMUS SULLIVAN, COUNTY MAYO. All day the idea of that card has been growing in him, a weighted restlessness in his chest, as he's been digging. He'll plant potatoes there when the time comes. It's no sin, he's sure, to take his pleasure privately now, thinking of himself as a man with gold in his field. No sin either to turn to his wife in bed tonight and take that pleasure as well; and when the time comes, when the washing up is done and the fire's banked and the two of them sigh into their rest, he does so, and she answers him gladly, a rare easy sweetness between them. As he falls asleep, his last thought is of the shimmering power of gold hidden in a field; hers is that these moments may get them a child.

Before that happens, back in the kitchen in Clonakilty, Mary Alice, weak in the knees, and Father Moran, utterly without a thought in his head, linger through the long moment of their kiss as if dependent for balance on their joined mouths, as if suspended from each other's lips, or from their hands on her cheek. And then, of course, they hear a sound from somewhere, a reminder that Aunt Margaret hasn't vanished from the earth, that priests and girls with pretty eyes aren't free to kiss in kitchens in this world, and they lurch apart. For a single second they stare at each other, blankly, and then the horror gathers. She turns and flies out of the house and down the narrow street of the town, eyes dry now and nearly blind. As soon as she's free of the houses, she turns off the road and sets out across the fields for home.

A mile or so along, as she's walking more slowly but still not daring to think of anything, she sees below her the ring of standing stones that people call the Druid's Altar. The light is failing fast, and the stones take on the look of giant shawled women, some standing, some kneeling. She takes herself down from the little ridge to them, between them, into the center of the circle.

"I've kissed a priest," she says aloud.

Maybe she sways with the enormity of what she has done, and it's just an illusion that the stone women stir, but Mary Alice O'Driscoll doesn't wait to see whether the women are welcoming her or casting her out. She takes to her heels, down across the fields in the twilight, and rushes into the kitchen, where her mother is getting the tea with a scowl on her face. Breathless, she says, "I'll marry him, Mother — I'll marry Jimmy if you say." What else could she do, a girl who would tempt a priest and bring stones to life by confessing it? If she didn't marry as quick as that, who knows what shame she might bring on them all?

So, say that was a Tuesday, in March of 1910. By Sunday, when the banns are read for Mary Alice O'Driscoll and James Patrick Curtin, Seamus Sullivan has been laid to rest (that weight in his chest was his heart failing, and he never knew, dreaming of his neighbors thumping his back in congratulation when the gold came pouring out of his land, and he may be dreaming it still, if heaven is as it should be), and Bridget's brother Pat has walked the three fields and found them poor, Seamus's plan for potatoes in the second field foolishness. He'll let it go back to grass and put his own sheep on it. He does that, and takes Bridget to keep house for him half a mile away, and when her son is born, in the winter, he'll be the one who insists the child be named Kevin, for their father, instead of Seamus, for his own. By that time, down in Cork, Mary Alice will be amazed to find herself a little in love with Jimmy Curtin, whose awkward chatter covers a thousand apt generosities, and when their first child is born, the next year, his name, without question, is James. Nor does the family hesitate when the chance comes for them (three more of them now, all strapping children), through the death of one cousin and the emigration of three others, to move to a small house in Galway. And of course the boys will follow their father and become fishermen. In fact, the only question that ever disturbs Mary Alice arises when her James comes to her at the age of fifteen and says, "Mother, I've a calling to be a priest." "You have not," she says, but he scowls and says, "Why not? I've the marks, and Father Kennedy says —" And what can she say but "I don't care what Father Kennedy says, you'll be no priest"? That's as close as she'll ever come to allowing herself to remember the forbidden salty kiss in the kitchen, and that's a story she'll never tell to a soul.

Seamus's story of finding the gold never gets told either, and the gold is never found, so when Bridget dies, with Kevin only eleven, his uncle Pat sees no reason not to take him off to America, where things will have to be better than they are at home with all the mess there is now. It's 1922, and who knows how things will turn out? So off they go, leaving the two houses to fall down around themselves, and if South Boston doesn't vault Pat into the prosperity he expected, it does vault young Kevin into a world of streetcorners and movies and — once he leaves school, at just fifteen — pubs and nicknames and fistfights. He's one of a gang of fellows on the corner of E Street and Bowen; they all live at home, work here and there on the docks and in the factories, fight about anything, spend their money foolishly, and try to impress girls. When Kevin's twenty, he falls mad in love with a girl five years older, and before he knows what he's about, he's going to be a father. It's 1931 now, and he sees no way to avoid taking his bride back to the cramped flat over the barbershop and Uncle Pat's vicious hospitality. He's twenty-one when his son, Lyle, is born, and twenty-two on Christmas Eve when, far gone in drink, he decides to swim the icy Charles River to sober up before going home to the wife and kid.

This same Christmas Eve, 1932, back in Galway City, James Curtin, who has put away his wish to be a priest as his mother once put away her wish to go to Switzerland, proposes marriage to Norah Silke, who turns him down. Two months later he marries her sister Maeve. They have a daughter, Róisín, and then another daughter, Mary, and then sons; before the sons are old enough to go out on the boat, which James has always hated, he sells the boat and buys a poor bit of land. But he has no talent as a farmer, and when his children offer to leave — Mary for America, one son to be a priest, another for Australia — he's glad to have them go. He's a harsh man, and real poverty makes him more so; but he's no worse than other fathers, better than some, which Maeve tells the children so often that even she believes it.

So when Lyle Sullivan and Mary Curtin meet at last, in 1960, at a huge company picnic on Cape Cod, they could have a load of stories to tell each other, but they don't. Mary doesn't work for the company; she has come with a girlfriend who does, and the girlfriend insists that Mary's perfectly welcome. Her whole life — she's twenty-four — Mary has worried about being where she doesn't belong, and she has never quite figured out where she does belong.

When she knew she was going to America, she was terrified and excited; once she got there, she was so homesick that she'd have gone back if she'd had the money, and if the ones at home hadn't needed the money she sent. She can't imagine living her whole life so far from home, but now that she's been here a year, she can't imagine what life she'd be living if she were still there. So even here, at a picnic, she doesn't dare go very far from her friend and doesn't join in conversations. That's where she is when Lyle first sees her.

He doesn't know that she looks a lot like his grandmother Bridget, who wore her long, dark, curling hair much the way Mary wears hers, in a soft bun high on her head, and whose mouth had a similar sweet patience. He doesn't know what Bridget looked like because he has never seen the one photograph of her, which his mother hoards, along with the eight other things that belonged to his father, Kevin, in a locked metal box in the back of her closet. He won't even find that box until after his mother's death, three years later; when Mary comes back from Ireland to marry him, she'll have cut her hair and taken to setting it on brush rollers for the bouffant effect that is the American style in 1963. This day on Cape Cod all he knows is that she looks good to him. He doesn't even think of her as pretty, although she is, and it's a good thing he doesn't. Long ago he developed the unconscious habit of avoiding anything that might distract him from his duty to his mother, so he never speaks to girls he thinks of as pretty. This isn't his mother's fault: she's not old in her mid-fifties, not bitter or pitiful. True, she has always tried to impress upon Lyle the dangers of drink and wild friends — but hasn't she good reason for that, since drink and wild friends killed her young husband and left her with a son to raise and no skills beyond laundry work, which she couldn't do anymore after she hurt her back, when Lyle was only seventeen? Not exactly her fault, or his, but it has come to this: Lyle lives the life of a middle-aged husband, although he's only twenty-eight. He's good at his office job with a hardware company, frugal, responsible. He likes some television programs, and he likes to drink a beer or, more rarely, a little whiskey and play a game or two of hearts in the evening with his mother in the oddly comforting cloud of her cigarette smoke. He's not unhappy, and he's not particularly eager to marry, but still, this pretty day on Cape Cod, the girl in the dark skirt and soft blouse looks good to him, and he keeps an eye on her, the way she's shy but cheery, and when he passes almost accidentally near enough to hear her talking with her friend, he hears that she's Irish, and he's a goner.

He doesn't recognize that he's a goner though. He has never been a goner before. As a teenager, back in Vermont, he kissed a few girls and longed in a shameful way for others, and once, after he brought his mother back to Boston to live, he dated one woman three times. But he hasn't been a goner. He thinks he feels sorry for this girl, so far from home, and that in itself is so unusual for him that it's almost dusk, almost time for the fireworks, before he finds a way to meet her.

She's alone at last — her friend has gone to get them some more lemonade. She's alone, crouching to spread the blanket where she and her friend will sit to watch the fireworks, and dusk is coming on, and the ocean is stirring, and she hasn't the least hint how appealing she looks to Lyle. He sees the domesticity of her task, and remembers the quick, dancing, foreign murmur of her voice. He isn't given to imagining (Mary's friend, who works in his department, calls him rude and bossy), but he imagines that she might be lonely, and that's what he means to ask her when he comes up beside her — he means to say something like "You're far from home," in the sort of joking tone he assumes men use with women they haven't met yet. Instead he says, "Hello — I'm Lyle Sullivan, from Production Control," just as if it were a staff meeting. Mary gives a little leap, she's so startled.

She has been thinking not of home but of underwear, actually — about the difference between Irish underwear and American underwear in her admittedly limited experience. Her job is minding the children of the Cunninghams, in Brookline, who lent her the fare to come over. The oldest of the Cunningham children is a girl, twelve, rather pretty, who has been teasing her mother for pettipants; for days now Mary has been wondering in odd moments just what pettipants might be, whether they're something she ought to buy. In April she finished paying her debt to the Cunninghams. She now sends half her small salary back to Róisín each month and saves most of the rest, but she has a bit she keeps out for pleasure, and she's wondering if the cost of pettipants (whatever they are) would match the pleasure of them. That's what she's wondering when this fellow comes up and startles her.

She blushes, because of the underwear and because he's the fellow she noticed earlier and asked her friend about and because he has recognized, as she knew someone would, that she has no right to be at the picnic.

He blushes, because he didn't mean to startle her and didn't mean to say such a stupid thing, but there they are.

Mary straightens up and puts out her hand. "I'm Mary Curtin, from Galway," she says, and she smiles, because she's relieved at last of the dread of discovery that has tagged behind her all day. "I don't work for the company," she says.

He's handsomer than she thought, though she thought him handsome enough in the sunshine and from a distance.

She's lovely, looking up at him with that smile, and the quick, cooing way she says *doon't* and *coompany;* he nearly forgets to shake her hand.

Maybe the first of the rockets goes up then and bursts in gold and silver in the sky. Or maybe Lyle gathers his wits and asks where Galway is, or where she does work, and they talk a little more before her friend comes back and Lyle takes his leave. They won't turn out to be the sort of couple that reminisces about their first meeting; years from now, when their younger son, Jimmy, asks her bitterly, "How did you end up with him, anyway?" she'll just say, "I met him at a picnic." If in saying that she remembers any of this — the fireworks, and how the crowd around her made a full, reverent chorus of their pleasure while she hugged to herself the thrilling certainty that shy, handsome Lyle Sullivan from Production Control fancied her — she won't say so.

It'll be their older son, Kevin, when he's about ten and curious, who asks his father, "Did Mom used to be pretty?" Maybe the question lurches Lyle back to this moment, standing in the dark beneath the brilliant, slow explosions of light, studying how straight her back is; then she turns and bends toward her friend and something in the tilting of her body wallops him with a desire so harsh he makes a sound. Maybe that's why his answer to his son is so harsh — "What difference does that make?" He can't answer his son directly, can he? Or tell how he was utterly certain, talking to her, that if he put out his hand and touched the spun darkness of the hair at her temple, her smile would only deepen?

So. No stories get told this night, and the story of this night will never be told, even between them, but it goes on for all that. Lyle goes home a goner, Mary goes home just as bad, and then the waiting part begins, because this is still 1960, long before young ladies began telephoning young men, and this is still Lyle, who hasn't stopped being cautious and mostly content just because of the way a girl he met says "It's grand, so," and makes him imagine touching her hair. When he can't get her voice out of his head but begins to be afraid that he doesn't remember it quite right, he still has to work his way around to finding out where she is, and that involves her friend in his department, and with one thing and another it's well into September before he telephones her and asks her to a movie. She says yes, and says yes when he calls her again, although it's October by then; this is the pattern of almost involuntary patience she'll never quite lose and he'll never quite recognize as patience, which will make him even more impatient with everyone else in his life, including his sons, who don't practice it in his behalf. But by the time he calls her again, to invite her to Thanksgiving dinner to meet his mother (things have gone that well, or that inevitably), she's gone.

Years later she'll tell stories of her childhood, of Irish people and Irish adventures, funny stories and inspiring stories and now and then a sad story, but she'll never tell the story of how she answered the doorbell and took the telegram that was addressed to Mary Curtin and stared at it as if it weren't her own name. She'll never explain how distant her own horror at herself seemed when she read the words MOTHER DYING and heard herself thinking *I'd be too late.* She'll never admit that she doesn't know what she'd have done next if her employer hadn't come into the corridor then and asked what was wrong.

But she doesn't have to know that, because Mrs. Cunningham does come into the corridor, so Mary does the right things. She explains, she apologizes; she has the price of the ticket back in her savings; she must go; she doesn't know if she'll come back. She does it all with dignity and calm, the telephoning, the packing, the leaving itself, and not until she's on the plane and night has fallen does the terrible thick guilt of it begin to squeeze her across the chest.

She lands at Shannon, takes the Galway bus, and gets out in the still early morning in Oranmore. A man happens to come up the footpath and sees her, and he says, "You'd be the Curtin girl, come back from America," and when she says, "Yes," he says, "Sorry for your trouble," so she knows, as she walks the last three miles, that she's too late, and she doesn't need the black ribbon on the door of the house to choke her with grief and regret, and she doesn't need Róisín's bitterness to make her feel the tug of the halter of shame at the nape of her neck, but she gets it anyway.

Róisín opens the door to her and turns back into the house without a word. It's left to Mrs. Joyce, who has come to help, to ask, "Would you see her?" So Mary steps unwelcomed and unembraced into the front room, still in her coat, and touches her mother's hand for the last time. She knows what her mother would say, what a load Róisín has carried alone this past year. As she stands there in the cold, Mary accepts Róisín's bitterness as just, and bearable. She believes that before spring she'll be back in America; if the Cunninghams don't want to sponsor her again, Father Martin may find her someone else. Or she can get some kind of work here and save.

But when she leaves that room, meaning to put her suitcase in a corner and take up some task in preparation for the wake, her father has come in the house, and Róisín dries her hands to embrace her. "I was taken strange," Róisín says, "seeing you there so American in your coat. You're welcome, Mary," she says, "you're welcome home again. The tea is on."

Mary's mortally tired; she hasn't slept for thirty hours. She kisses her sister and turns to kiss her father, who stands beside the fire. "It's good you've come," he says, "with Róisín off in Galway City now."

"Off?" Mary says.

"Oh," Róisín says, with the breath of a laugh, "I didn't write it to you, but Michael Joyce and I are being married. In Christmas week."

Mary stares, Róisín grins, Da folds his arms and snorts. "Did you think you were away?" he says.

For just that one moment Mary believes they have killed her, but in the next moment she is simply lost, unhappy, and at home.

Right then, without a cup of tea or a bit of rest, she accepts their tribal, intimate revenge, begins her penance for the sins of abandonment, hope, desire.

She takes on her mother's work and then her sister's, and protects her heart with prayer and exhaustion. She doesn't recognize the slow creep of hopelessness, doesn't know she's sinking, settling into the suffocating bog of it, until Lyle's letter arrives in mid-January and she finds herself unable to breathe.

It's only a letter, and rather short, though she reads it a dozen times. He writes about the weather, which is bad in Boston this winter, and says he's being promoted at work. He doesn't mention that his mother has had a stroke and that he spends his evenings now, after the nurse has gone, trying to pretend she isn't drooling, trying to pretend he doesn't understand her demands for cigarettes he'll have to hold for her. He never does tell Mary about that first year, or the guilt that stains his relief when he finally puts his mother into a nursing home and lives alone but still not free of her in the apartment they shared for so long. In the same way, Mary never tells him about Da's growing strangeness — the way he has taken to shouting up the chimney and hiding food and sometimes staring at her as if he suspects her of something — or Róisín's small, breezy cruelties. She writes instead of the weather and farming in Oranmore; he tells her about Irish politics, and she tells him droll bits about Irish people; she wonders about movies, and he tells her she's missing little. After the first year she asks him about world affairs, and he mentions his mother's illness; he writes vaguely of hoping to travel, and she mentions her sister's babies and her youngest brother's departure for work in England; she asks about his work, and he explains why buying a house is more sensible than renting. The courtship is odd and awkward, but it sustains their hearts through a long dark time.

And then one day in the third year, a week to the day after his mother's death, Lyle drives to a travel agency. His only idea is to be going somewhere, away from the empty apartment and the closet full of his mother's things, to be making arrangements, putting large and permanent things in motion and order. He writes a check; in four days he'll be on an airplane for Dublin, where he'll get a train to Galway and a bus to Oranmore. He figures he can take a taxi from there, or rent a bicycle, or walk if he has to. He doesn't question the propriety of paying an unannounced transatlantic call on a woman he has met only three times; he wants to see her, and she has always said yes, and he has nowhere else to go.

At the same moment — though it's late afternoon there on the small farm in County Galway — Mary is sitting on her bed dabbing a wet rag on the cut on her cheekbone Da's punch opened. She's panting, but not as badly as she was, and although she keeps a wary eye on her door, she isn't really afraid. Still, something will have to be done: she'll clean herself up and walk to Galway and speak with Róisín. She can't talk him past these sudden rages anymore, and with nobody left at home except her, he'll eventually knock down somebody who doesn't love him.

Five days later, as two elderly gardai lean smoking against their car with her suddenly cooperative father, Mary searches under his bed for the shoes he says he's got to have if he is to go with the lads to Saint Bridget's Hospital. She finds a plate of moldy potatoes, two copies of *Key of Heaven,* three knives, and a sock stuffed full of one- and five-pound notes. And the shoes. She runs to the car with the shoes, her heart pounding, and says, "Da," and he meets her eyes with his sly ones and winks. For an instant there in the thin sunshine he's the father of her best childhood mornings.

"Your mother made me them stockings," he says.

"Did she," she says.

"She did," he says, yawning. "Fine heavy stockings. I'm off, so," he says, and throws the cigarette away.

She watches the car down the yard, and she's crying, of course, but she'd hardly be human if some corner of her heart weren't preparing to wake into something new, if some corner of her mind weren't calculating how much money a sock could hold. So when she imagines that the fellow wobbling along the road now on a bicycle looks like Lyle Sullivan, she tells herself, *I'd not be human if I didn't think of him now,* but in penance for that humanity she stands a minute longer, waiting for him to pass by and prove her foolishness.

ALICE MATTISON

In Case We're Separated

FROM PLOUGHSHARES

"YOU'RE A BEAUTIFUL WOMAN, sweetheart," Edwin Friend began. His girlfriend, Bobbie Kaplowitz, paid attention: Edwin rarely spoke up and complimented her. He tipped his chair against her sink and glanced behind him, but the drainboard wasn't piled so high that the back of his head would start an avalanche today. He took a decisive drink from his glass of water and continued, "But in that particular dress you look fat."

It was a bright Saturday morning in October 1954. Edwin often visited Bobbie on Saturday mornings, and she had dressed up a little, anticipating. Now she didn't bother to speak. She reached behind to unfasten the hook and eye at the back of her neck, worked the zipper down without help, stepped out of the dress, and in her underwear took the sharp scissors. She cut a big piece of brown wrapping paper from a roll she kept next to the refrigerator, while Edwin said several times, "What are you doing?"

Bobbie folded the dress, which was chestnut brown with a rust- and cream-colored arrowlike decoration that crossed her breasts and pointed fetchingly down. She set the folded dress in the middle of the paper, wrapped and taped it, and addressed the package to her slimmer sister in Pittsburgh. Then she went into the bedroom and changed into something seriously gorgeous.

"Come, Bradley," she called, though Edwin would have babysat, but Bradley came quickly. He was a thin six-year-old with dark curls and the habit of resting his hands on his hips, so from the front he looked slightly supervisory and from the back his pointed elbows stuck out like outlines of small wings. They left Edwin looking surprised. At the post office, a considerable walk away, the clerk said the package had to be tied with string, but lent Bobbie a big roll of twine and his scissors. Bobbie was wearing high-heeled shoes, and she braced herself on the counter with one gloved hand. She was short, and the shoes made her wobble. She took the end of the twine in her mouth, grasped it between her teeth, and jerked her head back to pull it tight. It was brown twine, now reddened with her lipstick, and its taste was woody and dry. Fibers separating from the twine might travel across Bobbie's tongue and make her gag. For all she knew, her poor old teeth might loosen.

Much was brown: the twine, the paper around the package (even the dress inside, if one could see it), and the wooden counter with its darkened brass decorations. The counter was old enough to have taken on the permanent sour coloring possessed by wooden and metal objects in Brooklyn that had remained in one place — where any hand might close upon them — since the century turned. But Bobbie's lipstick, and the shoes she'd changed into, and her suit — which had a straight skirt with a kick pleat — were red. She wore a half-slip because she was a loose woman. Joke. Edwin's hands always went first to her bare, fleshy midriff. Then he seemed to enjoy urging the nylon petticoat down, sliding the rubber knobs up and out of the metal loops that attached her stockings to her girdle, even tugging the girdle off. She never let him take off her nylons because he wasn't careful.

Bobbie tied a firm knot. Then she changed her mind. She poked the roll of twine and the scissors toward the clerk with an apologetic wave, called to Bradley — who was hopping from one dark medallion on the tile floor to the next, flapping his arms — and went home. As Bobbie walked, one eye on Bradley, the package dangled from her finger on its string like a new purchase. At home she found Edwin taking apart her Sunbeam Mixmaster with her only tool, a rusty screwdriver.

"Didn't you say it wasn't working?" Edwin asked.

"There's nothing wrong with it. I didn't say anything."

Edwin was married. He had told Bobbie he was a bachelor who couldn't marry her because he lived with his mother, who was old, silly, and anti-Semitic. But his mother lived in her own apartment and was not silly or anti-Semitic, as far as he knew. Edwin had a wife named Dorothy, a dental hygienist. She'd stopped working when their first child was born — they had two daughters — but sometimes she helped out her old boss. Now, fumbling to put Bobbie's mixer back together, Edwin began to wonder uneasily whether it wasn't Dorothy, dressing for work in her uniform, who happened to mention a broken mixer. He had never confused the two women before in the years he'd been Bobbie's boyfriend.

Edwin's monkey business had begun by mistake. He was a salesman for a baking supply company, and Bobbie was in charge of the payroll at a large commercial bakery. Though Edwin didn't wear a ring, he believed that everyone in the firms through which he passed assumed he was somebody's husband. However, a clerk in Bobbie's office had moved to Brooklyn from Minneapolis. When this young woman, who had distinctive habits, asked him straight out, Edwin misheard the question and said no. He had heard, "Mr. Friend, are you merry?"

Edwin was good-natured but not merry, and the question puzzled him until he found himself having lunch with Bobbie, to whom the young woman from Minneapolis had introduced him. He realized that he was on a date. Bobbie seemed eager and attractive, while Dorothy liked to make love about as often as she liked to order tickets and go to a Broadway show, or invite her whole family for dinner, and with about as much planning. Not knowing exactly what he had in mind, Edwin suggested that Bobbie meet him for a drink after work, nervous that she'd refuse anything less than dinner and a movie. But she agreed. Drinking a quick whiskey sour in a darkened lounge, she suggested that next time he come to her house. So his visits began: daytime conversations over a glass of water or a cup of coffee; suppers followed by bed. Bobbie was always interested. She only needed to make sure Bradley was sleeping.

Bobbie rarely spoke of her marriage. Her husband had been a tense, mumbly man, a printer. He'd remained aloof from her family. At first he said she was nothing like her crude relatives. "I felt refined, but I didn't like it," Bobbie told Edwin. Later her husband began to say she was *exactly* like her family, and at last he moved her and Bradley, an infant, into a dark two-room apartment where nothing worked and there was hardly ever any hot water. He said he slept at his shop, and at first he brought her money, but soon that stopped. "I didn't have enough hot water to bathe the baby,"

Bobbie said. "Let alone my whole self." Edwin imagined it: naked Bobbie clasping a thin baby and splashing warm water on herself from a chipped, shallow basin. She'd moved back with her mother and got a job. Eventually she could afford the apartment on Elton Street where Edwin now visited her. When Bradley was two, she had taken him on the train to Reno, lived there for six weeks, and come home divorced, bringing her sisters silver pins and bracelets with Indian designs on them, arrows and stylized birds.

Bobbie's family wouldn't care much that Edwin wasn't Jewish, she assured him, and they'd understand that he couldn't be around often because of his mother. But they did want to know him. So Edwin had consented to an occasional Sunday lunch in Bobbie's kitchen with her mother or one of her sisters, eating whitefish and kippered salmon and bagels off a tablecloth printed with cherries, and watching the sun move across the table as the afternoon lengthened and he imagined Dorothy wondering. After the bagels they'd have coffee with marble cake from Bobbie's bakery. He'd tip his chair against the porcelain sink and consider how surprised his wife would be if she knew where he was, being polite to another woman's relatives. His own house was bigger and more up-to-date.

Dorothy would be even more surprised if she knew, right now, that Edwin was in that same kitchen, less sunny in the morning, fixing a mixer that wasn't broken. Edwin would have preferred to be a bigamist, not a deceiver. When he reassembled the mixer, it didn't work. He left the bowls and beaters and took the big contraption home in the trunk of his car. He'd work on it when Dorothy was out. She had promised Dr. Dressel, her old boss, a few hours in the coming week.

The day Edwin carried off the mixer, Bobbie's sister Sylvia and her kids, Joan and Richard, rang Bobbie's bell after lunch because they were all going to the Hayden Planetarium. Sylvia, a schoolteacher, had said, "Bradley's ready," as if she'd noticed blanks in his eyes where stars and planets belonged. Her own kids had often been to the planetarium. So the sisters walked to Fulton Street, urging along the children, who stamped on piles of brown sycamore leaves. Climbing the stairs to the elevated train, Bobbie was already tired. She'd have changed her shoes, but she liked the look of the red heels. They waited on the windy platform, Joan holding

Bradley's hand tightly. She and Richard were tall, capable children who read signs out loud in firm voices: NO SPITTING. MEET MISS SUBWAYS. They had to change trains, and as the second one approached, Sylvia said, "Does Bradley know what to do in case we're separated?"

"Why should we get separated?" said Bobbie.

"It can always happen," she said as the doors opened. The children squeezed into one seat, and Sylvia leaned over them. She had short curly hair that was starting to go gray. "Remember," she said, "in case we get separated, if you're on the train, get off at the next stop and wait. And if you're on the platform, just wait where you are, and we'll come back for you. Okay?"

Joan and Richard were reaching across Bradley to slap each other's knees, but Bradley nodded seriously. Bobbie rarely offered directives like that, and he probably needed them, yet she felt irritated. At the planetarium, Bradley tried to read aloud words on the curved ceiling that was covered with stars. The theater darkened. While the stars revolved swiftly, a slightly spooky voice spoke of a time so far back that Bobbie felt disjoined from herself: she in her red suit would surely never happen. Anything at all might be true.

Then Bradley whispered something. "Do you have to go to the bathroom?" Bobbie asked. "I can't go in with you." If Edwin would marry her, he'd be there to take Bradley to the bathroom! The size of Bobbie's yearning, like the age of the stars, was suddenly clear. But Bradley shook his head. "No. No. I can't remember what I do if you get off the train without me."

"I wouldn't do that, honey," she said, but of course he continued to worry. She could feel his little worry machines whirring beside her.

"You scared him," she said to Sylvia later, as they shuffled toward the exit with the crowd. "About being lost on the subway."

"He needs to know," Sylvia said, and Bobbie wondered if Sylvia would be as bossy if she didn't have a husband, Louis — an accountant, a good man; although Sylvia said he was quick in bed.

They spent an hour in the natural history museum — where Joan held Bradley's hand, telling him what Bobbie hoped were nonfrightening facts — before taking the long subway ride home again. At the stop before theirs, Bradley suddenly stood and ran toward the closing doors, crying out. Richard tackled him, knocking him to the dirty floor, and Bobbie took him on her lap. Bradley had thought a departing back was hers. "Oh, sweetie," she said, brushing him off and kissing him. She carried him as far as the stairs.

"Well, I shouldn't have said anything," said Sylvia as they reached the sidewalk and turned toward home. The train's sound grew faint behind them.

Bobbie said nothing. If she agreed, Sylvia would change her mind and defend what she'd said after all. Bobbie glanced back at the three kids, who were counting something out loud in exultant voices — passing cars, maybe. "Seven! No, nine!"

"I have chopped meat," said Sylvia at last, when their silence had lasted for more than a block. "I'll make mashed potatoes. Lou will drive you later, okay?"

"That would be nice," said Bobbie. They reached the corner of Sylvia's street and turned that way.

"Unless you have a date?" Sylvia added.

But it was cruel to make Bobbie say what was apparent. "No such luck."

"That guy has a problem," said Sylvia. "It's Saturday night!"

"Edwin says I look fat in that brown dress," Bobbie said. She never let herself think about Saturday nights. Edwin said his mother cooked corned beef and cabbage then, and minded if he went out. "Remember that dress? With the design down the front?"

"That gorgeous dress!" Sylvia said. "To tell the truth, you do look a little hefty in it, but who cares?"

In the dark, Bobbie cried. She hoped her sister would notice and maybe even put an arm around her, but that wasn't their way. Maybe Sylvia did notice. "I'll make a nice salad. You like salad, don't you?" she said soothingly.

Edwin's house was empty when he came home on Tuesday. Dorothy was working, and the girls were at a neighbor's. He spread newspaper on the dining room table and fixed Dorothy's mixer, the one that had been broken in the first place. It was not badly broken. A wire was loose. Then it occurred to him that the mixers looked alike, with bulbous arms to hold the beaters, and curved white bases on which bowls rotated. He'd bought Dorothy's after seeing Bobbie's. Edwin set aside Dorothy's bowls and beaters. He carried Dorothy's fixed mixer out to his car, then returned and put Bobbie's broken one on the sheet of newspaper.

He jumped when he heard Dorothy and the girls arriving, but there was nothing to worry about. Dorothy asked, "Did you fix it?" and Edwin truthfully said, "Not yet." She stood behind him watching as he took apart Bobbie's mixer. By this time it was hard to remember that the broken mixer was the one he had broken himself, not the one Dorothy had reported broken, and he listened attentively while she told him what she'd been about to mix when it didn't work. As he listened, his back to his wife, he suddenly felt love and pity for her, as if only he knew that she had a sickness. He looked over at Dorothy in her thin white hygienist's uniform, her green coat folded over her arm. She had short blond hair and glasses.

The girls had begun to play with a couple of small round dentist's mirrors that Dorothy had brought from Dr. Dressel's office. Mary Ann, the younger one, brought her mirror close to her eye. "I can't see anything," she said.

"Wait a minute," said Eileen. Her light hair was in half-unraveled braids. Eileen turned her back on Edwin and Dorothy and positioned her mirror just above her head. "I'm a spy," she said. "Let's see . . . oh, Daddy's putting poison in the mixer." Eileen would say anything.

"I'm a spy too," said Mary Ann, hurrying to stand beside her sister and waving her mirror. "Show me. Show me how to be a spy."

Edwin couldn't fix Bobbie's mixer, and it stayed broken, on a shelf in Edwin and Dorothy's kitchen, for a long time. Meanwhile, Dorothy's working mixer was in the trunk of Edwin's car, and it was a natural thing to pretend it was Bobbie's and take it to her house the next time he visited.

On many Thursdays Edwin told Dorothy a story about New Jersey, then arranged a light day and drove to Brooklyn to visit Bobbie. Bobbie prepared a good dinner that tasted Jewish to Edwin, though she said she wasn't kosher. Little Bradley sat on a telephone book, and still his face was an inch off the plate, which he stared at, eating mostly mashed potatoes. "They're better the way Aunt Sylvia makes them, with the mixer," Bobbie said on this particular Thursday, the Thursday on which Edwin had brought her his wife's Sunbeam Mixmaster and pretended it was hers.

"I'm sorry I couldn't bring it sooner, babe."

"Oh, I didn't mean that. I just don't bother, the way Sylvia does."

Edwin watched Bradley. With the mental agility born of his mixer exchange, Edwin imagined carrying Bradley off in similar fashion and replacing him, just temporarily, with talky Eileen. If her big sister was out of the way, Mary Ann would play with Bradley, while Bobbie would enjoy fussing with a girl.

"What are you thinking about?" said Bobbie.

"I wish I could take Bradley home to meet my mother."

"Take both of us. She won't be against Jewish girls once she sees me," said Bobbie. "I don't mean I'm so special, but I don't do anything strange."

She hurried to clean up and put Bradley to bed, while Edwin, who hadn't replied, watched television. He couldn't help thinking that his family was surely watching the same show, with Groucho Marx. Over the noise of Groucho's voice and the audience's laughter, Edwin heard Bobbie's voice now and then as she read aloud. "'Faster, faster!' cried the bird," Bobbie read. Soon she came in, and Edwin reached for her hand, but she shook her head. She always waited until Bradley was asleep, but that didn't take long. When she checked and returned smiling, Edwin turned off the set and put his hands on her shoulders, then moved them down her back and fumbled with her brassiere through her blouse. Dorothy wore full slips. Edwin pulled Bobbie's ruffled pink blouse free and reached his hand under it. Even using only one hand, he'd learned that if he worked from bottom to top, pushing with one finger and pulling with two others, he could undo all three hooks of her brassiere without seeing them. In a moment his hand was on her big round breast, and she was laughing and opening her mouth for him, already leading him toward her bed.

Edwin forgot that Dorothy had promised Dr. Dressel she'd work Saturday morning. As he dressed in Bobbie's dark bedroom on Thursday night, she asked, "Will you come Saturday?"

"Sure, babe," he said. He had fallen asleep, but he could tell from Bobbie's voice that she'd remained awake, lying naked next to him. He leaned over to kiss her, then let himself out, rubbing his hand on his lips and checking for lipstick stains.

But on Saturday he had to stay with Eileen and Mary Ann, then pick up Dorothy at Dr. Dressel's office. He was more at ease with the girls in the car than at home. Made restless by his broken promise to Bobbie, he left too early, then had to look after his children in the dentist's waiting room. He didn't know how to braid Eileen's hair, and it had not been done that morning; Edwin noticed as he reread the dentist's posters, which urged him to eat carrots and apples, that one of yesterday's rubber bands still dangled off Eileen's mussed hair. He called to her and tried to remove the band without pulling. "You're hurting me," she said, though he didn't think he was.

At last Dorothy came out in her coat. "I heard them whooping it up," she said, but she sounded amused. She took two rubber bands from the receptionist's desk and swiftly braided Eileen's hair. Leaving the car where it was, they walked to a nearby luncheonette. Dorothy took Edwin's hand. Sometimes she spoke to him in baby talk; it was a kind of game. "I am going to teach you to bwaid hair," she said. But he didn't know how to answer, so she spoke again, now taking his part, in a gruff voice like the Three Bears. "*How on earth do you braid hair?*" He let go of her hand and put his arm around her shoulders as she answered with elaborate patience, "Well, first you make a center part . . ." Edwin imagined Bobbie watching them, not jealously. "Squeeze," the imaginary Bobbie said, and Edwin squeezed his wife's taut shoulder through the green coat.

Bobbie didn't use her mixer often. She was not sufficiently interested in its departure and return to put it away, so she left it on the extra chair next to the kitchen table where Edwin had put it. On Saturday morning she put on makeup and stockings, but he didn't come. Ordinarily, if Edwin didn't appear by a quarter to ten, Bobbie took Bradley out, rather than brooding. This Saturday, though, Bradley had a cold. To distract herself, Bobbie called Sylvia, who asked, "Does he have a temperature?" Bobbie's thermometer was broken, so Sylvia brought hers over. Bobbie made coffee. Bradley sat on the floor in his pajamas, wiping his nose on his sleeve while putting together a jigsaw puzzle, a map of the United States.

Bobbie offered Sylvia a cookie, and she and Bradley said together, "Before lunch?" but then everyone took a Mallomar, since Bobbie said a cookie might cheer her up. Bradley licked his fingers and then placed Florida in the puzzle correctly.

"Edwin didn't come today?" Sylvia said, playing with her spoon.

"Sometimes he's busy on Saturdays."

"You need more."

"I manage," Bobbie said. If Sylvia knew all Edwin's ways, she thought, she wouldn't object to him. "He's worth it."

Sylvia laughed, stretching her arm and actually taking a second cookie. "Oh, I know what you mean," she said. She interrupted herself to supervise Bradley's placement of California. "I know what you see in your Edwin. I see the way he looks at you."

"When you've been married a long time," Bobbie said, "I guess it's not so exciting."

Sylvia laughed. "I know how you feel," she said again, not scolding.

"You mean you felt that way about Lou once."

"Well, I suppose."

"What *did* you mean?" Bobbie said.

"Oh, I shouldn't say anything," Sylvia said. She tipped the bowl of her spoon with one finger, making the handle rise.

"He's not listening," Bobbie said, tilting her head toward Bradley. "You mean — someone?"

"Someone I met at an in-service course."

"Another teacher? A man."

"He teaches at Midwood."

"A high school teacher. You — have feelings?" Bobbie said.

"Did this ever happen to you?" Sylvia said, now glad — it seemed — to talk. "At night, you know, picturing the wrong person?"

Bobbie thought she knew what Sylvia meant. She wasn't sure what an in-service course was, whether it consisted of one occasion or several. "How many times have you seen him?"

"Wait a minute," said Sylvia, but then she crouched on the floor. "Doesn't Colorado belong where you put Wyoming, Bradley?" Wyoming was nice and tight. "Could the map be wrong?"

"Did you have lunch with him?"

"Oh, I'm exaggerating, it's nothing," Sylvia said. She remained on the floor, helping Bradley with a few more states. Then she got up, reaching out a hand to steady herself on the extra chair. She gave the Mixmaster a pat. "Hey, you didn't just buy this, did you?"

"No, I've had it for a while."

"I might have been able to get you a discount. A client of Lou's . . ."

"I bought it last year."

"Oh, right." Sylvia seemed to expect Bobbie to explain why the mixer was on the chair, so Bobbie told in full the story Sylvia had heard only in part: the story of the dress, the walk to the post office, and her return to find Edwin fixing a mixer that wasn't broken.

"He took it home? Why did he do that?" Sylvia asked.

"At home he has tools."

"Maybe he took it to a repair place."

"Oh, no. I'm sure he fixed it himself," said Bobbie.

"You're sure he brought back the same mixer?"

"You mean he bought me a new one? I hope not!" Bobbie said.

"Or he could have bought a used one," said Sylvia.

"Oh, stop being so suspicious." She liked the more tremulous Sylvia who had spoken of the teacher from Midwood High School. She wasn't ready, yet, for the usual Sylvia. "Of course it's mine."

But as she spoke, as she insisted it was hers, Bobbie suddenly sensed that the mixer on the chair might never have been in her house before, and then, looking hard, she was certain. It was the same, but somehow not the same. It had been cleaned differently, maybe with a sponge, not a dishrag. But that thought was ridiculous. It had been handled in a way that was not Jewish. An even more ridiculous thought.

Bradley had abandoned the puzzle and left the room. Maybe Sylvia would say more. "Did you have lunch with him?" Bobbie asked again.

But Sylvia would not be deterred. "Maybe Edwin has another girlfriend," she said, "and this is her mixer. Hey, maybe he has a wife!" She gave a short laugh.

"He has a mother . . . ," said Bobbie. His mother didn't sound like someone who'd plug in a mixer and mix anything. She now remembered that the metal plate with the Sunbeam insignia on her mixer was chipped. She looked, and this one was whole. She looked again. "I *trust* Edwin," she said.

"I know you do. Boy, that would be something," Sylvia said. "If it turned out Edwin was married."

But Bobbie was experiencing one of those moments when one discovers the speed of thought by having several in an instant. First she felt ashamed of being stupid. Of course there had been plenty of hints that Edwin was married. Once she allowed herself to consider the possibility, she was sure it was so. Bobbie didn't need to know whose mixer it was to know that Edwin was married. Then, however, Bobbie felt something quite different. It wasn't anger at Sylvia, at her sister's gossipy curiosity.

She was not angry at Sylvia. She felt sorry for Sylvia, a little superior to Sylvia. All her life, Bobbie had known that Sylvia was smart, so Bobbie must be smart too, even Bobbie who carried her clothing back and forth to the post office. Once they knew Edwin was married, Sylvia would imagine there was only one way to behave — to laugh bitterly — but Bobbie understood that there were two.

That there were two different ways to think about Edwin's marriage — like thinking about the stars, which might be spots of light, close together, and might be distant, wild fireworlds — struck Bobbie with almost as much force as her sorrow. Sylvia's way would be to laugh bitterly and tell everyone the story. Edwin's marriage might be a bad joke on Bobbie, but then Edwin would no longer tip his chair against her sink, or walk her to her bed while his hands grasped all of her body he could reach under her loosened clothes. His marriage might be a bitter joke — or it might be something Bobbie just had to put up with.

Bobbie would never marry Edwin, but Bobbie had the mixer that worked. She stood and plugged it in, and it made its noise. The years to come, during which she'd keep Edwin's secret, not letting him know she knew — because it would scare him away — and not letting her sisters know she knew — because they'd scream at her to forget him — became real in her mind, as if she could feel all their length, their loneliness, at once. She would be separated from Edwin, despite Thursday evenings and Saturday mornings. Bobbie turned off the mixer and wept.

"Oh, of course he's not married," Sylvia said, and Bobbie didn't say that wasn't why she was crying. "Me and my big mouth, as usual," Sylvia continued. She stood up and put her arms around Bobbie, and then the sisters were hugging and smiling. "Edwin married," Sylvia said. "If there's one man on earth who couldn't manage being a two-timer, it's Edwin. Sorry, baby, I love the guy, but that swift he's not." And she went on and on, hugging her sister and calling her baby. Baby! The unaccustomed sweetness, like the cookie, comforted Bobbie for a while. Maybe she and Sylvia both had secrets, like Edwin. Maybe life required secrets. What an idea.

JILL McCORKLE

Billy Goats

FROM BOMB

WE USED to all come outside when the streetlights came on and prowl the neighborhood in a pack, a herd of kids on banana seat bikes and minibikes. The grownups looked so silly framed in their living room and kitchen windows. They complained about their days and sighed deep sighs of depression and loss. They talked about how spoiled and lucky children are these days. *We will never be that way,* we said, *we will never say those things.* We popped wheelies in pursuit of the mosquito truck, which was a guarantee on humid summer nights. We rode behind the big gray truck, our laughter and screams lost in the grinding whir of machinery, our vision blurred by the cloud of poison. We were lightheaded as we cruised our town — the dark deserted playground of the elementary school, the fluorescent-lit gas stations out on the service road of the interstate that scarred the rural landscape, past the rundown apartment complex where transient military families lived, past houses that were identified by histories of death, divorce, disaster. Sometimes we rode up to the hospital, a three-story red brick building that stayed lit throughout the night. We hid in the shrubbery of what was known as the lawyers' parking lot, a spot near the courthouse rumored to be the scene of many late-night rendezvous between people you would be shocked to see — mothers and fathers you would never suspect doing such things while their spouses and children lay asleep in their beds.

We rode way out past the tobacco warehouses and the railroad tracks, past the small footbridge where we used to play Billy Goats Gruff, our idea of who was scary enough to be the troll ever changing. We rode on, out to the local kennel, where one imitation bark could set off a satisfying round of howls that continued long after we'd ridden off in the direction of Bell's Econo Lodge, where we slipped fully clothed into the warm green water of the fenced-in pool, our cutoffs and T-shirts weighing us down as we bobbed and paddled back and forth. Sometimes we just floated there, buoyed by the constant rush of cars on the interstate and the still patterns of stars overhead.

One night we stopped and sat in a circle under the streetlight on my corner. We avoided the gaping storm drain across from us, home of many lost baseballs and bracelets and shoes. Only a few of us had ever been brave enough to go down into the dark muddy box in search of lost items. Those who did surfaced with vows never to do it again. This night we talked about *Laugh-In* and took turns imitating the stars: "sock it to me" and "one ringy-dingy" and "verrry interesting." One boy, tall with a freckled complexion and ears that stuck out from his head, was a bit of an outcast at the junior high school. But here in the neighborhood where he had lived his entire life, he fit in. This night, he told how he had ridden his bike to the emergency room earlier in the day and seen a woman whose face was torn away, a child with a broken leg that dangled from its hip like a bruised banana, another woman who had tried to kill herself on aspirin and failed. He said he heard them pump her stomach. He heard her vomiting and begging to die behind a curtain meant for child patients, its little farm animals in primary colors swaying back and forth with the movement of the tall oscillating fan in the corner. "It was so weird," he told all of us, who hung on his every word. "The incongruity of it all." His acute observations and large vocabulary, which brought laughter and scorn in the classroom, were accepted — really expected — by the neighborhood crowd. We counted on him to bring us the kind of news that left us weak in the knees and too nervous to sleep.

One girl was planning to stay out this whole night. Her parents were out of town and her older brother didn't give a damn what she did as long as she didn't tell that his girlfriend was going to sleep upstairs in his lower bunk. If she wanted to, she could smoke cigarettes and rummage through her parents' drawers for signs of their sex life. She could drink some wine and watch TV all night, go door-to-door at dawn stealing the milk and the Krispy Kreme doughnuts that were delivered to doorsteps.

We talked that night, as usual, about the murder-suicide house, which was just two blocks away, a tidy brick colonial with a bricked-in herb garden — long untended — complete with a sundial. Some nights we dared to creep into the yard and collect sprigs of mint and lavender, which we would rub and sniff for a long time after. We knew all the details of the house's story even though everything had happened a whole generation before, when our parents were growing up here. There was the murdered woman, an accomplished violinist. It had been her desire to teach the violin, but when there was no real interest in town (who, after all, actually owned a violin?), she taught voice and piano lessons. There was her husband, the suicide man, who had once lived in Chicago, a detail that was always included to mark him as an outsider no matter how many years he had lived in town. There was their one son, who came back from his home in California to bury them both in an expensive mausoleum at the center of Hollydale Cemetery. Before the son left town, never to be heard from again, he told people that his parents had made a suicide pact. We were left wondering which was worse: to have one parent a murderer or to have both parents choose to depart this earth without a thought about how it might affect your life. Theirs were not the only suicides in our town; there were more than we would ever have guessed, but we took turns telling what we knew about reported hunting accidents and accidental overdoses, whispering as if the deceased might suddenly step from the thick pine woods behind us.

We also talked about the famous Hank Carter, said to have been a genius who "crossed the line." None of the parents explained exactly what the line was or how crossing it happened or if there were warning signs. All we knew was that Hank was proof you could go from being a clean, well-dressed high school student who solved difficult calculus problems and aspired to be a NASA engineer to being a disheveled, bearded man who wore a cowboy hat and boots and rode around on a moped with a pistol and other weaponry attached to his belt and a Bible tied to the handlebars. Sometimes Hank threatened to shoot dogs and cats and the tires of expensive cars, and other times he preached, though no church in town had ever claimed him as one of its own.

We were discussing it all this night in July 1970, the summer of the Jeffrey MacDonald hearing. Jeffrey MacDonald was the man charged with murdering his whole family — two little girls and a pregnant wife — on the army base nearby. He claimed to have seen a band of hippies enter his darkened home. He said he heard them saying things like *acid is groovy* and *kill the pigs* just before performing an atrocious reenactment of the Manson Family murders. It had happened back in February and it was what the grownups discussed over their highballs and cigarettes, coffee and Jell-O, and Saturday night T-bones ever since. Had this good-looking surgeon, brilliant enough to have gone to Princeton, really butchered his young family? Was it possible that someone so smart and skillful could lose his mind, just snap and go into a bloodbath frenzy? To tell the truth, many kids had not slept through a night since February. Our minds were full of images of the beautiful young and blond Mrs. MacDonald and of her babies and with the bits of gory detail the adults stopped describing whenever we passed through a room.

"My God," the tall freckled boy said. "Like we don't read the newspapers too." And then he recited newspaper accounts of the state of the bodies, leaving us more lightheaded than the mosquito truck had.

"Hank Carter has crossed over; he might snap even more," one of us inevitably said, and though the whole town had proclaimed Hank harmless, there being no reports whatsoever of his ever hurting any person or pet, I could never look him in the eye, even when he yelled in a booming, slow-as-molasses voice, "I say, girl, have you got the correct Eastern Standard Time?"

Back then, when I wanted the time, I went to the phone and dialed 739-3241 and a man would say, *The correct time is eight-oh-two P.M. and forty seconds.* I must have called him twenty times a day. He became a security blanket of sorts. Even now, almost thirty years later, I can close my eyes and hear every beat of his mechanical voice.

We were too old for kick-the-can and too young to make out. We were restless. We had learned a lot about murder that year. We knew that most of the time a person knows the person killing them. We had learned that alcohol and cigarettes would begin to kill off people we loved. Some of the grownups who sheltered us were disappearing from their windows like fade-outs, images lifted from the earth in poofs of smoke, puddles of drink. We were learning that to be lost, a brain didn't have to be blown out all over a ceiling like in the murder-suicide house at the edge of town. We knew people whose brains were slipping down a long easy slope. There was a teacher we loved who got us confused with our parents. There was a man well loved in town for entertaining at children's birthday parties (a mediocre magician with an aging pet monkey) who had ended his own life.

"He was queer," said some older boys who had taken to hanging out in our neighborhood. "He was an old cocksucker." These were the same older boys who, one dark night that very summer, forced the freckle-faced boy to go down on them and then told us about it. They called him queer and they called him cocksucker and it didn't seem to occur to them that they were the ones who had demanded the act of him, that they were the ones who had pulled his serious young face into their damp bitter crotches and issued their orders. Did it occur to us?

So we did have to wonder about death. The slow poisoning of lungs and livers and brains. The pact a couple might make to end it all. The savage stabbing a man might fly off and commit. A kid — never the hunter, always the prey — whose only crime was that he was scared and too tired to fight back and who, when he could no longer live with the pressure building up in his mind, chose to treat himself with a gun barrel forced down his throat. But the boys who promised to share a beer with him out in the dark woods near the highway probably didn't make that connection. They probably grew up to drink their own highballs while their own children played outdoors, riding their bikes past the latest sites of domestic unrest.

As grownups, you have to stop and wonder what people are thinking, or not thinking. Do those boys, grown into the bodies of men, carry that death around in their pockets? Do they ever, at the height of sexual climax, see that boy there, his sad eyes pleading *Let me go?*

And the suicide-pact story, who knows if it was true? There was the note the son found, but how do we know the son didn't write it himself as a way to protect his dead parents? Or maybe the husband wrote it after he killed her. Maybe it was a murder of hatred, a murder of passion, and then he left behind a legacy of mutual love and decision. We will never know.

*

There was another house in town, a beautiful Victorian with a little circular tower. It was surrounded by an ornate fence, each iron picket the shape of an arrow. I loved the house and its fence until I heard that there had once been a terrible car crash on the corner. A young passenger, a boy, was thrown through the windshield and onto those iron arrows. It had happened twenty years earlier, when my parents were teenagers, back when the interstate didn't exist, back when people didn't know the danger of smoking the very tobacco that so many had helped to harvest. I tried to get the image of the speared boy out of my mind, but I was never able to pass that house without seeing him pinned there under the blue sky of a beautiful October afternoon.

That image, and the one of the middle-aged woman, violin in hand, son living elsewhere, begging for her life, hang on in my imagination. Sometimes the violinist's face gets confused with that of Mrs. Colette MacDonald. The stories of one person begging, another taking, run parallel.

It is said the MacDonald house remained vacant and untouched for years. The food in the freezer, the valentines out on display. I could not imagine my father in such a fit of rage, but some of my friends said they could imagine theirs that way. Some kids had seen their parents drunk. All of us had overheard at least one really bad argument. Most of us had seen our parents cry, and even for those who glimpsed only the briefest losses of control, the memories remained vivid. Our parents were as vulnerable as we were. Anyone, grownups and children alike, could die at any minute. They could disappear as quickly as a car crashed into a tree, or a trigger was pulled, an overdose or undetected cancer cell flowed through the bloodstream; their hearts, livers, or lungs might shut down, some with warnings, others without.

We all had experienced the desire for breath, the burning ache of our lungs when we shot up from the deep end of the motel pool to the surface of light and gasped for air, when we tumbled from our bikes, dizzy and high, to roll in someone's front yard and spit out the taste of mosquito poison. The wonder of that first full breath. Jeffrey MacDonald claimed in his trial to have given mouth-to-mouth to his wife. He claimed that he could hear the breath exit through her chest as quickly as he delivered it. Too late.

*

The last time I ever saw Hank Carter he was directing traffic around an accident at an intersection near the high school. We all stopped to watch him there, cowboy hat pulled low, beard long and unkempt, billy club swinging from his belt. He wore mirrored sunglasses and moved quickly, pushing bystanders over toward the curb as he tried to make the two men involved in the fender-bender sit down and breathe into paper bags. When he was dismissed from his post by a policeman, he reluctantly returned to his motorbike, which a crowd of us stood around. It was old and rusty. Ropes, flashlights, and fast-food bags were crammed in the basket on the back along with the Bible, yellowed and swollen from exposure to the weather.

"What's doin' Hank?" one of the boys yelled in a slow mimic. "Shot anything lately?" Traffic was moving by then, and we were ready to move on ourselves. We were in high school. We had afternoon jobs and study dates. We had a prom to plan and decorate.

"Nothin' but some old mean blue jays," he called back, mounting his bike as if it were a horse. "There weren't nothin' left but a few feathers and some bird gut." He pulled a blue feather from his back pocket and waved it back and forth, laughing until he began to cough and wheeze, a cigarette burning to ash between two fingers of his waving hand.

The boys liked to keep Hank talking. They liked to get him riled up over some topic far removed from the moment. They wanted his ranting and raving but not directed at them. It was a fine line they walked; a minefield of topics guaranteed to set him off. He hated dogs that barked when he rode past them. He'd like to see their vocal cords tied up into knots. That would leave them silent. "I hate a damn barking dog," he said. "I hate 'em like I hate a communist. I'd shoot me some dog if the law would allow it. They should've let me loose in Vietnam." He didn't believe that men had gone to the moon. He said all that stuff was filmed right down near the coast. "Down where you girls strip naked and grease your bodies to get that tan. The Lord would not like that." He laughed and shook his head. "The Lord would not like that one damn bit." He thought that women should not be allowed to drive cars, especially the really young women and the really old women and the foreign women. "A woman is good for one thing," he said, and the boys egged him on. "Not for *cooking*," he said, and adjusted his mirrored sunglasses, which made it hard to know what he was staring at. "Though I'd not turn myself down a meal of fried chicken and mashed potatoes. Don't need one for cleaning, neither," he said. "I can operate me a Hoover as good as any old woman. Got me a Hoover so goddamned powerful I can use it to rake up yards if I take a notion."

"So, you got yourself a woman, Hank?" one of the boys asked. Asking this kind of question was like playing Russian roulette. He might laugh, but he was just as likely to fire his pistol into the air and command some goddamn respect for the weaker sex. He often preached about Adam and Eve, which was exactly what the boys were hoping for. He could go on for hours about how that naked harlot was put there in the garden for one thing and one thing only until she took up with that devil snake and got it in her evil mind that she wanted herself some knowledge other than making some babies to populate the earth. "She was nothing but a rib," he said, "and Adam had every right to kick her ass." He said, "The great and almighty plan was not supposed to take such a turn."

Everyone knew that as a high school student he had dated Emma Mosby, a girl who grew up to marry another town boy, one who went off to school and then to the Korean War and then back to school and became a surgeon and then chief of staff at the hospital. They lived in an old house in the center of town, a block Hank circled endlessly. He was dating Emma Mosby when he began to cross over. One day he was telling her how much he loved her and explaining how suspension bridges are built, and the very next week he arrived at her house suited up like someone going to a rodeo and complained of all the racket the dogs were making, those cussing belligerent damned dogs. Emma Mosby's time in love with Hank Carter was something that everyone knew about but no one discussed. "Emma doesn't deserve to have that dredged up," the grownups would say.

But that day at the accident was the last time I ever saw him. The boys hoped for an angry answer, but Hank just shook his head and laughed. "For me to know and you to find out," he said. "You find out and I'm likely to reward you with a dollar bill or two." He mounted his bike, and the group cleared a path for him.

"Hey there, girl," he drawled when he saw me standing there. "Do I know you?" He lifted his sunglasses to reveal clear blue, much younger-looking eyes than I would ever have expected. "Are you the one been calling up to my house and hanging up? Or asking is my Frigidaire running or have I got Prince Albert in the can?" I shook my head, my face hot. I wanted to look away from him, but I was afraid of making him mad.

"Not me," I said, while a chorus of boys behind me sang out things like *Yeah right. Sure. You want us to believe that?*

"If that's what she says, then that's what she means, you bunch of stupid boys." He turned on them then, patted the big gun strapped to his hip. "You all look like a pack of mean old junkyard dogs to me. Damn Nazi mongrels." Everyone froze while he twirled his gun and then eased it back into the holster on his belt, alongside his big silver flashlight and the billy club. "The good Lord hates the Nazis and the commies and the ignoramuses, and I've been put here to keep a watch. Ain't nobody gettin' by me." He laughed his loud laugh and then turned back to me. "I've known you forever, girl," he said. "I know your whole life like a book. I always have and I always will." He shook his head and dropped his glasses back in place. "Don't you ever forget that." He made a clicking sound from the corner of his mouth, the kind of sound that someone might use to accompany a wink, though now his pale blue young eyes were hidden again. I nodded. No one spoke until he cranked his bike and rode well past the intersection as he headed out toward the service road.

I was a senior in college when I got word that Hank Carter had died. I was two hours and light-years away; I was in a place where my memories were something I could bend and shape into a suitable representation of who I was. I hung out at an old house at the edge of campus where there was always a gathering of students listening to music and drinking beer, discussing philosophy and religion and the fate of the world. My hometown paper said Hank died of a heart attack. Those among the huge outpouring of viewers said he looked small lying in his coffin without his hat and boots, his face shaved smooth. They said he looked like a normal person. Receding hairline. Wrinkles around his eyes and on his pale white throat that had always been protected by a red bandanna and the scraggly beard. They said he died at twelve noon, and for several months after that, when the bell of the Methodist church chimed the hour, people would pause over their lunches to comment how they missed seeing Hank riding through town. Until he died, they hadn't taken into account how many times a week they saw him — helping at accidents or collecting litter along the highway or just riding his motorbike through town.

As a child, I had a contest with myself to see how many times I could call the time service before the minute lapsed. It was a reassuring thing to do. And now other numbers I called often crowd my mind like secret codes: 3642 and 5756. If I could be in a *Twilight Zone* episode, it would be the one where the phone line has fallen down onto a grave so that calls are placed from beyond. If I could write my own episode, it would involve a phone line that could connect us back to those old places. Just dial and you get your grandfather in his wheelchair, his tired old collie curled beside him; your grandmother in her kitchen with Mason jars sterilized and ready to receive tomatoes and pear preserves; the neighbor saving her mail so when you got home from kindergarten you could use her jewel-handled letter opener — razor sharp — to slit the white envelopes of her bills and the pale ones of letters; the old aunt who kept a jar of peppermints for children and who always spoke with her hand covering poor dental work, her head tilted just slightly; fathers walking up from the eighteenth hole on late Sunday afternoons while mothers bundled their children into big warm towels as they stepped from the pool, eyes red and stinging from the chlorine; the freckle-faced boy, waiting on his bike, ready to race through the summer night with the sound of an ambulance on the highway. *Won't one of you please, please, please go with me?*

I would call the people I knew growing up who have since died. I would ask how life had taken them there. Did they beg or did they pass in silence? Did they embrace life or reject it? Were there memories that at the very last minute filled their minds and swaddled their fears? And like a director, I would call for lights to come on in every house in town and for every person who had ever lived there to step outside and take a long deep breath on this average summer night.

TOM McNEAL

Watermelon Days

FROM ZOETROPE

EARLY ONE AUGUST EVENING in Philadelphia in 1926, Doreen Sullivan paid her fifteen-cent admission to the Aldine at Nineteenth and Chestnut. The attraction was *Beau Geste* with Ronald Colman. Doreen was early. She lingered over the encased posters in the downstairs lobby (for a long moment she stared frankly into the eyes of Ramon Novarro), then took one of the curving marble staircases to the upper lobby and sat down in a brocaded armchair. No one else was there. Doreen lit her own cigarette, something she was rarely required to do in a public place, and from her handbag unfolded a letter she'd already read three or four times. It was a funny and disturbing letter from Lulu Schmidt, her sometimes best friend who almost two years before had run off to New Orleans with Clarence Nottingham and had not been heard from since.

It began, *Dear Dory — if you receive this you must be at the same old address living with Aggie and still wasting away in Phil-a-delph-eye-aye! I got disentangled thank you from Clarence Nottingham (a big drip and how!) and you'll never guess where I am now Yankton South Dakota — Ha! This town is full of hoot and holler — you've got bridge builders and train men and best of all cowboys and even a few Indians but now they dress just like us. Here's the good part though — the males outnumber the girls 3 to 1! which means they walk up to you and tell you how you look like Lillian Gish only more so! Ha!* The letter went on for three skittering pages. It ended with *Come see for yourself Dory, there's jobs and men galore who if they think I'm Lillian Gish will think you're Greta Garbo Ha!* She'd signed, *Your everlasting friend Lulu Schmidt.*

People had begun to mass in the upper lobby, their talk light and expectant. Beyond the auditorium doors the pipe organ was playing. A boy materialized beside Doreen and said, "How 'bout I escort you in?" He was hatless with his hair slicked back and parted down the middle. He was neither good-looking nor bad. He looked, in fact, more or less like all the other boys Doreen saw every day. Coolly, she said, "No, thank you, I'm waiting for someone," which was true in only the most abstract sense, but she didn't give the boy another look.

Thirty minutes into the movie, Doreen went out to the lobby for popcorn. When she got to the counter she was surprised to find that she not only didn't want popcorn but didn't want to return to the movie. She drifted outside. Normally Doreen came out of the moviehouse refreshed, and the lights and voices and laughter of the street would slip into her bloodstream like alcohol, but tonight everything seemed worn out by familiarity. The warm night air smelled faintly sour. She wore a thin, sleeveless dress over a light camisole, but the stares of men, which she usually craved, had no effect on her. There were places to go — there were always places to go — but she felt only like returning home, where Aggie would likely be entertaining one of what she called her gents.

Doreen had grown up believing her mother to be dead and Aggie to be her older sister, but one day when Doreen was fourteen she came upon a box of documents that included her own birth certificate. The space for the father's name was blank. Agnes Lee Sullivan was listed as the mother. When confronted with the document, Aggie didn't blush or stammer. She said, "Why, you little snoop!" And then, "Well, now you know." And finally, "It's kind of funny, this morning you didn't have a mother, and presto, tonight you do!" (In truth, little had changed — Doreen still called Aggie Aggie.)

When Doreen stepped into the flat tonight, there was a man's hat on the center table. It was a snap-brim fedora with a nicely creased crown. Doreen picked it up and did what Aggie always did when handed a coat or hat to hang. She ran her fingers over the material — soft felt — and checked the label — Lord & Taylor. Not Saks Fifth Avenue, Aggie would've said, but not bad.

Doreen glanced at Aggie's door. It was closed. If she waited for it, she would hear a laugh. In men, Aggie looked for what she called the three *m*'s — married, moneyed, and merry — and she gazed upon the boys Doreen brought home with a frozen smile of disapproval. Aggie had produced the same smile a few weeks before when Doreen told her she'd taken a new job at Kresge. "Managed by a man and staffed by girls?" Aggie asked. Doreen's cheeks pinkened and Aggie pressed her advantage. "Twenty cents an hour?" she said, and Doreen, glancing away, had murmured, "Fifteen."

Doreen used the bathroom and went to her room. She double-bolted the door from within (surprisingly often the merry men returning from the bathroom would try the wrong door). The room felt close. Doreen shed everything but her camisole and slip, switched on a black table fan, and opened wide the room's two windows. She pulled back the bedcover and lay atop the sheets with three pillows plumped behind her bare back. She lit a cigarette, drew the smoke deep into her lungs, and held it for a moment before exhaling, reaching for her handbag, and again unfolding Lulu Schmidt's funny letter.

When Doreen Sullivan started work at WBDY in downtown Yankton three weeks later, she brought with her from Philadelphia an attunement to fashion that the citizens of Yankton had rarely seen outside of magazines — her bobbed hair was marceled into deep horizontal waves, she wore a wide ribbon in her felt cloche, and she sported a scarf with a King Tut motif. She also used a scarlet lipstick to form her lips into a fresh cupid's bow that both her male and female coworkers, privately and for different reasons, found unsettling. Shortly after Doreen arrived, a station employee named Monty Longbaugh came in early one morning and very slightly repositioned his desk so he would have an unobstructed view of her as she worked.

In the early twenties, Monty Longbaugh had not quite made a name for himself as a cowboy balladeer and then had looked around for stabler employment. For the past two years he'd been reading the WBDY weather and farm reports in a consoling voice perfectly suited to solemn stories. In 1925, when he started at the station, Yankton was a river town of just under six thousand, set out on tableland that gently sloped down to the Missouri, the town's uncertain southern boundary. Monty liked the town. He liked living in one of its neat, white-fenced neighborhoods, and he liked working in one of the stout red stone buildings that dotted its commercial district.

The Stapleton Building had housed the Birney Seed & Nursery Company since 1913, and it was Henry Birney, the founder's son, who had grasped the happy commercial implications of radio transmission and quickly purchased the license and frequency designation for WBDY, had built its facilities on the Stapleton Building's third floor, and, when the station's transmitters were fortified to five hundred watts, had himself hit upon its first slogan: "WBDY, Your Big Buddy on the Great Plains."

Weekday mornings the station aired a show called *Neighbor Macy, the Farmwife's Companion,* hosted by an amiable woman who dispensed budget-stretching recipes and practical domestic tips. She also sold a number of household products available only by mail-order from WBDY. For the past four months, and with growing boredom, Doreen had been processing these orders. One day she noticed a red envelope among the shifting sackful of white. It was addressed to *Neighbor Macy, Mail Order,* but off to the side of the address, neatly printed, were the words *Attention Doreen.* Doreen slid her letter knife under the sealed flap. On the enclosed sheet of paper — also red — were the words *I must talk to you before another sun sets. Signed, Monty Longbaugh.* When Doreen looked up and searched out Monty Longbaugh sitting at the far reach of two dozen desks, he was staring back with an expression that somehow seemed both hopeful and forlorn. Doreen had seen the look before. Nothing important had ever come of it, but it had been the source of some nice presents.

They walked down the street to Wilkemeyer's Drugs. It was cold. In the street, wheel tracks ridged the frozen mud. He ordered coffee and she sipped lemon Coke from a glass that was soon printed with lipstick. In a tight voice, he asked her about the weather and why she'd come to Yankton and how she liked living there and what her relations thought of it. Doreen kept her responses breezy. She told him if it got any muddier she thought the whole town would slip into the Missouri and she'd only come to Yankton because her friend Lulu Schmidt had written letters singing its praises but then two weeks after she got here Lulu Schmidt went back to a man in New Orleans named Clarence Nottingham, who, it turned out, was Lulu's husband! She said her sister Aggie in Philadelphia was her only living relative and that her sister Aggie thought Yankton was just across the crusty bog from Timbuktu. After the last of these answers, Doreen gave Monty Longbaugh a saucy smile and said, "Was that the reason you needed to talk to me before another sun sets?"

Monty Longbaugh shoved his coffee away. He spread his hands and ironed them along his thighs, twice, which made Doreen think of a comic movie where a rural type was about to go after the greased pig at a state fair. Monty cleared his voice and lowered his eyes. "Well," he said in a low voice, "it's like all my life up until now I've been sleepwalking, and now I'm wide awake."

Monty Longbaugh lifted his eyes and allowed them to rest fully on hers. They were black-brown and their wet glisten made her think of a staring deer. None of the three *m*'s applied to him, and the *m* for money never would. Aggie would've said, "Would you excuse me half a half a minute?" and left without looking back. Doreen said, "What was it that woke you up?"

His gaze broke from hers and shifted to the plate glass window that gave onto the street. To Doreen, his long smooth pure white face seemed suddenly and shockingly handsome. "Why, you were, of course," he said. "What woke me up was you."

The sauciness slipped from Doreen's smile. She didn't know what to say. She said, "I never expected to be anybody's Prince Charming before."

He turned and gave her an open smile. "Well, I never knew I'd been asleep," he said. He'd reclaimed his normal voice. It was a nice voice, low and assuring, his radio voice.

She leaned forward. She spoke in a whisper. She said, "Wait till I kiss you. Then you'll know what waking up is."

When Monty proposed marriage five weeks later, Doreen thought, *I don't know,* and said yes. "Next Sunday?" Monty said. Doreen nodded. The union was witnessed only by the officiating judge's wife. Monty made the informal public announcements, often with Doreen standing uneasily nearby. She kept the news from Aggie — she knew the kind of judgments her return questions would contain — and was relieved when their already haphazard correspondence ceased completely.

To Doreen, the marital state seemed different, but not unpleasant, and she did her best to do exactly what Aggie had never done. She made curtains for their rented house (crooked, though she hemmed them twice) and painted its dingy rooms (in the morning she noticed that drips had hardened on walls and trim boards alike). In the spring she spaded a garden, but the carrots bent as if they'd hit metal and slugs tattered the lettuce. Winter nights, she tried to teach herself knitting, then began weaving rag rugs, which were homely but at least freed her from the reading of unfathomable directions. Doreen began to realize that she missed going to work. She missed going to dances. She missed putting on her camisoles and beaded chiffon dresses and feeling goose bumps in the cold. She began to hate housework and laundry and cooking horrid meals her husband indiscriminately praised. In the first weeks of their courtship, she had loved sitting naked inside Monty's old wool robe and listening to him sing his cowboy tales — "Little Joe the Wrangler," "The Strawberry Roan" — but he had proven a heedless, exuberant lover, one who, even when he chanced upon some happy ministration, seemed never to remember it on later occasions, and over time Doreen had grown first indifferent and then secretly hostile to the sentimental stories his ballads contained.

Two winters passed, one longer than the next. The stock market crash meant little to most citizens of Yankton (few had had money to invest), but it was the latest in a long line of bad news stretching back almost ten years, the cumulative effect of which Monty reported in his daily farm report. He might try a joke or anecdote afterward, but when he reported Chicago wheat at ninety-seven cents a bushel or feeder calves at a nickel a pound, his voice was low and somber.

In the third summer of their marriage, a record drought hit the northern plains. The wind blew. Dust settled over fields and houses. Gardens, lawns, and pastures browned. Temperatures shot up and seemed not to fall. At night families laid out blankets on Ohlman Hill, hoping for some refreshment. One night when Monty and Doreen both lay awake in their screened sleeping porch, he rose to look at the thermometer and then went to the kitchen. When he came back he said, "It's 2:40 A.M. and eighty-six degrees." After that they didn't speak. He'd wrapped some chipped ice in a wetted washcloth. He lifted her gown and began damping her ankles and legs with the cool cloth. The pleasantness of this surprised her. She closed her eyes and lifted her buttocks so he could push the nightgown past and made murmuring sounds of a type Monty had never before heard. The hot spell continued, and several other nights Doreen, without opening her eyes, would in a whisper ask him to go fetch his iced cloth and he, as if in a dream, would begin moving about.

Doreen became pregnant. She told no one, and didn't quite believe it herself until the fact became undeniable. When finally she announced the news to Monty, he was so pleased that his expression collapsed, his eyes moistened, and he had to turn away in embarrassment. This had a strange effect on Doreen. "I'll need to slow down," she said. "I'll need to do less around the house."

"I can cook," Monty said. The sudden expansion of his spirits nearly seemed visible. "I know a couple of pretty good camp meals."

Doreen almost felt Aggie's presence in the room. She seated herself carefully. "And the cleaning," she said. "Someone will have to clean."

The town's two baby doctors were Carlton Johnston, a genial but clumsy man, and Jennie Murphy, whose custom of presenting herself in men's suits made some citizens standoffish, but Doreen preferred the gynecological intrusions of an eccentric woman to a butterfingered man, so it was Dr. Jennie Murphy who delivered the baby in the early-morning hours of April 5, 1931. Toward the end, between coaxings to push, Dr. Murphy repeatedly muttered, "That's the stuff!" and "Now we're cooking!" When finally the baby was expelled, it was taken quickly away by the nurse while Dr. Murphy did some stitching and daubing, then removed the soiled bedding. A minute or two later she returned, adjusted her suspenders, buttoned her sleeves, and slipped into her suit coat. She laid a hand on Doreen's forehead to check for temperature. Then, making to go, she looked down at her patient and said, "You did splendidly, Doreen," which for no reason whatsoever made Doreen want to cry. Monty returned with the baby swaddled and pinkly clean. "Girl," he announced, beaming. "A dandy little girl." Doreen looked at the baby's squinchy face, wept hopefully, and fell into a hard sleep. Some indeterminate time later, she awakened confused. The room was dark and the windows were rattling gently. In a faraway room a baby was crying. The clock said one-fifteen, but the dark was not the darkness of night. Doreen called suddenly for Monty, and after a time a nurse appeared. She closed the door quickly behind her to muffle the sound of the baby's crying. "Where's Monty?" Doreen asked.

"He's gone to the station on account of the storm," the nurse said. She was stout, middle-aged, and veiny in the cheeks and nose. "It's terrible dust. Middle of an afternoon and the autos outside are passing with their lights on. Mr. Longbaugh on the radio called it a black blizzard and I thought, *Well, that's close enough.*" The window glass shuddered. A moment later Doreen became again aware of the dim, stretched-out cries of a baby. The nurse said, "It's a funny storm. Edna Arlene don't like it."

"Edna Arlene?"

"Your baby. Mr. Longbaugh said that was her name, after his deceased mother." She waited a second. "Should I bring the baby in now?"

The nurse thought Doreen would say yes, and so did Doreen, but when she opened her mouth she heard herself say, "Not for a bit yet."

"You just rest then," the nurse said, and when she came close to arrange Doreen's bedcovers she brought with her the faint smell of liquor. Doreen closed her eyes. Outside, behind the wind, there was a steady drone that became a kind of silence.

Doreen had no experience whatever with babies, and to the degree she'd thought of them at all, she'd sketched them in as sleepy, genial creatures, pleasing to dress up and roll about in buggies, but Edna Arlene was none of these things. She was drooly, colicky, and overly covetous of her mother's touch. At night she would not sleep alone — Doreen would rock her to sleep, but the moment she set her down in the cradle and let go, Edna Arlene awakened screaming, so Doreen finally brought the baby to bed, where she slept between her and Monty. During the day, the baby cried when awake and napped only when held. Doreen's exhaustion was complete.

She hadn't exchanged a word with Aggie for over two years, but now dashed off a penny postcard. *Did I mention I was a missus and a momma? Edna Arlene is my baby girl, cute as a button but a demon for ceaseless screaming. Advice? Love, D.* The return card read, *Dear Yoked Up in Yankton, Must be in the bloodlines — you were a Banshee yourself and saved from sacrifice only by use of earplugs! Love, A.*

One day when Monty was off at the station and Edna Arlene's shrill cries were like a strafing, Doreen wanted more than anything to clamp her hand over the baby's mouth and face but instead laid her down screaming among pillows on the floor. She went out on the front porch and closed the door, but the cries pierced the walls. She began to walk. When she reached the corner of Fifth and Mulberry, she stood for a full minute meaning to go back, but didn't. Instead she walked the five blocks more to Wilkemeyer's Drugs and bought a package of Lucky Strikes. When she thought the girl at the register was staring at her, she said, "The neighbor's watching my baby." Doreen made a little laugh. "That baby's a handful. It's awful nice to be out for a minute or two." She hurried back to the house, uphill, breathless, and was at first terrified when she heard nothing at all from the room where she'd left the baby. But Edna Arlene was nestled among pillows, sleeping so calmly she seemed hardly to breathe. Doreen lay down on the floor beside the girl and on an impulse leaned close to lightly kiss her smooth forehead, which snapped Edna Arlene awake and started a fresh course of screaming.

By the second year the crying had somewhat abated. Edna Arlene would play quietly as long as Doreen or Monty was within eyeshot. And though the girl made syllable-like sounds, they didn't evolve into intelligible words. If she was hungry or otherwise needed something, she made a series of urgent guttural squeals that Doreen couldn't help but think of as piggish. When Doreen raised the subject with Monty, he was unalarmed. He said that he himself hadn't spoken until his fourth year and that big tongues ran in his family. "Big tongues?" Doreen said. She'd never heard of tongues hereditarily big. She considered writing Aggie about it, but instead took the girl to Dr. Murphy, who peered into Edna's mouth and, pinching the tip of the suspect tongue, waggled it side to side. Then she released it and said, "Well, it's good-sized all right." She smiled at the girl and turned to Doreen. "Your daughter will talk when she's ready. She might lisp and she might not, but in any case it's nothing to worry about." In all other ways, Dr. Murphy said, Edna Arlene was perfectly normal.

When Edna Arlene began to talk, shortly before her fourth birthday, she did in fact lisp, which her father found endearing. He began to use it on the radio. After reporting, for instance, that the WPA boys were in town cleaning Marne Creek and widening Main Street, he said, "Well, as my baby daughter likes to say, 'Thank goodneth for Mitha Woothevelt.'" Listeners responded favorably, and the observations Monty Longbaugh passed as his lisping daughter's soon became the standard closing element in his news summaries.

Edna Arlene liked hearing her father's voice on the radio, and enjoyed it when he talked in the funny lisping voice. One morning, at the end of the eleven-thirty market, weather, and news, Monty Longbaugh said, "Well, as my baby girl said just the other night, 'God muth not've been payin attenthin when he made up gwathhoppeth.'" Doreen, sitting smoking a cigarette, didn't laugh, but Edna Arlene did. Then she asked her mother why Papa didn't bring that baby girl home to visit.

Doreen asked what baby girl she was talking about, and Edna Arlene said *the one on the radio that talks like that.*

Doreen stared for a moment at Edna Arlene, then began to laugh. It had become a husky, hollow laugh, rattly, as if there were in her throat tiny dry leaves she couldn't expel. Edna Arlene's first five years had corresponded with drought and other assorted maladies. Hopper swarms defoliated fields and formed horny encrustments on the walls and porches of lighted houses. Whole herds of anthrax-infected cattle were shot and bulldozed into mass graves. Civic-minded hunters brought to the Red Cross bloodstained flour sacks weighted with rabbits for the hungry. Barbers gave free haircuts to those who couldn't pay, and the town's two banks consolidated. At night, tramps congregated around cookfires along the riverbank south of Burleigh Street. It was a life as distant from Philadelphia as Doreen could imagine. She said, "Edna Arlene, the girl your papa's imitating on the radio is you." She wanted to stop, but couldn't. She said, "It's you everybody's laughing at."

Edna Arlene's body stiffened. Her face contorted and her lower lip doubled downward. She was about to cry, but instead she did something surprising. She turned stoic. Her eyes settled. Her face became itself again. "No," she said, "thath not twue."

Doreen's voice softened. "The world's full of hard truths, little miss, and the sooner you learn it, the better."

Edna Arlene went to the sewing room and slipped into the knee well of her mother's Singer. From there she could see what her mother couldn't. It was true that Monty Longbaugh on the radio was her father, but not exactly, because Monty Longbaugh on the radio was always someplace different, where he was somebody different and where he had his own radio family that was different too. That baby girl her father talked about on the radio couldn't be herself, Edna Arlene, because she didn't sound like that girl her father talked about, not one bit, and besides, she never said the things the radio girl said. She'd never said anything about God not paying attention when he made grasshoppers, for example.

To a surprising degree, Edna Arlene was able to believe what she told herself that day. Still, she began to talk more quietly and less often, so people wouldn't make the same mistake her mother had.

One Sunday afternoon in mid-August, while Monty was at work, Doreen sat on the front porch with Edna Arlene. It was hot and dry and gritty. Doreen had damp-ragged the dust from the porch chair before she sat in it. Edna Arleen played with a miniature car, painted orange, except where the metal showed through. She ran the car slowly along the top porch rail, one end to the other and back again, something she could do for an hour, trancelike, without uttering a word.

In the center of town, a watermelon festival was in progress, and its distant music pulled at Doreen. "Let's go to the festivities," she said, and Edna Arlene stopped her car and turned around to stare. Doreen said, "There'll be music and carnival acts and pyramids of melon."

Edna Arlene quickly tucked her car into her pocket to indicate she was ready to go.

Doreen took the girl's hand and walked toward the music. In the park there were sack races, seed-spitting contests, and free melon, all of which interested Edna Arlene, but Doreen was drawn to the pavement dance. It was the accordion player and his Honolulu Fruit Gum Orchestra. Doreen positioned herself among the encircling fringe of onlookers and after a while stepped onto the pavement and pulled Edna Arlene out with her, trying by her own example to coax the girl into dancing, but Edna Arlene stood miserably with her eyes down until Doreen gave up and slipped back among the nonparticipants.

Doreen bent down and said in a tight whisper, "Little miss is a horrible lump."

Edna Arlene held tightly to her mother's print skirt with one hand and her orange car with the other, and peered straight ahead.

They'd watched perhaps three dances when a man in a cowboy hat broke free from the opposite fringe and started working his way through the dancers toward Doreen. He was a complete stranger, a tall loose-jointed man, pleasing to look at as he moved easily through the dancers, smiling and apologizing politely, nodding and touching the brim of his dress Stetson, but all the while keeping his gaze fixedly in Doreen's direction. Doreen thought, *Oh, Lord,* and didn't know whether she was hoping he was going to ask her to dance or hoping he wasn't. He was handsome. He was handsome, and how. As he moved nearer, Edna Arlene's grip on Doreen's leg began to tighten and Doreen herself was suddenly overcome with something that seemed equal parts panic and exhilaration. He wore a neatly pressed pearl-buttoned green shirt. His smile seemed playful. But his eyes, which had seemed fixed on Doreen's face, seemed to shift just to her side. He was looking beyond her. His shirtsleeve grazed Doreen's bare hand as he slipped past her. Behind her, she heard him say, "Well, if it ain't Gordy McAllister! And here I thought you musta succumbed ages ago."

A big laugh issued forth, presumably from Gordy McAllister.

Doreen took Edna Arlene to the free-watermelon line and found herself a bench in the shade. She waved when Edna Arlene turned to wave from the line, and again when the girl turned happily as she neared the men handing out slices. Doreen felt all-overish. She closed her eyes and opened them again when a woman passing by hummed a tune vaguely familiar to Doreen. *I'm Billy Jones, I'm . . .* something something . . . *and we're a —* . Doreen couldn't remember it.

Across the square Edna Arlene was eating her melon with another girl, who then led her off to a small group of girls playing a game Doreen couldn't fathom. The girls sat stock-still in a circle for a time and then, out of the blue, two of them would suddenly stand, race to touch a nearby tree trunk, and return shrieking to the circle. The one who lost was consigned to run again against someone else. It was plain that Edna Arlene, slow and clumsy, would be doing a lot of running.

The girls grew silent as they noticed Doreen drawing close. "It's okay," Doreen said, "don't stop your game. I just wanted to tell Edna Arlene that I'm running a tiny errand and will be back in a little bit."

Doreen had thought she might go home for something to settle her stomach, but gravitated instead to Wilkemeyer's, away from the hubbub. There were a few other customers, but Doreen met no one's eyes. She seated herself in the same booth she'd shared long ago when Monty Longbaugh had to speak to her before the next sunset. She ordered a seltzer and saltines. While she waited she took a pen from her purse. She printed her maiden name on a napkin — DOREEN SULLIVAN — and stared at it in hopes of remembering what it meant to be that person with that name, but all she saw now were oddly familiar letters; the feelings that defined the name had slipped away completely. Doreen was crying before she knew it, and when a waitress she knew came over and in a kindly voice said, "You all right, darlin'?" Doreen snufflingly nodded and said, "Oh, you know, it's just one of those days."

The waitress waited a second or two. "Monty was in a little bit ago, beaming like a bride. He said if you came in to tell you he had some news that might interest you."

Doreen snufflingly laughed. *Well, I've got a little news for him too,* she thought, but what she said was "Well, I'll be looking forward to his news flash."

The waitress said, "He probably spent the morning dreaming up some new way for you to make him money. That's what my Donald does."

A few minutes later, while Doreen was sipping her water, the waitress came to the table with a rolled magazine, which she presented to Doreen. It was the new *Photoplay,* with a sultry James Stewart staring out from the cover. (In a circle superimposed on his shoulder were the words *Born to Dance!*) Doreen looked at the waitress.

"Keep it," the waitress said. "I've already read it."

The elusive tune streamed again through Doreen's mind — *I'm Billy Jones, I'm blankety-blank* — and she gave her head a quick shake to dispel it. It was a novelty song, she was pretty sure, and she didn't like novelty songs. She paid her bill in change, then stood for a moment outside the pharmacy wondering if Edna Arlene was still playing with those girls. She decided to walk up to the station to hear Monty's news, but when she got there she walked by and kept walking until she found herself in Foerster's Park, strangely quiet with the citizenry drawn to the festivities in town. She seated herself at a shady table near the rock amphitheater and pretended not to see three tramps standing and drinking some distance away, also in the shade. She read her magazine for a minute or two, then lay her arms on the table and her head on her arms. She closed her eyes. Even when she heard a crack of twigs and the definite tamp of footsteps, she kept her head down and eyes closed.

"Everything all right, miss?"

A male voice, a little high in pitch.

Doreen didn't speak.

"You sick or something?"

As Doreen raised her head, the tramp removed his cap. He was surprisingly young, a boy in fact. His cheeks were pink and smooth. "What do you want?" she said.

He shrugged. "You looked like something might be wrong."

"There's not, though."

The boy stood where he was.

Doreen said, "Aren't you awful young for a tramp?"

The boy, with some spine in his voice, said, "I'm full sixteen." Doreen doubted this, but didn't say so. The boy said, "And I just think of myself as an unfunded traveler." Then he said, "I used to have a job in Omaha killing chickens, but that ran out." He said, "A lot of the old guys ride up in the boxcars, but I ride underneath, on the connecting rods. You never get caught riding down there."

Doreen gave the boy her first full and direct look. "What're you and your unfunded-traveler buddies over there drinking?"

"I'm not drinking nothing," the boy said. "I made a promise I wouldn't till I was eighteen."

Doreen said, "Who was that promise to?"

The boy for the first time looked down.

From town a rousing cheer carried.

The boy lifted his head and said cheerfully, "Guess the prizefighting's started."

They were both quiet, as if listening, but no other cheers followed.

Abruptly, Edna Arlene came to Doreen's mind, but then she thought, *Edna Arlene is fine.* To the boy she said, "One day from our front window I watched a tramp working his way down our street. He stopped and knocked at some houses and others he left alone. Why do you think he did that?"

The boy's eyes moved to Doreen's as if pulled. "Did he come up to your house?"

He had, but Doreen said he hadn't.

"Oh," the boy said. The news seemed to disappoint him.

She suddenly wanted a cigarette, but knew that lighting one in the presence of this tramp would seem to an onlooker familiar. Yankton was a good-sized town, but it was small at heart. She said, "You hungry?"

"I could go for something to eat, sure."

"I don't cook," Doreen said. She opened her purse, found her package of cigarettes, and tapped one out. She made a wry face and said, "Reach for a Lucky instead of a sweet." She was searching for her matchbook when the boy said, "I got it." He held a lighted match in his cupped hands. She leaned close, took the smoke into her lungs, and leaned away. She exhaled and stared forward. She said, "My husband does all the cooking, every bit of it, and the cleanup too." She inhaled again, and this time released the smoke through her nose. "He made me promise I'd never tell that to a soul" — here she fixed the boy with her eyes — "and now I have."

The boy said, "I'm good at keeping secrets." He said this so smoothly Doreen tried to look behind his eyes to see if he meant something by it, but all she found was more earnestness. She said, "What other sins did you forswear until age eighteen?"

"Tobacco."

"That all?"

The color rose in the boy's pink cheeks.

Doreen said, "So I guess there's one other thing."

The boy said, "Yes, ma'am."

Doreen laughed. "And it's not snuff."

The boy shook his head and said blandly, "Snuff's included with tobacco."

The boy's simpleness was both an annoyance and an enticement to Doreen, and in the past few seconds she'd experienced a strange effusion of feeling that, while unshaped, she knew at bottom to be illicit. Without looking at the boy she said, "In my coin purse there's maybe seventy-five cents. It's all I've got. Go ahead and take it."

The boy didn't move. She looked at him. He said, "I'd rather you handed it to me, if it's all the same to you. So I wouldn't be removing it from your purse."

She poured the coins into his cupped hands. The boy said, "Thank you, lady." The term had a deflating effect. Doreen smoked for a few seconds, then she said, "So how'd that tramp know? How'd he know to go to just the nice houses?"

The boy shrugged. "There's probably marks on the gatepost or under the letterbox or something. A circle means good for a handout and a circle with rising squiggles means good cook." The boy made an odd, crooked grin. "A circle with a crosshatch means a cranky lady or bad dog."

As the boy was leaving, Doreen said, "It was your mother who made you promise those things, wasn't it?"

The boy stopped. He took a quick glance at his companions as if to judge whether they might overhear. He returned a few steps and kept his voice low. "It wasn't my mother. It was the mother of a pal of mine. In Omaha. This was two years ago, just before him and me were going off to Oklahoma to start up with a harvesting crew. She made us both promise." The boy had a sheepish smile, as if he was trying to explain something unexplainable. "She was just my pal's mother, so I didn't think it would matter, but then I found it did."

The sun was low in the sky when Doreen returned to the Watermelon Days. Almost everyone was gone, but there were more flies than Doreen had ever before seen in one place. Edna Arlene was alone, slowly walking among picnic tables, eating pink remnants from discarded rinds. When she looked up and saw her mother, she dropped the rind at hand and ran over crying. Her chin was pink and dripping with juice and her cheeks were dirty with tears. "Momma," she said, and Doreen leaned down to take her into her arms. The girl held on as if for dear life. Doreen held and soothed her until she felt the dampness of her sleeve beneath Edna Arlene's buttocks, then she set her down at once. "You've wetted yourself," she said. She took her to the water fountain, and while the girl cried in humiliation took off her clothes and bathed her. The girl bawled and trembled uncontrollably. "Wheah wuh you?" she said. "Wheah wuh you?" and for a flashing instant Doreen wanted to say in a mimicking whisper, *Wheah wuh you? Wheah wuh you?*, but by this time there were onlookers, two women, not close by but within possible earshot. "I wasn't far," Doreen said. "I wasn't far at all. I was right over there all the time."

When they got home and opened the front door, the air was rich with frying meat. Monty stood at the stove tending wienerwurst and onion slices in a black skillet. Doreen in a flat voice said, "I thought Sundays were meatless." This referred to a belt-tightening strategy Monty himself had initiated.

"Well, we're celebrating," Monty said, turning. He was wearing an apron over his faded street clothes. "I've got some good news."

"Me too," Doreen said, "but you first."

But Monty Longbaugh's eyes were now fixed on his daughter, who stood whimpering in her damp blue dress. She held her wet underdrawers in front of her, pinched between two fingers. Her face was contorted from efforts not to weep. He said, "What happened to Edna?"

Doreen shrugged. "That's part of my good news. She ate too much melon and wetted herself so completely I had to clean her up in a public water fountain."

Monty Longbaugh looked at the girl and said, "Oh, sweetie."

Edna Arlene said, "Some boyth took Tootie." Her orange metal car.

Monty said, "I know where we can get another Tootie. I know just where." He turned off the stove and took her hand. "But right now let's find you some fresh clothes," he said sweetly, almost crooning. "Then we can come back and all of us have a wienerwurst sandwich." In her smallest voice, Edna Arlene asked if she could have a puddle of ketchup in the middle of the plate, and her father said, "Sure you can, sweetie. Smack dab in the middle."

In their absence, Doreen forked a sausage and several coils of fried onion onto a slab of bread, folded it, and ate it quickly over the sink, washed down with a room-temperature Schlitz. Then she went to the front porch and smoked. It was early evening, but still hot. She sat back in the shadows, watching boys pass by on bicycles, the occasional automobile, citizens on constitutional walks. From somewhere a man yelled, "Cyrus, where are you?" Doreen recrossed her legs and waited, for what she had no idea. She thought about going in for another Schlitz but didn't. The man called again for Cyrus.

Eventually Monty stepped onto the porch and quietly set the screen door closed behind him, which meant Edna Arlene was asleep. He settled into the chair beside Doreen. After a time, he said, "She seemed kind of shaky."

Doreen didn't speak until she'd finished her cigarette and

flicked the stubbed butt over the porch rail. She said, "Somebody whose voice I don't recognize keeps calling for somebody named Cyrus. Who do you suppose he is, this Cyrus?"

Monty wasn't interested in Cyrus. "Edna Arlene said you left and told her you'd be back in a little bit but you didn't come back."

Doreen hadn't looked at Monty since he'd come out, and she didn't now. In a flat, recitative voice, she said, "After I left Edna Arlene at the little melonfest, I thought I was going to come home, but instead I went to Wilkemeyer's for a lemon Coke and a magazine. Then I was going to come see you at the station but instead walked on to Foerster's Park to sit in the shade. While I was there I talked to a tramp who was sixteen and had taken an oath against all sin. After that I came home and read my *Photoplay* in the bathtub until I remembered Edna Arlene. I'd just added hot water and I wanted to finish reading the magazine, so I did, and then I went and got her." For Doreen, telling her husband this version of things in this voice provided a kind of repudiative satisfaction — it made her think of the childhood pleasure of carving a swear word into a park bench.

Monty Longbaugh said, "You went alone to Foerster's and talked to a tramp?"

Doreen had to laugh. "Why? Did the town council write up a rule against that?"

Sullenly Monty said, "They didn't have to." He waited a few seconds. "So how long was Edna Arlene alone at the watermelon festival?"

Doreen hadn't thought of it that way, and gave it a quick computation. Two hours, and then some. "A while," she said. "I wasn't keeping a logbook." Then she said, "Look, if what you're trying to point out is that I'm not the tip-toppest mother, don't bother. I can see my shortcomings." Another silence developed. Finally Doreen in a quieter voice said, "Which brings us to my own bit of news." She made an unhappy smile and kept her eyes forward. "It turns out I'm just a little bit pregnant."

She felt him staring at her, but she still didn't turn. "And that's not all the good news," she said. "It also turns out that our good citizens have run out of town the only abortionist who kept her kitchen clean."

A second or two passed, then he said, "Abortionist? What in God's name are you talking about, Doreen?"

She said, "I'm talking about the present situation as I see it."

Someone was again calling for Cyrus.

Monty said in a small voice, "Well, whose —" but Doreen cut him off. "It's yours, Monty. Don't worry your pretty little head about that."

"Then . . ." His voice trailed off.

She said, "I'm bad with one child, Monty. I'll be worse with two. And these aren't exactly halcyon days, if you've been paying attention. There's not a lot of loose change lying around."

Monty Longbaugh had turned from her and was staring out toward the street. "We'll be all right," he said, almost more to himself than to her.

A full minute of black silence passed. Then Doreen said, "Okay, so what's your big news then?"

Monty seemed jerked back from some distant place. "What?"

"When we came home you said you had some big news. You never said what."

In a low voice he said, "I didn't say it was big news, Doreen."

"I just figured it must be, what with your breaking out the wienies and all." *Wienies,* she knew, was a term her husband didn't like.

He said, "It seemed like bigger news at the time."

"Well, either you tell me your news or I'm going to walk down to the river to cool off." When he didn't speak, Doreen stood up.

"I won the new-slogan contest for the station," he said, flat-voiced. "'WBDY, your Midwest address for CBS.' Mr. Birney said the vote was almost unanimous. He said there was over five hundred entries."

Doreen said, "What did you win?"

"A treasury bond," he said. "Just a small one." Then he said, "It's for five dollars."

Doreen stepped around him and walked toward the street. At the sidewalk she stopped to look back. Their house faced west. The last slanting light turned the white fence and gateposts a buttery yellow. She looked at one gatepost and then the other. There, a few inches above the ground, was some penciling. She bent close. A circle with vapors rising. She looked up at Monty sitting perfectly still on the porch beyond the light, a hobo's idea of a good cook.

She began to walk.

He called after her. "Take a coat, Doreen."

She pretended not to hear. It wasn't cold and she didn't look pregnant. She took a meandering route to the river, waiting for dark. She felt the grip within her loosen. It was what she used to feel long ago after evenings in the Aldine, the unencumbering conversion of light to darkness, of known to unknown. She liked the river best when everything slipped up from darkness, the heavy rush of the water, its murmurings and shiftings, the woodsmoke from the cookfires attended by tramps standing in half-light, laughter without cheer, songs she knew were bawdy but could not quite hear. To the side of the pilings, a landing overlooked the river. A lamp fixed to the underside of the bridge's truss beam shone down on the overlook. When she paused a few moments to stand in that illumination with her hands folded below the waist and her back straight, she could sense a stillness coming over the camps, and feel herself pulling imaginations up out of darkness.

An hour or so after setting out, Doreen returned to the house. Monty sat waiting in the same place. He'd known she'd be back. She often walked; she always came home, usually with her spirits improved. She unlatched the gate. She seated herself on the porch next to him, and after perhaps a minute had gone by, she said, "Pretty down there tonight." Meaning the river.

He didn't speak. As they sat, the voice again called out for Cyrus.

Doreen in a low voice said, "I think maybe it's time Cyrus should get his little hindquarters home."

Monty's laugh was sudden and caught him by surprise. It changed his mood slightly, caused some mysterious ignition of hope. He said, "Maybe Cyrus is doing something real important," and was glad when Doreen threw in with a little laugh of her own.

"Real important like what?" she said.

In a low, loose voice Monty said, "Well, maybe Cyrus and somebody are conjugating a certain verb."

Doreen laughed easily and slid down just a bit in her chair. The tune came again to mind, and she hummed it for Monty, breaking in with the words she knew.

"Yeah," he said when she was done, "It's that song from the Happiness Boys."

How do you do? How do you do?
Gee, it's great to see all of you
I'm Billy Jones

I'm Ernie Hare
And we're a silly-looking pair,
How do you doodle doodle do?

He sang it slow tempo in his low pleasant voice, his radio voice. It was a novelty song all right, but the way he sang it, it didn't sound like one. "One more time," she said. Doreen closed her eyes and had a hard time opening them again. There was a handbill from Monty's singing-cowboy days. It presented his long, smooth, almost equine face framed top and bottom by a dark kerchief and a black Stetson, and that's who, turning toward him in the dark, he seemed now to be.

LEONARD MICHAELS

Nachman from Los Angeles

FROM THE NEW YORKER

IF NACHMAN WAS GIVEN fifteen cents too much in change, he'd walk half a mile back to the newsstand or grocery store to return the money. It was a compulsion — to make things right — that extended to his work in mathematics. He struggled with problems every day. When he solved them, he felt good, and he also felt that he was basically a good man. It was a grandiose sensation, even a mild form of lunacy. But Nachman wasn't smug. He had done something twenty years before, when he was a graduate student at UCLA, that had never felt right and that still tugged at his conscience. The memory of it came to him, virtually moment by moment, when he went to the post office or when he passed a certain kind of dark face in the street. And then Nachman would brood on what had happened.

It had begun when Nachman saw two men standing in front of the library on the UCLA campus. One was his friend Norbert, who had phoned the night before to make a date for coffee. Norbert hadn't mentioned that he was bringing someone, so Nachman was unprepared for the other man, a stranger. He had black hair and black eyes, a finely shaped nose, and a wide sensuous mouth. A Middle Eastern face, aristocratically handsome. Better-looking than a movie star, Nachman thought, but he felt no desire to meet him, only annoyance. Norbert should have warned Nachman, given him the chance to say yes or no. Nachman would have said no. He had the beginning of a cold sore in the middle of his upper lip. Nachman wasn't normally vain, but the stranger was not merely handsome. He was perfect. Comparisons are invidious,

Nachman thought, but that doesn't make them wrong. Compared with the stranger, Nachman was a gargoyle.

"Nachman, this is Prince Ali Massid from Persia," Norbert said, as if introducing the prince to a large audience and somehow congratulating himself at the same time. "The prince has a problem. I told him you could help and I mentioned your fee, which I said is in the neighborhood of a thousand bucks."

Nachman assumed that Norbert was joking, but the prince wasn't smiling. With modest restraint, the prince said, "Norbert thinks of me as an exotic fellow. He tells people I am from Persia or Jordan or Bahrain. I've lived mainly in Switzerland. I went to school in Zurich, where there were a dozen princes among my classmates. I have noble relations, but in America I am like everyone else. My name is Ali. How do you do, Nachman? It is a pleasure to meet you."

Nachman said, "Oh?"

The little word, "Oh," seemed embarrassing to Nachman. What did he mean by "Oh"? He added, "How do you do? I'm Nachman from Los Angeles."

Norbert said, "What is this, the UN? Switzerland, Persia, Jordan — who cares? Ali's problem is about a term paper. He'll explain it to you."

Norbert walked away, abandoning Nachman and Ali. Nachman grinned at Ali and shrugged, a gesture both sheepish and ingratiating. "I don't always know when Norbert is joking. I thought I was meeting him for coffee. He didn't mention anything else."

"I understand. Norbert was indiscreet. He is like a person at a séance who speaks beyond himself. He has no idea how these things are done."

What things? Nachman wondered.

Ali smiled in a knowing manner, and yet he seemed uncertain. The smile flashed and, before it was fully formed, vanished. "Norbert is in my city-planning class, and we talk about this and that. The other day I mentioned my problem, you see, and Norbert said that he had a friend who could write papers. He insisted that I meet his friend. So here I am — you know what I mean? — and here you are. I want to ask you to write a paper, you see."

"I see."

"I cannot write well, and I have done badly in one class, which is called Metaphysics. I should never have taken this class. I imagined it had to do with mysticism. Please don't laugh."

"Who's laughing?"

"It happens that this class has nothing to do with mysticism, only with great thinkers in metaphysics. I am not interested in metaphysics, you see."

Ali nodded his beautiful head as though he were saying yes, yes, providing a gentle obbligato to his soft voice, and his hands made small gestures, waving about and chasing each other in circles. It was distracting. Nachman wanted to say, "Stop doing that. Talk with your mouth." Only Ali's eyes remained still, holding Nachman's eyes persistently, intimately.

"But I don't write well about anything, not even about mysticism, you see, and I have no desire to try to write about metaphysics."

"Why don't you drop the class?"

"Good question. I should drop the class, but it's now too late. I was hoping the professor would eventually talk about mysticism. There are people, you know, who talk and talk and never come to the point. The professor is a decent man and he is doing his best, but if I fail I won't graduate. This would ruin my plans for work and travel. Your friend Norbert said that you would be sympathetic. He said that you could write about metaphysics."

"I don't know anything about metaphysics. I don't even know what it is. I'm a student in mathematics."

"Norbert said that you could write about anything. He was sincere."

Ali sounded as if he were sliding backward down a hill he had just struggled to climb. Nachman felt sympathy, because of Ali's looks, but also because he seemed to engage Nachman personally. It wasn't strictly correct to write a paper for someone, but Nachman already knew that he was willing to try.

"I'm sure Norbert was sincere," Nachman said. "Norbert wants to start a paper-writing business. Did he tell you that?"

"No. But I applaud this idea. Many students need papers. You will be partners with Norbert?"

"I never said that, but you have to let a friend talk. Talking is Norbert's way of life. He is always broke, but he doesn't think about getting a job. He schemes day and night. And he dollars me. You know the expression? 'Nachman, lend me a dollar.' He never pays me back. He had the idea about the paper-writing business. I don't need the money. I have a scholarship that covers books and living expenses."

"Even so, you must go into business with Norbert. Because of your friendship. Norbert loves you, and he had a splendid idea. Norbert brings you poor students like me, and you write the papers. He gets a percentage and soon he will owe you nothing. Will you do it? A thousand dollars."

"It's not a question of money. If I write a paper, it will be a good paper."

"So you will help me?"

"What was the assignment? Let me think about it."

"I need a paper on the metaphysics of Henri Bergson. About twenty pages. It's due in three weeks."

"Bergson writes about memory, doesn't he?"

"See, Nachman, you already know what to write. If a thousand dollars isn't enough, I'll pay more. Will you do it?"

"I don't know."

"Don't know if you will do it? Or if a thousand isn't enough?"

"One, I don't know. Two, I also don't know. The money is Norbert's department. Talk to him about the money."

"So we have a deal?"

With a fantastic white smile on his dark face, Ali put forth his hand. Reflexively, Nachman accepted it. A line had been crossed. Nachman hadn't noticed when he crossed it. Maybe Ali had moved the line so that, to Nachman's surprise, it now lay behind rather than in front of him. Ali's expression was deeply studious, as if he were reading Nachman's heart and finding reciprocity there, a flow of sympathy equivalent to his need. For Nachman the reciprocity was too rich in feeling and too poor in common sense. He felt set up, manipulated. But he'd shaken hands.

"I'll phone you," Ali said. He nodded goodbye. Nachman nodded too, and walked into the library, went to the card catalogue, and pulled out a drawer. He found cards with the name Henri Bergson printed on them, and he copied the titles of several books onto call slips.

Nachman's apartment was in the basement of a house in the Hollywood Hills, near Highland Avenue. It had a bedroom and a living room, a tiny kitchen, and low ceilings. It was cramped, but not unpleasant. The windows, approximately at ground level, looked down a steep hillside to a narrow winding street. Nachman could see ice plants, cacti, rosebushes, and pine trees.

Sitting at the kitchen table, he picked up a book by Henri Bergson. According to the jacket, Bergson had won a Nobel Prize in literature and had influenced the intellectual and spiritual life of the modern age. He was a French Jew who had intended to convert to Catholicism, but when the Nazis began rounding up Jews he decided not to convert. His story was heartbreaking, but irrelevant to Nachman from Los Angeles. To Nachman, religious institutions were frightening. He believed, so to speak, in mathematics.

That evening, when the phone rang, Nachman picked it up and shouted, "Norbert, are you out of your mind?"

"A thousand dollars, Nachman."

"Ali wants me to write a paper about Henri Bergson."

"Who is Henri Bergson?"

"You wouldn't be interested and I don't want to talk about him. If you think writing a paper is easy, you do it."

"Nachman, I once tried to keep a diary. What could be easier? Little girls keep diaries. Every night I opened my diary and I wrote 'Dear Diary.' The next thing I wrote was 'Goodnight.' Nothing comes to me. I'm a talker. Believe me, Nachman, I can talk with the best, but I can't write."

"What does that have to do with me, Norbert? You did a number on me."

"Come on, man. A thousand dollars. We'll take a trip to Baja, hang out on the beach. It'll be great."

Norbert's voice had a wheedling, begging tone. It was irritating, but Nachman forgave him. He knew that his friend needed money. Norbert carried books and went to classes, but wasn't a registered student because he couldn't pay his fees. Norbert's father refused to help. He'd been alienated when Norbert got a small tattoo on the side of his neck. Norbert's father, an eminent doctor, considered tattoos low class. Norbert still lived at home in Beverly Hills and drove one of the family cars, a Mercedes convertible. He paid for gas with his mother's credit card. But until the tattoo was removed he would receive no money. Now he wandered about campus with his tattoo. He didn't want to look for a job. He felt he could survive in an original manner. He had business ideas.

"I don't know anything about metaphysics," Nachman said.

"What do you have to know? It's all in a book. You read the book and copy out sentences and make up some bullshit. *Finito.* That's a paper. Do me a favor, Nachman. Look at a couple of books. Flip through the pages and you'll know all you need."

"I've been reading for hours."

"That's good, that's good."

"Norbert, have you ever read a book?"

"Ali told me you promised. He is very happy."

"I said I'd try. It's not for the money, and not because I want to go to Baja and hang out on a beach."

"I understand."

"I'm doing it because I like Ali. He's a nice guy."

"I feel the same way about him."

"After this, no more. I'll do this one time."

"You're okay, Nachman."

"You're an idiot, Norbert."

"I'm glad you feel that way. But don't get too sentimental about Ali and forget the money part. Ali is very rich, you know. I would write a paper for Ali every day, but I can't write. You should see Ali's girlfriend, by the way. Georgia Sweeny. You ever go to football games? She's a cheerleader. An incredible piece. I'd let her sit on my face, man."

Nachman hung up.

Norbert was shockingly vulgar. Nachman almost changed his mind about writing the paper, but then he remembered the look in Ali's eyes. It had had nothing to do with the cheerleader or with being rich. Nachman's resentment faded. He went back to the books and read through the night.

For the next three days, he did none of his own work. He read Henri Bergson.

At the end of the week, Ali phoned.

"How are you, Nachman?"

"Okay."

"That's wonderful news. Have you given some thought to the paper?"

"I've been reading."

"What do you mean, reading?"

"I can't just start to write. I'm in math. It's not like philosophy.

Math you do. Philosophy you speculate. Did you ever hear of Galois? He was a great mathematician. He fought a duel. The night before the duel, he went to his room and did math, because he might be killed in the duel and not have another chance."

"Was he killed?"

"Yes."

"What a pity. Well, I agree completely. You must read and speculate. But is it coming along?"

"Don't worry."

"I'm sorry if I sound worried. I am confident that you will write the paper. A good paper, too. Do you mind if I phone now and then?"

"Phone anytime," Nachman said.

He liked Ali's voice — the way feelings came first and sense followed modestly behind. It was consistent with Ali's looks. Nachman wanted to ask, jokingly, if Ali had a sister, but of course he couldn't without embarrassing both Ali and himself.

"Can I invite you to dinner?" Ali asked. "You can't speculate all the time. It will give us a chance to talk."

"Sure. Next week."

Nachman went back to the reading.

Metaphysics was words. Nachman had nothing against words, but as a mathematician, he kept trying to read through the words to the concepts. After a while he believed he understood a little. Bergson raised problems about indeterminate realities. He then offered solutions that seemed determinate. Mathematicians did that too, but they worked with mathematical objects, not messy speculations and feelings about experience. But then — My God, Nachman thought — metaphysics was something like calculus. Bergson himself didn't have much respect for mathematics. He thought it was a limited form of intelligence, a way of asserting sovereignty over the material world, but still, to Nachman's mind, Bergson was a kind of mathematician. He worked with words instead of equations, and arrived at an impressionistic calculus. It was inexact — the opposite of mathematics — but Bergson was a terrific writer; his writing was musical, not right, not wrong, just beautiful and strangely convincing.

By Monday of the second week, Nachman had read enough. He

would reread, and then start writing. He would show that Bergson's calculus was built into the rhythm and flow of his sentences. Like music, it was full of proposals and approximations, and it accumulated meaning, which it built into crescendos of truth.

Ali phoned.

Nachman said, "No, I haven't started, but I know what I'm going to say. I love this stuff. I'm glad I read it. Bergson is going to change my life."

"I'm glad to hear that. You are marvelous, Nachman. I think the writing will go quickly. Perhaps you will be finished by tomorrow, almost two weeks ahead of time. I never doubted that you would do it."

Ali's faith in Nachman was obviously phony. He was begging Nachman to start. Despite his assertions, Ali lacked confidence. More troubling was Ali's indifference to Nachman's enthusiasm. That he didn't care about metaphysics was all right, but he also didn't care that Nachman cared. Nachman's feelings were slightly hurt.

"It's only been a week, Ali. Tomorrow is too soon. I still have two weeks to write the paper. I could tell you what I'll say. Do you want to hear?"

"I am eager to hear what you will say. So we must have dinner. The telephone is inappropriate. At dinner you can tell me, and I can ask questions. How about tonight? We will eat and talk."

"I'm busy. I have my own classes to think about. My work."

Surprised by his own reproachful tone — was he objecting to a dinner invitation? — Nachman tried to undo its effect. "Tomorrow night, Ali. Would that be good for you?"

"Not only good, it will be a joy. I will pick you up. I have in mind dinner at Chez Monsieur. The one in Brentwood, of course, not Hollywood."

"I've never heard of Chez Monsieur in Brentwood or Hollywood. But no restaurant music. I can't talk if I have to hear restaurant music." Nachman sighed. He was being a critical beast. Couldn't he speak in a neutral way? "Oh, you decide, Ali. If you like restaurant music, I'll live with it."

"I'll tell the maître d' there must be no music. Also no people at tables near ours."

"Do you own the place?"

"Tomorrow night I will own the place. Have no fear. We will be able to converse. When I make the reservation, I will also discuss our meal with the maître d', so we will not have to talk to a waiter. What would you like, Nachman? I can recommend certain soups, and either fowl or fish. Chez Monsieur has never disappointed me in these categories. I don't want to risk ordering meat dishes. I've heard them praised many times by my relatives, but personally, I'd rather not experiment."

"Ali, please order anything you like."

"But this is for you, not me. I want you to enjoy the meal."

Ali's solicitousness made Nachman uncomfortable. He wasn't used to being treated with such concern. "I'll trust your judgment."

"And the wine?"

"The wine?"

"You would like me to decide on the wine?"

"If they run out of wine, I'll settle for orange soda."

"Orange soda. That's very funny. I'll come for you at eight. Give me your address."

Promptly at eight, Nachman stood outside the house. The limousine appeared one minute later. A door opened. Nachman saw that Ali was wearing a dinner jacket.

Nachman was wearing his old gray tweed jacket, jeans, and a white shirt open at the collar. He hadn't been able to find his tie. In jacket, shirt, jeans, and no tie, Nachman climbed into the limousine.

Ali greeted him in a jolly spirit. "As you see, Nachman, I'm incapable of defying convention," he said. "Not even in California, where defiance is the convention. I must tell you a story. It will make you laugh."

There was no uncertain smile. There was nothing apologetic or needy in his manner. The limousine went sliding down Highland Avenue into the thrill of the city's billion lights, and Ali talked cheerily. Nachman sank into the embrace of soft gray leather and studied the back of the driver's head. The limousine smelled good. It seemed to fly. Tinted windows made Nachman invisible to the street. Such privilege and sensuous pleasure. He felt suspicious of it, as if he were being made to believe that he liked something he didn't like and could never have.

Ali said, "One evening not long ago — this was after I came to America — when I first started to go out with Sweeny . . . Have I told you about Sweeny?"

"No."

"She is my girlfriend. Do you go to football games? You would know who she is."

"She plays football?"

Ali paused. He lost his storytelling momentum and seemed to sneer faintly, but the expression quickly changed, became a smile.

"Sweeny is a cheerleader."

Nachman had been unable to resist the joke. The limousine, Ali's dinner jacket, and Nachman's embarrassment at his inappropriate attire had made him feel — yes, he named it — like a jerk. Hence he became a comedian, keeping his dignity by sacrificing it.

"As I was saying, Nachman, I picked Sweeny up at her apartment and I arrived wearing jeans. She shrieked. *Why is Sweeny shrieking?* I asked myself. It was because my jeans had been ironed, you see. I laughed. I was being a good sport, laughing at myself. In my heart, I was bitterly ashamed. When she stopped shrieking, Sweeny was able to explain. Ironed jeans, you see, are horrifying. An American would know this, but I had just arrived and I had never before worn jeans. Naturally, I had had them ironed. Can you imagine my shame?"

Ali wanted to make Nachman feel that his outfit was all right, and Nachman appreciated Ali's intention, but the word *shame* was telling. Ali thought Nachman looked shameful.

The limousine stopped in front of a white stucco building. There was no sign, no window, no doorman. Ali led Nachman through an ordinary wooden door, and *voilà,* Chez Monsieur, a restaurant for those in the know. It was two rooms, one opening into the other, neither very large. The décor was subtly graded tones of gray and ivory. A panel of black marble, like a belt, swept around the rooms. A man appeared and shook hands with Ali, then led them through the first room, which had a bar and several tables occupied by men and women in beautiful evening clothes. Not one head turned to look at Nachman, despite his shameful attire. This crowd, Nachman thought, is as cool as the décor. In the other room, Nachman saw empty tables. All had cloths and plates and napkins, but only one was set with silverware and glasses. Ali had reserved the entire room.

Waiters came and went. Dishes were placed before Nachman, wine was poured, dishes were removed. Everything was done with speed and grace, in silence. Ali chattered happily from one course to the next, describing the preparation of the soup and the fish. He was playing the gracious host. Nachman glanced up now and then and said, "Good."

"I'm so pleased you like it," Ali said.

Nachman was beginning to feel resentful again. He disliked the feeling. It had surprised him repeatedly in the past few days. That afternoon, before meeting Ali, he had prepared with excitement to talk about the paper. But Ali was absorbed by the idea of himself as a man who knew where and how to eat. Nachman thought the restaurant seemed too old for Ali, who was in the prime of life, the lover of the mythical Georgia Sweeny. Did he really care so much about food? Nachman remembered Norbert's comment about Sweeny. It had shocked him, but it now seemed less vulgar than healthy.

They finished a bottle of wine. Another bottle was set on the table. Ali had signaled for it with a nod or a glance. Nachman hadn't noticed. He'd already had a lot to drink. His attention was diffuse. He forgot about the paper. Ali now talked about Sweeny. He wanted to spend some years in Tehran, but Sweeny refused to live with restrictions on how she could dress. It was a perplexity. The chador was peasant attire, but even at the higher levels some women found it pleasing. Ali laughed at the idea of Sweeny in a chador. After all, she appeared nearly naked before a hundred thousand people on Saturday afternoons. Nachman laughed too, though he wasn't sure why. Intermittently, he said things like "I see" and "Is that so?" He was hypnotized by pleasant boredom. It struck him that lots of people go through life without ever talking seriously about anything, let alone Bergson's metaphysics.

The table was cleared, the cloth swept clean and reset with fresh glasses and an ashtray. Ali ordered port. He settled back in his chair. A fine sheen of perspiration appeared below his dark eyes. The port arrived in a black bottle with a dull yellow label. It was held over a small flame and decanted. The taste was thick and sweet. Ali offered Nachman a cigar. Nachman didn't smoke, but he accepted it anyway. They clipped the ends. Ali held a cigarette lighter to Nachman's cigar and said, "Tell me, Nachman. It must be nearly finished, am I right?"

Nachman drew against the flame. He flourished the cigar and exhaled a stream of white smoke. "It's finished," he said, an air of superiority in his tone.

"Marvelous. I've been dying to hear about it."

"Hear about what?"

"The paper."

"Right. Well, it's coming along."

"You just said it was finished."

"I mean in my head. Writing is a tedious chore. I'll put it in the mail by Friday."

Ali reached into the inside pocket of his jacket and withdrew a small card. He handed it to Nachman. Ali's name, address, and telephone number were inscribed in brilliant black ink. He said, "Could you give me a sense of the paper?"

Nachman cleared his throat and brushed his napkin across his lips. Earlier, he'd been eager to talk about the paper. He had no heart for it now. Ali sensed Nachman's reluctance. His dark eyes enlarged by a tiny degree and his mouth shaped itself with feeling. A subtle swelling, almost a pout, appeared in the lower lip. Nachman suddenly felt an intense desire to give Ali a pleasure that was worth ten thousand dinners, the undying pleasure of an idea. Nachman decided to say everything, to make it felt.

"I will begin the paper with a discussion of Zeno's paradox, and then I will move swiftly to Leibniz's invention of calculus. Then, then comes the metaphysics, but a good deal, Ali, depends on how I imitate Bergson's musical style, particularly as I elucidate his idea of intuition. I could put it all in a simple logical progression, but the argument would be sterile, unnatural, and unconvincing. Don't misunderstand me. Bergson is not some kind of rhetorician, but it is critical to understand what he means when he talks about intuition, and for this you must see why his style, his music, his way of advancing an argument by a sort of layering —"

Ali interrupted. He said, "I told Sweeny about your extraordinary grasp of metaphysics."

Nachman hesitated. Ali raised an eyebrow and smiled. His expression intimated that, speaking man to man, Sweeny was relevant to metaphysics.

"She said that she would love to meet you."

"Me?" Nachman flushed, his mind filling with a confusion of hurt and rage.

"It isn't inconceivable that you would enjoy her company."

The remark had a provocative thrust.

"I don't object to meeting Sweeny."

"You sound reluctant, Nachman." Ali was teasingly ironic, with an edge of contempt.

"I wasn't thinking about meeting anyone."

"Sweeny would be the first to admit that she isn't an intellectual. Don't imagine otherwise. She has no pretensions of that sort. Perhaps you object to wasting time with people who aren't intellectuals."

"I know plenty of people who aren't intellectuals."

"Sweeny has other virtues. There is more to life than intellect."

"I'm not crazy about intellectuals. Norbert is my best friend and he is an idiot. What are Sweeny's other virtues?"

"She is a woman who exists for the eyes. Some things shouldn't be described in words; among them are women like Sweeny. It cannot be done without desecration. That's the reason for the chador. A man shouldn't share his woman with other men, but I will make an exception for you. The three of us will go out some evening. Do you like to dance?"

"I can't dance."

"Perhaps it isn't intellectual enough."

"I also can't swim. These things are related."

"How are they related?"

"I'm deficient in buoyancy, you know what I mean? To dance, you must be light on your feet. Buoyant, as in water."

"There is something heavy in your nature, Nachman."

"I can't even float, Ali. If I lie down in the water, I sink."

"Well, you don't have to dance. It would be enough to talk to Sweeny about metaphysics. She will be delirious with excitement. She has never met a man who could tell her about metaphysics."

The conversation was more like a game of Ping-Pong than a fight with knives, and yet the hostility was obvious. Ali didn't want to hear about the paper. Ali didn't want to hear about Bergson or metaphysics. He was flaunting Sweeny, even giving her to Nachman, though not quite as he had given him the superb dinner. Ali's generosity had been reduced to an insulting message. Nachman could have wine and port and a Cuban cigar. Some night he could dance with Sweeny. But with all the metaphysics in the world, he could never have a girlfriend like her.

There was no business with the check. There was no check. Ali simply stood and walked away from the table. Nachman followed him. The limousine was waiting. They climbed inside. It slipped away from the building and gained a dreamlike speed. Nachman felt an impulse to lean over the seat in front of him and look at the driver's face. But what if there was no face, only another back of a head?

He wondered how much Ali had paid for the dinner. The room at Chez Monsieur must have cost at least a few thousand dollars. And the dinner itself? Another two thousand? A bottle of wine could be five hundred. Nachman was guessing, but he couldn't be far off. Two bottles of wine, and then the port. There was also the tip.

"Ali, do you mind if I ask a question? How much did you tip the headwaiter and the others?"

"One doesn't tip servants."

Nachman should have known that waiters were servants. He was embarrassed, but he was also high, and he continued blithely thinking about the cost of dinner. Even if Ali didn't tip servants, he'd probably spent five thousand dollars, and not even the faintest shadow of a thought related to the cost of anything had appeared in his eyes. Nachman suddenly felt illuminated by a truth. Why not spend five thousand dollars on dinner? They had eaten well. The service had been magical. They had sipped port and puffed on their cigars, which must have cost a fortune, perhaps even the lives of the Cubans who smuggled them past the Coast Guard. Nachman felt that he was on the verge of grasping the complexities at the highest levels of the universe.

Ali looked splendid and triumphant. He had allowed Nachman to see him as a man who knows how to live and how to include a person like Nachman in the experience of living. He hadn't listened to anything about the paper. He'd made Nachman feel meaningless. The idea of himself as meaningless compared with Ali made Nachman chuckle.

Ali said, "What's funny?" He was smiling, ready to enjoy Nachman's funny thought.

"I've never had an evening like this. Thanks, Ali."

"We must do it again soon. With Sweeny."

Nachman was awakened the following day by the telephone. He slid out of bed and stood naked with the phone in his hand.

"I wish you'd been there, Norbert," he crowed. "You wouldn't believe how much Ali spent on dinner."

"How much?"

"Eleven, maybe twelve."

"Twelve hundred. Wow."

"Thousand."

There was silence.

Nachman continued, "As for the paper, by the end of the week it will be in the mail to Ali."

"That's fantastic, Nachman, but don't bother mailing it. I'll come pick it up. You've done enough."

Nachman detected a strain of reservation in Norbert's voice. What a person says isn't always what a person means. If Norbert were to say what he was thinking, fully and precisely, he would have to talk for an hour. And yet Nachman heard everything in that tiny reservation. Norbert was jealous. Ali had spent thousands on a dinner for Nachman. Norbert wanted to be the one to give the paper to Ali. Personally.

"No trouble, Norbert. Besides, I'm going out of town on Friday. My mother moved to San Diego. I have to see her new house. I'll stick the paper in the mail. When I return late Monday, Ali will have read the paper, and you'll have a thousand bucks."

"A percentage."

"Fifty percent."

"Too generous."

"I wouldn't have met Ali if not for you. What's money? It's soon spent. A friendship never. What a dinner."

"Nachman. I don't know what Ali spent, but it wasn't eleven thousand dollars, so don't jerk me off. I'm not stupid. I'll accept an agent's percentage. Say, twenty-five percent."

"Are we in business, Norbert? If we're in business, we're partners."

Nachman enjoyed the heat of his feeling long after he said goodbye.

On Friday he didn't leave town. He hadn't finished writing the paper, but that was only because he hadn't begun.

Ali phoned on Monday.

"It didn't arrive?" Nachman said. "I mailed it from my mother's house in San Diego. She had a nice house in Northridge but decided to sell it, because real estate in her neighborhood went way up in value. She said to sleep in Northridge was like snoring money away. I used the address on your card. Is it correct?"

"Why would I put the wrong address on my card?"

"You sound angry."

"I am not a person who feels anger. Do you think the postal service is reliable?"

"We will go to the post office and initiate a search."

"The paper is lost?"

"Ali, if the paper doesn't arrive tomorrow, we will go to the post office and you will see a man who feels anger."

"Okay. I appreciate your sincerity."

Nachman stayed home the next day waiting for the phone to ring. The phone didn't ring. Nachman began to wonder why not. He was tempted to phone Ali and ask whether the paper had arrived. He glanced at the phone repeatedly but didn't touch it.

Late in the afternoon, there was a soft knock at the door. Nachman hurried to open it. It was a girl. She was average height, blond, very pretty. If Nachman had had to describe her to the police ten minutes from then, he could have said only that. Average height, blond, very pretty. She wore a blue cardigan the color of her eyes. She had left the cardigan open, revealing a skimpy bright-yellow cheerleader's outfit.

She said, "Hi."

"Hi."

"Are you Nachman?"

"Yes."

"Do you know who I am?"

"He sent you?"

"Can I come in?"

Nachman stepped back. She walked in, glanced around the apartment, and said, "This isn't bad. I mean, for a basement apartment. The light is nice. It could be real dark in here, but it isn't."

"Have a seat," Nachman said.

She sat on Nachman's sofa, her purse in her lap, her posture rather prim. She smiled pleasantly at Nachman and said, "Ali doesn't know what he did or said to offend you. But he is sorry. He hopes you'll forgive him."

"He is sorry?"

"Yes, he is sorry. He wants the paper."

"The paper didn't arrive?"

"Is this happening, Nachman?"

"What are you talking about?"

"What do you think? What am I doing in your apartment? Isn't this crazy?" She laughed. Her expression became at once pathetic and self-mocking. "Two men who, as far as I can tell, aren't brain-damaged can't talk to each other plainly. And I'm late for cheer-leading practice."

"Go, then," Nachman said.

"Don't you think you owe Ali something? He took you to dinner. He intends to pay you a thousand bucks for the paper."

"It's in the mail."

"Nachman, come on, be nice. Ali has an embassy job. He can't leave the country until he graduates. The paper is his passport. Won't you give it to me?"

"It's in the mail."

"Even a rough draft would do."

"Let's go to the post office."

"Oh, please, Ali went yesterday. I've been there twice today. Look, I brought a tape recorder." She took it out of her purse and held it up. "See this little machine? You talk to it. Tonight I'll type up what you've said."

Sweeny was clearly trying to seem amusing, but her voice was importunate and rather teary, and then she bent forward, her face in her hands. "I'm not good at this," she said. "It happens all the time. We go for a drive and Ali gets lost, so he pulls over at a streetcorner and tells me to ask some guys for directions. Man, we're in the barrio. I don't want to ask those guys anything. He says, 'You're a blond girl. They will tell you whatever you want to know.'"

Nachman wanted to embrace her and say "There, there," but worried that she would misinterpret the gesture.

She said, "I'm in the middle of this, Nachman. I don't even know what's going on. Ali is being mean to me. All I know is it's your fault. Do you hate Ali? He's suffered so much in his life."

"Suffered? Ali is a prince, isn't he?"

"Ali descends from the Qajar dynasty. It was deposed in 1921 by the shah's father, Reza Shah. Ali's father owned villages, and beautiful gardens around Tehran. So much was taken away. They're still multimillionaires, but they have sad memories. Can you imagine how much they lost? It's really sad. Don't laugh. How can Ali think about schoolwork? You're laughing, Nachman. Please give me the paper. I'm really late for cheerleading practice."

"I'm sorry."

Sweeny was on her feet. She said, "I guess I should go," and gave her head a small, defeated shake. "Ali tells me you're a smart guy, but I don't believe you understand the simplest thing."

Nachman said, "Practice can wait. I'll tell you about the paper."

Sweeny pursed her lips and frowned. "All right."

"Let's start with the idea of time. Tick tock, tick tock. That's how we measure time. With a clock. Do you follow me?"

"Yes."

"Each tick is separate from each tock. Each is a distinct and static unit. Each tock and tick is a particle that does not endure. It is replaced by another particle."

"Man, this is intense." She grinned. Her mood had changed radically. She was playing the moron for him. Nachman felt charmed. He began to adore her a little bit.

"Each particle occupies the space occupied by the previous particle, or tick or tock. Do you follow me?"

"Like 'hickory dickory dock.'"

"But the point is that 'tick tock' is an abstraction. A spatial idea about measuring time. It's nothing at all like the real experience of time. Real experience is fluid, as in a melody — la-la-la. Real human experience is different from the idea of experience. When you make love, time doesn't exist, isn't that true?"

"The paper is about sex?" Her mouth dropped open with mock amazement, and Nachman wondered about what could never happen between them.

"No. Making love is an example. I just thought of it. The nursery rhyme 'hickory dickory dock' is funny. It's mechanical. Love isn't funny. Love is an example of what's real."

"I'll just turn on the tape recorder."

"Sit down."

Sweeny sat.

Nachman was startled. He hadn't intended to order her to sit. But he had, and she had obeyed. There she was, a pretty blond Sweeny sitting on his sofa. Nachman felt a surge of gratification. Also power. He blushed and turned away so that she wouldn't witness her effect on him.

"As I was saying," he said, now addressing the ceiling. "We measure time by dividing it into tick tock, and this has nothing to do with . . . Look, if you can measure a thing, then you are talking about something that can change. Anything that can change is subject to death. The opposite of death is not life, it's love. How can I talk to you about Bergson? This won't do, Sweeny."

"Why can't you talk to me?"

"No damn tape recorder."

Nachman's voice had become hoarse. He felt a warmth in his chest and face, as if something had blossomed within because of this girl with her naked thighs and short yellow skirt. What he felt was the most common thing in the world, but Nachman didn't think it was uninteresting. He was inclined to do something. What? He could sit down beside her. The rest would take care of itself.

"Why not?"

Nachman was jarred. The question returned him to himself. He didn't sit down beside her.

"Why not?" Nachman sighed. "I don't know why not. I suppose it's because I want you to understand me. I mean, I want you to get it. This is all about intuition, which is about real experience, where everything begins. You simply have to get it. I don't know what I mean. Maybe I don't mean anything." Raising his voice, Nachman said, "Please put the tape recorder away."

Sweeny stood up, aghast, the tape recorder in hand. She whispered, "Do you have something to say or not?"

Nachman shouldn't have said *please.* He should have ordered Sweeny to put the tape recorder away. He'd been cowardly, unsure of his power. Now he had no power. He reached for the tape recorder and drew it slowly from her hand. She let it go. In the gesture of release, Nachman felt their connection falter. Sweeny's eyes enlarged as if to make a sky, a vastness wherein Nachman felt minuscule. Nachman was only a dot of being that subsisted within her blue light. A dot; no Nachman at all beyond what Sweeny perceived. He'd never been looked at that way by a woman. His knees trembled. He couldn't think. She said, "I don't believe you are interested in talking to me," and started toward the door.

Nachman called, "Hey!"

Sweeny stopped and looked back at him. He held the tape recorder toward her. She took it and said, "Ali ought to have his head examined." An instant later, she was gone.

Nachman sat at his small kitchen table and looked out the window. He rarely had visitors in his apartment, and yet he had never felt so alone. As the light failed, the trees became darker. Soon they were black shapes against the pink-green glow of sunset. Just before twilight became full night, a ghostly-looking dog appeared, sniffing about amid the ice plants. It sensed Nachman's eyes and lifted its head to face him. Nachman realized that it was a coyote, not a dog. He could see a glistening patina of moonlight on the coyote's nose. Nachman's heart beat with excitement, and his eyesight sharpened. His neck muscles stiffened as he met the coyote's stare.

The next morning Nachman went to the post office. He asked about an envelope addressed to Prince Ali Massid. The clerk was unable to find it, and called for the supervisor. Nachman told the supervisor about the envelope. The supervisor said he would initiate a search. Nachman returned the next day. There was no envelope. There was nothing the next day either. Nachman went regularly to the post office in the weeks that followed. He asked Norbert to go with him a few times. Norbert trudged along sullenly at Nachman's side. There was hardly any conversation. Once Nachman asked in a soft voice, "Did you really need that tattoo?"

"Did Ali really need a paper?" Norbert said. He sounded unhappy.

Eventually Norbert stopped going to the post office, and Nachman went less and less frequently. Then he too stopped. But over the years he continued to remember Ali's handsome face and Sweeny's beseeching expression, and he remembered the supervisor who had looked at him suspiciously and asked with a skeptical tone, "You're sure you mailed it?" Nachman wasn't sure, but then he hardly even remembered having written the paper, not one word.

ARTHUR MILLER

Bulldog

FROM THE NEW YORKER

HE SAW this tiny ad in the paper: "Black Brindle Bull puppies, $3.00 each." He had something like ten dollars from his house-painting job, which he hadn't deposited yet, but they had never had a dog in the house. His father was taking a long nap when the idea crested in his mind, and his mother, in the middle of a bridge game when he asked her if it would be all right, shrugged absently and threw a card. He walked around the house trying to decide, and the feeling spread through him that he'd better hurry, before somebody else got the puppy first. In his mind, there was already one particular puppy that belonged to him — it was his puppy and the puppy knew it. He had no idea what a brindle bull looked like, but it sounded tough and wonderful. And he had the three dollars, though it soured him to think of spending it when they had such bad money worries, with his father gone bankrupt again. The tiny ad hadn't mentioned how many puppies there were. Maybe there were only two or three, which might be bought by this time.

The address was on Schermerhorn Street, which he had never heard of. He called, and a woman with a husky voice explained how to get there and on which line. He was coming from the Midwood section, and the elevated Culver line, so he would have to change at Church Avenue. He wrote everything down and read it all back to her. She still had the puppies, thank God. It took more than an hour, but the train was almost empty, this being Sunday, and with a breeze from its open wood-framed windows it was cooler than down in the street. Below in empty lots he could see old Italian women, their heads covered with red bandannas, bent over and loading their aprons with dandelions. His Italian school friends said they were for wine and salads. He remembered trying to eat one once when he was playing left field in the lot near his house, but it was bitter and salty as tears. The old wooden train, practically unloaded, rocked and clattered lightly through the hot afternoon. He passed above a block where men were standing in driveways watering their cars as though they were hot elephants. Dust floated pleasantly through the air.

The Schermerhorn Street neighborhood was a surprise, totally different from his own, in Midwood. The houses here were made of brownstone, and were not at all like the clapboard ones on his block, which had been put up only a few years before or, in the earliest cases, in the twenties. Even the sidewalks looked old, with big squares of stone instead of cement and bits of grass growing in the cracks between them. He could tell that Jews didn't live here, maybe because it was so quiet and unenergetic and not a soul was sitting outside to enjoy the sun. Lots of windows were wide open, with expressionless people leaning on their elbows and staring out, and cats stretched out on some of the sills, many of the women in their bras and the men in underwear trying to catch a breeze. Trickles of sweat were creeping down his back, not only from the heat but also because he realized now that he was the only one who wanted the dog, since his parents hadn't really had an opinion and his brother, who was older, had said, "What are you, crazy, spending your few dollars on a puppy? Who knows if it will be any good? And what are you going to feed it?" He thought bones, and his brother, who always knew what was right or wrong, yelled, "Bones! They have no teeth yet!" Well, maybe soup, he had mumbled. "Soup! You going to feed a puppy *soup*?" Suddenly he saw that he had arrived at the address. Standing there, he felt the bottom falling out, and he knew it was all a mistake, like one of his dreams or a lie that he had stupidly tried to defend as being real. His heart sped up and he felt he was blushing and walked on for half a block or so. He was the only one out, and people in a few of the windows were watching him on the empty street. But how could he go home after he had come so far? It seemed he'd been traveling for weeks or a year. And now to get back on the subway with nothing? Maybe he ought at least to get a look at the puppy, if the woman would let him. He had looked it up in the *Book of Knowledge,* where they had two full pages of dog pictures, and there had been a white English bulldog with bent front legs and teeth that stuck out from its lower jaw, and a little black-and-white Boston bull, and a long-nosed pit bull, but they had no picture of a brindle bull. When you came down to it, all he really knew about brindle bulls was that they would cost three dollars. But he had to at least get a look at him, his puppy, so he went back down the block and rang the basement doorbell, as the woman had told him to do. The sound was so loud it startled him, but he felt if he ran away and she came out in time to see him it would be even more embarrassing, so he stood there with sweat running down over his lip.

An inner door under the stoop opened, and a woman came out and looked at him through the dusty iron bars of the gate. She wore some kind of gown, light-pink silk, which she held together with one hand, and she had long black hair down to her shoulders. He didn't dare look directly into her face, so he couldn't tell exactly what she looked like, but he could feel her tension as she stood there behind her closed gate. He felt she could not imagine what he was doing ringing her bell, and he quickly asked if she was the one who'd put the ad in. Oh! Her manner changed right away, and she unlatched the gate and pulled it open. She was shorter than he and had a peculiar smell, like a mixture of milk and stale air. He followed her into the apartment, which was so dark he could hardly make out anything, but he could hear the high yapping of puppies. She had to yell to ask him where he lived and how old he was, and when he told her thirteen she clapped a hand over her mouth and said that he was very tall for his age, but he couldn't understand why this seemed to embarrass her, except that she may have thought he was fifteen, which people sometimes did. But even so. He followed her into the kitchen, at the back of the apartment, where finally he could see around him, now that he'd been out of the sun for a few minutes. In a large cardboard box that had been unevenly cut down to make it shallower he saw three puppies and their mother, who sat looking up at him with her tail moving slowly back and forth. He didn't think she looked like a bulldog, but he didn't dare say so. She was just a brown dog with flecks of black and a few stripes here and there, and the puppies were the same. He did like the way their little ears drooped, but he said to the woman that he had wanted to see the puppies but hadn't made up his mind yet. He really didn't know what to do next, so, in order not to seem as though he didn't appreciate the puppies, he asked if she would mind if he held one. She said that was all right and reached down into the box and lifted out two puppies and set them down on the blue linoleum. They didn't look like any bulldogs he had ever seen, but he was embarrassed to tell her that he didn't really want one. She picked one up and said, "Here," and put it on his lap.

He had never held a dog before and was afraid it would slide off, so he cradled it in his arms. It was hot on his skin and very soft and kind of disgusting in a thrilling way. It had gray eyes like tiny buttons. It troubled him that the *Book of Knowledge* hadn't had a picture of this kind of dog. A real bulldog was kind of tough and dangerous, but these were just brown dogs. He sat there on the arm of the green upholstered chair with the puppy on his lap, not knowing what to do next. The woman, meanwhile, had put herself next to him, and it felt like she had given his hair a pat, but he wasn't sure because he had very thick hair. The more seconds that ticked away, the less sure he was of what to do. Then she asked if he would like some water, and he said he would, and she went to the faucet and ran water, which gave him a chance to stand up and set the puppy back in the box. She came back to him holding the glass, and as he took it she let her gown fall open, showing her breasts like half-filled balloons, saying she couldn't believe he was only thirteen. He gulped the water and started to hand her back the glass, and she suddenly drew his head to her and kissed him. In all this time, for some reason, he hadn't been able to look into her face, and when he tried to now he couldn't see anything but a blur and hair. She reached down to him and a shivering started in the backs of his legs. It got sharper, until it was almost like the time he touched the live rim of a light socket while trying to remove a broken bulb. He would never be able to remember getting down on the carpet — he felt like a waterfall was smashing down on top of his head. He remembered getting inside her heat and his head banging and banging against the leg of her couch. He was almost at Church Avenue, where he had to change for the elevated Culver line, before realizing she hadn't taken his three dollars, and he couldn't recall agreeing to it but he had this small cardboard box on his lap with a puppy mewling inside. The scraping of nails on the cardboard sent chills up his back. The woman, as he remembered now, had cut two holes into the top of the box, and the puppy kept sticking his nose through them.

His mother jumped back when he untied the cord and the puppy pushed up and scrambled out, yapping. "What is he doing?" she yelled, with her hands in the air as though she were about to be attacked. By this time he'd lost his fear of the puppy and held him in his arms and let him lick his face, and seeing this his mother calmed down a bit. "Is he hungry?" she asked, and stood with her mouth slightly open, ready for anything, as he put the puppy on the floor again. He said the puppy might be hungry, but he thought he could eat only soft things, although his little teeth were as sharp as pins. She got out some soft cream cheese and put a little piece of it on the floor, but the puppy only sniffed at it and peed. "My God in heaven!" she yelled, and quickly got a piece of newspaper to blot it up with. When she bent over that way, he thought of the woman's heat and was ashamed and shook his head. Suddenly her name came to him — Lucille — which she had told him when they were on the floor. Just as he was slipping in, she had opened her eyes and said, "My name is Lucille." His mother brought out a bowl of last night's noodles and set it on the floor. The puppy raised his little paw and tipped the bowl over, spilling some of the chicken soup at the bottom. This he began to lick hungrily off the linoleum. "He likes chicken soup!" his mother yelled happily, and immediately decided he would most likely enjoy an egg and so put water on to boil. Somehow the puppy knew that she was the one to follow and walked behind her, back and forth, from the stove to the refrigerator. "He follows me!" his mother said, laughing happily.

On his way home from school the next day, he stopped at the hardware store and bought a puppy collar for seventy-five cents, and Mr. Schweckert threw in a piece of clothesline as a leash. Every night as he fell asleep, he brought out Lucille like something from a secret treasure box and wondered if he could dare phone her and maybe be with her again. The puppy, which he had named Rover, seemed to grow noticeably bigger every day, although he still showed no signs of looking like any bulldog. The boy's father thought Rover should live in the cellar, but it was very lonely down there and he would never stop yapping. "He misses his mother," his mother said, so every night the boy started him off on some rags in an old washbasket down there, and when he'd yapped enough the boy was allowed to bring him up and let him sleep on some rags in the kitchen, and everybody was thankful for the quiet. His mother tried to walk the puppy in the quiet street they lived on, but he kept tangling the rope around her ankles, and because she was afraid to hurt him she exhausted herself following him in all his zigzags. It didn't always happen, but many times when the boy looked at Rover he'd think of Lucille and could almost feel the heat again. He would sit on the porch steps stroking the puppy and think of her, the insides of her thighs. He still couldn't imagine her face, just her long black hair and her strong neck.

One day his mother baked a chocolate cake and set it to cool on the kitchen table. It was at least eight inches thick, and he knew it would be delicious. He was drawing a lot in those days, pictures of spoons and forks or cigarette packages or, occasionally, his mother's Chinese vase with the dragon on it, anything that had an interesting shape. So he put the cake on a chair next to the table and drew for a while and then got up and went outside for some reason and got involved with the tulips he had planted the previous fall, which were just now showing their tips. Then he decided to go look for a practically new baseball he had mislaid the previous summer and which he was sure, or pretty sure, must be down in the cellar in a cardboard box. He had never really got down to the bottom of that box, because he was always distracted by finding something he'd forgotten he had put in there. He had started down into the cellar from the outside entrance, under the back porch, when he noticed that the pear tree, which he had planted two years before, had what looked like a blossom on one of its slender branches. It amazed him, and he felt proud and successful. He had paid thirty-five cents for the tree on Court Street and thirty cents for an apple tree, which he planted about seven feet away, so as to be able to hang a hammock between them someday. They were still too thin and young, but maybe next year. He always loved to stare at the two trees, because he had planted them, and he felt they somehow knew he was looking at them, and even that they were looking back at him. The back yard ended at a ten-foot-high wooden fence that surrounded Erasmus Field, where the semi-pro and sandlot teams played on weekends, teams like the House of David and the Black

Yankees and the one with Satchel Paige, who was famous as one of the country's greatest pitchers except he was a Negro and couldn't play in the big leagues, obviously. The House of Davids all had long beards — he'd never understood why, but maybe they were Orthodox Jews, although they didn't look it. An extremely long foul shot over right field could drop a ball into the yard, and that was the ball it had occurred to him to search for, now that spring had come and the weather was warming up. In the basement, he found the box and was immediately surprised at how sharp his ice skates were, and recalled that he had once had a vise to clamp the skates side by side so that a stone could be rubbed on the blades. He pushed aside a torn fielder's glove, a hockey goalie's glove whose mate he knew had been lost, some pencil stubs and a package of crayons, and a little wooden man whose arms flapped up and down when you pulled a string. Then he heard the puppy yapping over his head, but it was not his usual sound — it was continuous and very sharp and loud. He ran upstairs and saw his mother coming down into the living room from the second floor, her dressing gown flying out behind her, a look of fear on her face. He could hear the scraping of the puppy's nails on the linoleum, and he rushed into the kitchen. The puppy was running around and around in a circle and sort of screaming, and the boy could see at once that his belly was swollen. The cake was on the floor, and most of it was gone. "My cake!" his mother screamed, and picked up the dish with the remains on it and held it up high as though to save it from the puppy, even though practically nothing was left. The boy tried to catch Rover, but he slipped away into the living room. His mother was behind him yelling, "The carpet!" Rover kept running, in wider circles now that he had more space, and foam was forming on his muzzle. "Call the police!" his mother yelled. Suddenly the puppy fell and lay on his side, gasping and making little squeaks with each breath. Since they had never had a dog and knew nothing about veterinarians, he looked in the phone book and found the ASPCA number and called them. Now he was afraid to touch Rover, because the puppy snapped at his hand when it got close and he had this foam on his mouth. When the van drew up in front of the house, the boy went outside and saw a young guy removing a little cage from the back. He told him that the dog had eaten practically a whole cake, but the man had no interest and came into the house and stood for a moment looking down at Rover, who was making little yips now but was still down on his side. The man dropped some netting over him, and when he slipped him into the cage, the puppy tried to get up and run. "What do you think is the matter with him?" his mother asked, her mouth turned down in revulsion, which the boy now felt in himself. "What's the matter with him is he ate a cake," the man said. Then he carried the cage out and slid it through the back door into the darkness of the van. "What will you do with him?" the boy asked. "You want him?" the man snapped. His mother was standing on the stoop now and overheard them. "We can't have him here," she called over, with fright and definiteness in her voice, and approached the young man. "We don't know how to keep a dog. Maybe somebody who knows how to keep him would want him." The young man nodded with no interest either way, got behind the wheel, and drove off.

The boy and his mother watched the van until it disappeared around the corner. Inside, the house was dead quiet again. He didn't have to worry anymore about Rover doing something on the carpets or chewing the furniture, or whether he had water or needed to eat. Rover had been the first thing he'd looked for on returning from school every day and on waking in the morning, and he had always worried that the dog might have done something to displease his mother or father. Now all that anxiety was gone, and with it the pleasure, and it was silent in the house.

He went back to the kitchen table and tried to think of something he could draw. A newspaper lay on one of the chairs, and he opened it and inside saw a Saks stocking ad showing a woman with a gown pulled aside to display her leg. He started copying it and thought of Lucille again. Could he possibly call her, he wondered, and do what they had done again? Except that she would surely ask about Rover, and he couldn't do anything but lie to her. He remembered how she had cuddled Rover in her arms and even kissed his nose. She had really loved that puppy. How could he tell her he was gone? Just sitting and thinking of her he was hardening up like a broom handle, and he suddenly thought what if he called her and said his family was thinking of having a second puppy to keep Rover company? But then he would have to pretend he still had Rover, which would mean two lies, and that was a little frightening. Not the lies so much as trying to remember, first, that he still had Rover, second, that he was serious about a second puppy, and third, the worst thing, that when he got up off Lucille he would have to say that unfortunately he couldn't actually take another puppy because . . . Why? The thought of all that lying exhausted him. Then he visualized being in her heat again and he thought his head would explode, and the idea came that when it was over she might insist on his taking another puppy. Force it on him. After all, she had not accepted his three dollars and Rover had been a sort of gift, he thought. It would be embarrassing to refuse another puppy, especially when he had supposedly come back to her for exactly that reason. He didn't dare go through all that and gave up the whole idea. But then the thought crept back again of her spreading apart on the floor the way she had, and he returned to searching for some reason he could give for not taking another puppy after he had supposedly come all the way across Brooklyn to get one. He could just see the look on her face on his turning down a puppy, the puzzlement or, worse, anger. Yes, she could very possibly get angry and see through him, realizing that all he had come for was to get into her and the rest of it was nonsense, and she might feel insulted. Maybe even slap him. What would he do then? He couldn't fight a grown woman. Then again, it now occurred to him that by this time she might well have sold the other two puppies, which at three dollars were pretty inexpensive. Then what? He began to wonder, suppose he just called her up and said he'd like to come over again and see her, without mentioning any puppies? He would have to tell only one lie, that he still had Rover and that the family all loved him and so on. He could easily remember that much. He went to the piano and played some chords, mostly in the dark bass, to calm himself. He didn't really know how to play, but he loved inventing chords and letting the vibrations shoot up his arms. He played, feeling as though something inside him had sort of shaken loose or collapsed altogether. He was different than he had ever been, not empty and clear anymore but weighted with secrets and his lies, some told and some untold, but all of it disgusting enough to set him slightly outside his family, in a place where he could watch them now, and watch himself with them. He tried to invent a melody with the right hand and find matching chords with the left. By sheer luck, he was hitting some beauties. It was really amazing how his chords were just slightly off, with a discordant edge but still in some way talking to the right-hand melody. His mother came into the room full of surprise and pleasure. "What's happening?" she called out in delight. She could play and sight-read music and had tried and failed to teach him, because, she believed, his ear was too good and he'd rather play what he heard than do the labor of reading notes. She came over to the piano and stood beside him, watching his hands. Amazed, wishing as always that he could be a genius, she laughed. "Are you making this up?" she almost yelled, as though they were side by side on a roller coaster. He could only nod, not daring to speak and maybe lose what he had somehow snatched out of the air, and he laughed with her because he was so completely happy that he had secretly changed, and unsure at the same time that he would ever be able to play like this again.

MEG MULLINS

The Rug

FROM THE IOWA REVIEW

USHMAN KHAN doesn't like tourists. It is June, though, and tourist season in New York, and as he double-parks his van outside Mrs. Roberts's apartment building, they are everywhere. Dressed in T-shirts and sandals, fancy cameras dangling from their necks, they run for awnings and bus stops as a hard rain begins to fall. Watching the chaos, Ushman smiles. He holds a newspaper over his head and, nearly dry, makes his way through the crowd.

Mrs. Roberts's maid comes to the door, letting Ushman into the cool, dark apartment. The girl is young and squat and motions for Ushman to follow her into the den. He has been here before and walks silently through the expansive apartment. In nearly every room there is a rug from his small showroom on Madison Avenue. They are comforting to him, each one reminding him of his wife. She is still in Tabriz, where she selects and commissions hand-knotted wool and embroidered kilim from the women in the bazaar and private workshops. Every month she ships two or three rugs to Ushman with a note that reads *Sell, Sell, Sell, Your Wife, Farak.*

Last year, when Mrs. Roberts and her husband moved across the park, she commissioned Ushman to cover all the floors in the new apartment. The job enabled Ushman to absorb the increase in the rent for his shop and nearly double his inventory, but he never liked being in Mrs. Roberts's apartment, with its high, echoing ceilings and drafty, perfumed air. And she had not been easy to please. Ushman must have hauled two dozen rugs into and out of the apartment after Mrs. Roberts had lived with them for a few days, only to find their colors too muted, too bright, or just wrong. On these occasions she seemed perversely pleased, as if she enjoyed finding flaws. And then, when Ushman rolled out the rug that was eventually to stay, Mrs. Roberts would appear in the doorway grimacing. Ushman, sweating and impatient, would ask, "Not this one, either?"

She'd bite her bottom lip and place both hands on her hips. Then, as she turned away, she'd say, without looking back, "It's perfect. It stays."

After he'd finished the project, Mrs. Roberts still kept in touch. Often she would come by the shop with a friend of hers, winking at Ushman as the other woman knelt to admire an expensive silk. Or she would call asking about a rug's origin or care or something else that Ushman knew was on the appraisal documents he'd given her. This persistence made him anxious, made him think that maybe she would try to say he had cheated her or been dishonest. So when Mrs. Roberts called this morning and asked him to come to the apartment right away, Ushman felt nothing but dread.

He waits for her in the den, watching the rain fall in a dark haze over the park. It is an unusually cold day for late June, and Ushman shivers, even in long sleeves. From a bedroom off the den, Mrs. Roberts appears just as Ushman is looking at his watch. "You have somewhere to be," she says, more of a statement than a question.

"Yes, hello. An appointment." Then, with a gesture he learned from his father, Ushman raises his eyebrows and extends his arms toward her as if he were displaying a precious object. "But what may I do for you?"

Mrs. Roberts looks past him, out the window. "It's a terrible day to be working, Ushman," she says.

Ushman lowers his eyes, fiddles with the keys in his pocket. "You're right, a terrible day," he says.

Mrs. Roberts looks down at her feet. "I have grown a distaste for this rug," she says, walking across the center of it. "I want another."

Ushman smiles, tries hard to hide his irritation. "It's been over three months, Mrs. Roberts. The trial period is finished. You own the rug now."

"Oh, for goodness sakes, I know that. I don't want a refund, Ushman. This one will go to my niece, I think." She turns to look at the closed door from which she came, listens for a moment, and then turns back to Ushman. "But," she says, pacing the length of the rug, "I wanted to remind you of the space so you could pick out an appropriate few and show them to me."

Ushman nods, but cannot contain his disapproval. The royal blue and red silk from Karaja truly belongs in the room. As any good rug should, it makes the room appear bigger, warmer, more textured. But, most important, it gives the room weight.

"This rug, though, in this room, I have never seen a more perfect match . . ." he begins.

Mrs. Roberts waves her hand at Ushman, signaling for quiet. She turns her head again toward the closed bedroom door. Ushman hears it just as she does — a dull thud, followed by a thin, scared voice calling for help. Mrs. Roberts places her hand on her chest, as if she is trying to keep something in place. Ushman watches her jog awkwardly to the door, pull it open wide, and kneel next to a figure who is lying, nearly motionless, on the floor by the bed. He must have fallen out, Ushman thinks, and is startled by this part of Mrs. Roberts's life. Mrs. Roberts lifts the man's head into her lap, but he is still calling for help, his voice full of panic.

"I'm here, I'm here," she says, and in one motion rings a small brass bell by the nightstand, turns on the oxygen compressor, and positions the mask over the man's nose and mouth. The young maid comes running through the den and kneels next to Mrs. Roberts.

Ushman watches the two women as they try to negotiate the man back into bed. Not sure if he should look away in respect for their privacy or eagerly volunteer to help, Ushman approaches quietly. Standing in the doorway, he sees that the man is white-haired, pale, wearing navy silk pajamas that are wrinkled and twisted around his long, thin frame.

"I think we need his help," the maid says, gesturing toward Ushman.

Mrs. Roberts looks up at Ushman, her face flushed and tense. Ushman steps forward.

"Please, then," she acquiesces, moving away from the man's head. "My husband," she says, absently watching Ushman slide his arms beneath the man's armpits and lift him back onto the bed, the maid holding his feet.

"Who's this?" Mr. Roberts says, pulling the oxygen mask away for a moment.

Mrs. Roberts strokes the hair away from his temples. "This is the rug merchant, sweetheart," she says quietly.

Mr. Roberts looks at Ushman, his thick white eyebrows raised in comprehension. "Ushman," he says, closing his eyes, a brief smile crossing his lips.

"That's right. Ushman is going to find us another beautiful rug, sweetheart," she says, carefully pronouncing her words.

Mrs. Roberts stands, showing Ushman out of the room. She is composed again and all business. "Until tomorrow, then," she says, smoothing her hair into place. Ushman nods and closes the door.

The rain passes momentarily, but the afternoon remains cold and dark. Ushman drives through the park, feeling as though he's seen something he shouldn't have. He had been grateful for Mrs. Roberts's formality, ushering him out quickly, the look in her eyes assuring him that she would not want to speak of this again, that he should not have been witness to any of it. Ushman thinks of her husband's body, so small and weightless in his arms, and shudders, realizing what he had been trusted with, if only for a moment.

Witnessing the interaction between Mrs. Roberts and her husband reminds Ushman of his last days in Tabriz, before he came to America. He would stand and watch, through the open bedroom door, hoping to catch a glimpse of Farak's hands as she bathed his mother. Silently stroking a washcloth up and down a limp leg, Farak would not acknowledge Ushman, even if she saw him. She would simply squeeze the dirty water out the open window and start on the other leg.

Ushman could not see his mother's face, and should not have even seen her feet, bare and twisted. But as Farak worked her hands over his mother's body, conceding gracefully to her sharp demands, Ushman kept watching, hoping for a look of clemency from Farak as she scrubbed and wiped.

He merges into traffic on the Queensboro Bridge, not having felt so alone since his first days in America. He was living with his cousin in Howard Beach, across the expressway from Kennedy Airport. The roar of jets startled him at first — picture frames and ashtrays buzzed against tabletops like the beginnings of an earthquake. On the small balcony the three rugs Farak had sent him were wrapped and huddled like refugees, and Ushman had wondered if coming to America was the right thing. He missed Farak and worried that he would not be successful.

Each day had been the same, and each day he cringed to think of Farak seeing him this way: riding the G train, passing out business cards that read *carpet merchant* under his name, passengers mistaking him for a beggar and offering him change. Then one day he sold the first kilim to an Italian man for five thousand dollars. He counted the hundreds over and over and wished he could take Farak to the big department store on Fifth Avenue and let her pick out a dress or some jewelry. He begged Farak to come then, to bring his invalid mother with her and move into the small apartment he'd found in Flatbush. But she told him she would not come until it was a better life than in Tabriz, where the money he sent them bought fresh vegetables, black-market stockings, and all his mother's medications. Then last year, when he'd done the job for Mrs. Roberts and could promise Farak a two-bedroom apartment, she'd told him she still wasn't sure that America was the place for her. Ushman was beginning to understand, though, that it was not the country but Ushman himself with whom she wasn't sure she belonged.

Yesterday Ushman brought a privately owned kilim to his shop, on inspection, and decided to buy it from the owner in Jackson Heights for twelve thousand dollars, knowing that it would bring nearly twenty in his shop. He has the cashier's check in his satchel and the rug in the back of his van. Ushman does not bargain. If the man will not accept the twelve thousand, he will give him back the rug and drive away.

As he turns the corner onto the man's block, Ushman notices a single ambulance, its lights flashing brightly against the dullness of the day. Approaching the house, he sees a stretcher being carried out of the same front door from which Ushman took the kilim yesterday. There is a figure on the stretcher, but it is covered by a thick white sheet. Ushman parks the van across the street and watches the paramedics load the stretcher, turn off the flashing lights, and drive away.

There is a young man standing in the yard next door, smoking a cigarette. Ushman gets out of his van and asks the man what has happened.

"Heart attack. Quick and brutal," he says, snapping his fingers loudly, "like that."

"I'm so very sorry," Ushman says, backing away.

The young man shrugs, stamps out his cigarette. "Didn't know the dude," he says, and turns to go inside.

Ushman sits in his van with both the money and the rug, his feet tingling. He cannot believe this turn of events, his good fortune. The man lived alone, probably has children living in another state who are just now being lifted by the gentle roar of a jet, and whose last concern will be a rug of which even their father didn't realize the value.

Impulsively, he drives away, back across the Queensboro Bridge, remembering the makeshift stretchers that his village had made out of the kilim, and how, that day two and a half years ago, he found Farak still crouched, afraid to move, and bloodied when he finally rode back into Tabriz. Feeling as though it is that day again, and as though now he might be able change that day's events, he drives even faster.

Farak had had her fifth miscarriage early that morning, just before the earthquake. When the house began to shudder Farak knelt in the bathroom doorway, already weeping, and watched the roof crumble on either side of her. Ushman's mother was in bed still, and her spine was crushed beneath the weight of the dirt roof.

Ushman had been in Karaja, a small mountain village near Tabriz that has no road access, where he ran another small workshop. He had two Karaja rugs tethered to his saddlebags and was descending the mountain when the camel stopped and sat down.

Hours later, when Ushman found his damaged house and saw Farak so bloody, he was afraid that she had been badly hurt. She was crying, though, and he knew that was a good sign. But as he held her to him, dragging her out of the rubble, he understood that beneath her whimpers she was saying, *The baby, the baby.*

Kneeling in front of a loom for all of her childhood, at the demand of Ushman's father, had misshapen Farak's pelvis so badly that doctors told her a baby's skull would be crushed if she attempted vaginal childbirth. Farak had accepted this fact, but so far she had not even been able to carry a fetus beyond the first trimester. Though the doctors could offer no medical explanation for this, Farak insisted it must have the same origin as her misshapen pelvis.

More than thirty-five thousand people were killed in the earthquake, and Ushman wanted to blame the miscarriage on it as well.

"No," Farak said as they stood over his mother's hospital bed, "it happened before the earthquake."

"We will try again," Ushman said, placing his hand on Farak's back.

"It's no good, Ushman. I will lose the baby each time. Don't make me lose another one to prove it to you," Farak said, and lowered her head.

Ushman spent the week before they brought his mother home from the hospital rebuilding his own roof and helping other men in the village begin the cleanup. Both of Ushman's workshops were destroyed, and four of his weavers were dead. There was no electricity, so Ushman spent the evenings lying in bed, hoping Farak would understand that the miscarriage was his sorrow too. But she would come in late from speaking with neighbor women in the courtyard, and take Ushman's cigarette from between his fingers, grinding it into the dirt floor without a word.

After the earthquake, Ushman decided to try his hand as a merchant. It would be costly for him to rebuild his workshops, and he knew the merchants sold the rugs in Tehran and Kashan for twice what they paid Ushman. Farak suggested America. "They are rich there. You can sell the kilim for four times what we get here."

They were finishing a dinner of lentil stew. Ushman looked up from his bowl. "I cannot go to America alone. I have responsibilities here."

"Your mother is my responsibility. You can go and I will send you the kilim each month."

"You will get cheated," Ushman said, and lifted the bowl to his face, pouring the remaining lentil broth down his throat.

"I will buy from the women. They will not cheat me."

"And when my mother dies you will come?" Ushman asked under his breath.

"Don't talk of that," Farak said, and cleared away their bowls. Three months later Ushman was sleeping on a mat in his cousin's apartment in Queens.

Last year in a letter from his mother, Ushman learned of the Turkish tailor from Tehran who had come to the house. His mother told Ushman that the tailor had visited Tabriz three times that fall, and that each time she could hear him and Farak talking in the dim courtyard while her own neck cramped up, long overdue for her nightly massage. Ushman wished his mother would die.

His store is nothing more than a desk, a chair, and a small stack of rugs. Ushman sets the stolen rug down near his desk, still unable to believe the afternoon's events. He unrolls the rug, though, and is startled by its beauty. It is a Kashan Ardabil Shrine design carpet, semi-antique, probably made in the late 1960s. Ushman notices that the first two stanzas of Shiraz's ghazal that were woven into the border of the original Ardabil Shrine carpet in 1539 are typed in English on a sheet of stationery and stitched to the back. Ushman reads over the verses, remembering having to learn them in grade school.

When he examined the rug last night, he knew immediately that it was authentic and had only checked the fibers to verify its age and condition. Now, in the daylight of his shop, the rug's golden red tones are brilliant. He does not regret his decision. In its weave, he sees the marketplace of Tabriz, the early days of his marriage, the easy way in which Farak would lay their dinner dishes, light a candle, steep his tea, all while holding his gaze across the kitchen table. Anyway, he tells himself, the Ardabil rug would have been sold for a fraction of its value at some early-morning estate sale where it could never mean as much to the buyer as it does to Ushman. The rug had been meant for him.

Excited and lonely, he cannot help himself from placing the call to Tabriz, though he knows it will wake her.

"Farak?" he says to the sleepy distant voice that picks up.

"Ushman, what has happened to you?"

He instinctively changes the story a little. "I got an Ardabil kilim for free today. I was going to give him twelve thousand for it, but . . . he left town, Farak. A twenty-thousand-dollar kilim, he leaves it behind." When she is silent, Ushman adds, "With me."

"Nothing is for free, Ushman."

"How is my mother?" Ushman replies.

"Like a sack of bones," Farak says. "If you sell the Shrine rug, perhaps you will then have enough money to pay a nurse." He has not expected this. Ushman is afraid his mother is right, that Farak has a lover in Tehran who will never make her touch another kilim as long as she lives. Perhaps it is only her duty that keeps her in Tabriz, caring for Ushman's invalid mother. But then, it is also her duty to love him, Ushman reasons, and he holds on to this thought as he invents other ways to spend the money.

"I could use a bigger shop," Ushman says, and Farak doesn't reply. "Or perhaps I could come for a visit, like a vacation."

"Since when is Tabriz a vacation spot, Ushman? Come if you have to, not for the scenery."

He does not know what to say, but is glad that he cannot see her eyes, which, even on the morning he left Tabriz for his long journey to America, had been full of blame. She had allowed him to lift her veil and place one kiss on her dry lips before she covered her face again. It was their only act of marital intimacy since the earthquake, as she was still in mourning for the lost baby.

Ushman had hoped for children, but he did not need them if he had Farak. Though he understood why she held him and his family's workshops responsible, he did not agree. The kilim had been good to Ushman and his family. The kilim had brought Farak to him the first time, and he was sure that the Ardabil would bring her back again.

Farak had been a weaver in Ushman's father's workshop in Tabriz from the time she was seven years old. Her small hands maneuvered the thread expertly, spinning and dying wool in the evening and weaving every day. When Ushman was thirteen he accompanied his father into the workshop to inspect the women's progress. Farak was squatting over the loom, her veil hanging low over her forehead, tying the tight little knots that Ushman's father and the merchants from Tehran raved about.

Outside one day soon after, Ushman spotted Farak sketching a design in the dirt. He approached, and told her she had lovely technique, the highest compliment Ushman had ever heard his father give to a woman. She was humbled by his attention and lowered her eyes in respect. His big feet, the toes clumsily hanging over the edge of each leather sandal, must have moved her, and she dared to let a smile spread beneath her veil before returning to her work.

When his father died, Ushman married Farak and took over the workshops. She continued to weave for him until the workshops were destroyed.

Unsure what to do, Ushman rolls the Ardabil rug back up and places it in a corner. If he sells the rug for what it's worth, he can afford to pay a nurse for the rest of his mother's life. He can almost afford it now. But the only reason for a nurse is to set Farak free, and Ushman, although he has not seen her for two years, cannot imagine that.

He never should have told Farak about the rug, Ushman thinks to himself. He must be more careful of his urges.

The next morning summer is back and the air is thick with humidity. The hot months are always slow, but Ushman has not even read the headlines of his morning paper before someone rings at the door. It is Mrs. Roberts, dressed in white linen. She waves at Ushman through the glass door, and he buzzes her in. He did not expect her until later; she has never come before noon.

She greets him as if she has not seen him in weeks. He bows, relieved that they are back on familiar territory. She looks around his shop, then to the window. He turns and follows her gaze across the street to a man and woman arguing over a taxicab.

"I must confess," she finally says, removing a compact from her handbag, "I'm a terrible voyeur. We live so high that people on the street become nothing more than movement. But here, you're so close to the street, it's really quite mesmerizing, isn't it?"

Mrs. Roberts looks at Ushman with strangely bright eyes. It makes him suspicious, this look. He watches as she drags the thick powder across her nose. There is something terribly ugly about her face, Ushman thinks, something wide and shameful. He has never liked the looks of American women. He thinks of Farak: her delicate face, strong hands, and the small feet which crossed the dirt floor of their bedroom at night in hushed strides.

Abruptly Mrs. Roberts closes her compact, turns away from the window, and looks around her at the few rugs hanging and the stack just behind her. Then Ushman sees her eyes rest on the Ardabil rug, rolled tightly in the corner. "So," she says with her face already in a firmly established smile, "is this the one you've found for me?"

He is not prepared for this, has not yet decided just what he will do with the rug. But he understands there is no way to deny her. She smiles insistently. Ushman pulls the rug into the middle of the room, then gives it a kick and watches as it unrolls. It has one large medallion in the center surrounded by a sea of delicate flowers. The threads are warm shades of red and gold.

Mrs. Roberts's smile fades into some sort of astonishment. Ushman is proud of the rug's effect.

"It is a replica of one of the Ardabil Shrine rugs, woven in the sixteenth century. The original is in the Victoria and Albert Museum in London."

"It's the most wonderful-looking thing I've ever seen," Mrs. Roberts says, kneeling to touch the rug. Ushman kneels next to her, pleased that she appreciates the rug's value. Whatever anxiety Ushman has around Mrs. Roberts, she also makes him feel proud of his shop, his rugs. He wishes that Farak could see the way Mrs. Roberts looks at the kilim, at him. Perhaps such an important woman's esteem would change the way Farak feels about Ushman and the rugs.

As Mrs. Roberts extends a hand to touch the Ardabil, Ushman notices the skin, wrinkled and spotted, her fingers beginning to bend under the force of swollen knuckles. He looks at her face, smooth and covered in a heavy layer of makeup, which, instead of giving her a more youthful appearance, Ushman thinks, makes her look raw and somehow vulnerable.

"What's this?" she asks, looking at the small yellowed paper stitched to the backside.

"It was woven into the original," Ushman says quietly.

She reads aloud, *"Except for your threshold, there is no refuge in this world for me; except for this door, there is no shelter for my head. When the enemy's sword is drawn, I throw down my shield in flight because I have no weapon except weeping and sighing."* She looks at Ushman. "It takes your breath away, doesn't it?"

"They are nice verses," Ushman says, and stands. "We studied them as children, but I was never very good in school."

"What is the price?" Mrs. Roberts suddenly asks, standing next to him, her eyes wide with desire.

Ushman panics. She is close to him, her lipstick melting into the wrinkles around her mouth, a hint of staleness creeping into her minty breath.

Impulsively, Ushman names his price. "Thirty thousand."

Mrs. Roberts's face relaxes into a frown, but she doesn't flinch.

She has never questioned Ushman's fairness. "Fine," she says, disappointed. Then, with a pleading in her voice, she asks, "Why do you make it so easy for me, Ushman?"

"What do you mean?" he says, astonished that she has agreed to such a high figure.

"You always find the perfect rug. This one, it's like nothing I could have even imagined."

"You are a good customer," Ushman says, turning his gold signet ring around and around. He is elated at the thought of so much money. He cannot believe that such wealth will not change Farak's mind. "I can see you love the rug," he says, feeling as though he is finally in control of his fortune.

Mrs. Roberts's face is quiet, though, even stern, and Ushman thinks maybe she's changed her mind. He tempers his own emotion, afraid of betraying himself. She looks at him hard.

"I thought that maybe it wouldn't even be for sale," she says quietly, turning away from Ushman and the rug. He intuits that something has happened, and he's sure that it must be his fault, but Ushman just stands looking at the ridges of her shoulder blades moving beneath her tunic as she shifts in distress. Though her eyes are clear and dry when she turns to face him again, Ushman begins to understand that wanting is its own luxury.

And suddenly Ushman is sure of what Mrs. Roberts is asking him to do. He feels generous, standing over the rug, the sun making his shop warm and bright. "You're right," Ushman begins, watching her face for a response, "it is special to my family." She raises her eyebrows, alert, encouraging. "I'll have to check with my wife, you know," he continues. "Give me a few days."

Mrs. Roberts seems quite pleased with this revelation, and her eyes fix on the rug with what Ushman recognizes as longing. They stand in silence for a moment, and then, with the artificial formality that occurs between two people aware of a lie, Ushman and Mrs. Roberts say their goodbyes.

The next evening Ushman sits in his bedroom with the window open, listening to his downstairs neighbor practice the clarinet. He is drinking coffee. At midnight he will call Farak, as he does each month. It will be morning there, his mother barking out requests from her bed. Ushman has no nostalgia for his mother. He knows that each time Farak lays her hands on the old woman's greasy skin, massaging a stiff neck or arm, Farak's disdain for him hardens. If his mother hadn't been crippled, he might have brought Farak to America with him and let the fresh flowers and hot dogs on streetcorners lull her into forgiveness. It would be easier to love him here, where the rumblings outside are planes and trucks and where doctors work miracles every day. She could watch the talk shows on TV and see that there are men much worse than he. And they could sit together in the shop on the rugs from their past and dream about the people on the street they wished they were, but would not know how to be.

Ushman still believes in that dream. He did not come to America to lose his wife; he came to make a better life for both of them. He knows that after he plays her game, Mrs. Roberts will give him thirty thousand for the rug, and with that money Ushman can give Farak what she wants.

In the dark, Ushman feels close to her and sure of himself. When it is time, he places the call. He can hear the radio in the background as Farak answers.

"Ushman," she says, "how are you?"

"I'm well. How are you?"

"Your mother has a bit of a cold, but she is fine. She is sleeping now."

"What are you listening to?"

"The Beatles. Semah loaned me the tape."

"I could send you some tapes. Elvis, too."

"That would be nice. What happened with the Ardabil rug, Ushman?"

"Oh. One of my customers is very interested, and she will even pay more than the rug is worth. She's a little crazy, Farak."

"Crazier than you and me?"

"She's very rich. She can have anything she wants."

"To be crazy like that, Ushman. Oh, if only we were crazy like that."

Ushman listens to Farak's lazy voice, the tinny *yeah, yeah, yeah* of the Beatles in the background. He thinks of Mrs. Roberts and how she had been able to make him understand that she wanted to lose sleep over the rug, to worry that she might not be able to have it for her own. He wants to tell Farak that they can be crazy like that;

that they will be rich and crazy together in America. But something stops him. Ushman longs to see Farak — her face, her hands, her eyes. If he could see her, maybe he could understand her too. Finally, in a hesitant voice, he asks what he's never before dared, what he realizes he's never known. "What is it that you want, Farak?"

The line is silent except for the music and Farak's quiet breathing. "It's not that easy, Ushman. Things just happen, no matter what you want."

"Tell me what's happened, then," Ushman says, his heart racing.

The music clicks off and Farak's voice quivers. "I'm carrying a baby again, Ushman."

Ushman listens to the little sobs she tries to muffle. "The Turk's?" he finally asks.

She doesn't say anything.

"You will lose it like the rest," Ushman spits into the phone. He can hear a small whine of pain and then there is quiet.

"Farak?" Ushman says, looking out his window, wondering why he ever left Tabriz.

She breathes heavily into the phone but does not respond. "There's your mother calling," Farak says finally, her voice weak. "I've got to get her pills, Ushman."

He calls her name again, but she hangs up.

Ushman's chest heaves in anger. He stands up, as if movement will calm the burning in his stomach where her words have nested. He stomps his feet and shakes his head, fighting back tears until he is worn out and the cries of a child next door startle him into silence.

He gets to the shop before the morning has really gotten started. Bicycles whir through the streets unhindered, and dogs pee on the corner of every mailbox and newsstand as their owners follow sleepily in sneakers and sweatpants. The Ardabil rug is in the center of the shop, its brilliant red and gold threads taunting Ushman.

In the quiet of night, when the breeze still blew hot through the window and Ushman's body was limp on the bed, he realized that the rug had tested him. How far, it had asked, would he go for Farak? He had been thinking of nothing but her and of the earthquake as he drove back into the city, the dead man's rug in the back of his van. He'd thought the rug was a stroke of luck. That's why he had played Mrs. Roberts's game and that's why he had called Farak to tell her of his find, and that's why he'd had the nerve to ask her what he never had before. And that stupid lucky feeling made him a bigger fool now than ever.

Looking at the rug, he thinks of the dead man, whose face he cannot even remember. He thinks of the thousands of knots, the fingers that tied them, fingers like Farak's that have stroked the skin of another man. He rolls up the rug, heaves it onto his shoulder, and stands on the avenue, waiting.

He knows their schedule, and the truck pulls up just as he's beginning to break a sweat. The streets are still empty, but they're at the end of their route and the truck is nearly full. He places the rug on top of the six trash bags and watches as the sanitation worker stops to inspect the rug.

"It's trash," Ushman says, "terrible stains. Worthless, really."

Wiping his brow, the man looks at Ushman, then at the rug again.

"Please," Ushman says, and raises his voice to a tone of urgency, "just take it."

The worker shrugs. "Whatever, guy," he says, and throws the Ardabil up and into the compactor. Ushman stands listening to the motor, and he imagines the rug crushed between eggshells and dirty diapers, its proud design soiled by other people's filth.

As he's sure she would, Mrs. Roberts shows up before noon, inquiring about the rug.

Ushman notices that she is bright, hopeful that the rug may continue to be out of her reach for a little longer. It makes Ushman angry, that to want something she can't have is an indulgence, a fantasy he was willing to humor. He no longer feels generous or kind, and so he turns to her with a somber face and says, "It's gone. You cannot covet it or pretend to covet it any longer."

"Oh," she says, shocked by his tone. "Well, I certainly didn't mean to offend you." She stands her ground and makes no move to leave.

"I am not playing," Ushman says. "It's really gone. So go try to find something else in this city that you can't have."

Mrs. Roberts smiles stiffly at Ushman. He remembers that she is older than her face looks; he remembers that her husband is at home, dying, and yet she's here, with him.

Having been up all night is beginning to make his head buzz, his knees feel loose. He sits down on the small stack of rugs, stretches his arms out the way his father taught him, and pleads, "What do you want?"

She doesn't answer but steps out of her shoes, walks across the room, and sits next to him. Exhausted, he lies down, turning his back to her. Without speaking, Mrs. Roberts moves her body close to Ushman, careful not to touch him. She lies there next to him, the way a wife would, in silence. Ushman closes his eyes. He thinks of the window on the other side of the room, and of the people who, seeing the two of them there, like lovers on the small pile of rugs, are undoubtedly longing to trade places.

ALICE MUNRO

Family Furnishings

FROM THE NEW YORKER

ALFRIDA. My father called her Freddie. The two of them were first cousins and lived for a while on adjoining farms. One day they were out in the fields of stubble playing with my father's dog, whose name was Mack. The sun was shining but did not melt the ice in the furrows. They stomped on the ice and enjoyed its crackle underfoot.

"How could you remember a thing like that?" my father said. "You made it up."

"I did not."

"You did so."

"I did not."

All of a sudden they heard bells pealing, whistles blowing. The town bell and the church bells were ringing. The factory whistles were blowing, in the town three miles away. The world had burst its seams for joy, and Mack tore out to the road, because he was sure a parade was coming. It was the end of the First World War.

Three times a week, we could read Alfrida's name in the paper. Just her first name — Alfrida. It was printed as if written by hand, a flowing fountain-pen signature. Round and About the Town, with Alfrida. The town mentioned was not the one close by but the city to the south, where Alfrida lived, and which my family visited perhaps once every two or three years.

> Now is the time for all you future June brides to start registering your preferences at the China Cabinet, and I must tell you that if I were a

> bride-to-be — which, alas, I am not — I might resist all the patterned dinner sets, exquisite as they are, and go for the pearly-white, the ultra-modern Rosenthal . . .
>
> Beauty treatments may come and beauty treatments may go, but the masks they slather on you at Fantine's Salon are guaranteed — speaking of brides — to make your skin bloom like orange blossoms. And to make the bride's mom, and the bride's aunts and, for all I know, her grandmom, feel as if they had just taken a dip in the Fountain of Youth.

You would never have expected Alfrida to write in this style, from the way she talked. She was also one of the people who wrote under the name of Flora Simpson on the Flora Simpson Housewives' Page. Women from all over the countryside believed that they were writing their letters to the plump woman with crimped gray hair and a forgiving smile who was pictured at the top of the page. But the truth — which I was not to tell — was that the notes responding to each of the letters were produced by Alfrida and a man she called Horse Henry, who also did the obituaries. The women who wrote in gave themselves such names as Morning Star and Lily of the Valley and Little Annie Rooney and Dishmop Queen. Some names were so popular that numbers had to be assigned to them — Goldilocks 1, Goldilocks 2, Goldilocks 3.

"Dear Morning Star," Alfrida or Horse Henry would write. "Eczema is a dreadful pest, especially in this hot weather we're having, and I hope that the baking soda does some good. Home treatments certainly ought to be respected, but it never hurts to seek out your doctor's advice. It's splendid to hear that your hubby is up and about again. It can't have been any fun with *both* of you under the weather."

In all the small towns of that part of Ontario, housewives who belonged to the Flora Simpson Club would hold an annual summer picnic. Flora Simpson always sent her special greetings but explained that there were just too many events for her to show up at all of them, and she did not like to make distinctions. Alfrida said that there had been talk of sending Horse Henry done up in a wig and pillow bosoms, or even Alfrida herself, leering like the witch of Babylon (not even she, at my parents' table, would quote the Bible accurately and say "whore"), with a ciggie-boo stuck to her lipstick. "But, oh," she said, "the paper would kill us. And anyway it would be too mean."

She always called her cigarettes "ciggie-boos." When I was fifteen or sixteen, she leaned across the table and asked, "How would you like a ciggie-boo too?" The meal was finished, and my father had started to roll his own. He shook his head.

I said thank you and let Alfrida light me a cigarette and smoked for the first time in front of my parents. They pretended that it was a great joke.

"Ah, will you look at your daughter?" my mother said to my father. She rolled her eyes and clapped her hands to her chest and spoke in an artificial, languishing voice. "I'm like to faint."

"Have to get the horsewhip out," my father said, half rising in his chair.

This moment was amazing. It was as if Alfrida had transformed us into new people. Ordinarily my mother would have said that she didn't like to see a woman smoke. And when she said in a certain tone that she didn't like something, it was as if she were drawing on a private source of wisdom, which was unassailable and almost sacred. It was when she reached for this tone, and the expression of listening to inner voices that accompanied it, that I particularly hated her.

As for my father, he had beaten me, in that very room, not with a horsewhip but with his belt, for running afoul of my mother's rules and wounding her feelings. Now it seemed that such beatings could occur only in another universe.

My parents had been put in a corner by Alfrida — and also by me — but they had responded so gamely and gracefully that it was really as if all three of us, my mother and my father and myself, had been lifted to a new level of ease and aplomb. In that instant, I could see them — particularly my mother — as being capable of a kind of lightheartedness that was hardly ever on view.

All thanks to Alfrida.

In my family, Alfrida was always referred to as a "career girl." This made her seem younger than my parents, though she was about the same age. She was also said to be a city person. And "the city," when it was spoken of in this way, meant the one where she lived and worked. But it meant something else as well. It was not just a distinct configuration of buildings and sidewalks and streetcar lines, or even a crowding together of people; it was something more abstract, something like a hive of bees — stormy but organized, sometimes dangerous. Most people went into such a place only when they had to and were glad when they got out. Some, however, were attracted to it — as Alfrida must have been, long ago, and as I was now, puffing on my cigarette and trying to hold it in a nonchalant way, although it seemed to have grown to the size of a baseball bat between my fingers.

My family did not have a regular social life — friends did not come to the house for dinner, let alone for parties. It was a matter of class, maybe. The parents of the boy I married — about five years after this scene at the dinner table — invited people who were not related to them to dinner, and they went to afternoon parties, which they spoke of, unselfconsciously, as cocktail parties. Theirs was a life I had read of in magazines, and it seemed to me to place my in-laws in a world of storybook privilege.

What our family did was put boards in the dining room table two or three times a year in order to entertain my grandmother and my aunts — my father's two older sisters — and their husbands. We did this at Christmas or at Thanksgiving, when it was our turn, and perhaps also when a relative from another part of the province showed up on a visit.

My mother and I would start preparing for such dinners a couple of days ahead. We ironed the good tablecloth, which was as heavy as a bed quilt, and washed the good dishes, which had been sitting in the china cabinet collecting dust, and wiped down the legs of the dining room chairs, as well as making the jellied salads, the pies and cakes, that had to accompany the roast turkey or baked ham and bowls of vegetables. There had to be far too much to eat, and most of the conversation at the table concerned the food, with the company saying how good it was and being urged to have more, and saying that they couldn't, they were stuffed, and then relenting, taking just a little more, and saying that they shouldn't, they were ready to bust. And dessert still to come.

There was hardly any idea of general conversation, and in fact there was a feeling that conversation that passed beyond certain limits might be a disruption, a form of showing off. My mother's understanding of the limits was not reliable, and she sometimes couldn't wait out the pauses or honor the common aversion to follow-up. So when somebody said, "Seen Harley upstreet yesterday. Harley Cook," she was liable to say, perhaps, "Do you think a man like Harley is a confirmed bachelor? Or he just hasn't met the right person?" As if, when you mentioned seeing Harley Cook, you were bound to have something further to say about him, something *interesting.*

Then there might be a silence, not because the people at the table meant to be rude but because they were flummoxed. Until my father said, with embarrassment and oblique reproach, "He seems to get on all right by hisself." (If his family had not been present, he would more likely have said "himself.")

And everybody else went on cutting, spooning, swallowing, in the glare of the fresh tablecloth and the bright light pouring in through the newly washed windows. These dinners were always in the middle of the day.

The people at that table were quite capable of talk. Washing and drying the dishes in the kitchen, the aunts would talk about who had a tumor, a septic throat, a bad mess of boils. They would tell how their own digestions, kidneys, nerves were functioning. Intimate bodily matters never seemed to be so out of place, or suspect, as the mention of a fact read in a magazine, or an item in the news, or anything, really, that was not material close at hand. Meanwhile, resting on the porch, or during a brief walk out to look at the crops, the aunts' husbands would pass on the information that somebody was in a tight spot with the bank, or still owed money on an expensive piece of machinery, or had invested in a bull that was a disappointment on the job.

It could have been that they felt clamped down by the formality of our dining room, the presence of bread-and-butter plates and dessert spoons, when it was the custom to put a piece of pie right onto a dinner plate that had been cleaned up with bread. (It would have been an offense, however, for us not to set things out in this proper way, and in their own houses, on like occasions, they would put their guests through the same paces.) It may have been just that eating was one thing and talking was something else.

When Alfrida came, it was another story altogether. The good cloth would be spread and the good dishes would be out. My mother would have gone to a lot of trouble with the food, and she'd be nervous about the results — probably she would have abandoned the usual turkey and stuffing and mashed potatoes and made something like chicken salad surrounded by mounds of molded rice with cut-up pimentos, and this would be followed by a dessert involving gelatin and egg whites and whipped cream which took a long, nerve-racking time to set because we had no refrigerator and it had to be chilled on the cellar floor. But the constraint, the required pall over the table, was quite absent. Alfrida not only accepted second helpings, she asked for them. And she did this almost absent-mindedly, tossing off her compliments in the same way, as if the food, the eating of the food, were a secondary though agreeable thing, and she were really there to talk and make other people talk, and anything you wanted to talk about — almost anything — would be fine.

She always visited in summer, and usually she wore some sort of striped, silky sundress, with a halter top that left her back bare. Her back was not pretty, being sprinkled with little dark moles, and her shoulders were bony and her chest was nearly flat. My father would always remark on how much she could eat and remain thin. (One thing that was not considered out of place in our family was direct comment, to somebody's face, about fatness or skinniness or pallor or ruddiness or baldness.)

Alfrida's dark hair was done up in rolls above her face and at the sides, in the style of the time. Her skin was freckled and netted with fine wrinkles, and her mouth wide, the lower lip rather thick, almost drooping, painted with a hearty lipstick that left a smear on her teacup and water tumbler. When her mouth was opened wide — as it nearly always was, talking or laughing — you could see that some of her teeth had been pulled, at the back. Nobody would have said that she was good-looking — any woman over twenty-five seemed to me to have pretty well passed beyond the possibility of being good-looking, or at least to have lost the right to be so, and perhaps even the desire — but she was fervent and dashing and she lit up a room.

Alfrida talked to my father about things that were happening in the world, about politics. My father read the paper, he listened to the radio, and he had opinions about these things but rarely got a chance to talk about them. The aunts' husbands had opinions too, but theirs were brief and unvaried and expressed an everlasting distrust of all public figures and particularly all foreigners, so that most of the time all that could be got out of them was grunts of dismissal. My grandmother was deaf — nobody could tell how much she knew or what she thought about anything — and the aunts themselves seemed fairly proud of how much they didn't know or didn't have to pay attention to. My mother had been a schoolteacher, and she could readily have pointed out all the countries of Europe on the map, but she saw the world through a personal haze, with the British Empire and the royal family looming large and everything else diminished, thrown into a jumble heap that was easy for her to disregard.

Alfrida's views were not really so far removed from the uncles'. Or so it appeared. But instead of grunting and letting the subject go, she gave her hooting laugh and told stories about prime ministers and the American president and John L. Lewis and the mayor of Montreal — stories in which they all came out badly. She told stories about the royal family too, but there she made a distinction between the good ones, like the king and queen and the beautiful duchess of Kent, and the dreadful ones, like the Windsors and old King Eddy, who, she implied, had a certain disease and had marked his wife's neck by trying to strangle her, which was why she always had to wear her pearls. This distinction coincided pretty well with one my mother made but seldom spoke of, so she did not object — though the reference to syphilis made her wince.

I smiled at it, knowingly, and with a foolhardy composure.

Alfrida called the Russians funny names. Mikoyan-sky. Uncle Joe-sky. She believed that they were pulling the wool over everybody's eyes, and that the United Nations was a farce that would never work, and that Japan would rise again and should have been finished off when there was the chance. She didn't trust Quebec, either. Or the pope, whom she called "the poop." And there was a problem for her with Senator McCarthy — she would have liked to be on his side, but his being a Catholic was a stumbling block.

Sometimes it seemed as if she was putting on a show — a display, maybe, to tease my father. To rile him up, as he himself would have said, to get his goat. But not because she disliked him or even wanted to make him uncomfortable. Quite the opposite. She seemed to be tormenting him almost as young girls torment boys at school, where arguments are a peculiar delight to both sides and insults are taken as flattery. My father argued with her always in a mild steady voice, and yet it was clear that he too had the intention of goading her on. Sometimes he would do a turnaround and say that maybe she was right — that with her work on the newspaper, she must have sources of information that he didn't have. "You've put me straight," he'd say. "If I had any sense, I'd be obliged to you." And she'd say, "Don't give me that load of baloney."

"You two," my mother said, in mock despair and perhaps in real exhaustion, and Alfrida told her to go and have a lie-down — she deserved it after this splendiferous dinner, and Alfrida and I would manage the dishes. My mother was subject to a tremor in her right arm, a stiffness in her fingers, that she believed came when she got overtired.

While we worked in the kitchen, Alfrida talked to me about celebrities — actors, even minor movie stars, who had made stage appearances in the city where she lived. In a lowered voice broken by wildly disrespectful laughter, she told me rumors about their bad behavior, the private scandals that had never made it into the magazines. She mentioned queers, artificial bosoms, household triangles — all things I had found hints of in my reading but felt giddy to hear about, even at third or fourth hand, in real life.

Alfrida's teeth always got my attention, so that even during these confidential recitals, I sometimes lost track of what was being said. Her front teeth were all of a slightly different color, no two alike. Some tended toward shades of dark ivory; others were opalescent, shadowed with lilac, and gave out fish-flashes of silver rims, occasionally a gleam of gold. People's teeth then seldom made such a solid, handsome show as they do now — unless they were false — but Alfrida's were unusual in their individuality, clear separation, and size. When Alfrida let out some jibe that was especially, knowingly outrageous, they seemed to leap to the fore like jolly spear fighters.

"She always did have trouble with her teeth," the aunts said. "She had that abscess, remember — the poison went all through her body."

How like them, I thought, to pick on any weakness in a superior person, to zoom in on any physical distress.

"Why doesn't she just have them all out and be done with it?" they said.

"Likely she couldn't afford it," my grandmother said, surprising everybody, as she sometimes did, by showing that she had been keeping up with a conversation all along.

And surprising me with the new, everyday sort of light this shone on Alfrida's life. I had believed that Alfrida was rich, at least in comparison with the rest of the family. She lived in an apartment — I had never seen it, but to me that fact conveyed at least the idea of a very civilized life — and she wore clothes that were not homemade, and her shoes were not Oxfords like the shoes of practically all the other grownup women I knew; they were sandals made of bright strips of plastic. It was hard to know whether my grandmother was simply living in the past, when getting your teeth done was the solemn, crowning expense of a lifetime, or whether she really knew things about Alfrida's life that I would not have guessed.

The rest of the family was never present when Alfrida had dinner at our house. She did go to see my grandmother, who was her aunt, her mother's sister, and who lived alternately with one or the other of my aunts. Alfrida went to whichever house my grandmother was staying in at the time, but the meal she took was always with us. Usually she came to our house first and visited awhile, and then gathered herself up, as if reluctantly, to make the other visit. When she came back later and we sat down to eat, nothing derogatory was said outright, against the aunts and their husbands, and certainly nothing disrespectful about my grandmother. In fact, it was the way that Alfrida spoke of my grandmother — with a sudden sobriety and concern in her voice (what about her blood pressure, had she been to the doctor lately?) — that made me aware of the difference, of the coolness or restraint with which she asked after the others. There would be a similar restraint in my mother's reply, and an extra gravity in my father's — almost a caricature of gravity — that showed how they all agreed about something they could not say.

On the day I smoked the cigarette, Alfrida decided to take this routine a bit further, and she said somberly, "How about Asa then? Is he still as much of a conversation-grabber as ever?"

My father shook his head sadly, as if the thought of his brother-in-law's garrulousness must weigh us all down.

"Indeed," he said. "He is indeed."

Then I took my chance.

"Looks like the roundworms have got into the hogs," I said. "Yup."

Except for the "yup," this was just what my uncle had recently said, and he had said it at this very table, being overcome by an uncharacteristic need to break the silence or to pass on something important that had just come to mind. And I said it with just his stately grunts, his innocent solemnity.

Alfrida gave a great approving laugh, showing her festive teeth.

My father bent over his plate, as if to hide how he was laughing too, but of course not really hiding it, and my mother shook her head, biting her lips together, smiling. I felt a keen triumph. Nothing was said to put me in my place, no reproof for what was sometimes called my "sarcasm," my "being smart." The word "smart," when it was used about me, in the family, might mean intelligent, in which case it was used rather grudgingly — "Oh, she's smart enough some ways" — or it might be used to mean pushy, attention-seeking, obnoxious. *Don't be so smart.*

Sometimes my mother said, "You have a cruel tongue."

Sometimes — this was a great deal worse — my father was disgusted with me. "What makes you think you have the right to run down decent people?"

This day nothing like that happened. I seemed to be as free as a visitor at the table, almost as free as Alfrida, and flourishing under the banner of my own personality.

But a gap was about to open, and perhaps that was the last time, the very last time, that Alfrida sat at our table. Christmas cards continued to be exchanged, possibly even letters — as long as my mother could manage a pen — and we still saw Alfrida's name in the paper, but I cannot recall any visits during the last couple of years I lived at home.

It may have been that Alfrida had asked if she could bring her friend and been told that she could not. If she was already living with him, that would have been one reason, and if he was the same man she lived with later, the fact that he was married would have been another. My parents would have been united in this. My mother had a horror of irregular sex or flaunted sex — of any sex, you might say, for the proper, married kind was not acknowledged at all — and my father too judged these matters strictly, at that time in his life. He might have had a special objection also to any man who could get a hold over Alfrida. She would have made herself cheap, in my parents' eyes.

But she may not have asked at all; she may have known enough not to. During the time of those lively visits there may have been no man in her life, and then, when there was one, her attention may have shifted entirely.

Or she may have been wary of the special atmosphere of a household where there is a sick person who will go on getting sicker and never get better. Which was the case with my mother, whose odd symptoms joined together, and turned a corner, and instead of an inconvenience became her whole destiny.

"The poor thing," the aunts said.

And as my mother was changed from a mother into a stricken presence around the house, the other, formerly so restricted females in the family seemed to gain some little liveliness and increased competence in the world. My grandmother got herself a hearing aid — something nobody would have suggested to her. One of the aunts' husbands — not Asa, but the one named Irvine — died, and the aunt who had been married to him learned to drive a car and got a job doing alterations in a clothing store and no longer wore a hairnet.

They called in to see my mother, and always saw the same thing — that the one who had been better-looking, who had never quite let them forget that she was a schoolteacher, was growing month by month slower and stiffer in the movements of her limbs and thicker and more importunate in her speech, and that nothing was going to help her.

They told me to take good care of her. "She's your mother," they reminded me. "The poor thing."

Alfrida would not have been able to say those things, and she might not have been able to find anything to say in their place. Her not coming to see us was all right with me. I didn't want people coming. I had no time for them. I had become a furious housekeeper, waxing the floors and ironing even the dishtowels, and it was all done to keep some sort of disgrace (my mother's deterioration seemed to be a unique disgrace that infected us all) at bay. It was done to make it seem as if I lived in a normal family in an ordinary house, but the moment somebody stepped in our door and saw my mother they saw that this was not so and they pitied us. A thing I could not stand.

*

I won a scholarship, and I didn't stay home to take care of my mother or of anything else. The college I went to was in the city where Alfrida lived. After a few months she invited me to supper, but I couldn't go, because I worked every evening of the week except Sundays — in the city library, downtown, and in the college library, both of which stayed open until nine o'clock. Sometime later, during the winter, Alfrida asked me again, and this time the invitation was for a Sunday. I told her that I couldn't come because I was going to a concert.

"Oh — a date?" she said, and I said yes, but at the time it wasn't true. I would go to the free Sunday concerts in the college auditorium, with another girl, or two or three other girls, for something to do and in the faint hope of meeting some boys.

"Well, you'll have to bring him around sometime," Alfrida said. "I'm dying to meet him."

Toward the end of the year I did have someone to bring, and I had actually met him at a concert. But I would never have brought him to meet Alfrida. I would never have brought any of my new friends to meet her. My new friends were people who said, "Have you read *Look Homeward, Angel*? Oh, you have to read that. Have you read *Buddenbrooks*?" They were people with whom I went to see *Forbidden Games* and *Les Enfants du Paradis* when the Film Society brought them in. The boy I went out with, and later became engaged to, had taken me to the Music Building, where you could listen to records at lunch hour. He introduced me to Gounod, and because of Gounod I loved opera, and because of opera I loved Mozart.

When Alfrida left a message at my rooming house, asking me to call back, I never did. After that she didn't call again.

She still wrote for the paper. Occasionally I glanced at one of her rhapsodies about Royal Doulton figurines or imported ginger biscuits or honeymoon negligees. But now that I was living in the city, I seldom looked at the paper that had once seemed to me to be the center of its life — and even, in a way, the center of our life at home, sixty miles away. The jokes, the compulsive insincerity, of people like Alfrida and Horse Henry now struck me as tawdry and boring.

I did not worry about running into her, even in this city that was not, after all, so very large. I never went into the shops that she mentioned in her column, and she lived far away from my rooming house, somewhere on the south side of town.

Nor did I think that Alfrida was the kind of person to show up at the library. The very word *library* would probably make her turn down her big mouth in a parody of consternation, as she used to do at the books in the bookcase in our house — some of them won as school prizes by my teenage parents (there was my mother's maiden name, in her beautiful, lost handwriting), books that seemed to me not like things bought in a store at all but like presences in the house, just as the trees outside the window were not plants but presences rooted in the ground. *The Mill on the Floss, The Call of the Wild, The Heart of Midlothian.* "Lot of hot-shot reading in there," Alfrida had said. "Bet you don't crack those very often." And my father had said no, he didn't, falling in with her comradely tone of dismissal, and to some extent telling a lie, because he did look into them once in a long while, when he had the time.

That was the kind of lie I hoped never to have to tell about the things that really mattered to me. And in order not to, I would pretty well have to stay clear of the people I used to know.

At the end of my second year, I was leaving college — my scholarship had covered only two years there. But it didn't matter. I was planning to be a writer anyway. And I was getting married.

Alfrida had got word of this, and she got in touch with me again.

"I guess you must've been too busy to call me, or maybe nobody ever gave you my messages," she said.

I said that maybe I had been, or maybe they hadn't.

This time I agreed to visit. A visit would not commit me to anything, since I was not going to be living in this city in the future. I picked a Sunday in the middle of May, just after my final exams were over, when my fiancé was going to be in Ottawa for a job interview. The day was bright and sunny, and I decided to walk. There were parts of the city that were still entirely strange to me. The shade trees along the northern streets had just come out in leaf, and the lilacs, the ornamental crabapple trees, and the beds of tulips were all in flower, the lawns like fresh carpets. But after a while I found myself walking along streets where there were no shade trees, streets where the houses were hardly an arm's reach from the sidewalk, and where such lilacs as there were — lilacs will grow anywhere — were pale, as if sun-bleached, and their fragrance did not carry. On these streets, in addition to the houses, there were narrow apartment buildings, only two or three stories high, some with the utilitarian decoration of a rim of glass bricks around their doors, and some with raised windows and limp curtains falling out over their sills.

Alfrida's apartment was the whole upstairs of a house. The downstairs — at least the front part of the downstairs — had been turned into a shop, which was closed, it being Sunday. It was a secondhand shop — I could see through the dirty front windows a lot of nondescript furniture with stacks of old dishes and utensils set everywhere. The only thing that caught my eye was a honey pail, exactly like the honey pail with a blue sky and a golden beehive in which I had carried my lunch to school when I was six or seven years old. I could remember reading over and over the words on its side: "All pure honey will granulate."

I had no idea what *granulate* meant, but I liked the sound of it — it seemed ornate and delicious.

I had taken longer to get there than I had expected, and I was very hot. I had not thought that Alfrida, inviting me to lunch, would present me with a meal like the Sunday dinners at home, but it was cooked chicken and vegetables I smelled as I climbed the outdoor stairway.

"I thought you'd got lost," Alfrida called out above me. "I was about to get up a rescue party."

Instead of a sundress, she was wearing a pink blouse with a floppy bow at the neck, tucked into a pleated brown skirt. Her hair was no longer done up in smooth rolls but cut short and frizzed around her face, its dark brown now harshly touched with red. And her face, which I remembered as lean and summer-tanned, had got fuller and somewhat pouchy. In the noon light, her makeup stood out on her skin like orange-pink paint.

But the biggest difference was that she had got false teeth, of a uniform color, slightly overfilling her mouth and giving an anxious edge to her old expression of slapdash eagerness.

"Well — haven't you plumped out," she said. "You used to be so skinny."

This was true, but I did not like to hear it. Along with all the girls at the rooming house, I ate cheap food — copious meals of Kraft

Dinner and packages of jam-filled cookies. My fiancé, so sturdily and possessively in favor of everything about me, said that he liked full-bodied women and that I reminded him of Jane Russell. I did not mind his saying that, but I was affronted when other people had anything to say about my appearance. Particularly when it was somebody like Alfrida, somebody who had lost all importance in my life. I really believed that such people had no right to be looking at me, or forming any opinions about me, let alone stating them.

The house was narrow across the front but long from front to back. There was a living room, whose ceilings sloped at the sides and whose windows overlooked the street, a hall-like dining room with no windows at all, a kitchen, a bathroom also without windows that got its daylight through a pebbled-glass pane in the door, and, across the back of the house, a glassed-in sunporch.

The sloping ceilings made the rooms look makeshift, as if they were only pretending to be anything but bedrooms. But they were crowded with serious furniture — dining room table and chairs, kitchen table and chairs, living room sofa and recliner — all meant for larger, proper rooms. Doilies on the tables, squares of embroidered white cloth protecting the backs and arms of the sofa and chairs, sheer curtains across the windows and heavy flowered curtains at the sides — it was all more like the aunts' houses than I would have thought possible. And on the dining room wall — not in the bathroom or the bedroom but in the dining room — there hung a picture that was a silhouette of a girl in a hoop skirt, all constructed of pink satin ribbon.

Alfrida seemed to guess something of what I was thinking.

"I know I've got far too much stuff in here," she said. "But it's my parents' stuff. It's family furnishings, and I couldn't let it go."

I had never thought of her as having parents. As far as I knew, Alfrida's mother had died when she was six years old, and she had been brought up by my grandmother, who was her aunt.

"My dad and mother's," Alfrida said. "When Dad went off, your grandma stored it all in her back room and the basement and the shed, because she thought it ought to be mine when I grew up, and so here it is. I couldn't turn it down, when she went to that trouble."

Now it came back to me — the part of Alfrida's life that I had forgotten about. Alfrida's father had married again. He had left the farm and got a job working for the railway. He had had some other children, and sometimes Alfrida used to mention them, in a joking way that had something to do with how many children there had been and how quickly they had followed one another.

"Come and meet Bill," Alfrida said.

Bill was out on the sunporch. He sat as if waiting to be summoned, on a low couch or daybed that was covered with a brown plaid blanket. The blanket was rumpled — he must have been lying on it recently — and the blinds on the windows were pulled down to their sills. The light in the room — the hot sunlight coming through rain-marked yellow blinds — and the rough blanket and faded, dented cushion, even the smell of the blanket and of the masculine slippers, old, scuffed slippers that had lost their shape and pattern, reminded me, just as much as the doilies and the heavy polished furniture in the inner rooms had done, of my aunts' houses. There too you could come upon a shabby male hideaway with its furtive yet insistent odors, its shamefaced but stubborn rejection of the female domain.

Bill stood up and shook my hand, however, as the uncles would never have done with a strange girl. Or with any girl. No specific rudeness would have held them back — just a dread of appearing ceremonious.

He was a tall man with wavy, glistening gray hair and a smooth but not youthful face. A handsome man, with the force of his good looks somehow drained away by indifferent health or bad luck or lack of gumption. But he still had a worn courtesy, a way of bending toward a woman, which suggested that the meeting would be a pleasure, for her and for himself.

Alfrida directed us into the windowless dining room, where the lights were on in the middle of this bright day. I got the impression that the meal had been ready some time ago, and that my late arrival had delayed their usual schedule. Bill served the roast chicken and dressing, Alfrida the vegetables. Alfrida said to Bill, "Honey, what do you think that is beside your plate?" and then he remembered to pick up his napkin.

He did not have much to say. He offered the gravy; he inquired as to whether I wanted mustard relish or salt and pepper; he followed the conversation by turning his head toward Alfrida or toward me. Every so often he made a little whistling sound between his teeth, a shivery sound that seemed meant to be genial and appreciative and that I thought at first might be a prelude to some remark. But it never was, and Alfrida never paused for it. I have since seen reformed drinkers who behaved somewhat as he did — chiming in agreeably but unable to carry things beyond that, helplessly preoccupied. I never knew whether Bill was one of them, but he did seem to carry around a history of defeat, of troubles borne and lessons learned, and he had an air, too, of gallant accommodation for whatever choices had gone wrong or chances hadn't panned out.

These were frozen peas and carrots, Alfrida said. Frozen vegetables were fairly new at the time.

"They beat the canned," she said. "They're practically as good as fresh."

Then Bill made a whole statement. He said that they were better than fresh. The color, the flavor, everything was better than fresh. He said that it was remarkable what they could do now and what would be done by way of freezing things in the future.

Alfrida leaned forward, smiling. She seemed almost to hold her breath, as if he were her child taking unsupported steps, or a first lone wobble on a bicycle.

There was a way they could inject something into a chicken, he told us, a new process that would have every chicken coming out the same — plump and tasty. No such thing as taking a risk on getting an inferior chicken anymore.

"Bill's field is chemistry," Alfrida said.

When I had nothing to say to this, she added, "He worked for Gooderhams."

Still nothing.

"The distillers," she said. "Gooderhams whiskey."

The reason that I had nothing to say was not that I was rude or bored (or any more rude than I was naturally at that time, or more bored than I had expected to be) but that I did not understand that I should ask questions — almost any questions at all, to draw a shy male into conversation, to shake him out of his abstraction and set him up as a man of a certain authority, and therefore the man of the house. I did not understand why Alfrida looked at him with such a fiercely encouraging smile. All my experience of women with men — of a woman listening to her man and hoping that he will establish himself as somebody that she can reasonably be proud of — was in the future. The only observation that I had made of couples was of my aunts and uncles and of my mother and father, and those husbands and wives seemed to have remote and formalized connections and no obvious dependence on each other.

Bill continued eating as if he had not heard this mention of his profession and his employer, and Alfrida began to question me about my courses. She was still smiling, but her smile had changed. There was a little twitch of impatience and unpleasantness in it, as if she were just waiting for me to get to the end of my explanations so that she could say — as she did say — "You couldn't get me to read that stuff for a million dollars.

"Life's too short," she went on. "You know, down at the paper we sometimes get somebody that's been through all that. Honors English. Honors philosophy. You don't know what to do with them. They can't write worth a nickel. I've told you that, haven't I?" she said to Bill, and Bill looked up and gave her his dutiful smile.

"So what do you do for fun?" Alfrida said, sometime later.

A Streetcar Named Desire was playing at a theater in Toronto at that time, and I told her that I had gone down on the train with a couple of friends to see it.

Alfrida let her knife and fork clatter onto her plate.

"That filth!" she cried. Her face leapt out at me, carved with sudden anger and disgust. Then she spoke more calmly but still with a virulent displeasure.

"You went all the way to Toronto to see that filth."

We had finished the dessert, and Bill picked that moment to ask if he might be excused. He asked Alfrida, then with the slightest bow he asked me. He went back to the sunporch and in a little while we could smell his pipe. Alfrida, watching him go, seemed to forget about me and the play. There was a look of such stricken tenderness on her face that when she stood up, I thought she was going to follow him. But she was only going to get her cigarettes.

She held them out to me, and when I took one, she said, with a deliberate effort at jollity, "I see you kept up the bad habit I got you started on." It seemed as if she had remembered that I was not a child anymore and that I did not have to be in her house and there was no point in making an enemy of me. And I wasn't going to argue — I did not care what Alfrida thought about Tennessee Williams. Or what she thought about anything else.

"I guess it's your own business," Alfrida said. "You can go where you want to go." And she added, "After all — you'll be a married woman pretty soon."

By her tone, this could have meant "I have to allow that you're grown up now" or "Pretty soon you'll have to toe the line."

We got up and started to collect the dishes. Working close to each other in the small space between the kitchen table and counter and the refrigerator, we soon developed, without speaking about it, a certain order and harmony of scraping and stacking and putting the leftover food into smaller containers for storage and filling the sink with hot, soapy water. We brought the ashtray out to the kitchen and stopped every now and then to take a restorative, businesslike drag on our cigarettes. There are things women agree on or don't agree on when they work together in this way — whether it is all right to smoke, for instance, or preferable not to in case some migratory ash might find its way onto a clean dish, or whether every single thing that has been on the table has to be washed, whether it has been used or not — and it turned out that Alfrida and I agreed. Also, the thought that I could get away, once the dishes were done, made me feel more relaxed and generous. I had already said that I had to meet a friend that afternoon.

"These are pretty dishes," I said. They were cream-colored, almost yellowish, with a rim of blue flowers.

"Well, they were my mother's wedding dishes," Alfrida said. "That was one other good thing your grandma did for me. She packed up all my mother's dishes and put them away until the time came when I could use them. Jeanie never knew they existed. They wouldn't have lasted long, with that bunch."

Jeanie. That bunch. Her stepmother and the half-brothers and -sisters.

"You know about that, don't you?" Alfrida said. "You know what happened to my mother?" Of course I knew. Alfrida's mother had died when an oil lamp exploded in her hands — that is, she died of the burns she got when a lamp exploded in her hands — and my aunts and my mother had spoken of this regularly. Nothing could be said about Alfrida's mother or about Alfrida's father, and very little about Alfrida herself, without that death being dragged in and tacked onto it. It was the reason that Alfrida's father left the farm (somewhat of a downward step morally, if not financially). It was a reason to be desperately careful with coal oil, and a reason to be grateful for electricity, whatever the cost. And it was a dreadful thing for a child of Alfrida's age, whatever. (That is, whatever she had done with herself since.)

If it hadn't've been for the thunderstorm, she wouldn't ever have been lighting a lamp in the middle of the afternoon.

She lived all that night and the next day and the next night, and it would have been the best thing in the world for her if she hadn't've.

Just the year after that the hydro came down their road, and they didn't have the need of the lamps anymore.

The aunts and my mother seldom felt the same way about anything, but they shared a feeling about this story. The feeling was in their voices whenever they said Alfrida's mother's name. The story seemed to be a horrible treasure to them, a distinction our family alone could claim. To listen to them had always made me feel as if there were some obscene connivance going on, a fond fingering of whatever was grisly or disastrous.

Men were not like this, in my experience. Men looked away from frightful happenings as soon as they could and behaved as if there was no use, once things were over with, in mentioning them or thinking about them ever again. They didn't want to stir themselves up, or stir other people up.

So if Alfrida was going to talk about it, I thought, what a good thing it was that my fiancé had not come. What a good thing that he didn't have to hear about Alfrida's mother, on top of finding out about my mother and my family's relative — or maybe considerable — poverty. He admired opera and Laurence Olivier's Hamlet, but he had no time for the squalor of tragedy in ordinary life. His parents were healthy and good-looking and prosperous (though he said, of course, that they were dull), and it seemed that he had not had to know anybody who did not live in fairly sunny circumstances. Failures in life — failures of luck, of health, of finances — all struck him as lapses, and his resolute approval of me did not extend to my ramshackle background.

"They wouldn't let me in to see her, at the hospital," Alfrida said, and at least she was saying this in her normal voice, not preparing the way with any greasy tone of piety. "Well, I probably wouldn't have let me in either, if I'd been in their shoes. I've no idea what she looked like. Probably all bound up like a mummy. Or if she wasn't she should have been. I wasn't there when it happened. I was at school. It got very dark, and the teacher turned the lights on — we had the electric lights at school — and we all had to stay until the thunderstorm was over. Then my Aunt Lily — well, your grandmother — she came to meet me and took me to her place. And I never got to see my mother again."

I thought that that was all she was going to say, but in a moment she continued, in a voice that had actually brightened up a bit, as if she were preparing for a laugh.

"I yelled and yelled my fool head off. I wanted to see her. I carried on and carried on, and finally, when they couldn't shut me up, your grandmother said to me, 'You're just better off not to see her. You wouldn't want to see her, if you knew what she looks like now. You wouldn't want to remember her this way.' I guess I already knew that she was going to die, because it didn't seem strange to me to hear her talk about remembering her. But you know what I said? I remember saying it. I said, 'But she would want to see me.' *She would want to see me.*"

Then Alfrida really did laugh, or made a snorting sound that was evasive and scornful.

"I must've thought I was the cat's p.j.s, mustn't I? *She would want to see me.*"

This was a part of the story that I had never heard.

And the minute that I heard it, something happened. It was as if a trap had snapped shut to hold these words in my head. I did not exactly understand what use I would have for them. I knew only how they jolted me and released me, right away, to breathe a different kind of air, available only to myself.

She would want to see me.

The story I wrote, with these words in it, would not exist until years later, not until it had become quite unimportant to think about who had put the idea into my head in the first place.

I thanked Alfrida. I said that I had to go. Alfrida went to call Bill to say goodbye to me, but came back to report that he had fallen asleep.

"He'll be kicking himself when he wakes up," she said. "He enjoyed meeting you."

She took off her apron and accompanied me all the way down the outside steps. At the bottom of the steps was a gravel path leading around to the sidewalk. The gravel crunched under our feet, and she stumbled in her thin-soled house shoes.

She said, "Ouch. God damn it," and caught hold of my shoulder.

"How's your dad?" she said.

"He's all right."

"He works too hard."

I said, "He has to."

"Oh, I know. And how's your mother?"

"She's about the same."

She turned aside, toward the shop window.

"Who do they think is ever going to buy this junk? Look at that honey pail. Your dad and I used to take our lunch to school in pails just like that."

"So did I," I said.

"Did you?" She squeezed me. "You tell your folks I'm thinking about them, will you do that?"

Alfrida did not come to my father's funeral. I wondered if that was because she did not want to see me. As far as I knew, she had never made public what she held against me. But my father had known about it. When I was home visiting him and learned that Alfrida was living not far away — in my grandmother's house, in fact, which she had inherited — I had suggested that we go to see her. This was in the flurry between my two marriages, when I was in an expansive mood, newly released and able to make contact with anyone I chose.

My father said, "Well, you know, Alfrida was a bit upset."

He was calling her Alfrida now. When had that started?

I could not even think at first what Alfrida might be upset about. My father had to remind me of the story, published several years ago, and I was surprised, even impatient and a little angry, to think of Alfrida's objecting to something that seemed now to have so little to do with her.

"It wasn't Alfrida at all," I said to my father. "I changed it. I wasn't even thinking about her, it was a character. Anybody could see that."

But as a matter of fact, there was still the exploding lamp, the mother in her charnel wrappings, the staunch bereft child.

"Well," my father said. He was in general quite pleased that I had become a writer, but he had some reservations about what might be called my character. About the fact that I had ended my marriage for personal — that is, wanton — reasons, and about the way I went around justifying myself, or perhaps, as he might have said, weaseling out of things. But he would not say so — it was not his business anymore.

I asked him how he knew that Alfrida felt this way.

He said, "A letter."

A letter, though they lived not far apart. I did feel sorry to think that he had had to bear the brunt of what could be taken as my thoughtlessness, or even my wrongdoing. Also that he and Alfrida seemed now to be on such formal terms. I wondered what he was leaving out. Had he felt compelled to defend my writing to Alfrida, as he had to other people? He would do that now, though it was never easy for him. In his uneasiness, he might have said something harsh.

There was a danger whenever I was on home ground. It was the danger of seeing my life through someone else's eyes — comparing it, even, with the rich domesticity of others, their pileup production of hand-knitted garments and buttery cakes. Of seeing my own work as ever-increasing rolls of inky-black barbed wire — intricate, bewildering, uncomforting. So that it might become harder to say that writing was worth the trouble.

Worth my trouble, maybe, but what about anyone else's?

My father had said that Alfrida was living alone now. I asked him what had become of Bill. He said that all of that was outside his jurisdiction. But he believed that there had been a bit of a rescue operation.

"Of Bill? How come? Who by?"

"Well, I believe there was a wife."

"I met him at Alfrida's once. I liked him."

"People did. Women."

I had to consider that the rupture might have had nothing to do with me. My father had remarried, and my stepmother had urged him into a new sort of life. They went bowling and curling and regularly joined other couples for coffee and doughnuts at Tim Hortons. She had been a widow for a long time before she married him, and she had many friends from those days who became new friends for him. What had happened with him and Alfrida might have been simply one of the changes, the wearing out of old attachments, that I understood so well in my own life but did not expect to happen in the lives of older people — particularly in the lives of people at home.

My stepmother died just a little while before my father. After their short, happy marriage, they were sent to separate cemeteries to lie beside their first, more troublesome partners. Before either of those deaths, Alfrida had moved back to the city. She didn't sell my grandmother's house; she just went away and left it. "That's a pretty funny way of doing things," my father wrote to me.

There were a lot of people at my father's funeral, a lot of people I didn't know. A woman came across the grass at the cemetery to speak to me. I thought at first that she must have been a friend of my stepmother's. Then I saw that the woman was only a few years past my own age. The stocky figure and puffed-up, hairdresser-blond curls and floral patterned jacket made her look older.

"I recognized you by your picture," she said. "Alfrida used to always be bragging about you."

I said, "Alfrida's not dead, is she?"

"Oh, no," the woman said, and went on to tell me that Alfrida was in a nursing home in a town just north of Toronto.

"I moved her down there so's I could keep an eye on her."

Now it was easy to tell — even by her voice — that she was somebody of my own generation, and it came to me that she must be a member of the other family, a half-sister of Alfrida's, born when Alfrida was almost grown up.

She told me her name, and it was of course not the same as Alfrida's — she must have married. And I couldn't recall Alfrida's ever having mentioned any of her half-family by their first names.

I asked how Alfrida was, and the woman said, Cataracts in both eyes, but when they ripened they could be taken off. And she had a serious kidney problem, which meant that she had to be on dialysis twice a week.

"Other than that?" she said, and laughed. I thought, *Yes, a sister,* because I could hear something of Alfrida in that reckless tossed laugh.

"So she doesn't travel too good," she said. "Or else I would've brought her. She still gets the paper from here, and I read it to her sometimes, and that's where I saw about your dad."

I wondered out loud, impulsively, if I should go to visit at the nursing home. The emotions of the funeral — all the warm and relieved and reconciled feelings opened up in me by the death of my father at a reasonable age — prompted this suggestion. It would have been hard to carry out. My husband — my second husband — and I were flying to Europe in two days on an already delayed holiday.

"I don't know if you'd get so much out of it," the woman said. "She has her good days. Then she has her bad days. You never know. Sometimes I think she's putting it on. Like, she'll sit there all day and whatever anybody says to her, she'll just say the same thing. 'Fit as a fiddle and ready for love.' That's what she'll say all day long. 'Fit as a fiddle and ready for love.' She'd drive you crazy. Then, other days, she can answer all right."

Again the woman's voice and laugh, this time half submerged, reminded me of Alfrida's, and I said, "You know, I must have met you. I remember once, when I was over at my grandmother's house and Alfrida's stepmother and her father dropped in, or maybe it was only her father and some of the children —"

"Oh, that's not who I am," the woman said. "You thought I was Alfrida's sister? Glory. I must be looking my age."

I started to say that I could not see her very well, and it was true. In October the afternoon sun was low, and it was coming straight into my eyes. The woman was standing against the light, so that it was hard to make out her features or her expression.

She twitched her shoulders nervously and importantly. She said, "Alfrida was my birth mom."

Mawm. Mother.

Then she told me, at not too great length, the story that she must have told often, because it was about an emphatic event in her life and an adventure that she had embarked on alone. She had been adopted by a family in eastern Ontario — they were the only family she had ever known ("and I love them dearly") — and she had married and had her children, who were grown up before she got the urge to find out who her own mother was. It wasn't too easy, because of the way records used to be kept, and the secrecy ("It was kept one-hundred-percent secret that she had me"), but a few years ago she had tracked down Alfrida.

"Just in time, too," she said. "I mean, it was time somebody came along to look after her. As much as I can."

I said, "I never knew."

"No. Those days, I don't suppose too many did. They warn you, when you start out to do this, it could be a shock when you show up. Older people, it's still heavy-duty. But I don't think she minded. Earlier on, maybe she would have."

There was a sense of triumph about the woman, which wasn't hard to understand. If you have something to tell that will stagger someone, and you've told it, and it has done that, you must experience a balmy moment of power. In this case, it was so complete that she felt a need to apologize.

"Excuse me, talking all about myself and not saying how sorry I am about your dad."

I thanked her.

"You know, Alfrida told me that your dad and her were walking home from school one day — this was in high school. They couldn't walk all the way together because, you know, in those days, a boy and a girl, they would just get teased something terrible. So if he got out first he'd wait just where their road went off the main road, outside of town, and if she got out first she would do the same, wait for him. And one day they were walking together and they heard all the bells starting to ring and you know what that was? It was the end of the First World War."

I said that I had heard that story too. "Only I thought they were just children."

"Then how could they be coming home from high school, if they were just children?"

I said that I had thought they were out playing in the fields. "They had my father's dog with them. He was called Mack."

"Maybe they had the dog, all right. Maybe he came to meet them. I wouldn't think she'd get mixed up on what she was telling me. She was pretty good on remembering anything that involved your dad."

Now I was aware of two things. First, that my father had been born in 1902, and that Alfrida was close to the same age. So it was much more likely that they were walking home from high school than that they were playing in the fields, and it was odd that I had never thought of that before. Maybe they had said they were in the fields, that is, walking home across the fields. Maybe they had never said "playing."

Also, that the feeling of apology or friendliness, the harmlessness that I had felt in this woman a little while before, was not there now.

I said, "Things get changed around."

"That's right," the woman said. "People change things around. You want to know what Alfrida said about you?"

Now. Now.

"What?"

"She said you were smart but you weren't ever quite as smart as you thought you were."

I made myself keep looking into the dark face against the light. Smart, too smart, not smart enough. Joke on you.

I said, "Is that all?"

"Except she said you were a cold fish, sort of. That's her talking, not me. I haven't got anything against you."

That Sunday, after the lunch at Alfrida's, I set out to walk all the way back to my rooming house. Walking both ways, I reckoned that I would cover about ten miles, which ought to offset the effects of the meal I had eaten. I felt overfull, not just of food but of everything that I had seen and sensed in the apartment. The crowded, old-fashioned furnishings. Bill's silences. Alfrida's love, stubborn as sludge, and inappropriate, and hopeless — as far as I could see — on the ground of age alone.

After I had walked for a while, my stomach did not feel so heavy. I made a vow not to eat anything for the next twenty-four hours. I walked north and west, north and west, on the streets of the tidily rectangular small city. On a Sunday afternoon, there was hardly any traffic, except on the main thoroughfares. A bus might go by with only two or three people in it. People I did not know and who did not know me. What a blessing.

I had lied. I was not meeting any friend. My friends had mostly gone home to wherever they lived. My fiancé would be away until the next day — he was visiting his parents, in Cobourg, on the way home from Ottawa. There would be nobody in the rooming house when I got there — nobody I had to bother talking or listening to. I had nothing to do.

When I had walked for over an hour, I saw a drugstore that was open. I went in and had a cup of coffee. The coffee was reheated, black and bitter — its taste was medicinal, exactly what I needed. I was already feeling relieved, and now I began to feel happy. Such happiness, to be alone. To see the hot late-afternoon light on the sidewalk outside, the branches of a tree just out in leaf, throwing their skimpy shadows. To hear from the back of the shop the sounds of the ballgame that the man who had served me was listening to on the radio. I did not think of the story that I would write about Alfrida — not of that in particular — but of the work I wanted to do, which seemed more like grabbing something out of the air than like constructing stories. The cries of the crowd came to me like big heartbeats, full of sorrows. Lovely, formal-sounding waves, with their distant, almost inhuman assent and lamentation.

This was what I wanted, this was what I thought I had to pay attention to, this was how I wanted my life to be.

AKHIL SHARMA

Surrounded by Sleep

FROM THE NEW YORKER

ONE AUGUST AFTERNOON, when Ajay was ten years old, his elder brother, Aman, dove into a pool and struck his head on the cement bottom. For three minutes, he lay there unconscious. Two boys continued to swim, kicking and splashing, until finally Aman was spotted below them. Water had entered through his nose and mouth. It had filled his stomach. His lungs collapsed. By the time he was pulled out, he could no longer think, talk, chew, or roll over in his sleep.

Ajay's family had moved from India to Queens, New York, two years earlier. The accident occurred during the boys' summer vacation, on a visit with their aunt and uncle in Arlington, Virginia. After the accident, Ajay's mother came to Arlington, where she waited to see if Aman would recover. At the hospital, she told the doctors and nurses that her son had been accepted into the Bronx High School of Science, in the hope that by highlighting his intelligence she would move them to make a greater effort on his behalf. Within a few weeks of the accident, the insurance company said that Aman should be transferred to a less expensive care facility, a long-term one. But only a few of these were any good, and those were full, and Ajay's mother refused to move Aman until a space opened in one of them. So she remained in Arlington, and Ajay stayed too, and his father visited from Queens on the weekends when he wasn't working. Ajay was enrolled at the local public school and in September he started fifth grade.

Before the accident, Ajay had never prayed much. In India, he and his brother used to go with their mother to the temple every Tuesday night, but that was mostly because there was a good *dosa* restaurant nearby. In America, his family went to a temple only on important holy days and birthdays. But shortly after Ajay's mother came to Arlington, she moved into the room that he and his brother had shared during the summer and made an altar in a corner. She threw an old flowered sheet over a cardboard box that had once held a television. On top she put a clay lamp, an incense-stick holder, and postcards depicting various gods. There was also a postcard of Mahatma Gandhi. She explained to Ajay that God could take any form; the picture of Mahatma Gandhi was there because he had appeared to her in a dream after the accident and told her that Aman would recover and become a surgeon. Now she and Ajay prayed for at least half an hour before the altar every morning and night.

At first she prayed with absolute humility. "Whatever you do will be good because you are doing it," she murmured to the postcards of Ram and Shivaji, daubing their lips with water and rice. Mahatma Gandhi got only water, because he did not like to eat. As weeks passed and Aman did not recover in time to return to the Bronx High School of Science for the first day of classes, his mother began doing things that called attention to her piety. She sometimes held the prayer lamp until it blistered her palms. Instead of kneeling before the altar, she lay face down. She fasted twice a week. Her attempts to sway God were not so different from Ajay's performing somersaults to amuse his aunt, and they made God seem human to Ajay.

One morning as Ajay knelt before the altar, he traced an Om, a crucifix, and a Star of David into the pile of the carpet. Beneath these he traced an *S*, for Superman, inside an upside-down triangle. His mother came up beside him.

"What are you praying for?" she asked. She had her hat on, a thick gray knitted one that a man might wear. The tracings went against the weave of the carpet and were darker than the surrounding nap. Pretending to examine them, Ajay leaned forward and put his hand over the *S*. His mother did not mind the Christian and Jewish symbols — they were for commonly recognized gods, after all — but she could not tolerate his praying to Superman. She'd caught him doing so once several weeks earlier and had become very angry, as if Ajay's faith in Superman made her faith in Ram ridiculous. "Right in front of God," she had said several times.

Ajay, in his nervousness, spoke the truth. "I'm asking God to give me a hundred percent on the math test."

His mother was silent for a moment. "What if God says you can have the math grade but then Aman will have to be sick a little while longer?" she asked.

Ajay kept quiet. He could hear cars on the road outside. He knew that his mother wanted to bewail her misfortune before God so that God would feel guilty. He looked at the postcard of Mahatma Gandhi. It was a black-and-white photo of him walking down a city street with an enormous crowd trailing behind him. Ajay thought of how, before the accident, Aman had been so modest that he would not leave the bathroom until he was fully dressed. Now he had rashes on his penis from the catheter that drew his urine into a translucent bag hanging from the guardrail of his bed.

His mother asked again, "Would you say, 'Let him be sick a little while longer'?"

"Are you going to tell me the story about Uncle Naveen again?" he asked.

"Why shouldn't I? When I was sick, as a girl, your uncle walked seven times around the temple and asked God to let him fail his exams just as long as I got better."

"If I failed the math test and told you that story, you'd slap me and ask what one has to do with the other."

His mother turned to the altar. "What sort of sons did you give me, God?" she asked. "One you drown, the other is this selfish fool."

"I will fast today so that God puts some sense in me," Ajay said, glancing away from the altar and up at his mother. He liked the drama of fasting.

"No, you are a growing boy." His mother knelt down beside him and said to the altar, "He is stupid, but he has a good heart."

Prayer, Ajay thought, should appeal with humility and an open heart to some greater force. But the praying that he and his mother did felt sly and confused. By treating God as someone to bargain with, it seemed to him, they prayed as if they were casting a spell.

This meant that it was possible to do away with the presence of

God entirely. For example, Ajay's mother had recently asked a relative in India to drive a nail into a holy tree and tie a saffron thread to the nail on Aman's behalf. Ajay invented his own ritual. On his way to school each morning, he passed a thick tree rooted half on the sidewalk and half on the road. One day Ajay got the idea that if he circled the tree seven times, touching the north side every other time, he would have a lucky day. From then on he did it every morning, although he felt embarrassed and always looked around beforehand to make sure no one was watching.

One night Ajay asked God whether he minded being prayed to only in need.

"You think of your toe only when you stub it," God replied. God looked like Clark Kent. He wore a gray cardigan, slacks, and thick glasses, and had a forelock that curled just as Ajay's did.

God and Ajay had begun talking occasionally after Aman drowned. Now they talked most nights while Ajay lay in bed and waited for sleep. God sat at the foot of Ajay's mattress. His mother's mattress lay parallel to his, a few feet away. Originally God had appeared to Ajay as Krishna, but Ajay had felt foolish discussing brain damage with a blue god who held a flute and wore a dhoti.

"You're not angry with me for touching the tree and all that?"

"No. I'm flexible."

"I respect you. The tree is just a way of praying to you," Ajay assured God.

God laughed. "I am not too caught up in formalities."

Ajay was quiet. He was convinced that he had been marked as special by Aman's accident. The beginnings of all heroes are distinguished by misfortune. Superman and Batman were both orphans. Krishna was separated from his parents at birth. The god Ram had to spend fourteen years in a forest. Ajay waited to speak until it would not appear improper to begin talking about himself.

"How famous will I be?" he asked finally.

"I can't tell you the future," God answered.

Ajay asked, "Why not?"

"Even if I told you something, later I might change my mind."

"But it might be harder to change your mind after you have said something will happen."

God laughed again. "You'll be so famous that fame will be a problem."

Ajay sighed. His mother snorted and rolled over.

"I want Aman's drowning to lead to something," he said to God.

"He won't be forgotten."

"I can't just be famous, though. I need to be rich too, to take care of Mummy and Daddy and pay Aman's hospital bills."

"You are always practical." God had a soulful and pitying voice, and God's sympathy made Ajay imagine himself as a truly tragic figure, like Amitabh Bachchan in the movie *Trishul.*

"I have responsibilities," Ajay said. He was so excited at the thought of his possible greatness that he knew he would have difficulty sleeping. Perhaps he would have to go read in the bathroom.

"You can hardly imagine the life ahead," God said.

Even though God's tone promised greatness, the idea of the future frightened Ajay. He opened his eyes. There was light coming from the street. The room was cold and had a smell of must and incense. His aunt and uncle's house was a narrow two-story home next to a four-lane road. The apartment building with the pool where Aman had drowned was a few blocks up the road, one in a cluster of tall brick buildings with stucco fronts. Ajay pulled the blanket tighter around him. In India, he could not have imagined the reality of his life in America: the thick smell of meat in the school cafeteria, the many television channels. And, of course, he could not have imagined Aman's accident, or the hospital where he spent so much time.

The hospital was boring. Vinod, Ajay's cousin, picked him up after school and dropped him off there almost every day. Vinod was twenty-two. In addition to attending county college and studying computer programming, he worked at a 7-Eleven near Ajay's school. He often brought Ajay hot chocolate and a comic from the store, which had to be returned, so Ajay was not allowed to open it until he had wiped his hands.

Vinod usually asked him a riddle on the way to the hospital. "Why are manhole covers round?" It took Ajay half the ride to admit that he did not know. He was having difficulty talking. He didn't know why. The only time he could talk easily was when he was with God. The explanation he gave himself for this was that just as he couldn't chew when there was too much in his mouth, he couldn't talk when there were too many thoughts in his head.

When Ajay got to Aman's room, he greeted him as if he were all right. "Hello, lazy. How much longer are you going to sleep?" His mother was always there. She got up and hugged Ajay. She asked how school had been, and he didn't know what to say. In music class, the teacher sang a song about a sailor who had bared his breast before jumping into the sea. This had caused the other students to giggle. But Ajay could not say the word *breast* to his mother without blushing. He had also cried. He'd been thinking of how Aman's accident had made his own life mysterious and confused. What would happen next? Would Aman die or would he go on as he was? Where would they live? Usually when Ajay cried in school, he was told to go outside. But it had been raining, and the teacher had sent him into the hallway. He sat on the floor and wept. Any mention of this would upset his mother. And so he said nothing had happened that day.

Sometimes when Ajay arrived his mother was on the phone, telling his father that she missed him and was expecting to see him on Friday. His father took a Greyhound bus most Fridays from Queens to Arlington, returning on Sunday night in time to work the next day. He was a bookkeeper for a department store. Before the accident, Ajay had thought of his parents as the same person: MummyDaddy. Now, when he saw his father praying stiffly or when his father failed to say hello to Aman in his hospital bed, Ajay sensed that his mother and father were quite different people. After his mother got off the phone, she always went to the cafeteria to get coffee for herself and Jell-O or cookies for him. He knew that if she took her coat with her, it meant that she was especially sad. Instead of going directly to the cafeteria, she was going to go outside and walk around the hospital parking lot.

That day, while she was gone, Ajay stood beside the hospital bed and balanced a comic book on Aman's chest. He read to him very slowly. Before turning each page, he said, "Okay, Aman?"

Aman was fourteen. He was thin and had curly hair. Immediately after the accident, there had been so many machines around his bed that only one person could stand beside him at a time. Now there was just a single waxy yellow tube. One end of this went into his abdomen; the other, blocked by a green bullet-shaped plug, was what his Isocal milk was poured through. When not being used, the tube was rolled up and bound by a rubber band and tucked beneath Aman's hospital gown. But even with the tube hidden, it was obvious that there was something wrong with Aman. It was in his stillness and his open eyes. Once, in their house in Queens, Ajay had left a plastic bowl on a radiator overnight and the sides had drooped and sagged so that the bowl looked a little like an eye. Aman reminded Ajay of that bowl.

Ajay had not gone with his brother to the swimming pool on the day of the accident, because he had been reading a book and wanted to finish it. But he heard the ambulance siren from his aunt and uncle's house. The pool was only a few minutes away, and when he got there a crowd had gathered around the ambulance. Ajay saw his uncle first, in shorts and an undershirt, talking to a man inside the ambulance. His aunt was standing beside him. Then Ajay saw Aman on a stretcher, in blue shorts with a plastic mask over his nose and mouth. His aunt hurried over to take Ajay home. He cried as they walked, although he had been certain that Aman would be fine in a few days: in a Spider-Man comic he had just read, Aunt May had fallen into a coma and she had woken up perfectly fine. Ajay had cried simply because he felt crying was called for by the seriousness of the occasion. Perhaps this moment would mark the beginning of his future greatness. From that day on, Ajay found it hard to cry in front of his family. Whenever tears started coming, he felt like a liar. If he loved his brother, he knew, he would not have thought about himself as the ambulance had pulled away, nor would he talk with God at night about becoming famous.

When Ajay's mother returned to Aman's room with coffee and cookies, she sometimes talked to Ajay about Aman. She told him that when Aman was six he had seen a children's television show that had a character named Chunu, which was Aman's nickname, and he had thought the show was based on his own life. But most days Ajay went into the lounge to read. There was a TV in the corner and a lamp near a window that looked out over a parking lot. It was the perfect place to read. Ajay liked fantasy novels where the hero, who was preferably under the age of twenty-five, had an undiscovered talent that made him famous when it was revealed. He could read for hours without interruption, and sometimes when Vinod came to drive Ajay and his mother home from the hospital it was hard for him to remember the details of the real day that had passed.

One evening when he was in the lounge, he saw a rock star being interviewed on *Entertainment Tonight.* The musician, dressed in a sleeveless undershirt that revealed a swarm of tattoos on his arms and shoulders, had begun to shout at the audience, over his interviewer, "Don't watch me! Live your life! I'm not you!" Filled with a sudden desire to do something, Ajay hurried out of the television lounge and stood on the sidewalk in front of the hospital entrance. But he did not know what to do. It was cold and dark and there was an enormous moon. Cars leaving the parking lot stopped one by one at the edge of the road. Ajay watched as they waited for an opening in the traffic, their brake lights glowing.

"Are things getting worse?" Ajay asked God. The weekend before had been Thanksgiving. Christmas soon would come, and a new year would start, a year during which Aman would not have talked or walked. Suddenly Ajay understood hopelessness. Hopelessness felt very much like fear. It involved a clutching in the stomach and a numbness in the arms and legs.

"What do you think?" God answered.

"They seem to be."

"At least Aman's hospital hasn't forced him out."

"At least Aman isn't dead. At least Daddy's Greyhound bus has never skidded off a bridge." Lately Ajay had begun talking much more quickly to God than he used to. Before, when he had talked to God, Ajay would think of what God would say in response before he said anything. Now Ajay spoke without knowing how God might respond.

"You shouldn't be angry at me." God sighed. God was wearing his usual cardigan. "You can't understand why I do what I do."

"You should explain better, then."

"Christ was my son. I loved Job. How long did Ram have to live in a forest?"

"What does that have to do with me?" This was usually the cue for discussing Ajay's prospects. But hopelessness made the future feel even more frightening than the present.

"I can't tell you what the connection is, but you'll be proud of yourself."

They were silent for a while.

"Do you love me truly?" Ajay asked.

"Yes."

"Will you make Aman normal?" As soon as Ajay asked the question, God ceased to be real. Ajay knew then that he was alone, lying under his blankets, his face exposed to the cold dark.

"I can't tell you the future," God said softly. These were words that Ajay already knew.

"Just get rid of the minutes when Aman lay on the bottom of the pool. What are three minutes to you?"

"Presidents die in less time than that. Planes crash in less time than that."

Ajay opened his eyes. His mother was on her side and she had a blanket pulled up to her neck. She looked like an ordinary woman. It surprised him that you couldn't tell, looking at her, that she had a son who was brain-dead.

In fact, things were getting worse. Putting away his mother's mattress and his own in a closet in the morning, getting up very early so he could use the bathroom before his aunt or uncle did, spending so many hours in the hospital — all this had given Ajay the reassuring sense that real life was in abeyance, and that what was happening was unreal. He and his mother and brother were just waiting to make a long-delayed bus trip. The bus would come eventually to carry them to Queens, where he would return to school at P.S. 20 and to Sunday afternoons spent at the Hindi movie theater under the trestle for the 7 train. But now Ajay was starting to understand that the world was always real, whether you were reading a book or sleeping, and that it eroded you every day.

He saw the evidence of this erosion in his mother, who had grown severe and unforgiving. Usually when Vinod brought her and Ajay home from the hospital, she had dinner with the rest of the family. After his mother helped his aunt wash the dishes, the two women watched theological action movies. One night, in spite of a headache that had made her sit with her eyes closed all afternoon, she ate dinner, washed dishes, sat down in front of the TV. As soon as the movie was over, she went upstairs, vomited, and lay on her mattress with a wet towel over her forehead. She asked Ajay to massage her neck and shoulders. As he did so, Ajay noticed that she was crying. The tears frightened Ajay and made him angry. "You shouldn't have watched TV," he said accusingly.

"I have to," she said. "People will cry with you once, and they will cry with you a second time. But if you cry a third time, people will say you are boring and always crying."

Ajay did not want to believe what she had said, but her cynicism made him think that she must have had conversations with his aunt and uncle that he did not know about. "That's not true," he told her, massaging her scalp. "Uncle is kind. Auntie Aruna is always kind."

"What do you know?" She shook her head, freeing herself from Ajay's fingers. She stared at him. Upside down, her face looked unfamiliar and terrifying. "If God lets Aman live long enough, you will become a stranger too. You will say, 'I have been unhappy for so long because of Aman, now I don't want to talk about him or look at him.' Don't think I don't know you," she said.

Suddenly Ajay hated himself. To hate himself was to see himself as the opposite of everything he wanted to be: short instead of tall, fat instead of thin. When he brushed his teeth that night, he looked at his face: his chin was round and fat as a heel. His nose was so broad that he had once been able to fit a small rock in one nostril.

His father was also being eroded. Before the accident, Ajay's father loved jokes — he could do perfect imitations — and Ajay had felt lucky to have him as a father. (Once, Ajay's father had convinced his own mother that he was possessed by the ghost of a British man.) And even after the accident, his father had impressed Ajay with the patient loyalty of his weekly bus journeys. But now his father was different.

One Saturday afternoon, as Ajay and his father were returning from the hospital, his father slowed the car without warning and turned into the dirt parking lot of a bar that looked as though it had originally been a small house. It had a pitched roof with a black tarp. At the edge of the lot stood a tall neon sign of an orange hand lifting a mug of sudsy golden beer. Ajay had never seen anybody drink except in the movies. He wondered whether his father was going to ask for directions to somewhere, and if so, to where.

His father said, "One minute," and they climbed out of the car.

They went up wooden steps into the bar. Inside, it was dark and smelled of cigarette smoke and something stale and sweet. The floor was linoleum like the kitchen at his aunt and uncle's. There was a bar with stools around it, and a basketball game played on a television bolted against the ceiling, like the one in Aman's hospital room.

His father stood by the bar waiting for the bartender to notice him. His father had a round face and was wearing a white shirt and dark dress pants, as he often did on the weekend, since it was more economical to have the same clothes for the office and home.

The bartender came over. "How much for a Budweiser?" his father asked.

It was a dollar fifty. "Can I buy a single cigarette?" He did not have to buy; the bartender would just give him one. His father helped Ajay up onto a stool and sat down himself. Ajay looked around and wondered what would happen if somebody started a knife fight. When his father had drunk half his beer, he carefully lit the cigarette. The bartender was standing at the end of the bar. There were only two other men in the place. Ajay was disappointed that there were no women wearing dresses slit all the way up their thighs. Perhaps they came in the evenings.

His father asked him if he had ever watched a basketball game all the way through.

"I've seen the Harlem Globetrotters."

His father smiled and took a sip. "I've heard they don't play other teams, because they can defeat everyone else so easily."

"They only play against each other, unless there is an emergency — like in the cartoon, when they play against the aliens to save the Earth," Ajay said.

"Aliens?"

Ajay blushed as he realized his father was teasing him.

When they left, the light outside felt too bright. As his father opened the car door for Ajay, he said, "I'm sorry." That's when Ajay first felt that his father might have done something wrong. The thought made him worry. Once they were on the road, his father said gently, "Don't tell your mother."

Fear made Ajay feel cruel. He asked his father, "What do you think about when you think of Aman?"

Instead of becoming sad, Ajay's father smiled. "I am surprised by how strong he is. It's not easy for him to keep living. But even before, he was strong. When he was interviewing for high school scholarships, one interviewer asked him, 'Are you a thinker or a doer?' He laughed and said, 'That's like asking, "Are you an idiot or a moron?"'"

From then on they often stopped at the bar on the way back from the hospital. Ajay's father always asked the bartender for a cigarette before he sat down, and during the ride home he always reminded Ajay not to tell his mother.

Ajay found that he himself was changing. His superstitions were becoming extreme. Now when he walked around the good-luck tree he punched it, every other time, hard, so that his knuckles hurt. Afterward, he would hold his breath for a moment longer than he thought he could bear, and ask God to give the unused breaths to Aman.

In December, a place opened in one of the good long-term care facilities. It was in New Jersey. This meant that Ajay and his mother could move back to New York and live with his father again. This was the news Ajay's father brought when he arrived for a two-week holiday at Christmas.

Ajay felt the clarity of panic. Life would be the same as before the accident but also unimaginably different. He would return to P.S. 20, while Aman continued to be fed through a tube in his abdomen. Life would be Aman's getting older and growing taller than their parents but having less consciousness than even a dog, which can become excited or afraid.

Ajay decided to use his devotion to shame God into fixing Aman. The fact that two religions regarded the coming December days as holy ones suggested to Ajay that prayers during this time would be especially potent. So he prayed whenever he thought of it — at his locker, even in the middle of a quiz. His mother wouldn't let him fast, but he started throwing away the lunch he took to school. And when his mother prayed in the morning, Ajay watched to make sure that she bowed at least once toward each of the postcards of deities. If she did not, he bowed three times to the possibly offended god on the postcard. He had noticed that his father finished his prayers in less time than it took to brush his teeth. And so now, when his father began praying in the morning, Ajay immediately crouched down beside him, because he knew his father would be embarrassed to get up first. But Ajay found it harder and harder to drift into the rhythm of sung prayers or into his nightly conversations with God. How could chanting and burning incense undo three minutes of a sunny August afternoon? It was like trying to move a sheet of blank paper from one end of a table to the other by blinking so fast that you started a breeze.

On Christmas Eve his mother asked the hospital chaplain to come to Aman's room and pray with them. The family knelt together beside Aman's bed. Afterward the chaplain asked her whether she would be attending Christmas services. "Of course, Father," she said.

"I'm also coming," Ajay said.

The chaplain turned toward Ajay's father, who was sitting in a wheelchair because there was nowhere else to sit.

"I'll wait for God at home," he said.

That night, Ajay watched *It's a Wonderful Life* on television. To him, the movie meant that happiness arrived late, if ever. Later, when he got in bed and closed his eyes, God appeared. There was little to say.

"Will Aman be better in the morning?"

"No."

"Why not?"

"When you prayed for the math exam, you could have asked for Aman to get better, and instead of your getting an A, Aman would have woken."

This was so ridiculous that Ajay opened his eyes. His father was sleeping nearby on folded-up blankets. Ajay felt disappointed at not feeling guilt. Guilt might have contained some hope that God existed.

When Ajay arrived at the hospital with his father and mother the next morning, Aman was asleep, breathing through his mouth while a nurse poured a can of Isocal into his stomach through the yellow tube. Ajay had not expected that Aman would have recovered; nevertheless, seeing him that way put a weight in Ajay's chest.

The Christmas prayers were held in a large, mostly empty room: people in chairs sat next to people in wheelchairs. His father walked out in the middle of the service.

Later, Ajay sat in a corner of Aman's room and watched his parents. His mother was reading a Hindi women's magazine to Aman while she shelled peanuts into her lap. His father was reading a thick red book in preparation for a civil service exam. The day wore on. The sky outside grew dark. At some point Ajay began to cry. He tried to be quiet. He did not want his parents to notice his tears and think that he was crying for Aman, because in reality he was crying for how difficult his own life was.

His father noticed first. "What's the matter, hero?"

His mother shouted, "What happened?" and she sounded so alarmed it was as if Ajay were bleeding.

"I didn't get any Christmas presents. I need a Christmas present," Ajay shouted. "You didn't buy me a Christmas present." And then, because he had revealed his own selfishness, Ajay let himself sob. "You have to give me something. I should get something for all this." Ajay clenched his hands and wiped his face with his fists. "Each time I come here I should get something."

His mother pulled him up and pressed him into her stomach. His father came and stood beside them. "What do you want?" his father asked.

Ajay had no prepared answer for this.

"What do you want?" his mother repeated.

The only thing he could think was "I want to eat pizza and I want candy."

His mother stroked his hair and called him her little baby. She kept wiping his face with a fold of her sari. When at last he stopped crying, they decided that Ajay's father should take him back to his aunt and uncle's. On the way, they stopped at a mini-mall. It was a little after five, and the streetlights were on. Ajay and his father did not take off their winter coats as they ate, in a pizzeria staffed by Chinese people. While he chewed, Ajay closed his eyes and tried to imagine God looking like Clark Kent, wearing a cardigan and eyeglasses, but he could not. Afterward, Ajay and his father went next door to a magazine shop and Ajay got a bag of Three Musketeers bars and a bag of Reese's peanut butter cups, and then he was tired and ready for home.

He held the candy in his lap while his father drove in silence. Even through the plastic, he could smell the sugar and chocolate. Some of the houses outside were dark, and others were outlined in Christmas lights.

After a while Ajay rolled down the window slightly. The car filled with wind. They passed the building where Aman's accident had occurred. Ajay had not walked past it since the accident. When they drove by, he usually looked away. Now he tried to spot the fenced swimming pool at the building's side. He wondered whether the pool that had pressed itself into Aman's mouth and lungs and stomach had been drained, so that nobody would be touched by its unlucky waters. Probably it had not been emptied until fall. All summer long, people must have swum in the pool and sat on its sides, splashing their feet in the water, and not known that his brother had lain for three minutes on its concrete bottom one August afternoon.

JIM SHEPARD

Love and Hydrogen

FROM HARPER'S MAGAZINE

IMAGINE FIVE OR SIX city blocks could lift, with a bump, and float away. The impression the 804-foot-long *Hindenburg* gives on the ground is that of an airship built by giants and excessive even to their purposes. The fabric hull and main frame curve upward sixteen stories high.

Meinert and Gnüss are out on the gangway ladder down to the starboard #1 engine car. They're helping out the machinists, in a pinch. Gnüss is afraid of heights, which amuses everyone. It's an open aluminum ladder with a single handrail extending eighteen feet down into the car's hatchway. They're at 2,000 feet. The clouds below strand by and dissipate. It's early in a mild May in 1937.

Their leather caps are buckled under their chins, but they have no goggles. The air buffets by at eighty-five miles per hour. Meinert shows Gnüss how to hook his arm around the leading edge of the ladder to keep from being blown off as he leaves the hull. Even through the sheepskin gloves the metal is shockingly cold from the slipstream. The outer suede of the grip doesn't provide quite the purchase they would wish when hanging their keisters out over the open Atlantic. Every raised foot is wrenched from the rung and flung into space.

Servicing the engines inside the cupola, they're out of the blast but not the cold. Raising a head out of the shielded area is like being cuffed by a bear. It's a pusher arrangement, thank God. The back end of the cupolas is open to facilitate maintenance on the blocks and engine mounts. The engines are 1,100 horsepower diesels four feet high. The propellers are twenty feet long. When the men are down on their hands and knees adjusting the vibration dampers, those props are a foot and a half away. The sound is like God losing his temper, kettledrums in the sinuses, fists in the face.

Meinert and Gnüss are both Regensburgers. Meinert was in his twenties and Gnüss a child during the absolute worst years of the inflation. They lived on mustard sandwiches, boiled kale, and turnip mash. Gnüss's most cherished toy for a year and a half was a clothespin on which his father had painted a face. They're ecstatic to have found positions like this. Their work fills them with elation, and the kind of spuriously proprietary pride that mortal tour guides might feel on Olympus. Meals that seem giddily baronial — plates crowded with sausages, tureens of soup, platters of venison or trout or buttered potatoes — appear daily, once the passengers have been served, courtesy of Luftschiffbau Zeppelin. Their sleeping berths, aboard and ashore, are more luxurious than any other place they've previously laid their heads.

Meinert and Gnüss are in love. This complicates just about everything. They steal moments when they can — on the last Frankfurt to Rio run, they exchanged an intense and acrobatic series of caresses 135 feet up inside the superstructure when Meinert was supposed to have been checking a seam on one of the gasbags for wear, their glue pots clacking and clocking together — but mostly their ardor is channeled so smoothly into underground streams that even their siblings, watching them work, would be satisfied with their rectitude.

Meinert loves Gnüss's fussiness with detail, his loving solicitude with all schedules and plans, the way he seems to husband good feeling and pass it around among his shipmates. He loves the celebratory delight Gnüss takes in all meals, and watches him with the anticipatory excitement that an enthusiast might bring to a sublime stretch of *Aida.* Gnüss has a shy and diffident sense of humor that's particularly effective in groups. At the base of his neck so it's hidden by a collar he has a tattoo of a figure eight of rope: an infinity sign. He's exceedingly well proportioned.

Gnüss loves Meinert's shoulders, his way of making every physical act worthy of a Johnny Weissmuller, and the way he can play the irresponsible daredevil and still erode others' disapproval or righteous indignation. He's open-mouthed at the way Meinert flaunts the sort of insidious and disreputable charm that all mothers warn against. In his bunk at night, Gnüss sometimes thinks, *I refuse to list all his other qualities,* for fear of agitating himself too completely. He calls Meinert "Old Shatterhand." They joke about the age difference.

It goes without saying that the penalty for exposed homosexuality in this case would begin at the loss of one's position. Captain Pruss, a fair man and an excellent captain, a month ago remarked in Gnüss's presence that he'd bodily throw any fairy he came across out of the control car.

Meinert bunks with Egk; Gnüss, with Thoolen. It couldn't be helped. Gnüss had wanted to petition for their reassignment as bunkmates — what was so untoward about friends wanting to spend more time together? — but Meinert the daredevil had refused to risk it. Each night Meinert lies in his bunk wishing they'd risked it. As a consolation, he passed along to Gnüss his grandfather's antique silver pocket watch. It had already been engraved "To My Dearest Boy."

Egk is a fat little man with boils. Meinert considers him to have been well named. He whistles the same thirteen-note motif each night before lights-out.

How much happiness is someone entitled to? This is the question that Gnüss turns this way and that in his aluminum bunk in the darkness. The ship betrays no tremor or sense of movement as it slips through the sky like a fish.

He is proud of his feelings for Meinert. He can count on one hand the number of people he's known he believes to be capable of feelings as exalted as his.

Meinert, meanwhile, has developed a flirtation with one of the passengers: perhaps the only relationship possible that would be more forbidden than his relationship with Gnüss. The flirtation alternately irritates and frightens Gnüss.

The passenger is one of those languid teenagers who own the world. She has a boy's haircut. She has a boy's chest. She paints her lips but otherwise wears no makeup. Her parents are briskly polite with the crew and clearly excited by their first adventure on an airship; she is not. She has an Eastern name: Tereska.

Gnüss had to endure their exchange of looks when the girl's family first came aboard. Passengers had formed a docile line at the base of the main gangway. Gnüss and Meinert had been shanghaied to help the chief steward inspect luggage and personal valises for matches, lighters, camera flashbulbs, flashlights, even a child's sparking toy pistol: anything that might mix apocalyptically with their ship's seven million cubic feet of hydrogen. Two hundred stevedores in the ground crew were arrayed every ten feet or so around the airship's perimeter, dragging slightly back and forth on their ropes with each shift in the wind. Meinert made a joke about drones pulling a queen. The late afternoon was blue with rain and fog. A small, soaked Hitler Youth contingent with two bedraggled Party pennants stood at attention to see them off.

Meinert was handed Tereska's valise, and Tereska wrestled it back, rummaging through it shoulder to shoulder with him. They'd given each other playful bumps.

The two friends finished their inspections and waited at attention until all the passengers were up the gangway. "Isn't she the charming little rogue," Gnüss remarked. "Don't scold, auntie," Meinert answered.

The first signal bell sounded. Loved ones who came to see the travelers off waved and shouted. A passenger unbuckled his wristwatch and tossed it from one of the observation windows as a farewell present. Meinert and Gnüss were the last ones aboard and secured the gangway. Two thousand pounds of water ballast was dropped. The splash routed the ranks of the Hitler Youth contingent. At 150 feet the signal bells of the engine telegraphs jangled, and the engines one by one roared to life. At 300 feet the bells rang again, calling for higher revolutions.

On the way to their subsequent duties, the two friends took a moment at a free spot at an observation window and watched the ground recede. The passengers were oohing and aahing as the mountains of Switzerland and Austria fell away to the south, inverted in the mirrorlike expanse of the lake. The ship lifted with the smoothness of planetary motion.

Aloft, their lives had really become a pair of stupefying narratives. Frankfurt to Rio in three and a half days. Frankfurt to New York in two. The twenty-five passenger cabins on A deck slept two in stateroom comfort and featured feather-light and whisper-quiet sliding doors. On B deck passengers could lather up in the world's first airborne shower. The smoking room, off the bar and double-sealed all the way round, stayed open until the last guests said goodnight. The fabric-covered walls in the lounge and public areas were decorated with hand-painted artwork. Each room had its own theme: the main salon, a map of the world crosshatched by the routes of famous explorers; the reading room, scenes of the history of postal delivery. An aluminum bust of General von Hindenburg sat in a halo of light on an ebony base in a niche at the top of the main gangway. A place setting for two for dinner involved fifty-eight pieces of Dresden china and silver. The handles of the butter knives were themselves mini-zeppelins. Complimentary sleeping caps were bordered with the legend *An Bord Des Luftschiffes Hindenburg*. Luggage tags were stamped *Im Zeppelin Uber Den Ozean* and featured an image of the *Hindenburg* bearing down, mid-ocean, on what looked like the *Santa Maria.*

When he can put Tereska out of his head, Gnüss is giddy with the danger and improbability of it all. The axial catwalk is 10 inches wide at its base, 782 feet long, and vertiginously high above the passenger and crew compartments below. Crew members require the nimbleness of structural-steel workers. The top of the gas cells can only be inspected from the top of the vertical ringed ladders running along the inflation pipes, sixteen stories up into the radial and spiraling bracing wires and main frame. Up that high, the airship's interior seems to have its own weather. Mists form. The vast cell walls holding the seven million cubic feet of hydrogen billow and flex.

At the very top of Ladder #4 on the second morning out, Meinert hangs from one hand. He spins slowly above Gnüss, down below with the glue pots, like a high-wire act seen at such a distance that all the spectacle is gone. He sings one of his songs from the war, when as a seventeen-year-old he served on the LZ 98 and bombed London when the winds let them reach it. His voice is a floating echo from above:

> In Paris people shake all over
> In terror as they wait.
> The Count prefers to come at night,
> Expect us at half-past eight!

Gnüss nestles in and listens. On either side of the catwalk, great tanks carry 143,000 pounds of diesel oil and water. Alongside the tanks, bays hold food supplies, freight, and mail. This is one of his favorite places to steal time. He and Meinert sometimes linger here for the privacy and the ready excuses — inspection or errands — that all this storage space affords.

Good news: Meinert signals that he's located a worn patch, necessitating help. Gnüss climbs to him with another glue pot and a pot of the gelatin latex used to render the heavy-duty sailmaker's cotton gas-tight. His erection grows as he climbs.

Their repairs complete, they're both strapped in on the ladder near the top, mostly hidden in the gloom and curtaining folds of the gas cell. Gnüss, in a reverie after their lovemaking, asks Meinert if he can locate the most ecstatic feeling he's ever experienced. Meinert can. It was when he'd served as an observer on a night attack on Calais.

Gnüss still has Meinert's warm sex in his hand. This had been the LZ 98, captained by Lehmann, Meinert reminds him. They'd gotten nowhere on a hunt for fogbound targets in England, but conditions over Calais had been ideal for the observation basket: thick cloud at 4,000 feet, but the air beneath crystalline. The big airships were much safer when operating above cloud. But then how to see their targets?

The solution was exhilarating: on their approach they throttled the motors as far back as they could while retaining the power to maneuver. The zeppelin was leveled out at 500 feet above the cloud layer, and then, with a winch and a cable, Meinert, as air observer, was lowered nearly 2,000 feet in the observation basket, a hollow metal capsule scalloped open at the top. He had a clear view downward, and his gondola, so relatively tiny, was invisible from the ground.

Dropping into space in that little bucket had been the most frightening and electric thing he'd ever done. He'd been swept along alone under the cloud ceiling and over the lights of the city, like the messenger of the gods.

The garrison of the fort had heard the sound of their motors, and all the light artillery had begun firing in that direction. But only once had a salvo come close enough to have startled him with its crash.

His cable had extended up above his head into the darkness and murk. It had bowed forward, the capsule canted from the pull. The wind had streamed past him. The lights had rolled by below. From his wicker seat he had directed the immense invisible ship above by telephone, and had set and reset their courses by eye and by compass. He had crisscrossed them over the fort for forty-five minutes, signaling when to drop their small bombs and phosphorus incendiaries. The experience had been that of a magician's, or a sorcerer's, hurling thunderbolts on his own. That night he'd been a regular Regensburg Zeus. The bombs and incendiaries had detonated on the railroad station, the warehouses, and the munitions dumps. When they'd fallen they'd spiraled silently out of the darkness above and had plummeted past his capsule, the explosions always carried away behind him. Every so often luminous ovals from the fort's searchlights had rippled the bottoms of the clouds like a hand lamp beneath a tablecloth.

Gnüss, still hanging in his harness, is disconcerted by the story. He tucks Meinert's sex back into the opened pants.

"That feeling comes back to me in memory when I'm my happiest: hiking or alone," Meinert muses. "And when I'm with you as well," he adds, after having seen Gnüss's face.

Gnüss buckles his own pants, unhooks his harness, and begins his careful descent. "I don't think I make you feel like Zeus," he says, a little sadly.

"Well, like Pan, anyway," Meinert calls out from above him.

That evening darkness falls on the ocean below while the sun is still a glare on the frames of the observation windows. Meinert and Gnüss have their evening duties, as waiters. Their stations are across the room from each other. The dining room is the very picture of a fine hotel restaurant, without the candles. After dinner, they continue to ferry drinks from the bar on B deck to thirsty guests in the lounge and reading rooms. Through the windows the upper surfaces of the clouds in the moonlight are as brilliant as breaking surf. Tereska is nowhere to be found.

Upon retiring, passengers leave their shoes in the corridor, as on shipboard. Newspaper correspondents stay up late in the salon, typing bulletins to send by wireless ahead to America. In the darkness and quiet before they themselves turn in, Gnüss leads Meinert halfway up Ladder #4 yet again, to reward him for having had no contact whatsoever with that teenager. Their continuing recklessness feels like Love itself.

Like their airship, their new home when not flying is Friedrichshafen, beside the flatly placid Lake Constance. The company's presence has transformed the little town. In gratitude the town fathers have erected a zeppelin fountain in the courtyard of the rathaus, the centerpiece of which is the count astride a globe, holding a log-sized airship in his arms.

Friedrichshafen is on the north side of the lake, with the Swiss mountains across the water to the south, including the snow-capped Santis, rising some 8,000 feet. Meinert has tutored Gnüss in mountain hiking, and Gnüss has tutored Meinert in oral sex above the tree line. They've taken chances as though cultivating a death wish: in a lift in the famous Insel Hotel, in rented rooms in the wood-carving town of Uberlingen and in Meersburg with its old castle dating back to the seventh century. In vineyards on the southern exposures of hillsides. Even, once, in a lavatory in the Maybach engine plant, near the gear-manufacturing works.

When not perversely risking everything they had for no real reason, they lived like the locals, with their coffee and cake on Sunday afternoon and their raw smoked ham as the ubiquitous appetizer for every meal. They maintained their privacy as weekend hikers, and developed the southerner's endless capacity for arguing the merits of various mountain trails. By their third year in Friedrichshafen their motto was "A mountain each weekend." They spent nights in mountain huts, and in winters they might ski whole days without seeing other adventurers. If Meinert had asked his friend which experience had been the most ecstatic of *his* young life, Gnüss would have cited the week they spent alone in a hut over one Christmas holiday.

Neither has been back to Regensburg for years. Gnüss's most vivid memory of it, for reasons he can't locate, is of the scrape and desolation of his dentist's tooth-cleaning instruments one rainy March morning. Meinert usually refers to their hometown as Vitality's Graveyard. His younger brother still writes to him twice a week. Gnüss still sends a portion of his pay home to his parents and sisters.

Gnüss knows that he's being the young and foolish one but nevertheless can't resist comparing the invincible intensity of his feelings for Meinert to his pride at serving on this airship — this machine that conquers two oceans at once, the one above and the one below; this machine that brought their country supremacy in passenger, mail, and freight service to the North and South American continents only seventeen years after the Treaty of Versailles.

Even calm, cold, practical minds that worked on logarithms or carburetors felt the strange joy, the uncanny fascination, the radiance of atmospheric and gravitational freedom. They'd watched the *Graf Zeppelin,* their sister ship, take off one beautiful morning, the sun dazzling on its aluminum dope as if it were levitating on light, and it was like watching a juggernaut float free of the earth. One night they'd gone down almost to touch the waves and scared a fishing boat in the fog, and had joked afterward about what the boat's crew must have experienced: looking back to see a great dark, whirring, chugging thing rise like a monster upon them out of the murky air.

They're both Party members. They were over Aachen during the national referendum on the annexation of the Rhineland, and helped the chief steward rig up a polling booth on the port promenade deck. The yes vote had carried among the passengers and crew by a count of 103 to 1.

Meals in flight are so relaxed that some guests arrive for breakfast in their pajamas. Tereska is one such guest, and Gnüss from his station watches Meinert chatting and flirting with her. *She's only an annoyance,* he reminds himself, but his brain seizes and charges around enough to make him dizzy.

The great mass of the airship, though patrolled by crew members, is off-limits to passengers except for those on guided tours. Soon after the breakfast service is cleared, Meinert informs him, with insufficient contrition, that Tereska's family has requested him as their guide. An hour later, when it's time for the tour to begin, there's Tereska alone, in her boyish shirt and sailor pants. She jokes with Meinert and lays a hand on his forearm. He jokes with her.

Gnüss, beside himself, contrives to approach her parents, sunning themselves by a port observation window. He asks if they'd missed the tour. It transpires that the bitch has forewarned them that it would be a lot of uncomfortable climbing and claustrophobic poking about.

He stumbles about belowdecks, only half remembering his current task. What's happened to his autonomy? What's happened to his ability to generate pleasure or contentment for himself independent of Meinert's behavior? Before all this he saw himself in the long term as first officer, or at least chief sailmaker: a solitary and much-admired figure of cool judgments and sober self-mastery. Instead, now he feels overheated and coursed through with kineticism, like an agitated and kenneled dog.

He delivers the status report on the ongoing inspection of the gas cells. "Why are you *weeping?*" Sauter, the chief engineer, asks.

Responsibility has flown out the window. He takes to carrying Meinert's grandfather's watch inside his pants. His briefs barely hold the weight. It bumps and sidles against his genitals. Does it show? Who cares?

He sees Meinert only once all afternoon, and then from a distance. He searches for him as much as he dares during free moments. During lunch the chief steward slaps him on the back of the head for gathering wool.

Three hours are spent in a solitary and melancholy inspection of the rearmost gas cell. In the end he can't say for sure what he's seen. If the cell had disappeared entirely, it's not clear he would have noticed.

Rhine salmon for the final dinner. Fresh trout from the Black Forest. There's an all-night party among the passengers to celebrate their arrival in America. At the bar the man who'd thrown away his wristwatch on departure amuses himself by balancing a fountain pen on its flat end.

They continue to be separated for most of the evening, which creeps along glacially. Gnüss sorts glassware for storage upon landing, and Meinert lends a hand back at the engine gondolas, helping record fuel consumption. Time seems out of joint, and Gnüss finally figures out why: a prankster has set the clock in the bar back, to extend the length of the celebration.

On third watch he takes a break. He goes below and stops by the crew's quarters. No luck. He listens in on a discussion of suitable first names for children conceived aloft in a zeppelin. The consensus favors Shelium, if a girl.

Someone asks if he's seen Meinert. Startled, he eyes the questioner. Apparently the captain's looking for him. Two machinists exchange looks.

Has Gnüss seen him or not? the questioner wants to know. He realizes he hasn't answered. The whole room has taken note of his paralysis. He says he hasn't, and excuses himself.

He finds Meinert on the catwalk heading aft. Relief and anger and frustration swarm the cockleshell of his head. It feels like his frontal lobe is in tumult. Before he can speak, Meinert tells him to keep his voice down, and that the party may be over. What does *that* mean? Gnüss wants to know. His friend doesn't answer.

They go hunting for privacy without success. A cross-brace near the bottom of the tail supports a card game.

On the way forward again, they're confronted by their two roommates, Egk and Thoolen, who block the catwalk as though they've formed an alliance. Perhaps they feel neglected. "Do you two *ever* separate?" Egk asks. "Night and day I see you together." Thoolen nods unpleasantly. One is Hamburg at its most insolent, the other Bremerhaven at its foggiest.

"Shut up, you fat bellhop," Meinert says. They roughly squeeze past, and Egk and Thoolen watch them go.

"I'm so in love!" Egk sings out. Thoolen laughs.

Gnüss follows his friend in silence until they reach the ladder down to B deck. It's a busy hub. Crew members come and go briskly. Meinert hesitates. He seems absorbed in a recessed light fixture. It breaks Gnüss's heart to see that much sadness in the contours of his preoccupation.

"What do you mean the party may be over?" Gnüss demands quietly.

"Pruss wants to see me. He says for disciplinary matters. After that, you know as much as I," Meinert says.

The radio officer and the ship's doctor pass through the corridor at the bottom of the stairs, glancing up as they go, without stopping their quiet conversation.

When Gnüss is unable to respond, Meinert adds, "Maybe he just wants me to tidy up my uniform."

At a loss, Gnüss finally puts a hand on Meinert's arm. Meinert smiles, and whispers, *"You are the most important thing in the world right now."*

The unexpectedness of it brings tears to Gnüss's eyes. Meinert murmurs that he needs to get into his dining room whites. It's nearly time to serve the third breakfast. They've served two luncheons, two dinners, and now three breakfasts.

They descend the stairs together. Gnüss is already dressed and so gives his friend another squeeze on the arm and tells him not to worry, and then goes straight to the galley. His eyes still bleary with tears, he loads linen napkins into the dumbwaiter. Anxiety is like a whirling pillar in his chest. He remembers another of Meinert's war stories, one whispered to him in the early morning after they'd first spent the night together. They'd soaked each other and the bed linens with love and then had collapsed. He woke to words in his ear, and at first thought his bedmate was talking in his sleep. The story concerned Meinert's captain after a disastrous raid one moonless night over the Channel. Meinert had been at his post in the control car. The captain had started talking to himself. He'd said that both radios were smashed, not that it mattered, both radiomen being dead. And that both outboard engines were beyond repair, not that that mattered, since they had no fuel.

Around four A.M., the passengers start exclaiming at the lights of Long Island. The all-night party has petered out into knots of people waiting and chatting along the promenade. Gnüss and Meinert set out the breakfast china, sick with worry. Once the place settings are all correct, they allow themselves a look out an open window. They see below that they've overtaken the liner *Staatendam,* coming into New York Harbor. She salutes them with blasts of her siren. Passengers crowd her decks, waving handkerchiefs.

They're diverted north to avoid a front of thunderstorms. All morning they drift over New England, gradually working their way back to Long Island Sound.

At lunch Captain Pruss appears in the doorway for a moment and then is gone. They bus tables. The passengers all abandon their seats to look out on New York City. From the exclamations they make, it's apparently some sight. Steam whistles sound from boats on the Hudson and East rivers. Someone at the window points out the *Bremen* just before it bellows a greeting. The *Hindenburg*'s passengers wave back with a kind of patriotic madness.

The tables cleared, the waiters drift back to the windows. Gnüss puts an arm around Meinert's shoulders, despair making him courageous. Through patchy cloud they can see shoal water, or riptides, beneath them.

Pelicans flock in their wake. What looks like a whale races to keep pace with their shadow.

In New Jersey they circle over miles of stunted pines and bogs, their shadow running along the ground like a big fish on the surface.

It's time for them to take their landing stations.

Sauter passes them on their way to the catwalk and says that they should give the bracing wires near Ladder #4 another quick check and that he'd noticed a little bit of a hum.

By the time they reach the base of #4, it's more than a little bit of a hum. Gnüss volunteers to go, anxious to do something concrete for his disconsolate beloved. He wipes his eyes and climbs swiftly while Meinert waits below on the catwalk.

Meinert's grandfather's pocket watch bumps and tumbles about his testicles while he climbs. Once or twice he has to stop to rearrange himself. The hum is up near the top, hard to locate. At their favorite perch, he stops and hooks on his harness. His weight supported, he turns his head slightly to try and make his ears direction-finders. The hum is hard to locate. He runs a thumb and forefinger along nearby cables to test for vibration. The cables are covered in graphite to suppress sparks. The slickness seems sexual to him. He's dismayed by his single-mindedness.

On impulse, he takes the watch, pleasingly warm, from his pants. He loops it around one of the cable bolts just so he can look at it. The short chain keeps slipping from the weight. He wraps it once around the nut on the other side of the beam. The nut feels loose to him. He removes and pockets the watch, finds the adjustable spanner on his tool belt, fits it snugly over the nut, and tightens it, and then, uncertain, tightens it again. There's a short, high-pitched sound of metal under stress or tearing.

Below him, his lover, tremendously resourceful in all sorts of chameleonlike self-renovations, and suffused with what he understands to be an unprecedented feeling for his young young boy, has been thinking to himself, *Imagine instead that you were perfectly happy.* Shivering, with his coat collar turned up as though he were sitting around a big cold aerodrome, he leans against a cradle of wires and stays and reexperiences unimaginable views, unearthly lightness, the hull starlit at altitude, electrical storms and the incandescence of clouds, and Gnüss's lips on his throat. He remembers his younger brother's iridescent fingers after having blown soap bubbles as a child.

Below the ship, frightened horses spook like flying fish discharged from seas of yellow grass. Miles away, necklaces of lightning drop and fork.

Inside the hangarlike hull, they can feel the gravitational forces as Captain Pruss brings the ship up to the docking mast in a tight turn. The sharpness of the turn overstresses the after-hull structure, and the bracing wire bolt that Gnüss overtightened snaps like a rifle shot. The recoiling wire slashes open the gas cell opposite. Seven or eight feet above Gnüss's alarmed head, the escaping hydrogen encounters the prevailing St. Elmo's fire playing atop the ship.

From the ground, in Lakehurst, New Jersey, the *Hindenburg* malingers in a last wide circle, uneasy in the uneasy air.

The fireball explodes outward and upward, annihilating Gnüss at its center. More than a hundred feet below on the axial catwalk, as the blinding light envelops everything below it, Meinert knows that whatever time has come is theirs, and won't be like anything else.

Four hundred and eighty feet away, loitering on the windblown and sandy flats weedy with dune grass, Gerhard Fichte, chief American representative of Luftschiffbau Zeppelin and senior liaison to Goodyear, hears a sound like surf in a cavern and sees the hull interior blooming orange, lit from within like a Japanese lantern, and understands the catastrophe to his company even before the ship fully explodes. He thinks: *Life, motion, everything was untrammeled and without limitation, pathless, ours.*

MARY YUKARI WATERS

Aftermath

FROM MANOA

IN IMAMIYA PARK the boys are playing dodge ball, a new American game. Behind them tall poplars rise up through the low-lying dusk, intercepting the last of the sun's rays, which dazzle the leaves with white and gold.

Makiko can hardly believe her son, Toshi, belongs with these older boys. Seven years old! Once, his growth had seemed commensurate with the passage of time. These last few years, however, with the war and surrender, the changes have come too fast, skimming her consciousness like pebbles skipped over water.

Makiko is grateful the war is over. But she cannot ignore a nagging sense that Japan's surrender has spawned a new threat — one more subtle, more diffuse. She can barely articulate it, even to herself; feels unmoored, buffeted among invisible forces surging all around her. As if caught up in these energies, her son's thin body is rapidly lengthening. Look! Within that circle in the dirt he is dodging, he is feinting; his body twists with an unfamiliar grace, foreshadowing that of a young man.

Toshi's growth is abetted by a new lunch program at school that is subsidized by the American government, which has switched, with dizzying speed, from enemy to ally. Each day her son comes home with alien food in his stomach: bread, cheese, bottled milk. Last week, in the pocket of his shorts Makiko found a cube of condensed peanut butter — an American dessert, Toshi explained — which he had meant to save for later. It was coated with lint from his pocket, which he brushed off, ignoring her plea to "get rid of that dirty thing."

And each day Toshi comes home with questions she cannot answer: Who was Magellan? How do you say "My name is Toshi" in English? How do you play baseball?

Makiko shows him the ball games her own mother taught her. She bounces an imaginary ball, chanting a ditty passed down from the Edo period:

> Yellow topknots
> of the Portuguese wives
>
> spiraled like seashells
> and stuck atop their heads,
>
> hold one up to your ear,
> shake it up and down —
>
> a little shrunken brain
> is rattling inside.

In the old days, she tells him, they used to put something inside the rubber balls — maybe a scrap of iron, she wasn't sure — that made a rattling noise. Toshi, too old now for this sort of amusement, sighs with impatience.

Just four years ago, Toshi's head had been too big for his body — endearingly out of proportion, like the head of a stuffed animal. Even then he had a manly, square-jawed face, not unlike that of a certain city council candidate appearing on election posters at the time. Her husband, Yoshitsune, nicknamed his son "Mr. Magistrate." Before going off to war, Yoshitsune had developed a little routine with their son. "*Oi,* Toshi! Are you a man?" Yoshitsune would prompt in his droll tone, using the word *otoko,* with its connotations of male bravery, strength, and honor. He would ask this question several times a day, often before neighbors and friends.

"*Hai,* Father! I am a man!" little Toshi would cry, stiffening at soldierly attention as he had been coached, trembling with eagerness to please. His short legs, splayed out from the knees as if buckling under the weight of his head, were still dimpled with baby fat.

"*Maaa!* An excellent, manly answer!" the grownups praised, through peals of laughter.

Makiko had laughed too, a faint constriction in her throat, for Yoshitsune had remarked to her, "When I'm out fighting in the Pacific, that's how I'm going to remember him." After that, she began watching their child closely, trying to memorize what Yoshitsune was memorizing. Later, when her husband was gone, it comforted her to think that the same images swam in both their minds at night. Even today, Toshi's three-year-old figure is vivid in her mind. On the other hand, she has not fully absorbed the war years, still shrinks from those memories and all that has followed.

Foreigners, for instance, are now a familiar sight. American army jeeps with beefy red arms dangling out the windows roar down Kagane Boulevard, the main thoroughfare just east of Toshi's school. "Keep your young women indoors," the neighbors say. Occasionally Makiko has seen a soldier offering chocolates or peanuts to little children, squatting down to their level, holding out the treat — it seems to her they all have hairy arms — as if to a timid cat. Just yesterday Toshi came home, smiling broadly and carrying chocolates — not one square but three. Bile had surged up in Makiko's throat, and before she knew it, she had struck them right out of his hand and onto the kitchen floor. "How could you!" she choked as Toshi, stunned, burst into sobs. "How could you! Those men killed your *father*!"

This evening Makiko has come to the park with a small box of caramels, bought on the black market with some of the money she was hoarding to buy winter yarn. "In the future," she will tell him, "if you want something so badly, you come to me. *Ne?* Not to them."

On a bench in the toddlers' section, now deserted, she waits for her son to finish his game with the other boys. All the other mothers have gone home to cook dinner. The playground equipment has not been maintained since the beginning of the war. The swing set is peeling with rust; the freestanding animals — the ram, the pig, the rooster — have broken-down springs, and their carnival paint has washed away, exposing more rusted steel.

Ara maaa! Her Toshi has finally been hit! Makiko feels a mother's pang. He is crossing the line to the other side now, carrying the ball. Makiko notes the ease with which the fallen one seems to switch roles in this game, heaving the ball at his former teammates without the slightest trace of disloyalty.

This year Makiko is allowing Toshi to light the incense each evening before the family altar. He seems to enjoy prayer time much more now that he can use matches. She also regularly changes which photograph of her husband is displayed beside the miniature gong. This month's photograph shows Yoshitsune in a cotton *yukata,* smoking under the ginkgo tree in the garden. Sometimes, in place of a photograph, she displays an old letter or one of his silk scent bags, still fragrant after a bit of massaging. To keep Toshi interested, Makiko presents his father in the light of constant renewal.

"Just talk to him inside your mind," she tells her son. "He wants to know what you're learning in school, what games you're playing. Just like any other father, *ne?* Don't leave him behind, don't ignore him, just because he's dead." She wonders if Toshi secretly considers his father a burden, making demands from the altar, like a cripple from a wheelchair.

"Your father's very handsome in this picture, *ne?*" she says tonight. Within the lacquered frame, her son's father glances up from lighting a cigarette, a bemused half-smile on his face, as if he is waiting to make a wry comment.

Toshi nods absently. Frowning, he slashes at the matchbox with the expert flourish of a second-grade boy. The match rips into flames.

"Answer properly! You're not a little baby anymore."

"*Hai,* Mother." Toshi sighs with a weary, accommodating air, squaring his shoulders in a semblance of respectful attention. Makiko remembers with sorrow the big head, the splayed legs of her baby boy.

It amazes her that Toshi has no memory of the routine he once performed with his father. "What *do* you remember of him?" she prods every so often, hoping to dislodge some new memory. But all that Toshi remembers of his father is being carried on one arm before a sunny window.

"*Maaa,* what a wonderful memory!" Makiko encourages him each time. "It must have been a very happy moment!"

When would this have taken place: which year, which month? Would even Yoshitsune have remembered it, this throwaway moment that, inexplicably, has outlasted all the others in their son's mind? She tries conjuring it up, as if the memory is her own. For some reason she imagines autumn, the season Yoshitsune sailed away: October 1942. How the afternoon sun would seep in through the nursery window, golden, almost amber, advancing with the viscous quality of Hiezan honey or of nostalgia, overtaking sluggish dust motes and even sound. She wishes Toshi could remember the old view from that upstairs window: a sea of gray tiled roofs drowsing in the autumn haze, as yet unravaged by the fires of war.

"I'm done," Toshi says.

"What! Already? Are you sure?"

"*Hai,* Mother." Already heading for the dining room, where supper lies waiting on the low table, he slides back the *shoji* door in such a hurry that it grates on the grooves. Makiko considers calling him back — his prayers are getting shorter and shorter — but the incident with the chocolates is still too recent for another reprimand.

She follows him into the dining room. "A man who forgets his past," she quotes as she scoops rice into his bowl, "stays at the level of an animal." Toshi meets her eyes with a guilty, resentful glance. "Go on," she says blandly, "eat it while it's hot."

Toshi falls to. In order to supplement their meager rice ration, Makiko continues to mix in chopped *kabura* radishes — which at least resemble rice in color — as she did during the war. Sometimes she switches to chopped turnips. At first, before the rationing became strict, Toshi would hunch over his rice bowl with his chopsticks, fastidiously picking out one bit of vegetable after another and discarding it on another plate. Now he eats with gusto. It cuts her, the things he has grown used to. As a grown man he will reminisce over all the wrong things, things that should never have been a part of his childhood: this shameful pauper food; a block of peanut paste covered with lint; enemy soldiers amusing themselves by tossing chocolate and peanuts to children.

Later, Toshi ventures a question. Makiko has noticed that nighttime — the black emptiness outside, the hovering silence — still cows him a little, stripping him of his daytime cockiness. After his goodnight bow, Toshi remains kneeling on the *tatami* floor. He says, "I was thinking, Mama, about how I'm seven — and how I only remember things that happened after I was three. So that means I've forgotten a whole half of my life — right?"

"That's right," Makiko says. He is looking up at her, his brows puckered in a look of doleful concentration, which reminds her of his younger days. "But it's perfectly normal, Toshi-*kun.* It's to be expected."

He is still thinking. "So when I get older," he says, "am I going to keep on forgetting? Am I going to forget you too?"

Makiko reaches out and strokes his prickly crewcut. "From this age on," she says, "you'll remember everything, Toshi-*kun*. Nothing more will ever be lost."

In the middle of the night, Makiko awakens from a dream in which Yoshitsune is hitting her with a fly swatter. She lies paralyzed under her *futon,* outrage buzzing in her chest. Details from the dream wash back into her mind: Yoshitsune's smile, distant and amused; the insolent way he wielded the swatter, as if she were hardly worth the effort.

A blue sheet of moonlight, slipping in through the space between two sliding panels, glows in the dark.

In the first year or two after his death, this sort of thing would happen often, and not always in the form of dreams. There were times — but hardly ever anymore; why tonight? — when, in the middle of washing the dishes or sweeping the alley, some small injustice from her past, long forgotten, would rise up in her mind, blocking out all else till her heart beat hard and fast. Like that time, scarcely a month after their wedding, when Yoshitsune had run into his old girlfriend at Nanjin Station and made such a fuss: his absurd, rapt gaze; the intimate timbre of his voice as he inquired after her welfare.

And there was the time — the only time in their entire marriage — when Yoshitsune had grabbed Makiko by the shoulders and shaken her hard. He'd let go immediately, but not before she had felt the anger in his powerful hands and her throat had choked up with fear. That too was early on in the marriage, before Makiko learned to tolerate his sending sizable sums of money to his mother each month.

What is to be done with such memories?

They get scattered, left behind. Over the past few years, more pleasant recollections have taken the lead, informing all the rest, like a flock of birds, heading as one body along an altered course of nostalgia.

She has tried so hard to remain true to the past. But the weight of her need must have been too great: her need to be comforted, her need to provide a legacy for a small, fatherless boy. Tonight she senses how far beneath the surface her own past has sunk, its outline distorted by deceptively clear waters.

*

Toshi has been counting the days till Tanabata Day. A small festival is being held at the riverbank — the first since the war. It will be a meager affair, of course, nothing like it used to be: no goldfish scooping, no *soba* noodles, no fancy fireworks. However, according to the housewives at the open-air market, there will be a limited number of sparklers — the nicest kind, Makiko tells her son — and traditional corn grilled with *shoyu,* which can be purchased out of each family's food allowance.

Because of an after-dark incident near Kubota Temple involving an American soldier and a young girl, Makiko's younger brother has come by this evening to accompany them to the festival. Noboru is a second-year student at the local university.

"*Ne,* Big Sister! Are you ready yet?" he keeps calling from the living room. Makiko is inspecting Toshi's nails and the back of his collar.

"Big Sister," Noboru says, looking up as Makiko finally appears in the doorway, "your house is too immaculate. I get nervous every time I come here!" He is sitting stiffly on a floor cushion, sipping homemade persimmon tea.

"Well," Makiko answers, "I hate dirt." She has switched, like most women, to Western dresses — they require less fabric — but it makes her irritable, having to expose her bare calves in public. She tugs down her knee-length dress.

"*Aaa,*" says young Noboru from his floor cushion, "but I, for one, am fascinated by it. The idea of it, I mean. What's that old saying — 'Nothing grows in a sterile pond'? Just think, Big Sister, of the things that come out of dirty water. A lotus, for example. Or a pearl. Just think: a pearl's nothing more than a grain of dirt covered up by an oyster! And life itself, Big Sister, billions of years ago — emerging from the primordial muck!"

"*Maa maa,* Nobo-*kun.*" She sighs, double-checking her handbag for coin purse, ration tickets, and handkerchief. "You seem to be learning some very interesting concepts at the university."

Toshi is waiting by the front door in shorts and a collared shirt, impatiently pulling the door open and then shut, open and then shut.

Finally they are on their way, strolling down the narrow alley in the still, muggy evening. The setting sun angles down on the east side of the alley, casting a pink-and-orange glow on the charred wooden lattices, where shadows stretch like the long heads of snails from the slightest of protrusions. In the shadowed side of the alley, one of the bucktoothed Kimura daughters ladles water from a bucket onto the asphalt around her door, pausing, with a good-evening bow, to let them pass. The water, colliding with warm asphalt, has released a smell of many layers: asphalt, earth, scorched wood, tangy dragon's beard moss over a mellower base of tree foliage; prayer incense and *tatami* straw, coming from the Kimuras' half-open door; and mixed in with it all, some scent from far back in Makiko's own childhood that falls just short of definition.

"We Japanese," Noboru is saying, "must reinvent ourselves. We must change to fit the modern world. We mustn't remain an occupied nation." He talks of the new constitution, of the new trade agreements. Makiko has little knowledge of politics. She is amused — disquieted too — by this academic young man, who before the war was a mere boy loping past her window with a butterfly net over his shoulder.

"Fundamental shifts . . . ," Noboru is saying, ". . . outdated pyramidal structures." He has just begun wearing hair pomade with an acrid metallic scent. It seems to suggest fervor, fundamental shifts.

"Toshi-*kun!*" Makiko calls. "Don't go too far." The boy stops running. He walks, taking each new step in exaggerated slow motion.

"So much change!" she says to Noboru as she tugs at her cotton dress. "And so fast. Other countries had centuries to do it in."

"*Sō, sō,* Big Sister!" Noboru says. "*Sō, sō.* But we have no choice — that's a fact. You jettison from a sinking ship if you want to survive."

The pair approaches Mr. Watanabe, watering his potted morning glories in the twilight. Holding his watering can in one hand, the old man gives them a genteel bow over his cane. "Yoshitsune-*san,*" he murmurs politely, "Makiko-*san.*" He then turns back to his morning glories, bending over them with the tenderness of a mother with a newborn.

"Poor Watanabe-*san, ne?*" Noboru whispers. "He gets more and more confused every time we see him."

Yes, poor Mr. Watanabe, Makiko thinks. Bit by bit he is being pulled back in, like a slowing planet, toward some core, some necessary center of his past. Laden with memory, his mind will never catch up to Noboru's new constitution or those trade agreements, or even the implications of that billboard with English characters

— instructions for arriving soldiers? — rising above the blackened rooftops and blocking his view of the Hiezan hills.

Oddly, Mr. Watanabe's greeting has triggered a memory: Makiko is strolling with Yoshitsune on a summer evening. For one heartbeat she experiences exactly how things used to be — their commonplace existence, before later events imposed their nostalgia — with a stab of physical recognition that is indefinable, impossible to call up again. Then it is gone, like the gleam of a fish, having stirred up all the waters around her.

They walk on in silence. "Toshi-*kun!*" she calls out again. "Slow down." Toshi pauses, waiting for them; he swings at the air with an imaginary bat. *"Striku! Striku!"* he hisses.

It occurs to Makiko how artificial this war has been, suspending people in the same, unsustainable state of solidarity. For a while everyone had clung together in the bomb shelter off Nijiya Street, thinking the same thoughts, breathing in the same damp earth and the same warm, uneasy currents made by bodies at close range. But that is over now.

Makiko thinks of her future. She is still full of life and momentum. There is no doubt that she will pass through this period and into whatever lies beyond it, but at a gradually slowing pace; a part of her, she knows, will lag behind in the honeyed light of prewar years.

"Toshi-*kun!*" she cries. "Wait!" Her son is racing ahead, his long shadow sweeping the sunlit fence as sparrows flutter up from charred palings.

Makiko stands out on the veranda, fanning herself with a paper *uchiwa.* Toshi is already asleep. The night garden is muggy; the mosquitoes are out in full force. She can hear their ominous whine from the hydrangea bush, in between the rasping of crickets, but they no longer target her as they did in her youth. She is thinner now, her skin harder from the sun, her blood watered down from all the rationing.

It was a wonderful festival. Shadowy adults bent over their children, helping them to hold sparklers over the glassy water. The sparklers sputtered softly in the dark, shedding white flakes of light. Makiko had watched from a distance; Toshi was old enough, he had insisted, to do it by himself. She had remarked to Noboru how there is something in everyone that responds to fireworks: so fleeting, so lovely in the dark.

It was a fine night for Toshi. “This corn is so *good, ne,* Mama?” he kept saying, looking up from his rationed four centimeters of corncob. “This sure tastes *good, ne?*” The joy on his face, caught in the glow of red paper lanterns, brought a lump to her throat.

Tonight there is a full moon. Earlier, at dusk, it was opaque and insubstantial. Now, through shifting moisture in the air, it glows bright and strong, awash with light.

For Makiko, the festival owed its luster to all that lay beneath, to all those other evenings of her life and their lingering phosphorescence. Which long-ago evenings exactly? They are slowly losing shape, merging together in her consciousness.

Perhaps Toshi will remember this night. Perhaps it will rise up again once he is grown. Some smell, some glint of light will bring texture and emotion to a future summer evening. As will his memory of praying before his father’s picture or being carried by his father before an open window.

Contributors' Notes

100 Other Distinguished Stories of 2001

Editorial Addresses

Contributors' Notes

MICHAEL CHABON was born in Washington, D.C., in 1963 and raised in Columbia, Maryland. He spent his twenties and thirties moving around — Laguna Beach, Seattle, Florida, New York, San Francisco, Los Angeles — but since 1997 he has stayed put in Berkeley, California, with his wife, Ayelet Waldman, who is also a novelist. They have three children and a Bernese mountain dog.

▪ This story came out of nowhere one night when I was supposed to be working on something else entirely. Before starting to work, I sat listening to "The Carpet Crawlers" by Genesis, a song I have listened to a thousand times before without any associations or strange effects coming to the fore. But for some reason that night the music triggered a deep feeling of mournfulness and regret. It was very mysterious. When I started to write, the story just pretty much fell out in one piece.

CAROLYN COOKE is the author of a short story collection, *The Bostons,* which earned her a 2002 PEN/Robert Bingham Fellowship for a first book. Her work has appeared once before in *The Best American Short Stories* and twice in *Prize Stories: The O. Henry Awards.* She lives in Point Arena, California, and is working on a novel.

▪ "The Sugar-Tit" is based on a true story of carrying a steaming roast of beef into the Boston Athenaeum on Beacon Street. The uncomfortable sense of judgment raining down, of carrying certain delusions and secret truths around like a hot bloody roast on a plate through a good library, helped me finally to relax into telling this story about a practical joke and a sudden death.

ANN CUMMINS was born in Durango, Colorado, and grew up in Shiprock, New Mexico. Her short stories have appeared in *McSweeney's, The New Yorker, The Prentice Hall Anthology of Women's Literature,* and *The Best American Short Stories.* Her story collection will be published next year by Houghton Mifflin.

▪ When I was about seven years old, I had a transforming experience with a jar of beans at a birthday party. I gleaned that there was more to that jar than met the eye — beans behind the visible beans — and as a result, I won a bean-counting contest. The incident stuck in my memory. At some point the bean jar evolved in my mind from an image of three-dimensionality to a metaphor for the hidden world, the world of secrets — the unspeakable and taboo — a world I try to mine in fiction. In "Red Ant House" I gave my bean jar event to Leigh, the protagonist, and let the story grow around her. Leigh is a child I wish I'd been: vocal, cunning, full of spit.

EDWIDGE DANTICAT is the author of *Breath, Eyes, Memory; Krik? Krak!; The Farming of Bones; Behind the Mountains,* a young adult novel; and a nonfiction book, *After the Dance: A Walk Through Carnival in Jacmel.* She is also the editor of *The Butterfly's Way: Voices from the Haitian Dyaspora in the United States* and *The Beacon Best of 2000.*

▪ I began writing "Seven" while working on a nonfiction book about carnival in Haiti. During my research, I observed how many carnival traditions had parallels in everyday life but were wildly exaggerated during the celebrations. When I came back to New York, I became haunted by the image of a woman who is left behind by her lover after carnival. Her strongest memories of him, and his of her, are of the time they spent together performing a mock marriage ritual at carnival. Since they never spent long periods of time together, they cherish these memories even more, making these moments a paradigm for a relationship that would eventually have to endure a seven-year separation. At first I didn't want to write the story, fearing that this was not enough of a plot. However, I soon let go of my reservations about plot, giving that space instead to the silence that eventually becomes a central part of the relationship when the couple is finally reunited. Once I began the actual writing of the story, many other elements streamed in, such as the police assault on Abner Louima and the killing of Patrick Dorismond, a Haitian American youth from Brooklyn, New York, where the couple eventually makes their home. I also included the extramarital affairs that both the unnamed husband and the wife were involved in while they were apart, burdening their reacquaintance period with an extra layer of guilt. In the end, however, it all came back to the carnival, which in the course of their relationship is transformed from a symbol of celebration to one of sorrow and loss.

E. L. DOCTOROW's work has been published in thirty languages. His novels include *Welcome to Hard Times, The Book of Daniel, Ragtime, Loon Lake, Lives of the Poets, World's Fair, Billy Bathgate, The Waterworks,* and *City of God.* Among his honors are the National Book Award, two National Book Critics Circle Awards, the PEN/Faulkner Award, the Edith Wharton Citation for Fiction, the William Dean Howells Medal of the American Academy of Arts and Letters, and the National Humanities Medal (conferred by the president). He lives and works in New York.

▪ There is a tabloid history behind this tale: In Chicago around the turn of the last century, a Norwegian immigrant named Belle Paulson took to murdering members of her family after buying insurance policies on their lives. She then repaired to La Porte, Indiana, to expand her enterprise. To this day the locals speak of La Porte's "murder farm." It seemed to me that no one could commit to so many barbarous acts over an extended time if she did not have some mental mechanism that resolved everything she did as necessary and normal. Surely such criminal insanity, amounting to a total worldview, would have charismatic powers. Enter Earle, my narrator. Of course, his mama, Dora, is not the immigrant Belle Paulson (who had daughters but no sons), and the events of the story do not coincide with the history. I think the relationship of mother and son is the heart of the composition, though I'm not at all sure that any recent mother-son criminal team was on my mind when I found Earle. It is more what the title may suggest — some of our houses are not right; a house on the plains, a house in the suburbs, but always seeming inevitably to be integral to the American landscape.

RICHARD FORD was born in Jackson, Mississippi, in 1944, and was raised there and in Little Rock. He has written five novels and three collections of stories. Among these are *The Sportswriter, Independence Day, Rock Springs, Wildlife,* and most recently, in 2002, *A Multitude of Sins,* from which the story "Puppy" is taken.

▪ I usually don't remember much about how any story of mine came to be written. Once the raw material gets combined into the story, not only does the material itself become denatured, but the course of the story's composition almost always grows indistinct to me. Often I completely misremember things — where details came from, what I originally had in mind (if anything), where the title popped up. Sometimes Kristina will have been in on a story's beginnings, and she can set things straight. But not always. And this seems all right. The new "set" of the material really ought to abolish the old, if the story is at all unique. And in general I'm still of the old, literature-as-magic school, whose chief tenet is that saying very much about how a story got written is usually misleading or banal or both, and, perhaps more important, can threaten to make the "product" story seem a little too mechanistic. ("What you need to build your tower, Monsieur Eiffel, is all these pieces of steel and a big ladder . . .") Something remarkable, even mysterious, does occur in any good story's writing, causing it to exceed its parts, its origins, its author's biography — its explanation.

With that said, however and alas, someone did abandon a little dog in our garden on Bourbon Street. And its presence occasioned a lot of tumultuous feelings in Kristina and me. I recognized the event as a possible premise for a story right away: "What if someone left a puppy in someone's garden . . ." Eventually these strong emotions — which were complex and not conventionally identifiable — began to draw me in the way that potential stories do, so that my response was to dedicate language to the feeling of attraction, using the factual events, and quite a few nonfactual ones that came from someplace else, as *hearers* for advancing the story's inquiry: *If* someone did leave a puppy in someone's garden, *then* what might happen . . .

"Puppy" is only the second story I've written since 1975 that has a southern setting. So spooked was I about setting it in New Orleans (spooked that I would be inhabited and crippled by some other writer's spirit, style, preoccupations) that I wrote the story entirely without mentioning New Orleans, and only after it was written felt okay about putting in the name of where it's set. Seems silly, in a way. But there you are.

MELISSA HARDY was born and raised in Chapel Hill, North Carolina. She graduated from the University of North Carolina at Chapel Hill with an honors degree in creative writing, did graduate work in history at the University of Toronto, and now lives in Canada, where she works as a communications specialist. She published her first novel, *A Cry of Bees,* in 1970, when she was sixteen, and *Constant Fire* in 1995. In 1995 she won the Journey Prize for the best piece of short fiction to be published in Canada in that year; more recently, she was a finalist for a 1999 Western Magazine Foundation Award. Her work has been included in a number of anthologies, including *The Best Canadian Short Stories, The Best American Short Stories 1999,* and *The Year's Best Fantasy and Horror,* forthcoming in 2002. Her most recent collection of short stories, *The Uncharted Heart,* was published in the spring of 2001. She is married to Ken Trevenna. Between them, they have five children and one dog.

▪ "The Heifer" was written as part of the collection *The Uncharted Heart,* set in the Porcupine region of northeastern Ontario, my husband's homeland. This remote bush country, which lies well beyond the arctic watershed, was settled very suddenly and from all corners of the globe early in the twentieth century, when first silver and then gold was discovered in the region. I had set out to craft a literary portrait of the Porcupine by writing a series of stories, each of which focused on one of the groups that settled in the region — French trappers, prospectors, and surveyors from Upper Canada, Scottish factors, Cornish miners, Chinese "paper sons," and, in the case of "The Heifer," Finnish farmers. Since very little has been written about northeastern Ontario, either fictional or nonfictional, I was forced to rely on self-published memoirs, obtained through interlibrary loans, for a great deal of my research. The seed of this story came from one of these memoirs — an account of how a farmer got a cow to walk across glare ice. The fire that ravages Aina's farm was, in fact, historically accurate, and I drew much of the description of the devastation it wreaked from personal accounts. Aina's last encounter with Olga was impossibly difficult to write, and my father swears he will never forgive me for putting him through the agony of reading it.

KARL IAGNEMMA is a research scientist in the mechanical engineering department at MIT. His short stories have received the *Playboy* College Fiction Award and the *Paris Review* Discovery Prize. "Zilkowski's Theorem" is part of his first collection of stories, *On the Nature of Human Romantic Interaction,* which will be published in 2003. He lives in Cambridge, Massachusetts.

▪ I wrote this story while I was a graduate student and was going through a phase where I would occasionally be overcome with an (I hoped) irrational fear that my thesis research was completely, totally wrong. Alternately, I worried that at my thesis defense, someone would stand up and point out that my work had been blatantly plagiarized. These feelings were the basis for "Zilkowski's Theorem." There's something about engineering graduate school that seems to bring out a bitter edge in people, and Henderson is a composite of many of my bitter but goodhearted colleagues and friends. He probably also contains a fair amount of myself.

While I was writing this story I was also thinking about the way that religion can provoke both selfless and selfish acts, sometimes simultaneously. Luckily, I've had more experience observing the selfless side of religion, which is why this story was written for and is dedicated to my mother.

JHUMPA LAHIRI was born in London, England, and grew up in Rhode Island. She is the author of *Interpreter of Maladies,* a collection of short stories, which was awarded the Pulitzer Prize for fiction in 2000. She lives with her husband in New York City.

▪ I spent most of my twenties in Boston. In my eight years there, I moved a total of eight times. For the majority of those years I shared apartments with people whom, initially, I didn't know at all. I usually found them through newspaper ads or word of mouth. Needless to say, it was always something of a gamble. Apart from the bedrooms, everything in those households was communal. It felt normal then, but it's hard to imagine now, living in such proximity with perfect strangers. This story was inspired by the unexpected glimpses one sometimes has of the intimate lives of others.

BETH LORDAN directs the creative writing program at Southern Illinois University at Carbondale. She is the author of a novel, *August Heat,* and a collection of stories, *And Both Shall Row.* Her research in Ireland has been made possible by the Irish and Irish Immigration Studies Program, directed by Dr. Charles Fanning, at SIUC. She lives with her family in Carbondale.

▪ Sometimes a story just arrives. I suppose that sometimes when that happens, the writer is paying attention. More often, I suspect, we're not: instead, we're working on something else, busily imagining that we create the stories. If we're fortunate, the story hangs around and waits, more or less patiently.

The opening of "Digging" showed up in the imagination of a potential daughter-in-law for Mary and Lyle, musing on what she'd seen in the National Museum as she traveled on the train from Dublin to Galway. That story didn't go (or hasn't arrived yet), but Seamus and his gold were nice enough to keep, not because I really thought I'd use them — I've abandoned whimsy, I don't do history — but just because the sentences had come out so nicely, the tone was so easy. So I kept him in a little file marked "Seamus." For a year. Now and then he'd make a little murmur, rattle his hovel against the gold cup, and I'd explain again that I had work to do, stories to invent.

And then I read Alice McDermott's miraculous story "Enough," a breathless romp through eighty-some years of the life of the unnamed central character, executed in insanely long and busy sentences mostly in the imperative voice; there's no conventional scene, and the story is somehow both a biography and a philosophical definition and hedonistic celebration of the joys of desire via ice cream, in about eight pages. This, I need not point out, cannot be done: she did it, and took my breath away. And the voice that had handed Seamus his shovel and sent him up the field said, quite firmly, "Ahem."

Welty said, "Read you story: your story will help you." Buried treasure equals secrets; I mentioned the buried treasure to a friend, who mentioned Seamus Heaney's poem "Digging," which led me to his poems about the bodies found in bogs, and about the complexities of leaving and staying and returning, and I have borrowed shamelessly from him. If burial was the occasion, then secrets were the point, and Mary Alice hurried up. And then the story was in charge. I wrote it in seven weeks, far more quickly than I usually manage to get out of the way of a story, and I've never had more fun writing.

ALICE MATTISON'S most recent book is a novel, *The Book Borrower.* She is the author of two previous novels, including *Hilda and Pearl* (recently reprinted in paperback), three collections of stories, and a book of poems. She lives in New Haven, Connecticut, and teaches in the low-residency MFA program at Bennington College. She is now writing a novel and a book of short stories.

▪ "In Case We're Separated" was the first story I wrote for a collection, still unfinished, to be called *Brooklyn Sestina.* A note about the stories I hoped to write says I wanted them to be "direct, corny, and simple," but I also had in mind a book in which stories would relate to one another in a literary pattern (which isn't visible when they are read singly), using repetition in something like the way a sestina does. I think I wanted to reproduce the divided feelings of my college years, when I lived at home in Brooklyn amid an extended family of immigrant and second-generation secular Jews while taking the el train to college every day to study English literature, ancient Greek, and Latin. In this story, Sylvia's the one who knows about something beyond life at home, and maybe Bobbie does, finally, as well.

JILL MCCORKLE is a native of Lumberton, North Carolina. She is the author of five novels and three short story collections, most recently *Creatures of Habit,* which includes the story "Billy Goats." She has taught creative writing at the University of North Carolina at Chapel Hill, Tufts, Harvard, and Brandeis. She is currently on the faculty of the MFA program at Bennington College.

▪ "Billy Goats" began as an exercise to set the small-town stage of my story collection. I wrote it as a kind of mood piece, incorporating mentions of various characters who appear in greater depth in later stories in the collection. I wanted to capture the experience of my own childhood summers in a small southern town — the freedom we had on those nights the neighborhood kids banded together on bikes and took off without any fear or warnings from our parents. We chased the mosquito truck, dipped into the motel pools along I-95, and played endless games of kick-the-can or cops and robbers. There was a kind of security within the town that I don't think kids these days are able to experience in the same way. We knew our town and everyone in it. My parents had grown up there, as had one set of grandparents, so I knew the way our town had looked two generations before. There was a shared sense of history: the ice storm in 1964 that kept us home from school for over a week; Hurricane Hazel in 1954, the wreckage of which adults referred to often when describing the landscape; the Lumbee Indians, famously surrounding and scaring off the Klan with sawed-off shotguns; right on back to when Sherman rode through downtown Lumberton and got lost in the swamp.

But as I was writing about the familiar, I discovered what I always tell my students, which is that it is impossible to sit down and start writing and *not* tell a story. And I was telling the story about a loss of security and innocence, that age when the stories are not fanciful and far back in time but immediate and closer than we'd ever dared to think. The setting is the summer of the Jeffrey MacDonald hearings, which took place just thirty miles away in Fort Bragg. In looking back, I realized that this summer was a milestone, one where I began seeing the potential for darkness and danger where I had never seen it before. The result was that the narrator then began to look much closer into the lives surrounding her, seeking out the darkest details.

For me, the story itself became a kind of milestone, as it set the tone for a group of stories I had wanted to write for a very long time — stories that center on loss and grief. I am someone who always looks under the bed and behind the shower curtain, with the idea that I want to find *it* (whatever it may be) before *it* finds me. There is strength in knowledge — particularly the disturbing kind — because it keeps the imagination from running completely wild. There is the feeling, especially in childhood, I think, that if you can see what's threatening and name it, you are more protected than those who refuse to look.

Ultimately this story is about both the survivor and the victim, and the image of the billy goat was a natural fit. I had in mind the story where the billy goats must scramble over the dangerous bridge to safety (a story we often acted out in my neighborhood), but I also had in mind the simple wide-spaced stare of the creature, his eyes set so that he can see predators from both directions. I felt while writing this story that my eyes adjusted to the dark and my vision expanded.

TOM MCNEAL's short fiction has appeared in *The Atlantic Monthly, Playboy,* and various literary journals and has been anthologized in the O. Henry and Pushcart Prize collections. His first novel, *Goodnight, Nebraska,* winner of the James A. Michener Memorial Prize, was published in 1998. With his wife, Laura, he has written two young adult novels, *Crooked,* which was listed among the American Library Association's Top Ten Young Adult Books of 2000, and *Zipped,* which is forthcoming. He lives in California with Laura and their sons, Sam and Hank, aged four and two.

▪ "Watermelon Days" started with an image of a sweet, somewhat ineffectual man working in a small town and laying eyes on a cosmopolitan-seeming woman newly arrived from the East Coast. I wanted the story (and the early sections of the novel from which it comes) placed where WNAX (the actual "Midwest address for CBS") originated, and that's Yankton. I've lived in northwest Nebraska but had never set foot in eastern South Dakota, let alone Yankton, so in 1999 my wife (pregnant) and son (aged one) more or less obligingly flew off with me to spend a Labor Day weekend there. We reconnoitered and took notes and got haircuts and photographed buildings and houses and just generally had such a good time that my wife started talking openly about us taking up residence there.

Much of the history that finds its way into the story comes from the local history section of the Yankton library, where I found several works by Bob Karolevitz, a Yankton native who not only has all his facts at hand, but also presents them with clarity and style. And perhaps this anecdote will make more comprehensible my weakness for small towns. When the librarian, Joyce Brunken, learned that I could use another day with the reference books, she offered to come in on Sunday and open the library for me. She was just going to quilt that day anyway, she said, and the library tables were perfect for laying out a quilt.

As for the story itself, I can't say what it's about. A misfitting woman, an uncertain man, a little girl with a big tongue. If somebody said, "It's about a funny couple finding the eyes to see themselves," that would be fine.

LEONARD MICHAELS lives in Italy. His most recently published books are a collection of stories called *A Girl with a Monkey* and *Time Out of Mind,* his journals from the sixties to the nineties. His work has appeared several times before in *The Best American Short Stories* and *The Best American Essays.*

▪ "Nachman from Los Angeles" was inspired by a friend's experience in graduate school when, in need of money, he wrote freshman themes and term papers for students who had no interest in any academic subject, no ideas, and no desire to go to the library to do research. Books depressed them. My friend pitied them, so it wasn't only for money that he became a ghostwriter. It was hard work, because the desperate students would often show up at his door in the middle of the night after failing to write a paper that was due the next morning. He would tell them to go away, and they would start to beg. He took pride in being able to guarantee a high grade, but that was impossible if he had to start writing at 3 or 4 A.M. and finish before their class met at 9 or 10 A.M. A few students were so grateful for any grade higher than D or F that they offered to do anything for him in return, or almost anything.

ARTHUR MILLER was born in New York City in 1915 and studied at the University of Michigan. He is the author of many plays, screenplays, stories, novels, and essays and of an autobiography, *Timebends.* His plays include *The Crucible, Death of a Salesman, All My Sons, After the Fall, The Ride Down Moran,* and a new one called *Resurrection Blues.* Among his screenplays are *The Misfits* and *The Crucible.* Among his many awards are three Tony Awards, two Emmy Awards, two New York Drama Critics Circle Awards, the John F. Kennedy Lifetime Achievement Award, the Prix Molière of the French Theater, the Dorothy and Lillian Gish Lifetime Achievement Award, and the Pulitzer Prize. He was the Jefferson Lecturer for the National Endowment for the Humanities in 2001.

▪ As much as anything else, "Bulldog" is a voyage backward to the Brooklyn I knew a long time ago. It isn't quite autobiographical, however — the mixture in it of recollection and invention is twisted, one around the other, and beyond my ability to untangle. It may, in fact, have arisen from a certain smell that wafted up from a pile of wet leaves.

MEG MULLINS was born in New Mexico in 1972. She attended Barnard College and received her MFA from Columbia University. "The Rug" was the first story to be published from her collection, *Trouble.* Others have appeared in *The Baltimore Review* and *Image.* She lives with her husband and their two children in Albuquerque, where she is at work on her first novel.

▪ My grandmother was a beautiful, elegant, witty, sensitive, and kind woman. She had a hat for nearly any occasion and wore heels and pearls every day. A true matriarch, she brought all branches of our diverse family together. My grandfather was a unique combination of intellectual curiosity and Western machismo. Fluent in Latin and an avid hunter, he was an eccentric spirit. Together, they were a glamorous and fascinating couple.

I was six when my grandmother died suddenly. Home alone, she had a heart attack and collapsed on the bedroom rug. The loss was so great for my grandfather that the family worried for many months that he would commit suicide. Her death continued to linger over him and our family like a tragedy of epic proportions. As I grew older and came to know my grandfather better, his sadness became even more painful to witness.

A few days after my grandmother's death, my grandfather rolled up the rug on which she had died. When she fell, she hit her head, and the wound left a small pool of her blood on the rug. This was all that was left of her. My grandfather silently carried the rug to the curb for the trash collector and stood there, waiting, until it was picked up and taken away.

"The Rug" was prompted by that image, and after many drafts, I was somewhat surprised to find that the final draft — so far from its original form and substance — actually contained a version of the image.

My husband, in one of many tales from his childhood, introduced me to Ushman Kahn. I thank him. I also owe a debt to Jonathan Franzen for assuring me that a character's flaws are compelling, to Helen Schulman for encouraging me to send Ushman out into the world, and to David Hamilton for seeing him and liking him, flaws and all.

ALICE MUNRO is a native of Maron County, Ontario, and has written many books and short stories.

▪ "Family Furnishings" is all built around the kernel incident — the mother dying of burns, the child saying, "But she would want to see *me,*" which is a true story that I have somewhat rearranged. Around this are layers of autobiographical half-truth, and handy invention, and then an entirely personal final bit in the drugstore.

AKHIL SHARMA'S novel, *An Obedient Father,* received the 2001 PEN/Hemingway Award and the Sue Kaufman Prize from the American Academy of Arts and Letters and was considered by more than eighty publications, including the *New York Times* and *USA Today,* as one of the best novels of 2000. His short stories have also been included in the 1996 and 1998 *Best American Short Stories.* Sharma lives in New York with his wife.

▪ "Surrounded by Sleep" is the only story where, even as I wrote, I thought I was doing a good job. The use of God to create a narrative spine is, I think, quite clever. There were lots of revisions as I worked — the story took about three months to write — but every afternoon as I went jogging, I felt pregnant. I sent the story to *The New Yorker,* and in the same happy, hazy way that everything with the story had been progressing, the magazine bought it and almost immediately published it. My luck continued, and the issue in which the story was published (the one with a map of Manhattan renamed with Afghani suffixes) sold the most copies of the year. Then I waited for *The Best American Short Stories.* I thought I had a good chance of getting in, because my work had been chosen for previous anthologies and so the editor probably remembered me. February, the month when I was notified the last two times, came and went. Sometime in the beginning of March, I read "Surrounded by Sleep" again, and I did not feel at all proud of what I was reading. Then, in mid-March, I got a letter telling me I had been accepted into the anthology. I read my story again and thought, "This is pretty good." Such is the madness of being a writer.

JIM SHEPARD is the author of five novels — *Flights, Paper Doll, Lights Out in the Reptile House, Kiss of the Wolf,* and *Nosferatu* — and two collections of short stories, *Batting Against Castro* and the forthcoming *Love and Hydrogen.* His short fiction has appeared in *Harper's Magazine, The New Yorker, The Atlantic Monthly, Esquire, The Paris Review, Playboy, DoubleTake,* and *Tin House,* among other places. He teaches at Williams College and in the Warren Wilson MFA program.

▪ "Love and Hydrogen" began when I was stuck for longer than I wanted to be in the children's book section of my local bookstore. I'd been trailing back and forth through it in the company of my four-year-old son, and he'd been not much interested in his father's conceptions of what constituted adequate browsing time. Sometimes he wanted to show me what he found; sometimes he wanted to poke through discoveries on his own. During one of the latter periods I came across a children's book about the *Hindenburg*. The oversized illustrations seemed startlingly evocative to me, though evocative of what, I wasn't sure. I was struck by the immensity of the ship's scale, which I'd known about intellectually but hadn't experienced viscerally. A sense of the hubris of the thing — building a lighter-than-air machine *that* immense, and then filling it with *hydrogen*, and then building into its belly a *smoking* room — touched off in me a sense of the apocalyptic, which, it's been recently pointed out, has been a longstanding fascination of mine in my fiction.

I started researching. The research enlarged my sense of just how bizarrely compelling this now-lost world of zeppelins was. I still needed something to lift the project beyond your average small boy's absorption with big things that blow up, however, and that something was provided when, surprising myself, I wrote, a page or so after having introduced my two protagonists, "Meinert and Gnüss are in love. This complicates just about everything." Which, I discovered happily, turned out to be the case.

MARY YUKARI WATERS is half Japanese and half Irish. Her stories have appeared in various magazines and have been anthologized in *The Pushcart Book of Short Stories* as well as *Prize Stories: The O. Henry Awards*. She is a 2002 recipient of a fellowship from the National Endowment for the Arts. Her first story collection will be published in the spring of 2003.

▪ I grew up listening to my Japanese grandmother tell stories from her past. Those stories were deliberately vague when it came to details of the war; my family considered the topic to be in bad taste. But what came through to me as a child — and has stayed with me through adulthood — was something of the unique mood of those times, a glimpse of what it was like, trying to lead ordinary lives after the surrender. This story was my attempt to transfer some of those feelings onto paper.

100 Other Distinguished Stories of 2001

COMPILED BY KATRINA KENISON

ACKERMAN, DIANE
Hummingbirds. *Ploughshares,* Vol. 27, No. 4.

ALMOND, STEVE
I Am as I Am. *The New England Review,* Vol. 22, No. 1.

BARKLEY, BRAD
Beneath the Deep, Slow Motion. *The Virginia Quarterly Review,* Vol. 77, No. 3.

BAUSCH, RICHARD
The Weight. *The Southern Review,* Vol. 37, No. 2.

BEATTIE, ANN
Find and Replace. *The New Yorker,* November 5.
That Last Odd Day in L.A. *The New Yorker,* April 16.

BENIOFF, DAVID
The Affairs of Each Beast. *Zoetrope: All Story,* Vol. 5, No. 4.

BETTS, DORIS
Aboveground. *Epoch,* Vol. 50, No. 3.

BIGUENET, JOHN
It Is Raining in Bejucal. *Zoetrope: All Story,* Vol. 5, No. 2.

BROCKMEIER, KEVIN
The Ceiling. *McSweeney's,* No. 7.

BURNS, DEBRA
By the Sea. *West Branch,* No. 48.

CHAON, DAN
I Demand to Know Where You're Taking Me. *Epoch,* Vol. 50, No. 1.

CLARK, GEORGE MAKANA
The Raw Man. *Transition,* No. 89.

COOKE, CAROLYN
The Bostons. *The New England Review,* Vol. 22, No. 1.

DAVIES, PETER HO
What You Know. *Harper's Magazine,* January.

DAY, CATHY
Wallace Porter Sees the Elephant. *The Southern Review,* Vol. 37, No. 1.

DELANEY, EDWARD J.
The Warp and the Weft. *The Atlantic Monthly,* November.

DIVAKARUNI, CHITRA
The Lives of Strangers. *Agni Review,* No. 53.

DOERR, ANTHONY
The Caretaker. *The Paris Review,* No. 159.
The Hunter's Wife. *The Atlantic Monthly,* May.

DORMAN, LESLEY
The Old Economy Husband. *The Atlantic Monthly,* December.

DYBEK, STUART
Blue Boy. *TriQuarterly,* Nos. 110 and 111.

EICHENBERGER, PETER
The Blue Couch. *Epoch,* Vol. 50, No. 3.

ELLISON, HARLAN
Incognita, Inc. *Hemispheres,* January.

ERDRICH, LOUISE
The Butcher's Wife. *The New Yorker,* October 15.
Sister Godzilla. *The Atlantic Monthly,* February.

FEITELL, MERRILL
Here Beneath Low-Flying Planes. *Book,* November-December.

FORD, RICHARD
Charity. *Tin House,* No. 9.

FRENCH, ELIZABETH KEMPER
Flamingo. *Ploughshares,* Vol. 27, Nos. 2 and 3.

FREUDENBERGER, NELL
Lucky Girls. *The New Yorker,* June 18 and 25.

FURMAN, LAURA
Beautiful Baby. *The Yale Review,* Vol. 89, No. 1.

GADOL, PETER
Line Up. *Tin House,* No. 9.

GAITSKILL, MARY
A Bestial Noise. *Tin House,* No. 9.

GATES, DAVID
George Lassos Moo. *Esquire,* December.

GAY, WILLIAM
Good 'Til Now. *The Oxford American,* No. 37.

GORDON, JAIMY
Polio Weather. *The Colorado Review,* Vol. 28, No. 2.

GRIMM, MARY
Here, At Last. *New Letters,* Vol. 67, No. 4.

HAGENSTON, BECKY
Arctic Circus. *The Threepenny Review,* No. 84.

HAMPL, PATRICIA
The Summer House. *TriQuarterly,* No. 109.

HANSEN, RON
My Communist. *Harper's Magazine,* November.

HODGEN, CHRISTIE
Sir Karl LaFong or Current Resident. *Bellingham Review,* Vol. 24, No. 1.

HOMES, A. M.
Do Not Disturb. *McSweeney's,* No. 7.

HYDE, CATHERINE RYAN
Bloodlines. *Ploughshares,* Vol. 27, No. 1.
The Man Who Found You in the Woods. *The Sun,* October.

IAGNEMMA, KARL
The Confessional Approach. *The Paris Review,* No. 160.

KING, STEPHEN
All That You Love Will Be Carried Away. *The New Yorker,* January 29.

LEE, ANDREA
The Birthday Present. *The New Yorker,* January 22.

LINNEY, ROMULUS
Tennessee. *The Southern Review,* Vol. 37, No. 2.

MACHART, BRUCE
The Last One Left in Arkansas. *Zoetrope: All Story,* Vol. 5, No. 2.

MASON, BOBBIE ANN
Three-Wheeler. *The Atlantic Monthly,* June.

McGuane, Thomas
Boom and Bust. *The Harvard Review,* No. 21.
McNeely, Thomas
Tickle Torture. *Ploughshares,* Vol. 27, No. 4.
Means, David
Lightning Man. *Esquire,* April.
Mina, V. K.
Reading. *Transition,* No. 89.
Mitchell, Judith Claire
Unknown Donor. *The Iowa Review,* Vol. 31, No. 2.
Montemarano, Nicholas
Note to Future Self. *Zoetrope: All Story,* Vol. 5, No. 4.
Mori, Kyoko
The World of Weather. *Prairie Schooner,* Vol. 75, No. 4.
Moss, Barbara Klein
Interpreters. *The Missouri Review,* Vol. 24, No. 2.
Munro, Alice
Comfort. *The New Yorker,* October 8.
What Is Remembered. *The New Yorker,* February 19 and 26.
Murphy, Roberta
What to Do About the Dead. *Nimrod,* Vol. 44, No. 2.

Nixon, Cornelia
Lunch at the Blacksmith House. *Ploughshares,* Vol. 27, Nos. 2 and 3.
Nolan, Jonathan
Memento Mori. *Esquire,* March.

Oates, Joyce Carol
Curly Red. *Harper's Magazine,* April.
O'Brien, Tim
Little People. *Esquire,* October.
Orringer, Julie
Pilgrims. *Ploughshares,* Vol. 27, No. 1.

Page, Patricia
Dios Nunca Muere. *Epoch,* Vol. 50, No. 1.
Pearlman, Edith
Neighbors. *Ascent,* Vol. 26, No. 1.
Unravished Bride. *Pleides,* Vol. 21, No. 2.
Phipps, Marilene
Down by the River. *Transition,* No. 86.
Powers, Sara
Dating a Dead Girl. *Zoetrope: All Story,* Vol. 5, No. 1.

Rock, Peter
Disentangling. *Zoetrope: All Story,* Vol. 5, No. 1.
Rooke, Leon
A Good Radio Voice. *Descant,* No. 113.
Roorbach, Bill
Big Bend. *The Atlantic Monthly,* March.

Schacochis, Bob
Sabo. *Harper's Magazine,* June.
Schlaks, Maximilian
Jingling Bracelets. *The Sun,* August.
Schmidt, Heidi Jon
Wild Rice. *Provincetown Arts,* No. 16.
Schwartz, Lynne Sharon
Sightings of Loretta. *Agni Review,* No. 53.
Shapiro, Dani
Plane Crash Theory. *Ploughshares,* Vol. 27, No. 1
Shepard, Karen
Popular Girls. *The Atlantic Monthly,* October.
Shoemaker, Karen Gettert
Playing Horses. *Prairie Schooner,* Vol. 75, No. 2.
Shonk, Katherine
Children's Verse. *Story Quarterly,* No. 37.
Singleton, George
Show and Tell. *The Atlantic Monthly,* July.
Small, Kate
Maximum Sunlight. *Nimrod International,* Vol. 45, No. 1.

SOLI, TATIANA
The Long Goodbye. *Nimrod International,* Vol. 45, No. 1.

STANTON, MAURA
Glass House. *Ploughshares,* Vol. 27, No. 2 and 3.

STRICKLAND, LEE
Paper Trail. *The Gettysburg Review,* Vol. 14, No. 1.

TALLENT, ELIZABETH
Code. *Zyzzyva,* Vol. 17, No. 1.

TREADWAY, JESSICA
Testimony. *Glimmer Train,* No. 37.

TREVOR, DOUG
Saint Francis in Flint. *The Paris Review,* No. 158.

UNGER, DOUGLAS
Leslie and Sam. *Southwest Review,* Vol. 86, Nos. 2 and 3.

UPDIKE, JOHN
Free. *The New Yorker,* January 8.
Guardians. *The New Yorker,* March 26.

VAZ, KATHERINE
Taking a Stitch in a Dead Man's Arm. *Bomb,* No. 77.

VOLLMER, MATTHEW
Oh Land of National Paradise, How Glorious Are Thy Bounties. *The Paris Review,* No. 158.

WATERMAN, DANIEL
A Lepidopterist's Tale. *Bomb,* No. 77.

WATERS, MARY YUKARI
Egg Face. *Zoetrope: All Story,* Vol. 5, No. 4.

WHITTY, JULIA
Jimmy Underwater. *Zoetrope: All Story,* Vol. 5, No. 2.

WILLIAMS, ANN JOSLIN
Before This Day There Were Many Days. *Ploughshares,* Vol. 27, Nos. 2 and 3.

YATES, RICHARD
The Canal. *The New Yorker,* January 15.

Editorial Addresses of American and Canadian Magazines Publishing Short Stories

African American Review
Department of English
Indiana State University
Terre Haute, IN 47809
web.indstate.edu/artsci/AAR
$30, Joe Weixlmann

Agni Review
Boston University Writing Program
236 Bay State Road
Boston, MA 02115
agni@bu.edu
$15, Askold Melnyczuk

Alaska Quarterly Review
University of Alaska, Anchorage
3211 Providence Drive
Anchorage, AK 99508
ayaqr@uaa.alaska.edu
$10, Ronald Spatz

Alligator Juniper
Prescott College
220 Grove Avenue
Prescott, AZ 86301
$7.50, Allyson Stack

American Letters and Commentary
850 Park Avenue, Suite 5b
New York, NY 10021
www.amletters.org
$8, Anna Rabinowitz

American Literary Review
University of North Texas
P.O. Box 311307
Denton, TX 76203-1307
www.engl.unt.edu/alr
$10, Lee Martin

Another Chicago Magazine
Left Field Press
3709 North Kenmore
Chicago, Il 60613
$8, Sharon Solwitz

Antietam Review
41 South Potomac Street
Hagerstown, MD 21740-3764
$5, Susanne Kass

Antioch Review
Antioch University
150 East South College Street
Yellow Springs, OH 45387
$35, Robert S. Fogarty

Apalachee Quarterly
P.O. Box 20106
Tallahassee, FL 32316
$15, Barbara Hamby et al.

Apalachee Review
P.O. Box 10469
Tallahassee, Fl 32302
$15, Laura Newton, Mary Jane Ryals, Michael Trammell

Appalachian Heritage
Berea College
Berea, KY 40404
$18, James Gage

Arkansas Review
Department of English and Philosophy
P.O. Box 1890
Arkansas State University
State University, AR 72467
$20, William Clements

Ascent
English Department
Concordia College
901 Eighth Street
Moorhead, MN 56562
olsen@cord.edu
$12, W. Scott Olsen

Atlantic Monthly
77 North Washington Street
Boston, MA 02114
www.theatlantic.com
$14.95, C. Michael Curtis

Baffler
P.O. Box 378293
Chicago, IL 60637
thebaffler.com
$24, Thomas Frank,

Bellingham Review
MS-9053
Western Washington University
Bellingham, WA 98225
$14, Robin Hemley, Brenda Miller

Bellowing Ark
P.O. Box 55564
Shoreline, WA 98155
$15, Robert Ward

Beloit Fiction Journal
Beloit College
P.O. Box 11
700 College Street
Beloit, WI 53511
$14, Clint McCown

Berkshire Review
P.O. Box 23
Richmond, VA 01254-0023
$8.95, Vivan Dorsel

Black Warrior Review
P.O. Box 862936
Tuscaloosa, AL 35486-0027
www.webdelsol.com/bwr
$14, Jennifer Davis

Bomb
New Art Publications
594 Broadway, 10th floor
New York, NY 10012
www.bombsite.com
$18, Betsy Sussler

Book
252 W. 37th st., 5th floor
New York, NY 10018
Jerome V. Kramer

Border Crossings
500-70 Arthur Street
Winnipeg, Manitoba
Canada R3B 167
$27, Meeka Walsh

Boston Review
Building E 53, Room 407 MIT
Cambridge, MA 02139
www.bostonreview.mit.edu
$17, Joshua Cohen

Boulevard
4579 Laclede Avenue, #332
St. Louis, MO 63108
$15, Richard Burgin

Brain, Child: The Magazine for Thinking Mothers
P.O. Box 1161
Harrisonburg, VA 22801
www.brainchildmag.com
$18, Jennifer Niesslein, Stephanie Wilkinson

Briar Cliff Review
3303 Rebecca Street
P.O. Box 2100
Sioux City, IA 51104-2100
$10, Phil Hey

Callaloo
Department of English
Texas A&M University
4227 TAMU
College Station, TX 77843-4227
$37, Charles H. Rowell

Calyx
P.O. Box B
Corvallis, OR 97339
calyx@proaxis.com
$19.50, Margarita Donnelly

Capilano Review
Capilano College
2055 Purcell Way
North Vancouver
British Columbia V7J 3H5
$25, Ryan Knighton

Carolina Quarterly
Greenlaw Hall 066A
University of North Carolina
Chapel Hill, NC 27514
$12, George Hovis

Carve Fiction Writers Association
SAO Box 187
University of Washington Box 352238
Seattle, WA 98195
www.carvezine.com
Melvin Sterne

Chariton Review
Truman State University
Kirksville, MO 63501
$9, Jim Barnes

Chattahoochee Review
Georgia Perimeter College
2101 Womack Road
Dunwoody, GA 30338-4497
$16, Lawrence Hetrick

Chelsea
P.O. Box 773
Cooper Station
New York, NY 10276
$13, Richard Foerster

Chicago Quarterly Review
517 Sherman Avenue
Evanston, IL 60202
$10, S. Afzal Haider, Jane Lawrence, Brian Skinner

Chicago Reader
11 East Illinois Street
Chicago, IL 60611
Alison True

Chicago Review
5801 South Kenwood
University of Chicago
Chicago, IL 60637
www.humanities.uchicago.edu/review
$18, Eirik Steinhoff

Cimarron Review
205 Morrill Hall
Oklahoma State University
Stillwater, OK 74078-0135
www.cimmaronreview.okstate.edu
$16, E. P. Walkiewicz

Colorado Review
Department of English
Colorado State University
Fort Collins, CO 80523
creview@vines.colostate.edu
$24, David Milofsky

Columbia
404 Dodge Hall
Columbia University
New York, NY 10027
$15, Ellen Umansky, Neil Azevedo

Comfusion / Lotus Foundation
304 South Third Street
San Jose, CA 95112
auer@comfusion.com
Victoria Auer

Connecticut Review
English Department
Southern Connecticut State University
501 Crescent Street

New Haven, CT 06515
Vivian Shipley

Cottonwood
Box J, 400 Kansas Union
University of Kansas
Lawrence, KS 66045
$15, Tom Lorenz

Crab Creek Review
P.O. Box 840
Vashon Island, WA 98070
$10, Carolyn Alessio

Crab Orchard Review
Department of English
Southern Illinois University at Carbondale
Carbondale, IL 62901
www.siu.edu/~crborchd
$10, Richard Peterson

Crucible
Barton College
P.O. Box 5000
Wilson, NC 27893-7000
Terrence L. Grimes

CutBank
Department of English
University of Montana
Missoula, MT 59812
cutbank@selway.umt.edu
$12, David Cohen

Daedalus
136 Irving Street, Suite 100
Cambridge, MA 02138
$33, James Miller

Denver Quarterly
University of Denver
Denver, CO 80208
$20, Bin Ramke

Descant
P.O. Box 314
Station P
Toronto, Ontario M5S 2S8
www.descant.on.ca
$25, Karen Mulhallen

Descant
Department of English
Box 32872
Texas Christian University
Fort Worth, TX 76129
$12, Lynn Risser, David Kuhne

Distillery
Division of Humanities & Social Sciences
Motlow State Community College
P.O. Box 8500
Tullahoma, TN 37388-8100
$15, Inman Majors

DoubleTake
55 Davis Square
Somerville, MA 02144
www.doubletakemagazine.org
$32, R. J. McGill

Elle
1633 Broadway
New York, NY 10019
$14, Ben Dickinson

Ellery Queen's Mystery Magazine
475 Park Avenue South
New York, NY 10016
$33.97, Janet Hutchings

Em
P.O. Box 194672
San Francisco, CA 94119-4672
$10, Brandon Mise

Epoch
251 Goldwin Smith Hall
Cornell University
Ithaca, NY 14853-3201
$11, Michael Koch

Esquire
250 West 55th Street
New York, NY 10019
www.esquire.com
$17.94, Adrienne Miller

Eureka Literary Magazine
Eureka College
300 East College Avenue

Eureka, IL 61530-1500
$15, Loren Logsdon

Event
Douglas College
P.O. Box 2503
New Westminster
British Columbia V3L 5B2
$22, Christine Dewar

Fantasy & Science Fiction
P.O. Box 3447
Hoboken, NJ 07030
GordonFSF@aol.com
$38.97, Gordon Van Gelder

Fiction International
Department of English and
Comparative Literature
San Diego State University
San Diego, CA 92182
$12, Harold Jaffe, Larry McCaffery

Fiddlehead
UNB P.O. Box 4400
Frederiction
New Brunswick E3B 5A3
$20, Mark Anthony Jarman

Five Points
Georgia State University
Department of English
University Plaza
Atlanta, GA 30303-3083
$15, Pam Durban, David Bottoms

Florida Review
Department of English, Box 25000
University of Central Florida
Orlando, FL 32816
www.pegasus.cc.ucf.edu/~english/
floridareview/home.htm
$10, Pat Rushin

Flyway
206 Ross Hall
Department of English
Iowa State University
Ames, IA 50011
$18, Sam Pritchard

Folio
Department of Literature
The American University
Washington D.C. 20016
$12, Geoffrey D. Witham

Fourteen Hills
Department of Creative Writing
San Francisco State University
1600 Holloway Ave.
San Francisco, CA 94132
Hills@sfu.edu
$12, Julian Kudritzki

Front Range Review
Department of English
Front Range Communtiy College
Larimer Campus
Fort Collins, CO 80527
Boliver@larimer.cccoes.edut
$10, Blair Oliver

Gargoyle
Paycock Press
c/o Atticus Books & Music
1508 U Street NW
Washington, DC 20009
$20, Richard Peabody, Lucinda Ebersole

Georgia Review
University of Georgia
Athens, GA 30602
www.uga.edu/garev
$24, T. R. Hummer

Gettysburg Review
Gettysburg College
Gettysburg, PA 17325
$24, Peter Stitt

glass tesseract
P.O. Box 702
Agoura Hills, CA 91376
editor@glasstesseract.com
$9, Michael Chester

Glimmer Train Stories
710 SW Madison Street
Suite 504
Portland, OR 97205

$32, Susan Burmeister-Brown, Linda Swanson-Davies

GQ
4 Times Square, 9th floor
New York, NY 10036
$19.97, Walter Kirn

Grain
Box 1154
Regina, Saskatchewan S4P 3B4
www.grain.mag@sk.sympatico.ca
$26.95, Elizabeth Philips

Granta
1755 Broadway, 5th floor
New York, NY 10019-3780
$32, Ian Jack

Great River Review
Anderson Center for Interdisciplinary Studies
P.O. Box 406
Red Wing, MN 55066
$12, Richard Broderick, Robert Hedin

Green Hills Literary Lantern
North Central Missouri College
Box 375
Trenton, MO 64683
$7, Sara King

Green Mountains Review
Box A58
Johnson State College
Johnson, VT 05656
$14, Tony Whedon

Greensboro Review
Department of English
University of North Carolina
Greensboro, NC 27412
www.uncg.edu/eng
$10, Jim Clark

Gulf Coast
Department of English
University of Houston
4800 Calhoun Road
Houston, TX 77204-3012
$22, Mark Doty

Gulf Stream
English Department
Florida International University
3000 NE 151st Street
North Miami, FL 33181
$9, Lynne Barrett

Harper's Magazine
666 Broadway
New York, NY 10012
$16, Lewis Lapham

Harvard Review
Poetry Room
Harvard College Library
Cambridge, MA 02138
$16, Christina Thompson

Hawaii Pacific Review
1060 Bishop Street, LB 402
Honolulu, HI 96813
hpreview@hpu.edu
Catherine Sustana, Patrice Wilson

Hawaii Review
University of Hawaii
Department of English
1733 Donaghho Road
Honolulu, HI 96822
$20, Michael Puleloa

Hayden's Ferry Review
Box 871502
Arizona State University
Tempe, AZ 85287-1502
www.haydensferryreview.org
$10, Julie Hensley, Bill Martin

Hemispheres
1301 Carolina Street
Greensboro, NC 27401
Free, Selby Bateman

High Plains Literary Review
180 Adams Street, Suite 250
Denver, CO 80206
$20, Robert O. Greer, Jr.

Hudson Review
684 Park Avenue
New York, NY 10021
$24, Paula Deitz, Frederick Morgan

Idaho Review
Boise State University
Department of English
1910 University Drive
Boise, ID 83725
$9.95, Mitch Wieland

Image
323 South Broad Street
P.O. Box 674
Kennett Square, PA 19348
www.imagejournal.org
$36, Gregory Wolfe

India Currents
P.O. Box 21285
San Jose, CA 95151
info@indiacur.com
$19.95, Arviund Kumar

Inkwell
Manhattanville College
2900 Purchose Street
Purchose, NY 10577
$14, Karen Sirabian

Iowa Review
Department of English
University of Iowa
308 EPB
Iowa City, IA 52242
www.uiowa.edu/~iareview
$18, David Hamilton

Iris
Women's Center
Box 323 HSC
University of Virginia
Charlottesville, VA 22908
$9, Virginia Moran

Italian Americana
University of Rhode Island
Providence Campus
80 Washington Street
Providence, RI 02903
$20, Carol Bonomo Albright

The Journal
Department of English
Ohio State University
164 West 17th Avenue
Columbus, OH 43210
$12, Kathy Fagan, Michelle Herman

Kalliope
Florida Community College
3939 Roosevelt Boulevard
Jacksonville, FL 32205
$12.50, Mary Sue Koeppel

Kenyon Review
Kenyon College
Gambier, OH 43022
www.kenyonreview.org
$25, David H. Lynn

Lililth
250 West 57th Street
New York, NY 10107
lilithmag@aol.com
$18, Susan Weidman Schneider

Literal Latte
61 East 8th Street, Suite 240
New York, NY 10003
litlatte@aol.com
$11, Jenine Gordon Bockman

Literary Review
Fairleigh Dickinson University
285 Madison Avenue
Madison, NJ 07940
www.theliteraryreview.org
$18, Rene Steinke

Louisiana Literature
Box 792
Southeastern Louisiana University
Hammond, LA 70402
$12, Jack B. Bedell

Lynx Eye
ScribbleFest Literary Group
542 Mitchell Drive
Los Osnos, CA 93402
$25, Pam McCully, Kathryn Morrison

The MacGuffin
Schoolcraft College
18600 Haggerty Road
Livonia, MI 48152
$15, Arthur J. Lindenberg

Madison Review
University of Wisconsin
Department of English
H. C. White Hall
600 North Park Street
Madison, WI 53706
$15, Jessica Agneessens, Meaghan Walker

Malahat Review
University of Victoria
P.O. Box 1700
Victoria, British Columbia V8W 2Y2
malahat@uvic.ca
$40, Marlene Cookshaw

Manoa
English Department
University of Hawaii
Honolulu, HI 96822
$22, Frank Stewart

Massachusetts Review
South College
Box 37140
University of Massachusetts
Amherst, MA 01003
www.massreview.com
$22, David Lenson, Mary Heath, Paul Jenkins

Matrix
1455 de Maisonneuve Boulevard West
Suite LB-514-8
Montreal, Quebec H3G IM8
matrix@alcor.concordia.ca
$18, R.E.N. Allen

McSweeney's
394A Ninth Street
Brooklyn, NY 11215
submissions@mcsweeneys.net
$36, Dave Eggers

Meridian
Department of English
P.O. Box 400145
University of Virginia
Charlottesville, VA 22904-4145
$10, Paula Younger

Michigan Quarterly Review
3032 Rackham Building
915 East Washington Street
University of Michigan
Ann Arbor, MI 48109
$25, Laurence Goldstein

Mid-American Review
Department of English
Bowling Green State University
Bowling Green, OH 48109
www.bgsu.edu/midamericanreview
$12, Michael Czyzniejewski

Minnesota Review
Department of English
East Carolina University
Greenville, NC 27858
$20, Jeffrey Williams

Mississippi Review
University of Southern Mississippi
Southern Station, Box 5144
Hattiesburg, MS 39406-5144
www.sushi.st.usm.edu/mrw
$15, Frederick Barthelme

Missouri Review
1507 Hillcrest Hall
University of Missouri
Columbia, MO 65211
www.missourireview.org
$19, Speer Morgan

Moment
4710 41st Street NW
Washington, D.C. 20016
editor@momentmag.com
$14.97, Herschel Shanks

Mondo Greco
34R South Russell Street, Suite 2B
Boston, MA 02114-3936
mondogreco@att.net
$19, Barbara Fields

Ms.
20 Exchange Place
New York, NY 10005

www.msmagazine.com
$35, Marcia Ann Gillespie

Nassau Review
English Department
Nassau Community College
One Education Drive
Garden City, NY 11530-6793
Paul A. Doyle

Natural Bridge
Department of English
University of Missouri, St. Louis
8001 Natural Bridge Road
St. Louis, MO 63121-4499
www.umsl.edu/~natural/index.htm
$15, Steven Schreiner

Nebraska Review
Writers Workshop
WFAB 212
University of Nebraska at Omaha
Omaha, NE 68182-0324
$15, James Reed

New England Review
Middlebury College
Middlebury, VT 05753
NEReview@middlebury.edu
$23, Stephen Donadio

New Letters
University of Missouri
5100 Rockhill Road
Kansas City, MO 64110
$17, James McKinley

New Orleans Review
P.O. Box 195
Loyola University
New Orleans, LA 70118
$15, Christopher Chambers

New Orphic Review
706 Mill Street
Nelson, British Columbia VIL 4S5
$25, Ernest Hekkanen

New Renaissance
26 Heath Road, #11
Arlington, MA 02474
wmichaud@gwi.net
$11.50, Louise T. Reynolds

New Yorker
4 Times Square
New York, NY 10036
$46, David Remnick, Bill Buford

New York Stories
English Department
La Guardia Community College
31-10 Thomson Avenue
Long Island City, NY 11101
$13.40, Daniel Lynch

Night Rally
P.O. Box 1707
Philadelphia, PA 19105
www.nightrally.org/interlo.htm
$21, Amber Dorko Stopper

Nimrod
Arts and Humanities Council of Tulsa
600 South College Avenue
Tulsa, OK 74104
nimrod@utulsa.edu
$17.50, Francine Ringold

Noon
1369 Madison Avenue
PMB 298
New York, NY 10128
noonannual@yahoo.com
$9, Diane WIlliams

North American Review
University of Northern Iowa
1222 West 27th Street
Cedar Falls, IA 50614
NAR@uni.edu
$22, Vince Gotera

North Dakota Quarterly
University of North Dakota
P.O. Box 8237
Grand Forks, ND 58202
ndq@sage.und.nodak.edu
$25, Robert Lewis

Northwest Review
369 PLC

University of Oregon
Eugene, OR 97403
$20, John Witte

Oasis
P.O. Box 626
Largo, FL 34649-0626
$22, Neal Storrs

Oklahoma Today
15 North Robinson, Suite 100
P.O. Box 53384
Oklahoma City, OK 73102
$16.95, Louisa McCune

One Story
P.O. Box 1326
New York, NY 10156
$21, Hannah Tinti

Ontario Review
9 Honey Brook Drive
Princeton, NJ 08540
www.ontarioreviewpress.com
$14, Raymond J. Smith

Open City
225 Lafayette Street
Suite 1114
New York, NY 10012
editors@opencity.org
$32, Thomas Beller, Daniel Pinchbeck

Other Voices
University of Illinois at Chicago
Department of English, M/C 162
601 South Morgan Street
Chicago, IL 60607-7120
www.othervoicesmagazine.org
$24, Lois Hauselman

Oxford American
P.O. Box 1156
404 South 11th Street
Oxford, MS 38655
www.oxfordamericanmag.com
$24.95, Marc Smirnoff

Oxygen
537 Jones Street, PMB 999
San Francisco, CA 94102
oxygen@slip.net
$14, Richard Hack

Oyster Boy Review
P.O. Box 77842
San Francisco, CA 94107
www.oysterboyreview.com
$20, Damon Sauve

Pangolin Papers
Turtle Press
P.O. Box 241
Norlond, WA 98358
$15, Pat Britt

Paris Review
541 East 72nd Street
New York, NY 10021
$34, George Plimpton

Parting Gifts
3413 Wilshire Drive
Greensboro, NC 27408-2923
Robert Bixby

Partisan Review
236 Bay State Road
Boston, MA 02215
www.partisanreview.org
$22, William Phillips

Passages North
English Department
Northern Michigan University
1401 Presque Isle Avenue
Marquette, MI 49007-5363
$10, Anne Ohman Youngs

Penny Dreadful: Tales & Poems
P.O. Box 719
Radio City Station
New York, NY 10101-0719
mpendragon@aol.com
$12

Pindeldyboz
25–53 36th Street, 2nd floor
Astoria, NY 11103
Jboison@earthlink.net
$12, Jeff Boison

Playboy
Playboy Building
919 North Michigan Avenue
Chicago, IL 60611
$29.97, Alice K. Turner

Pleiades
Department of English and Philosophy, 5069
Central Missouri State University
P.O. Box 800
Warrensburg, MO 64093
$12, R. M. Kinder, Kevin Prufer

Ploughshares
Emerson College
120 Boylston Street
Boston, MA 02116
www.emerson.edu/ploughshares
$22, Don Lee

Porcupine
P.O. Box 259
Cedarburg, WI 53012
ppine259@aol.com
$15.95, group

Potomac Review
P.O. Box 354
Port Tobacco, MD 20677
elilv@juno.com
$20, Eli Flam

Potpourri
P.O. Box 8278
Prairie Village, KS 66208
potpourripub@aol.com
$16, Polly W. Swafford

Prairie Fire
423-100 Arthur Street
Winnipeg, Manitoba R3B 1H3
prfire@escape.ca
$25, Andris Taskans

Prairie Schooner
201 Andrews Hall
University of Nebraska
Lincoln, NE 68588-0334
www.unl.edu/schooner/psmain.htm
$26, Hilda Raz

Prairie Star
P.O. Box 923
Fort Collins, CO 80522-0923
$10, Mark Gluckstern

Prism International
Department of Creative Writing
University of British Columbia
Vancouver, British Columbia V6T 1W5
prism@interchange.ubc.ca
$18, Chris Labonte, Andrea MacPherson

Provincetown Arts
650 Commercial Street
Provincetown, MA 02657
$10, Ivy Meeropol

Puerto del Sol
Department of English
Box 3E
New Mexico State University
Las Cruces, NM 88003
$10, Kevin McIlvoy

Quarry Magazine
P.O. Box 74
Kingston, Ontario K7L 4V6
goldfishpree@hotmail.com
$15, Andrew Griffin

Quarterly West
312 Olpin Union
University of Utah
Salt Lake City, UT 84112
$12, Aaron Sanders

Rain Crow
2127 W. Pierce Avenue, #2B
Chicago, IL 60622-1824
http://rain-crow.com/
$15, Michael manley

Rattapallax
532 LaGuardia Place, Suite 353
New York, NY 10012
ratapallax@hotmail.com
$14, George Dickerson

Reading Room
Great Marsh Press
P.O. Box 2144
Lenox Hill Station
New York, NY 10021
www.greatmarshpress.com
$65, Barbara Probst Solomon

REAL
School of Liberal Arts
Stephen F. Austin State University
Nacogdoches, TX 75962
$15, Dale Hearell

Red Rock Review
English Department, J2A
Community College of Southern Nevada
3200 East Cheyenne Avenue
North Las Vegas, NV 89030
$9.50, Richard Logsdon

Red Wheelbarrow
De Anza College
21250 Stevens Creek Boulevard
Cupertino, CA 95014-5702
www.deanza.fhda.edu/redwheelbarrow
$5, Randolph Splitter

Republic of Letters
120 Cushing Avenue
Boston, MA 02125-2033
rangoni@bu.edu
$25, Keith Botsford

River City
Department of English
University of Memphis
Memphis, TN 38152
$12, Scott McWaters

River Oak Review
734 Noyes Street, #M3
Evanston, IL 60201
maryleemock@mindspring.com
$12, Mary Lee MacDonald

River Sedge
Department of English
University of Texas
1201 W. University Drive, CAS 266
$12, Dorey Schmidt

River Styx
Big River Association
634 N. Grand Boulevard, 12th floor
St. Louis, MO 63103-1002
$20, Richard Newman

Room of One's Own
P.O. Box 46160
Station D
Vancouver, British Columbia V6J 5G5
www.islandnet.com/Room/enter
$25, Madeleine Thien

Salmagundi
Skidmore College
Saratoga Springs, NY 12866
$18, Robert Boyers

Salt Hill
English Department
Syracuse University
Syracuse, NY 13244
salthill@cas.syr.edu
$15, Maile Chapman, R. J. Curtis

Santa Monica Review
1900 Pico Boulevard
Santa Monica, CA 90405
$12, Andrew Tonkovich

Seattle Review
Padelford Hall, GN-30
University of Washington
Seattle, WA 98195
$9, Colleen McElroy

Seventeen
850 Third Avenue
New York, NY 10022
$14.95, Patrice G. Adcroft

Sewanee Review
University of the South
Sewanee, TN 37375-4009
$20, George Core

Shenandoah
Troubador Theater, 2nd floor
Washington and Lee University

Lexington, VA 24450-0303
www.wlu.edu/~shenando
$15, R. T. Smith

Songs of Innocence
Pendragon Publications
P.O. Box 719
Radio City Station
New York, NY 10101-0719
mpendragon@aol.com
$12, Michael M. Pendragon

Sonora Review
Department of English
University of Arizona
Tucson, AZ 85721
$12, Linda Copeland

South Carolina Review
Department of English
Clemson University
Strode Tower, Box 340523
Clemson, SC 29634-1503
$10, Wayne Chapman, Donna Haisty Winchell

Southeast Review
406 Williams Building
Florida State University
Talahassee, FL 32306-1036
sundog@english.fsu.edu
$10, C. V. Davis

Southern Exposure
P.O. Box 531
Durham, NC 27702
southern_exposure@i4south.org
$24, Jordan Green

Southern Humanities Review
9088 Haley Center
Auburn University
Auburn, AL 36849
www.auburn.edu/english/shr/home.htm
$15, Dan R. Latimer, Virginia M. Kouidis

Southern Review
43 Allen Hall
Louisiana State University
Baton Rouge, LA 70803
$25, James Olney, Dave Smith

Southwest Review
Southern Methodist University
P.O. Box 4374
Dallas, TX 75275
$24, Willard Spiegelman

Spindrift
1507 East 53rd Street, #649
Chicago, IL 60615
$10, Mark Anderson-Wilk, Sarah Anderson-Wilk

Story Quarterly
431 Sheridan Road
Kenilworth, IL 60043-1220
storyquarterly@hotmail.com
$12, M.M.M. Hayes

Sun
107 North Roberson Street
Chapel Hill, NC 27516
$34, Sy Safransky

Sycamore Review
Department of English
1356 Heavilon Hall
Purdue University
West Lafayette, IN 47907
www.sla.purdue.edu/academic/engl/sycamore/
$12, Barbara Lawhorn-Haroun

Talking River Review
Division of Literature and Languages
Lewis-Clark State College
500 Eighth Avenue
Lewiston, ID 83501
$14, Sandra Lantz

Thema
Box 74109
Metairie, LA 70033-4109
$16, Virginia Howard

Thin Air
P.O. Box 23549
Flagstaff, AZ 86002

www.nau.edu/english/thinair
$9, A. Vaughn Wagner

Third Coast
Department of English
Western Michigan University
Kalamazoo, MI 49008-5092
$11, Lisa Lishman, Libbie Searcy

Threepenny Review
P.O. Box 9131
Berkeley, CA 94709
$16, Wendy Lesser

Timber Creek Review
3283 UNCG Station
Greensboro, NC 27413
timber_creek_review@hoopsmail.com
$15, John Freiermuth

Tin House
P.O. Box 10500
Portland, OR 97296-0500
$39.80, Rob Spillman

Transition
69 Dunster Street
Harvard University
Cambridge, MA 02138
transition@fas.harvard.edu
$27, Kwame Anthony Appiah, Henry Louis Gates, Jr., Michael Vazquez

TriQuarterly
2020 Ridge Avenue
Northwestern University
Evanston, IL 60208
$24, Susan Firestone Hahn

Virginia Adversaria
Empire Publishing, P.O. Box 2349
Poquoson, VA 23662
Empirepub@hotmail.com
Bill Glose

Virginia Quarterly Review
One West Range
Charlottesville, VA 22903
$18, Staige D. Blackford

War, Literature, and the Arts
Department of English and Fine Arts
2354 Fairchild Drive, Suite 6D45
USAF Academy, CO 80840-6242
donald.anderson@usafa.af.mil
Donald Anderson

Wascana Review
English Department
University of Regina
Regina, Canada
$10, Jeanne Shami

Washington Square
Creative Writing Program
New York University
19 University Place, 2nd floor
New York, NY 10003-4556
washington.square.journal@nyu.edu
$6, Ben Rhodes

Water Stone
Graduate Liberal Studies Program
Hamline University
1536 Hewitt Avenue
St. Paul, MN 55104-1284
water-stone@gw.hamline.edu
$8, Mary Francois Rockcastle

Weber Studies
Weber State University
Ogden, UT 84408
$20, Sherwin Howard

West Branch
Bucknell Hall
Bucknell University
Lewisburg, PA 17837
$10, Paula Closson Buck

Western Humanities Review
University of Utah
255 South Central Campus Drive
Room 3500
Salt Lake City, UT 84112
$14, Barry Weller

Willow Springs
Eastern Washington University
705 West 1st Avenue
Spokane, WA 99201
$11.50, Christopher Howell

Wind
Wind Publications
P.O. Box 24548
Lexington, KY 40524
www.wind-wind.org
$15, Chris Green

Witness
Oakland Community College
Orchard Ridge Campus
27055 Orchard Lake Road
Farmington Hills, MI 48334
www.witnessmagazine.com
$15, Peter Stine

Wordwrights!
Argonne Hotel
1620 Argonne Place NW
Washington D.C. 20009
$10

Yale Review
P.O. Box 208243
New Haven, CT 06520-8243
$27, J. D. McClatchy

Yankee
Yankee Publishing, Inc.
Dublin, NH 03444
www.newengland.com
$22, Judson D. Hale

Zoetrope
The Sentinel Building
916 Kearney Street
San Francisco, CA 94133
www.all-story.com
$20, Adrienne Brodeur

Zyzzyva
P.O. Box 590069
San Francisco, CA 94104
editor@zyzzyva.org
$28, Howard Junker

THE B·E·S·T AMERICAN SERIES™

THE BEST AMERICAN SHORT STORIES® 2002

Sue Miller, guest editor • Katrina Kenison, series editor

"Story for story, readers can't beat the *Best American Short Stories* series" (*Chicago Tribune*). This year's most beloved short fiction anthology is edited by the best-selling novelist Sue Miller and includes stories by Edwidge Danticat, Jill McCorkle, E. L. Doctorow, and Akhil Sharma, among others.

0-618-13173-6 PA $13.00 / 0-618-11749-0 CL $27.50
0-618-13172-8 CASS $26.00 / 0-618-25816-7 CD $35.00

THE BEST AMERICAN ESSAYS® 2002

Stephen Jay Gould, guest editor • Robert Atwan, series editor

Since 1986, the *Best American Essays* series has gathered the best nonfiction writing of the year. Edited by Stephen Jay Gould, the eminent scientist and distinguished writer, this year's volume features writing by Jonathan Franzen, Sebastian Junger, Gore Vidal, Mario Vargas Llosa, and others.

0-618-04932-0 PA $13.00 / 0-618-21388-0 CL $27.50

THE BEST AMERICAN MYSTERY STORIES™ 2002

James Ellroy, guest editor • Otto Penzler, series editor

Our perennially popular anthology is a favorite of mystery buffs and general readers alike. This year's volume is edited by the internationally acclaimed author James Ellroy and offers pieces by Robert B. Parker, Joyce Carol Oates, Michael Connelly, Stuart M. Kaminsky, and others.

0-618-12493-4 PA $13.00 / 0-618-12494-2 CL $27.50
0-618-25807-8 CASS $26.00 / 0-618-25806-X CD $35.00

THE BEST AMERICAN SPORTS WRITING™ 2002

Rick Reilly, guest editor • Glenn Stout, series editor

This series has garnered wide acclaim for its stellar sports writing and top-notch editors. Now Rick Reilly, the best-selling author and "Life of Reilly" columnist for *Sports Illustrated,* continues that tradition with pieces by Frank Deford, Steve Rushin, Jeanne Marie Laskas, Mark Kram, Jr., and others.

0-618-08628-5 PA $13.00 / 0-618-08627-7 CL $27.50